C. M. Elliott [illegible] to Zimbabwe in the middle [illegible] er husband, pioneered a tourism business in the newly independent country, based in and around Hwange National Park. Elliott began writing seriously about three years ago – short stories to begin with and then moving on to what would eventually become *Sibanda and the Rainbird*. She now writes fulltime.

SIBANDA AND THE RAINBIRD

C.M. Elliott

CONSTABLE

First published in South Africa in 2013 by Jacana Media (Pty) Ltd

First published in Great Britain in 2019 by Constable
This paperback edition published in 2019 by Constable

1 3 5 7 9 10 8 6 4 2

A CIP catalogue record for this book is available from the British Library.

ISBN: 978-1-47213-049-5

Typeset by Initial Typesetting Services, Edinburgh
Printed and bound in Great Britain by Clays Ltd, Elcograf S.p.A.

Papers used by Constable are from well-managed forests and other responsible sources.

Constable
An imprint of
Little, Brown Book Group
Carmelite House
50 Victoria Embankment
London EC4Y 0DZ

An Hachette UK Company
www.hachette.co.uk

www.littlebrown.co.uk

Dedicated to the memory of
Jon and Pat Arscott

Chapter 1

Detective Inspector Jabulani Sibanda stood for some moments over what remained of the mutilated body. He stroked his chin several times, a habit which his fellow police officers understood to mean, 'Don't interrupt me, I'm thinking'.

'What happened in this remote patch of bush, Ncube?' he addressed his sergeant.

'Sir, it's an open and shut case. The victim has been attacked and killed by wild animals.' They both continued to stare at the disfigured corpse hardly recognisable as a human being. Sibanda glanced across at the flocks of vultures roosting in the nearby acacia grove. He controlled a wave of disgust. They had much to answer for, having digested this man's identity for breakfast.

Gubu Police Station had received the call early from the manager of Thunduluka Safari Lodge. 'We've found a body in the valley,' he had said over the crackling line. 'Our morning game drive came across it a few minutes ago. They've just radioed in. You'd better get here in a hurry. It's disappearing fast. The vultures have found it.'

Sergeant Ncube, who answered the phone, replied, 'Tell them to remain at the spot and guard the corpse. We will be sending a detail as soon as we can.' The sergeant had been on the night shift about to knock off. There would be no sleep for him today.

'Sorry Sergeant, I can't. The vehicle is full of sensitive clients. Our guide says they are talking "law suits" for exposure to "gratuitous carnage". They are on their way back to camp. We have litres of strong coffee and a trauma counsellor waiting.'

‘A trauma counsellor?’ Ncube hadn’t a clue what ‘trauma’ was or why anyone would need counselling.

‘My wife is a trained nurse. She adopts whatever terminology suits the moment. People seem to find security in titles.’ The manager continued to offer his apologies and assistance, but was eager to terminate the call and prepare for the arrival of his guests. They had seen an African kill they weren’t banking on. ‘Sorry we couldn’t be more help. We are always available to help if you need us,’ he said as he hung up.

Ncube stared at the phone for a moment, as if will power alone could erase the message and replay time until he had knocked off. He sighed and punched in the number of the detective about to come on duty. He would need a trauma counsellor himself by the end of the conversation. The man’s words often stung like a hive of angry hornets. They would pain the ears that had been preparing for the sweet welcoming murmurs of his wives. He relayed the gist to Detective Inspector Sibanda, home in the bathroom allowing the trickle of tepid water that passed as a shower to attempt to launch him into the day.

‘Listen Ncube,’ he said irritably, as he towelled himself dry, ‘phone the lodge back, advise them that we need to interview those clients. They must stay put.’ Tourists were a fickle lot: Here today, in the Serengeti tomorrow. The detective knew that an American and his planned itinerary are rarely parted.

‘And you stay put too, Ncube. Organise the transport,’ he hesitated for a moment before snapping, ‘and make sure it can get us as far as the crime scene.’ Ncube sensed a hint of future suffering infused in his words. Failure was not an option.

Sibanda arrived at the police station in near-record time. Speed was the crux. He estimated forty-five minutes to the scene. Scavengers and the blistering heat were going to destroy whatever evidence remained if they didn’t get a move on.

The rattletrap Land Rover serving Gubu Police was running when he arrived. Given its usual allergy to any form of locomotion, this was an auspicious start. He suspected Ncube had rounded up everyone within a couple of hundred metres of the station and had them pushing the obstinate beast up and down the road to coax a spark of compliance. He was grateful.

Sibanda drove as fast as the engine would allow. He had long ago, against the explicit instructions of police internal regulations (at best a maze of unfathomable, unworkable minutiae), hammered the governor into submission. It was now a flattened disc beneath the accelerator, unable to do its intended job of preventing the pedal from fully depressing, and the driver now had some semblance of acceptable forward motion.

As the detective approached the valley, he could see no need to call in at the lodge for directions. Vultures were circling high on the morning thermals. Beneath them would lie the ill-fated corpse.

'I suppose it's too much to ask that the safari vehicle might have come across the scene earlier, before the vultures had begun their feast. I doubt there's much evidence left,' he complained to Ncube, who had arrived a few minutes before him. He'd driven an even older Spanish Land Rover substitute. It travelled sideways like a crab, was shunned by most of the station staff and required exquisite driving skills to keep on the road. A real bitch. Not Sibanda's bitch if he could avoid it.

'Yes, sir,' replied Ncube, although he couldn't imagine what more evidence they needed. This unfortunate person had wandered off into the bush, maybe got lost, and died a hideous death in the deadly jaws of a lion. Much of the flesh was digesting in the vultures' guts and being passed in dollops of white droppings that splashed the branches and painted the leaves.

Sibanda reviewed what he knew of vulture feeding patterns. First the Bateleur eagles would arrive. At the vanguard of death, they were rewarded by the choice pickings of the eyes. Bateleurs and the heavy-bodied vultures only managed to get going when hot air formed thermals to support their soaring weight. They were late starters.

The huge lappet-faced vultures, from their mile-high cruising altitude, were often next at the kill. With three-foot wing spans and wickedly curved beaks, they did most of the butchering. Their beaks had become adapted over millennia to rip open even rhino hide, making it easier for their smaller cousins, the white-backed vultures, to move into the opened body cavity, eating away at the soft-tissue organs and entrails. Often hundreds of these birds and others of their ilk gathered at a large carcass and disposed of it in minutes. Sibanda realised they were lucky that anything at all of the body remained.

The detective closed his eyes. He imagined the scene. The internecine squabbling would have been ferocious as each bird jockeyed for position both on and in the body – a wrestle of competitive heaving, pulling and tugging. The body would have quickly given up its stinking gases and secret fluids to those featherless heads adapted over time for their internal task. He could hear the sucking noises as they fought to separate heart, liver and lungs from the thorax. He saw behind his lids the macabre tug-of-war over ropes of large and small intestine. Death was never pretty, but this was a gruesome final scene. Vultures feed only during the daylight hours. Sunrise had come at 5:11 am; thermals around 8 am. They had made short work of their victim in the hour that followed.

Ncube was restless. He was shifting from leg to leg. His left arm rested on his hip, his right scratched his head. Sibanda knew that his legendary and discerningly delicate digestive system would be complaining. Gore was not Ncube's forte. He had probably spent the night wolfing down his wives' baking along with an assortment of fizzy drinks as an antidote to night-shift boredom. A glutinous, volcanic concoction was now travelling down his gullet and along a well-worn path to his bloated abdomen. He would, no doubt, pay the price. Sibanda tried to distract him from the butchered body.

'Sergeant Ncube,' he asked, 'in your opinion, what caused the death of this individual?'

'Isilwane, a lion, sir,' replied Ncube with conviction.

'And why do you suppose the lion barely touched his supper, and allowed the vultures to finish it for him?' asked Sibanda, exasperation creeping into his voice.'

'He was disturbed perhaps?' ventured Ncube, beginning to sweat. He ran his finger between his neck and the stiff uniform collar in an attempt to loosen it and let in some air. The sun was high and the flies that were attracted to the putrefying corpse had recognised a ready source of moisture on his brow. Swatting had little effect on the swarms. He was nervous, expecting lions to attack from behind every tussock, shrub and anthill. Ncube had nearly died of fright when a partridge-like francolin had suddenly taken flight from its shelter in the long grass accompanied by a loud chek, chek, chek alarm call.

Sibanda's tone became patronising. He couldn't help the sarcasm, although he did recognise it as a diversionary tactic from his own frustration at the clueless scene. 'What animal do you suppose scared off the lion?'

'A pack of hyenas, sir?'

'Good man,' said Sibanda, in ominous tones, 'now you are starting to think – through your backside, you idiot,' he finished with a disparaging snarl, irritated by the Sergeant's ignorance and less concerned by his troubled bile duct. 'Now get yourself back to the vehicle and chase up the body box.'

Sibanda had allowed his frustration to erupt and he regretted it. It wasn't Ncube's fault that he had grown up in the city and had never seen a cow, let alone a lion. Why HQ insisted on posting urban dwellers to the bush he would never know. On the upside, though, Ncube was a good back-up man and he could keep that rubbish, skoroskoro, Land Rover on the road against all predictions of its demise.

On arrival at the scene, Sibanda had looked for the spoor of any major predator. Other than the small prints of a pair of side-striped jackals that must have chased off the vultures and tried to gain access to the body via the anus, there was nothing: No lion spoor, no hyena spoor. He searched for signs of the offal having been buried away from the kill; the first indication of big-cat activity. Before he even double-checked, he knew no lion had been anywhere near this corpse.

The musculature that remained indicated an African male, probably between twenty and forty years of age, but he couldn't be sure. Forensics would have to take care of that. They were going to have a hard time with identification. Nothing remained on the body, no personal items, just a few shreds of a cotton shirt and a strip of remnant denim from his jeans. No shoes. Fingerprints would not be an option, they had been torn away. The face had gone. Eyes, nose, lips and ears were all missing. The jaw and teeth remained, but this man had a perfect set of teeth that had never visited a dentist. Even his mother wouldn't recognise him, but as someone's son, brother, perhaps husband and father, he deserved an identity.

Sibanda had wanted to be alone with the victim. Solitude would help him concentrate. Sergeant Ncube and several policemen had already compromised the scene with their own genetic detritus and government-issue boots. Sibanda doubted any forensic breakthrough. The body-botherers would only approximate a time of death.

He sat on his haunches and examined the body once again. He stared down at the bloody mess that used to be a face. Featureless and ravaged, the scavenged bones gave up no clues, but something niggled Sibanda about this corpse like the persistent whine of a hungry mosquito.

Faces, even dead faces, fascinated Sibanda. The Pythagorean ratio, the golden ratio of 1.618 to 1, dictated the structure of the facial bones – where the nose sat in relation to the mouth, how close together the eyes. As long as a face conformed to those related numbers, give or take the odd millimetre, the look would be acceptable to fellow inhabitants of the earth. The closer to the proportion, the more symmetrical and handsome the owner.

He thought then about the most perfectly beautiful face he had ever seen. A familiar sick feeling churned in the pit of his stomach. Most times he kept the face from haunting his working day. What was the point anyway? Those perfect features were as lost to him as this corpse was to its family. Sibanda blanked out the image and refocused on the mauled visage in front of him. He mulled over characteristics. Did the victim's lip curl, his eyebrow arch? Did he frown, squint, scowl or was he a smiler? He would probably never know. Whilst on a scholarship at Nottingham Police College, the courses drummed into him that identity was the key to all crime.

'Identify the victim, identify the criminal: that's all there is to a murder,' the lecturer used to incant. 'Sound simple?' he would ask. 'Well it bloody well isn't, unless the victim has his wallet on him and the murderer leaves a calling card.'

Sibanda had dabbled in forensics and done his final paper on identity and anthropometry. He focused in particular on the work of Alfred V Iannerelli and his theory on ears and ear prints. No use here though. The victim was an African male. His eyes would have been brown – round or oval, prominent or sunken? Not even the eagle that had punctured them could tell him that. Were the lips full or mean? And the ears? Ears were recognised by Iannerelli, in his work, as one of the best indicators of identity. They had the most distinctive and unusual features. Every human ear was individual, like a fingerprint, hardly changing since birth. Lobes and whorling cartilage vary vastly in shape and size. Had this man's ears survived the onslaught they might have given up a clue, but there was nothing left on the side of the head, just some neat holes waiting for the first of the flies to deposit their larvae in the conveniently exposed openings.

'Agh,' the detective slapped his forehead with the heel of his hand, 'now who's the idiot? I should have picked this up earlier.' In an instant Sibanda mentally opened a murder docket.

This victim didn't just land in the middle of the valley. He must have been carried or dragged here without any help from carnivores. His breakfast-deprived, instinctive gut had known this all along.

Sibanda stood and glanced around. The morning had aged while he thought. The dew had dried. The light had softened, become sleepy. A buzz of insects hovered before setting off for pollen troves and water spots. Wasting no time, Sibanda tipped his head sideways. He used the rays and their angle to backlight the grass and any disturbance to the pattern. The sun was against him at this late hour, but there had to be spoor and tracks of some kind to indicate how the dead man reached this spot.

You can't fool grass. Before the rains arrived, the grass was brittle and inflexible with empty seed heads tangled and stalks muddled. They didn't spring back to their usual combed perfection and they always pointed in the direction of the traveller. No matter what anti-tracking techniques are used, grass is implacable.

He almost missed the signs in the climbing light. A slight but faint indent led from the dirt road to where the body lay. The grass still had a tinge of green, and had made a weary effort to return to the vertical, helped by some hand or hands eager to disguise their traces. Sibanda rose from his haunches and jogged back towards the dirt road, skirting the disturbance, looking for a possible entry point. In places the earth had been scuffed to camouflage shoe prints and the heel-drag of the victim. When he reached the dirt road, he turned back towards Ncube and the vehicles. His sergeant stood deeply engrossed in conversation with the other officers.

'I tell you, that man can be very disagreeable at times,' Ncube said to the nearest police officer, punctuating each word with a forced belch in an attempt to deflate the build-up of wind threatening to dislodge the contents of his unhappy paunch. 'He needs to eat more. Look at him, he's as lean as a village dog in a drought. That cannot be good for his disposition and he makes life too complicated, always looking for trouble, doubting his own eyes.'

'What do you mean, sir,' the young policeman asked, 'isn't he some kind of a genius at solving crimes?'

'Yes, yes,' said Ncube, dismissing the detective's remarkable reputation with a further swat at the flies that had followed him from the vultures' breakfast table, 'but anyone with eyes can see this was just an unfortunate incident. Here we are in the middle of lion territory with a corpse torn to shreds like a woman's monthly rags, and he doesn't want to believe it.'

The young officer flinched. 'A gruesome sight, sir?' he asked.

'Stay well away if you want to sleep without nightmares. You don't want to view a person's inner bits exposed and mangled in a soup of blood and shit. The smell is…' A piercing whistle halted Sergeant Ncube as he was about to entertain his audience with further unsavoury details. They both eyed the whistler.

'I think Detective Sibanda is calling you, sir.'

'I am not deaf, young man,' said Sergeant Ncube, and he turned and hurried as best as his weight would allow to where Sibanda was examining the ground. The grey perspiration-soaked shade of his shirt matched his sickly complexion. Sibanda took note, but had no time for sympathy. 'What do you think, Ncube? I followed those tracks back to the road,' Sibanda indicated the broken stems and bent clumps of grass he had picked out against the light. 'The body was dumped and whoever off-loaded it entered the valley right here.'

Ncube peered at the disturbance. He knew better than to question the detective's observation so he just nodded his head and watched as droplets of perspiration pitted the sandy ground.

'What do you make of those?' Sibanda asked, pointing to patterned imprints in the dust of the road.

'Desert Duellers,' the sergeant replied, like a schoolboy reciting his alphabet. Even he recognised the common print. Every second vehicle in the bush seemed to be a Toyota Land Cruiser with the same make of tyre on them. 'Sir, this isn't going to help,' he added. 'If, as you suggest,' and he laid heavy emphasis on the doubt implied, 'we are talking murder here, we'll never prove it, not from what is left of…' he hesitated, 'the thing in the valley.'

'How old are these tyre tracks, Ncube?' Sibanda asked, ignoring his sergeant's misgivings.

'I couldn't say, sir,' he replied. He certainly did not want to hazard a guess. The detective was a magician in the bush. He understood and observed things that a normal human person born of an earthly mother could not possibly know. Ncube remained tight-lipped. Another vague answer might anger him further.

Sibanda bit his tongue this time and held back the stinging comment he had at the ready. Ncube had township in his blood. He had never herded cattle and goats as a child, never needed to track them when they got lost or wandered off. A severe beating awaited he who put them at risk. You learned or you took a hiding. He knew he had something of a legendary reputation for his tracking skills. When asked how he had become so skilled, he replied, 'Ngangiselusa, I was a herd boy.'

'Take a good look, Ncube,' he said, bending closer to the tyre tracks, 'at how crisp the edges of the prints are. That tells us the sun hasn't dried them out yet. Once they become dry like dust, they start to crumble in on themselves and become less distinct. 'Here too,' he said moving further along the path of the track, 'the only spoor over the top of the Duellers is in miniature.' He pointed to a tiny pattern of dots sprinkled across the tyre tread. 'Those are mouse tracks, Ncube, and mice are nocturnal. Those tyre tracks were put down in the night. Given their definition, I would say this vehicle passed here in the early hours of this morning, maybe five or six hours ago. Now, if it had been a shrew…' but he decided he had dispensed enough detail for Ncube to take in at one go.

'We need to go back to the body,' said Sibanda, 'and I'll show you why I'm convinced,' the detective underlined his certainty, 'this man was murdered.' Ncube's face turned a bilious shade of putty. Sibanda recognised that Ncube didn't want to go back to the crime scene. He felt some remorse for his sergeant's troubled stomach, but would need to get the full picture for himself. He pulled up a long stalk of elephant grass as they backtracked, to use as a pointer.

'Examine the ears, Sergeant', he said, using the grass to touch the place where the ears used to be, 'look how clean and perfectly rounded those holes are. No ripping or nibbling. They have been severed cleanly with a knife. I expect the eyes, nose and lips were cut away too and the body dumped here in full knowledge that the vultures would do an expert clean-up job and disguise the handiwork.'

Ncube caught on immediately. 'So you suspect witchcraft then?' he sighed. He would get lumbered with all the paperwork. A witchcraft case involved endless reports and filing. It would be complex and worst of all sickening in its detail. He could see himself tied up at a desk for several weeks. Witchcraft-related murders had hogged the headlines in the last few months. The police had found decapitated victims. Heads were highly prized for umuthi, magic medicine, across the border and brought big rewards.

'Ncube, do you remember the incident last year at the Plumtree border post?'

'Yes, sir,' said the sergeant cradling his aching stomach at the memory, 'several men were arrested carrying three human heads in cooler boxes disguised under frozen slabs of beef.'

'Since then, the gang has clearly had to downsize, leave the head and just take the features. You could stuff bits of a face in one packet of frozen peas and no one would be the wiser,' said Sibanda. Ncube blanched further at this thought.

Sibanda motioned to his sergeant. 'Help me lift the torso, Ncube, I want to look underneath.'

'Are you sure that is necessary?' he protested, wanting nothing more to do with the human travesty at his feet, let alone move it. 'Isn't it highly irregular to disturb a murder scene before Forensics arrive?'

'Ncube, both you and I know it could be hours, even days, before that lot pitch up this far out in the bush, by which time this body will be maggot fodder and the trail will have gone cold.'

Together they levered the body using a couple of dead branches. A miasma of engorged flies swarmed up and buzzed angrily as the body moved. Copulating, and depositing eggs in such a rich incubator was opportune and not to be disturbed. Ncube gagged. He turned his head away, but not before he caught sight of a tiny blue speck. He wondered later if he couldn't, perhaps, have somehow disguised the splinter of paint clinging to the dead man's right shoulder, flicked it away with sleight of hand. Sibanda, with eyes that swivelled in all directions was on to it in a flash.

Why couldn't it have been white? Ncube inwardly wailed. Every man and his dog owned a white Toyota Land Cruiser. The kingfisher-blue metallic paint shard winking at them in the morning light indicated one owner. His name might as well have been tattooed on the victim's shoulder. The only Toyota Land Cruiser with such a distinctive paint job belonged to the most powerful politician in the district. He was both the governor and a highly connected minister in government.

Ncube had been in the area long enough to learn you didn't mess with Micah Ngwenya. The lump of fly-blown mincemeat at his feet had probably been a political thorn in Ngwenya's side. At least that would narrow down identification for whoever survived the fallout from this case. Everyone knew it didn't pay to be Ngwenya's enemy.

Ncube stared at Sibanda, who was stroking his chin again, and prayed against all odds his boss would forget what he had seen, but the detective's eyes were resolute.

'Why did I ever get up this morning?' the sergeant thought. 'In a few years' time I am to retire and fish to my heart's content. Now the only fishing I'm likely to experience is my head, on a line, trawling for injuzu', a mermaid-like fish that fed on gold at the bottom of the ocean and converted the fish bones to bullion. The mermaid could only be baited with a human head. Ncube had dreamed of such a catch since childhood. The sergeant's fearful thoughts continued, 'my private parts will be transported in a bag of frozen French fries and fed to some poor unfortunate impotent, my eyeballs sliced and fed to those in need of foresight, and my tongue dried, ground and sold as a powder to induce sweet words. I am going to be carrion.'

Ngwenya would never be arraigned. He would pay some poor AIDS victim to take the fall and lop a few months off his life in order to secure his family's future. For those who chose to test the governor's authority and attempted to get some mud to stick, the outcome would be bleak.

The terrified sergeant turned to his boss. 'Sir?' he queried out loud, and in his inflection he included many questions, not the least of which was: Can't we pretend a lion killed him?

Sibanda stared hard at his sergeant like a cheetah assessing an impala. Ncube thought for one moment there might even have been the hint of an apology and regret in those steely eyes. The moment passed. He said in a voice so unwavering it would have intimidated the great Mzilikazi, 'Sergeant, get a grip. We need to investigate this killing for the sake of the victim and his family.'

As he walked back to the Land Rover, Sibanda's concerns were less for vehicle paint colour and more for the personal difficulties he would face. Today he was to meet his fiancée's mother. It had been arranged for weeks, but crime had no respect for a cop's plans. He would contact his uncle, who was acting as his sodombo, his go-between, in the marriage negotiations. Changing arrangements would make Khanyi, his fiancée, anxious. He doubted there would be phone coverage here in this wild valley. It would have to wait until they reached Thunduluka Lodge.

'Come, Sergeant, you can hop in with me. Let's see where these tracks lead.' The sergeant sighed. He gingerly hauled himself into the passenger seat of the Land Rover. Travelling with the detective meant he could not loosen his belt or fart at will. Not even an impentsho, a little accidental squeak from between the buttocks. He would have to wait some time to dispense his gaseous burden.

The Land Rover started reluctantly. Sibanda recognised that any indication of life from this heap of junk was a miracle. He accepted the unexpected gift without comment. They travelled west following the tyre tracks until the blue Toyota turned off the bush road, out of the game park, through some ranch land and back on the tar, leaving no indication of direction.

'I'm heading back to Thunduluka,' said Sibanda. 'The governor will keep.' The tension in Ncube's body dissolved. Its prodigious bulk sank back into the seat with relief.

'Good idea, sir,' he said.

Chapter 2

The old woman clung to the stick with both hands. It braced her journey across the bare, sandy earth. Her shuffling gait indicated the arthritic stiffness in her joints and the pain in her muscles. When she reached her destination, she planted the stick in the ground with as much force as she could muster. She used it as a support to lower herself, painstakingly, onto the squat stool resting against the uneven wall of the kitchen hut. From here she could survey her small village. Here she would remain until nature prodded her bladder and gripped her bowels, or the night summoned her back to her bed.

As the early sun tipped the horizon, its welcome warmth seeped into the mud walls. They in turn released a soothing heat to her aching back. She discretely raised the well-worn, brightly printed wrap above her swollen knees giving them access to the dawn's early blessing. Heat was the only medicine she had for her crumbling bones. The warmer weather had come. She didn't think she could survive another winter. She wondered if she wanted to survive another winter.

She sensed stirrings from the other huts now. Her youngest sister was already shrieking at her brood of children, chivvying them to get up, get to their chores. Fetch water, collect wood, hurry to the bellowing cattle kraal and drive the beasts to the best forage for the day. Even one of the youngest, who could hardly walk herself, was sent out with the baby strapped to her back to lull and soothe. When the morning porridge was cooked she would feed the little scrap, and jiggle it to sleep, already a mother, in all but birth, at four years old.

Across the yard of tamped, swept earth the old lady fixed her eyes on the door of the hut directly opposite, waiting for signs of life. The occupant was still asleep. She moved on to the adjacent doorway where her nephew and his family slept. The chickens had begun their daily scavenge and pecked around the hut, gleaning scraps of last night's meal. The incumbent rooster's flame-coloured feathers outshone the dowdy hens as he chased them away from the choice morsels. He opened his chest, spread his wings, proclaimed sovereignty of his territory and harem with lusty throat, dusted himself down and went back to foraging. She suspected that might be his last display for the morning. The sun had already climbed over the thatched roofs and its fiery dominance would soon rule until it sank to sleep behind the distant hills. All living things would be stifled to submission by its searing arrogance.

The rooster's last shrieking effort had done its job. She heard the door to her nephew's hut scrape open just enough for his wife to poke her head through the gap and push the two little ones into the yard. They ran out in vests only, their tiny trouble-makers dangling free. They stopped at the side of the hut, arched their backs, thrust their pelvises forward and emptied the night's accumulation on the parched soil. Their mother, her wild, unbraided hair signalling another restless night, remained in the doorway long enough to lock eyes with the old lady. Her look spoke of two concerns – he's still alive, and watch the children please. She retreated into the darkness and coaxed the grudging door back into its jamb.

Her nephew had been sick for some months, but in these last few days he had become bedridden. Her practised eye told her he could not survive much longer. There would be another funeral. Already the mounds in the family burial ground in front of the kraal were growing at an alarming rate. Several cousins, a nephew, his wife, two nieces, their husbands, countless children and one of her own precious daughters lay rotting before their time in the same baked earth as their ancestors.

Anxiously now, with her stomach still digesting the foreboding of a disease that struck with no respect for the young, her eyes returned to the unopened door. Behind it slept her daughter Kanku. The door remained firmly shut. She sighed in resignation and busied her brain with other thoughts. The rainbird's raucous call interrupted. A composition of tuneless whistles, scrapes and cheeps heralded the first downpour of the season. Other cuckoos would follow in the next few weeks, but the Jacobin cuckoo was always the first, the herald of the rains. The strident call sparked uncomfortable memories. She suffocated them with a mental pillow kept ever ready and waiting. When the danger moment passed, she squinted into the unremitting blanched-blue sky. No clouds yet. It satisfied her to know they would soon arrive.

She had learned so much about birds. She recognised their calls and their place and time in the scheme of the bush. They added a comforting rhythm and certainty to the seasons, punctuated the changes of the earth's moods. Her personal favourite was the fiery-necked nightjar, the Mapostoli bird that had arrived last month. It reassured her sleepless hours with its mournful prayer repeated through the night like a lullaby for the troubled. Her sick nephew would be listening. Wherever he was, Mr Barton, Thandanyoni, the famous bird lover and safari guide, would be listening too. She remembered the day that bird calls became a part of her life…

'Do you hear that, Mantini?' Thandanyoni said.

'What, sir?' she asked, lending a cursory ear as she continued to let down the mosquito net and arranged order in the cluttered tent.

'Ssshh. Put that duster down, stop fidgeting, just listen,' he said. Thandanyoni was sitting at his desk, his ear tilted towards the open door flap. Nothing unusual sang in the night air. She shook her head, keeping the rest of her body motionless so as not to disturb the silence. And then, suddenly, the sound came to her, a haunting, whistling refrain, drifting on the shafts of moonlight creeping stealthily into the room unnoticed.

'That's the fiery-necked nightjar, Mantini, the first of the season. Can you hear what he's saying?' he whispered.

'No, sir, but he sings the song of the moon. He tells the story of her sadness,' she said, trying to put into words the mournful yet beautiful tune filling the night sky. 'It is a song of silver and sorrow.'

Thandanyoni looked closely at Mantini as though he had never seen her before. 'Most people say he is praying and singing *good Lord deliver us.* That's why he's nicknamed the litany bird.'

She listened again, mouthing the words to the cadence. They fitted perfectly. 'What is *litany*?' she asked. Her English was good. It had to be to get a job in this prestigious safari camp. *Litany* was new to her. Her curiosity was aroused and seduced by this moonlight supplicant.

'It's another word for the prayers and responses at a Christian church service,' he explained. 'The priest asks God for a blessing or request. The congregation reply in words set down in a book. They are the same each week.'

Mantini thought about this for a while, but something chafed with the rawness of an ill-fitting shoe. This bird would never be contained in four walls on a Sunday morning. This was a free spirit worshipping under the stars and praying to the moon. She remembered those flocks of worshippers who gathered outside in open land, dressed all in white, chanting throughout the night: The Apostolics. 'No,' she said, 'the name is wrong. This bird is the Mapostoli bird.'

Thandanyoni laughed heartily. He recognised the accuracy of the description. 'You are so right, Mantini, and from now on, in this camp at least, it will be the Mapostoli bird…'

The old woman came back to the present, stirred and shifted her position on the stool, moving it into the shade on the western side. Throughout the day she would circumnavigate the walls, chasing the shadow as it traced the sun's path to darkness. She still had Kanku's hut door in view. It remained shut. Her nephew's wife must have surfaced during her reverie though. She was already dressed, her hair neatly tamed in rows, scrubbing her complaining children with a sharp cloth.

Mantini was not startled at this loss of time. She often drifted off during the day. Memories were her salve. They rubbed balm into her aching knees and massaged her twisted back. She felt happiest these days sifting through the debris and undergrowth of her mind like a guinea fowl scratching in the leaf-litter for grubs. Some would be pounced upon and devoured while others were discarded as unappetising. In this way she built up a mosaic of laughter and pride, love and satisfaction, sustenance for her day. Again, she opened the lid of the memory jar and dipped into the comforting liniment…

She had left the routine of village life, once her children could stay alone with their grandmother, to look for a job. Her husband had abandoned them two years before to search for work in Johannesburg but had found women and alcohol instead. He never sent money for the children. He had a new life. She must look for her own.

Her children were scattered now to the excitable spring winds, bursting seeds dispersing. One daughter dead, one sweet, harmless boy who had never been right since birth wandered freely, an unfettered soul, one good-for-nothing, matshayinyoka in South Africa she rarely heard from, and one, heaven knows where. Only Kanku, the youngest, remained with her. Their loss was a heavy price to pay for working away from home, but they had needed food and education. After a moment, she brushed the thought aside. What alternative did she have?

Those were difficult days in Zimbabwe. Jobs were few during years of a crippling bush war, when the finest men and boys had slipped across the border into Zambia to train and fight for independence. The jubilation of victory had been short-lived. The Matabele boys returned to the bush to struggle for their tribe and the right to share in government.

The new life she found as a camp attendant in the blossoming safari industry helped. She could not afford to be picky. Paid employment was a rarity in those unstable and dangerous days. A town job was too far from home and her children, but employment deep in the Matabele bush had its own perils – a current civil war raging, the worst of them.

Mantini, a thorough sort of person, soon absorbed the eccentric ways of the white tourists. She learned of their need for a continual stream of fresh towels and clean laundry. They liked their iced drinks and water that came in sealed bottles costing more than bread. They craved bottomless coffee and perpetual wine.

She found a new interest too. She crept into the shadows each evening and listened to the bird lectures of Thandanyoni. It began, at first, because of her enchantment with the Mapostoli bird. It grew because she needed to know what obsessed her disturbed son, Mtabizi, to roam the bush from nest to nest, talking to the birds as he went, watching them for hours. He always wanted to share his secrets and bush finds with her. She tried to give him the time his relentless wanderings demanded, but she was mother to three other children, without a husband. It was she who ploughed and tilled the fields, planted the maize and attended to all the daily chores.

Now he had grown, her spiteful younger sister, child of her father's third and last wife, had demanded that she chain Mtabizi in a hut. He brought shame to the village, a filthy bag of disease, she said, but Mantini had faith in him. Mtabizi, her bringer of joy, would die if he were caged. She let him roam, left him to his grimy uniform, turning her back on the jibes. He always wandered home when he had a need, bringing his precious treasures wrapped in an endless smile.

Thandanyoni, the camp owner, had bewitched the American tourists who came to collect a list of African bird sightings. He had captivated her with his knowledge of the aerial creatures that soared effortlessly through the heavens and carolled each in its own tongue. She began to see what Mtabizi must see. She reasoned that if these rich tourists found them so worthy and spent a life's fortune just to come and tick them, there must be something to their existence.

'182,' said Thandanyoni, seated around the campfire with his American clients.

'Where did we see that?' came a southern drawl from across the fire.

'In the acacia grove, half way down the valley, just after we spotted 440,' he explained.

'OK, I didn't realise that was 182,' replied the southerner. There was a moment's silence as all the participants ticked the number on a sheet as though competing in some ecological bingo game.

The old woman chuckled to herself. She held her painful back remembering the scene. Confusion as number after number came up. Each person ticked, queried or confirmed its accuracy. What were they talking about? It was later she discovered the Bird Bible, a book written by a Mr Roberts numbering every bird.

'You see,' said Thandanyoni, 'we ornithologists are a stubborn and individual lot. Many of us from different regions have developed our own names for the same birds or at least variations of them. Over the years some of the birds have been classified incorrectly – put in the wrong Order. Their names get changed. It can be very confusing so we just use the number, which never changes.'

'Humph,' she replied, 'you mukiwas have strange habits. Don't you know numbers are for money, books are for stories and names are for living things?'

Thandanyoni laughed as he always did when she questioned him. He was a good man, full of joy and laughter. She liked working for him. 'I love your take on life, Mantini, you certainly have your priorities right.'

'Thank you, sir, I have learned from my son.' And she thought she was closer to understanding Mtabizi and his mindless wanderings than she had ever been.

Slowly she had collected species for herself and imprinted their calls, their shapes and the cut of their feathers in her memory. She didn't care for books or numbers or pages. She noted where they nested and marvelled at the handicraft and architectural variety of their homes. Fascinated by what they ate, she learned to attract them with titbits from the kitchen. She watched them raise their broods, and counted the numbers of chicks. At first she did this for Mtabizi, but slowly she realised it was for her.

Thandanyoni observed her growing curiosity and gave her an old pair of binoculars. They were battered. One eye piece couldn't focus, but she cherished them. Each afternoon during her free hours she would scan the branches and the nearby waterhole searching for new birds. The rest of the staff thought her stupid, wasting her free time staring into the bush.

'Mantini, come and lie in the shade and rest,' said Shadrek, the camp cook. He patted the blanket next to him, set beneath an ancient camel thorn acacia whose branches carved cool, contorted passageways through the stifling, mid-afternoon air. 'Leave those gundwane lesibhaka bhaka, those sky-rats. Come and lie down next to me. Here, I have reserved a place in the deepest cover.'

She was tempted. She could lie on her back and search in the overhead tangle for the myriad fire finches that flocked to the shade in between mercurial visits to the water. Nearby was a rare Bradfield's hornbill plastered into a hollow in the acacia trunk, ready to nest. The curved hornbill beak appeared through a carefully measured slit. Her devoted husband was feeding her while she moulted and produced her brood. Throughout, the naked bird remained behind the mud bars of her birthing prison, safe from all marauders. But, should her overworked, distracted husband die, perhaps in the talons of the peregrine falcon that called the neighbouring woodland home, it would mean a lingering death from starvation. Waiting patiently in the darkness for his return, she would be unable to break free in her vulnerable, featherless state.

'Birds have a lot to teach us, Shadrek,' she replied, brushing aside his advances, knowing that her own independence would be her best salvation.

The old woman came back to the present and shifted her stool again, now almost out of view of the hut door. She would allow the sun to bake her marrow dry before she let it disappear, out of sight, unopened. If only she still had those old binoculars. They disappeared, the day The Boys came.

The binocular memory was a mistake. She should never have allowed it to surface. The day had become suffocating, making her drowsy. With little energy left, bad memories were fighting to come alive, pushing like a baby whose waters had broken. When they arrived, it was with all the unstoppable fury and turmoil of birth pains and none of the rewards. She went back…

The day The Boys came, the rainbirds had already been calling for two weeks. Mantini had been watching a male displaying near the nest of a pair of bulbuls. His tail fanned, his wings flapping to attract their attention. In turn, the little birds darted from their nest. They bravely chased and harried the cuckoo until finally his ruse succeeded. Both parents left the nest unattended to see him off. In an instant the female Jacobin hopped into their home and deposited her single egg among the small bulbul clutch. Job done. Like those rich mukiwa ladies, the rainbird Jacobin had found herself a perfect nanny to feed and nurture her child.

Mantini had watched cuckoos at work before or at least seen their handiwork. Once the nestlings hatched, the baby cuckoo would evict the chicks, nudge them over the edge. If they survived the fall, they were devoured by a range of insects eating them alive as they struggled, still blind and bald, to make sense of their fate. The unwitting parents continued to feed this murderous invader, battling with all their skills to satisfy a chick sometimes three times their own adult size, unaware of the bloodthirsty drama unfolding beneath them.

Mantini had found a good vantage point to observe the nest by climbing a few feet into the acacia where several branches knotted to form a perfect observation deck. From here she looked down on the infiltrated home. She noted the three perfectly formed bulbul eggs splashed with red and purple on a bed of herbs and soft grasses patiently sewn together with cobwebs. In the middle lay a pure white cuckoo egg. Why did these birds accept such an obvious intruder that didn't even bother to camouflage its appearance? This was the question she must ask Thandanyoni when next redistributing the dust on his papers. She could not know she would never see Thandanyoni to speak to about birds again or to report to him what she observed next.

The eggs hatched in front of her monocled eye. She expected the much larger cuckoo to begin his evictions using his wing stubs and strong back to roll the victims out of the nest. Instead he squatted firmly on each of the three bulbul siblings in turn and calculatingly smothered them.

Life in the bird world could be brutal. With no insect accomplices to share the blame or scavenging lizards to hide the crime, the parents themselves were left to dispose of the corpses and raise the murderer of their progeny. Mantini shook her head to rid herself of the ruthless image. She fixed her skewed binoculars on the waterhole. At this time of day, the bull elephant groups often came to bathe and coat themselves in soothing mud, or a large buffalo herd might lumber in, stirring up dust clouds, desperate to slake their thirst.

There was something coming to the waterhole, but the heat-fog sliced through the image and distorted the shape. Her single lens obscured the outline of the vague and woolly silhouette. When she did focus it was the rifles that she saw first. From this distance, the arrivals were difficult to identify. As they emerged from the hazed pixilation, she noted four of them, all armed, AKs in their hands, bandoliers of ammunition and grenades across their chests…

The hut door, focus of all her waking attention, swung open and the familiar greeting 'Salibonani, Mama', brought her back to the present. 'Yebo, Kanku,' she responded. 'Livukanjani?' she asked, keen to know how her daughter was feeling this morning.

'Mama,, how many times have I asked you not to call me Kanku? My name is Khanyi!' Mantini chided herself for the mistake. This child would always be Kanku to her and anyway her mind had still been in the tree with the inkanku, the rainbird cuckoo, and The Boys. She had been caught off guard. She glanced across at Khanyi, standing tall and statuesque, carrying morning bathwater on her head, so different from her other children who had been wiry, scrawny, short and practical like herself. Kanku was a beauty and acknowledged as such by all who knew her. Her skin glowed with the burnt amber of wild imgongomtshani honey, her eyes were almond and deep like those of the kudu roaming the nearby forest and, as her elegant neck swayed to balance the heavy water bucket on her head, she transformed into a giraffe of long-limbed grace.

Giraffe had been standing around, waiting to come to the waterhole on that distant day at the camp. They held back, clustered in a tangle of extremities, staring down patrician noses, alarmed at their strange human drinking companions with their shiny killing kit. Even when the fighters melted into the bush, the giraffe remained alert, haughtily surveying the water, disdainful of their thirst, chary of the danger.

Mantini had scrambled down the tree, shredding her hands on the hooked thorns as she descended.

'Shadrek, armed men are heading this way, run and tell Thandanyoni,' she hissed. Shadrek shook himself and lifted his head off the blanket.

'What are you saying, Mantini?'

'The Boys are here, the dissidents, with guns. Go and warn Barton.' Louder and more urgently she spoke, her whisper breaking through into a hoarse squawk. She used Thandanyoni's real name knowing this rare usage would reinforce the menace of the situation.

'No!' he said. 'Barton must not know, he will get all of us killed.' Shadrek panicked. If they aided these men they would be arrested and tortured by the police. If they refused to help these bush warriors, they would be shot without excuse. 'Listen,' he continued, 'we should try and give them what they want. Maybe they will go away. Some beers and food might be enough to get rid of them. Thandanyoni will understand.'

She recognised the sense in what the cook said. Terror weakened her legs. Would they be strong enough to carry her to the staff quarters? Would her acting skills fool the dissidents?

'Don't run,' he pleaded, 'they will be watching us now. Act normally, stroll. Here, help me roll up the blanket.' Together they made their way to the kitchen tent. The Boys were there before them...

'Mama, Mama, you are dreaming again.' Khanyi woke her from the nightmare. 'You are in full sun and sweating, Mama,' she said, as she bathed her mother's brow with cool water. She moved Mantini's stool further around the rondavel into deep shade. 'You mustn't get too hot. You will not be in any fit state to welcome our guest.' Mantini paused to take in this statement, trying her best to remember the visitor. Why could she clearly remember the events of twenty-five years ago, but barely remember what had happened yesterday?

'Sibanda, Mama; Jabu. He is coming to meet the family,' Khanyi prompted.

Ah, yes, Kanku's isoka, her intended.

'Mama, here is porridge and a mug of cold water. When you have finished we must get you dressed and smart in your best, ready to meet Jabu and his uncle,' Khanyi wheedled. The old woman groaned at the thought of any disturbance to her aching bones, but she would suffer anything for Kanku. The visit would be a distraction from the day and her recent unwanted memories.

Chapter 3

The Land Rover chugged into the lodge car park and belched to a premature halt in a cloud of black diesel fumes. Sibanda got out. His mood was not helped by the comparison of his obdurate boneshaker to the row of immaculate safari vehicles lined up, polished and ready to take clients on their adventure tours into the park.

'Ncube,' he barked. 'Get under the bonnet of this thing and have a look. See if you can get it running again. Try and be discreet,' was his quiet admonition as he walked off towards reception, putting as much distance between himself and the cantankerous Land Rover as he could. He walked past the gleaming line-up of vehicles and noted they were all Land Cruisers shod with Desert Duellers.

As he approached the lodge, he marvelled at what could be achieved with canvas and a few poles. Before him, nestled in a confection of lawn and shady acacias, were several large, airy tents dotted beneath the trees. Each tent came with its own plunge pool, space and privacy. The ground fell away steeply at the front of the camp. Every tent veranda had a breathtaking view across the bush and grassland, extending for several kilometres and ending abruptly at a low ridge of hills. Even now, with his naked eye, he could see a small herd of impala nudging toward the waterhole at the base of the drop away. No doubt they would be followed by sable and kudu, grazing and browsing their way to a mid-morning drink. The puddled edges of the pan showed a favourite elephant haunt. The bulls would dawdle here, peppering themselves with mud blown from their trunks, siphoning up litres of water, standing in the shade, languidly fanning their ears and enjoying a well-earned rest from the relentless foraging needed to provide them with the tonnes of food they ingested daily.

Sibanda thought, not for the first time, that he had chosen the wrong profession. He could be living here, with this view every morning and a new vehicle to drive that started with the turn of a key. He imagined the wilderness on his doorstep and the companionship of international tourists who understood that the Pulitzer was not a make of towrope designed to assist in jump-starting recalcitrant Land Rovers.

'African hawk eagle. They have a nest in that large canopied teak to the left,' a voice from behind him interrupted his musings. He pulled his focus from the far to the middle distance and saw the eagle circling overhead. He recognised the black back, the white, streaked front and the distinctive white wing markings.

Sibanda turned and addressed the man who was now standing at his side, 'Perfect spot for them. They prefer to nest with sweeping views. They certainly have a magnificent vista here. Hieraaetus spilogaster,' he added, 'it means spotted stomach.' He was showing off and normally resented people who reeled off Latin names, but he felt the need to establish his credentials in this impossibly opulent setting.

'Hi, I'm John Berger, the manager here, and you are…?'

'Detective Inspector Sibanda, Gubu Police.'

'Yes, Detective, we have been expecting you. Follow me. We will find somewhere comfortable to talk.' Berger led him to a large pavilion tent and a deep leather armchair. 'Can I get you anything to drink or eat?' he asked.

Sibanda thought for a moment. He was ravenous, but had long ago made a pact never to accept food on the job. 'Just a glass of mineral water, thanks, and perhaps you could see that my sergeant gets a glass of soda water. He has had a rough morning.'

While Berger was away, Sibanda checked for phone signal. A morale-boosting three bars filled the screen. He should phone Khanyi and apologise for his delay. He dialled Gubu Station instead and connected with Constable Zanele Khumalo.

'Hi, Zee,' he addressed the station's best go-to officer, 'we've got a murder case on our hands this morning and very little to go on. The corpse has been severely mutilated by scavengers. We do have some paint at the scene, though. Phone around to all the 4x4 dealers. Find out how many blue vehicles, probably pick-ups, have been sold in the region in say… the last ten years.'

'What shade of blue should I ask for?'

Sibanda wanted to reply, a shade between the wing of a malachite kingfisher and the tail of a purple roller, two of the flashiest birds in the bush, but he knew she wouldn't know those birds, let alone the subtle shade.

'Something like the colour on the cover of the latest phone directory,' he explained. 'Tell them it has a metallic finish. That should narrow it a bit. Zee, this is urgent, drop everything.'

'Right, I'm on to it.'

Sibanda put his phone away and took in his surroundings. This main tent was enormous. It had the best views across the waterhole. The décor was simple with a neo-colonial flavour. Overhead, the canvas roof was draped with white muslin. Two crystal chandeliers hung on either side of a ceiling fan gently turning, wafting a soothing breeze throughout the room. The tent's cool elegance contrasted sharply with the raw ugliness of the site he had just left.

He wished Khanyi could be here sitting beside him. She would love the lavishness. They could sit quietly and watch the waterhole together, pointing out the animals coming in to drink. He could explain their behaviour. She would take pleasure from the sheer magnificence of the site. Khanyi knew very little about wildlife when he met her. She had never ventured into the park even though she lived almost on its boundary. Now she was beginning to learn the names of some of the trees and take an interest in the habitat. He loved her being a bit of a scaredy cat around elephants. Protecting her from these mostly gentle giants made him feel like a caveman, a primordial chest-beater. She reinforced his function as a man in this era of complex and confused gender roles. He was a lucky guy to have found her. His mother had nagged him to get a companion.

'You will end up a lonely old man if you don't find someone soon to share your joys and sorrows,' she said. 'Look at your brother, he is so settled now. With another child on the way, he has been truly blessed.'

Sibanda always suffered in comparison to his brother in his mother's eyes. She was very proud of Xolisani. He had gone to university, become a lawyer, married and produced a child in the perfect script of a perfect life. His mother's admonitions were gentle and always softened with love, but he knew he was something of a disappointment. She was not one to boast, but having a policeman as a son, particularly in these unstable political times, could not be easy for her. Several girlfriends had come and gone. He had even taken one or two home to meet his mother, but none of them put up with his frequent absences and the anti-social hours of crime. The relationships inevitably fizzled under a welter of disappointment and broken dates.

Khanyi was different, not needy and clinging or weepy when he didn't call. She understood the nature of his job. She accepted it was part of his life and he wasn't going to change it for anyone. He wouldn't be moving away from the bush and the game park to the neon life of the larger towns if he could avoid it.

Khanyi was tall and slender with an inbred grace that set her above the rest of the local girls. From the time they bumped heads over the Gubu General Supplies supermarket freezer and the frozen chicken thighs, they chatted easily in each other's company. The sex, when it happened, was a complete bonus – hot, unbridled and daring. Roll on the day she was in his bed every morning, not just the sneak previews he currently enjoyed.

Berger chose that moment to return. Sibanda hoped the glass of water would arrive soon. He was beginning to feel the heat. The thought of Khanyi in his bed hadn't cooled his temperature. Berger brought along a tall, athletically built, khaki-clad guide. Pythagoras had this man in mind when he formulated his golden ratio. He was in his prime, with prematurely grey hair – the silver-grey of a black-backed jackal pelt. Smooth skin, lightly tanned, was salted by a day-old beard. His Hollywood jaw could have come straight out of a deodorant advert.

'Detective, this is Barnaby Jones. He was guiding when they spotted the vultures circling. He'll be able to give you all the detail you need.'

'Mr Berger, I have to interview all the others on the vehicle,' said Sibanda. 'Please organise for them to be on standby.'

'Some of them are in a bad way, Detective. Can you come back later?'

Sibanda would have liked to give the tourists time to compose themselves and to come to grips with the image of the grisly corpse. He suspected it would have been their first de-sanitised brush with death. The stench, the flies, the mutilation were a far cry from an air-conditioned funeral parlour and a silk-lined coffin. The Land Rover rarely ventured out on more than one trip in twenty-four hours. After this it would need a day of rest. The indignity of being pushed around the lodge car park to get it going could not be repeated.

'I'm sorry, Mr Berger, I insist on seeing your clients in the next half an hour. Time is important.'

Berger addressed Barnaby Jones, 'Okay, Rubble, see to it the detective gets access to them after he has finished with you.'

Sibanda picked up on the 'Rubble' nickname. It was a *Flintstone* reference. He had heard it before somewhere else. It rang a dozen competing and discordant cow-bells in his brain. He stored the name away in his memory bank for later analysis.

'Mr Jones, let's start,' he said. 'Tell me everything about the morning game drive from the very beginning.'

'Call me Barney,' said the good-looking ranger and proceeded to give a brief account of the morning safari.

Sibanda made a few notes. 'Did you approach the valley from the north or south road?'

'We took the loop road around Sable Springs and came in from the north,' Barney replied. 'We got out of the vehicle near Ntundhla Pan and began our walk.'

'Were any other lodge vehicles or walks out yesterday morning?'

'No, just me. We are quiet at the lodge at the moment. The Bernstein family are the only clients in camp.'

'And you didn't travel on the road south of the valley at all?'

'No. Normally I would. The game is brilliant further along. We often get good lion sighting at Windmill Pan, but as soon as I came across the body, I headed back to the vehicle and radioed the lodge. We called the Gubu Police Station immediately.'

'Anything out of the ordinary on the drive?' asked Sibanda.

'Yes, we came across a snared warthog around seven-thirty,' replied Barney. 'The poor bastard must have been in the snare since yesterday or even the day before. In this heat…' He broke off to leave the suffering to the detective's imagination.

'You saw no signs of tracks?'

'No, the snare line could have been set weeks ago. We sweep the area with our patrols but this is a huge reserve, Detective, and sadly, we often miss the wires.'

'How close did you get to the body?'

'Not close at all. We didn't enter the valley. I looked through my binos from the north road, maybe thirty or forty metres from the scene. I could see there was a carcass, I didn't know it was a body. I wanted to check clearly that there were no predators lurking. We were on foot. The Bernstein family all have good binos and cameras. They got more than they bargained for.'

'You said that an anti-poaching patrol was out last night?'

'Yes, but I don't know where they were deployed. Speak to the manager about that. He is in charge of the anti-poaching team.'

'How long have you worked at this lodge, Barney?'

'About two years now.'

'And before that?'

'On my dad's ranch, Hunter's Rest.' Barnaby Jones dropped his eyes and looked away towards the waterhole. A group of giraffe had wandered up during the conversation. They were splaying their front legs, edging first the left then the right hoof further and further apart until they had lowered themselves sufficiently for their long necks to reach the water.

Barney pointed towards the waterhole. 'Do you know that they only have seven neck vertebrae, the same as all mammals?' he said.

Sibanda nodded his head, 'Giraffe have a special adaptation at the base of their skulls to offset the huge blood pressure surge that occurs when they drop those long necks to drink. The heart has to work hard to pump blood all the way up the extended necks to the head. In order to avoid blowing their brains out of their nostrils when they lower them, there is a mat of blood vessels that disperses the pressure.'

Barney raised his eyebrows. 'Interesting,' he said begrudgingly, aware of the aggressive atmosphere that was developing during the questioning. 'I'll go and bring the Bernstein family, if you have finished with me.' Sibanda nodded.

Sibanda reached for the glass of water that had arrived seamlessly and silently while he was in conversation. It was a piece of art unto itself. It sat on a padded coaster embossed in gold with the name Thunduluka Lodge and the stylised effigy of the wild plum tree the name represented. In the water amid a wealth of ice cubes lay a lemon wedge and a sprig of mint. By the side of the glass was placed a drinking straw cased in a sheath printed with the gold logo.

Sibanda's thoughts flew to his own village and his mother who still drew her water from a hand-pumped well several hundred metres away. Daily, and sometimes twice a day, she carried every drop of water for drinking and washing in a container on her ageing head. The bucket had no lid so his mother filled it with newly picked leaves and branches to prevent the formation of waves which would slop the water over the sides, wasting the precious cargo. He still marvelled at her ability to keep the bucket practically motionless as she walked with extraordinary grace over the uneven ground back to the village. It was a skill honed since childhood. Ice? Well, that was a dream. Sibanda picked up the straw and rolled it between his fingers. Africa was indeed a continent of startling contrasts.

The detective gulped the clear liquid down without a breath. For the second time in this lodge, he regretted reeling off arcane knowledge, but he had the humiliation of the car park to face shortly and somehow, subconsciously, this man and his cartoon nickname had tweaked his competitive streak. He wondered how Ncube was faring.

Sergeant Ncube was still in the car park, talking to himself with his head under the Land Rover's bonnet. The bonnet support had long ago rusted and disassociated itself from the underside of the hood. He had improvised with a branch broken from a nearby shade tree. Detective Inspector Sibanda, if he had been there, would have given him a lecture on the tree, its name, the properties of the bark, the roots, the leaves and whether it was best suited to the purpose he was using it for. As far as Ncube was concerned, it was wood and could hold up the bonnet lid, or so he hoped. He normally liked to have a helper around at times like these to keep an eye on the makeshift arrangement and intervene should the prop break while he was lost in the wondrous world of the diesel engine, but he was alone with a precariously balanced weight over his head. His concentration wasn't as intense as usual.

The Land Rover was well over twenty years old. It had come to Gubu Police Station from the Central Mechanical Engineering Department, the CMED, where it had been abandoned by some previous civil service branch. It had been battered and unloved. A bullet hole through the passenger door would tell a story of jealousy if it could talk. The windscreen was a collection of crazed shards. The driver's door was missing and the upholstery had split at every seam and rotted to a pile of dust. It had sat up on chocks and had been parasitised ruthlessly for spare parts.

The previous station transport, an aged Santana, had hit a cow in the pursuit of a stolen car. No one at Gubu Police Station had any political connections or clout to acquire one of the newer imports and the station was advised that it would 'have to get by' with the one vehicle it still had running. The situation was intolerable. Word had got around the village and surrounding areas that the police were running at half strength. There had been an immediate upsurge in petty theft.

Chief Inspector Stalin Mfumu, the Member-in-Charge, Gubu, could see his crime statistics suffering and with it any hope of promotion out of the godforsaken wilderness that he currently held sway over. He was from the ruling Shona tribe and when, at Independence, the Matabele refused subjugation, the government sent in troops to crush the populace. Very quickly, however, they learned that massacre bred resentment. There were many better options more powerful than the sword. One of their most successful ideas had been to flood the local civil service with the ruling tribe. Chief Inspector Mfumu's posting to Gubu in the Matabele heartland was part of that strategy.

Mfumu called his sergeant into the office one Thursday morning. 'Ncube, you were recently stationed in Bulawayo. I hear you have contacts in the CMED down there?'

'I have a brother who is a clerk in the office,' the sergeant replied.

'Right, you will catch the night train to Bulawayo tonight. By Monday morning you will have a vehicle back here at the station. I don't care what you have to do to get it. Do you understand? Don't come back without one.' Mfumu's voice rose from bass through baritone to tenor before coming to a screaming halt on a soprano note. There was no way this vehicle situation was going to undermine his escape strategy. The sergeant needed to understand that clearly.

Ncube relished the thought of getting back to civilisation if only for a couple of days, but he had visited the CMED workshops before. It was a wrecker's yard, full of rusting hulks, rotting tyres and twisted chassis. The task was hopeless.

As he and his brother wandered around the graveyard of abused and tangled bodies, cooked engines and smashed dreams, Ncube despaired. If he didn't get something to take back to Gubu, his life would be a misery of roadblock duty and domestic disputes. Standing for hours in the sun checking driving licences or vehicle defects was a torture devised to punish incompetent, unpopular officers. He had far too sensitive a nature to get involved in domestic violence. With three happy and contented wives, he could not begin to understand why fists and boiling water made their way into marriages. Ncube had almost abandoned the yard of wrecks and mentally donned the yellow, fluorescent vest of the roadblock when he spied the Land Rover in a corner. Under a pile of discarded exhausts, mufflers and oil filters, it still had the shape of a vehicle.

Ncube stowed away under a tarpaulin until all the staff had knocked off for the weekend and set to work. That night, he fixed up a light and worked until 4 am. His brother passed by with a plate of maize meal, stew and an ice-cold beer which he squeezed under a break in the chain-link fencing surrounding the yard.

'Howzit going, Bru?' he asked. Ncube's brother was young, trendy and spoke in the language of the street. Ncube looked him up and down and shook his head. The boy's jeans were low and baggy, held up by a belt decorated with lethal-looking silver studs. The jeans hung far below his hips and the waistband of his underpants was clearly visible in the interests of advertising some foreign name. His shoes, glossy and unscuffed, were so elongated as to be dangerous weapons and on his head he wore a cap with the peak studiously turned to protect his left ear rather than his face for which it was designed. He was ready for a big Friday night out. Ncube glanced down at his own greasy overalls, worn at the knee and with the arms sawn off and sighed. 'Be back here by tomorrow morning. I will have the list of parts for you to requisition.' With a nod of the head his brother melted into the night.

What Ncube was doing was not in any way illegal. Chief Inspector Mfumu had given him a letter of authority to acquire a vehicle, but if anyone were to suspect that a half-decent runner still existed in the system, someone with greater authority, or a distant cousin who was a politician, would take precedence. Stealth was of the essence.

Through the night Ncube scavenged what he could from other smashed wrecks strewn around the yard. A recent arrival gave up a set of side mirrors, two wheels with roadworthy tyres and a set of brake shoes. The windscreen was replaced by one with several chips, stars and cracks, but it was the closest thing to visibility in the yard. The Land Rover had been abandoned because of age, not collision. The chassis was straight and the axles were aligned. But it was the engine that was a thing of beauty to Ncube. Once he had washed it down and cleaned it off, he could see its potential. A diesel engine was the closest thing to eternal life. They ran forever and the longer they ran the looser and more efficient they became. This was an older-version Land Rover, forsaken when the shiploads of shiny new Santanas arrived just after Independence. It had outlasted most of them. It was British and built with pride and precision.

By Saturday afternoon Ncube's brother had filled out the paperwork, raided the stores and supplied most of the missing spares. He even managed two new tyres to fit a couple of battered rims that had taken some force to straighten. He was short of heater plugs, but it was summer. They could wait for the colder weather. A spare driver's door had been located and attached, although its delicate lavatory-green contrasted starkly with the robust green of the rest of the body. A school friend of Ncube's had welded, patched and cobbled together an exhaust pipe and muffler from the heap that had concealed the old Land Rover. His cousin resuscitated the radiator.

After a second mostly sleepless night, the old girl was starting to splutter into life. Ncube cajoled and coaxed, twiddled and tuned until the engine finally ran without dying. By Sunday afternoon he was on the road back to Gubu. There had been no time to fix the seats so he perched on a cushion borrowed from the CMED office. He had a plan to get the upholstery repaired if he could get back to Gubu in reasonable time.

The Land Rover behaved impeccably. He only stopped twice on the four-hour journey, once to readjust the timing and once to top up with oil. This latter was something of a worry. He would deal with it in the long term. Ncube pulled up outside Phiri's house in the village. The engine was a bit hot and the exhaust was coated in black soot deposited from the clouds of billowing smoke that continuously exited the exhaust pipe, but he had made it.

'Phiri, are you home?' he yelled. He put his hand on the hooter, which surprised him by delivering a very loud blast. An old man came out from the hut and greeted him.

'What do you want on a Sunday afternoon, Ncube?' Phiri asked, 'you are disturbing my rest.'

'I need a huge favour from you,' said the Sergeant, 'and my life depends on it.'

'On a Sunday?' Phiri protested.

'Yes, I need you to recover the seats in this old Land Rover,' he said, waving his hands over the remnant upholstery that still clung to the framework. 'And if you can get it done by tonight, I promise to show you my best fishing hole.'

Phiri was not only a brilliant tailor who could sew anything, he was also Ncube's fishing rival. He had been trying for months to get the sergeant to disclose the location of the huge bream he had been catching of late.

'Do you have any fabric?' the old Malawian asked.

'No, I had no time to get anything. You must have something that would do. Please,' he added in desperation.'

'Come back tonight and I will see what I can find,' said Phiri.

On Monday morning Ncube drove the Land Rover into the station yard to be appreciated by all. Even the candy-striped, deck-chair canvas that Phiri had used to cover the seats failed to dampen the universal admiration. Everyone realised with relief that life would now return to normal at the station. Chief Inspector Mfumu might regain his equilibrium.

Ncube had pinpointed the source of the Land Rover's current difficulty to an airlock in the fuel supply. He would bleed the system, which was a fairly simple operation, but it did require a second pair of hands, or rather feet, to pump the accelerator as he adjusted the bleed screw and eliminated the bubble. The sergeant gingerly extricated himself from under the potentially hazardous guillotine to see an opportune waiter headed in his direction.

'Here,' the waiter thrust a glass of something cold and fizzy under his nose. 'I have been sent to bring this to you.' Ncube grabbed the glass. He would have preferred a cola or a glass of the garish orange stuff that was his favourite tipple, but this might well settle the confusion in his digestive system.

'You have come at just the right moment,' said Ncube, 'hop behind the wheel.'

From the comfort of his armchair Sibanda heard the chesty diesel coughs of the Land Rover. His mood improved instantly. He was interviewing his way through the Bernstein family. Bill Bernstein had been clear and concise in his memory. He had nothing to add to the account received from Barney Jones. His wife Pearl was a mess and barely functioning. She would need expensive psychiatric analysis as soon as she got back to small-town America. Pearl was verging on hysteria and talking legal retribution.

'How could any agent send us to a place where wild animals can kill people?' she warbled in southern complaint. 'It's irresponsible. I'm going to see to it this lodge is closed down. It's plumb dangerous.' Her eye-witness account seemed unreliable and wildly exaggerated. She claimed to have seen a 'pack' of leopards pulling the victim down and devouring him. Leopards, as anyone knew, were secretive, solitary creatures that rarely socialised, rarely hunted during the day and never gathered in groups of more than two let alone cooperated in a hunting expedition. They also never attacked humans unless cornered or injured. Sibanda discounted her testimony, but listened to her account with interest. She demanded attention. He did not think now was the time to advise her that animals had played no part in the demise of the victim.

Their young son had an enthusiastic imagination. He had a similar story to his father and the guide. He was not in the least bothered by the gruesome scene. He lived on a diet of bloodthirsty horror movies and was convinced that the body had been the victim of a crazed zombie attack. Ironically, thought Sibanda, he was probably closest to the truth.

It was the daughter, Ruby, an intelligent but sullen teenager, who piqued his interest the most. She had attitude, and he suspected a severe dose of khaki fever. Given Barney's near-perfect looks, this was hardly surprising, but something had occurred to sour her opinion of the safari guide. He was keen to mine the discontent.

'I don't know why he got it into his head to traipse after those warthogs,' she said. 'We had had a pretty good morning up until then, and sighting the leopard charging the warthog group was really cool.

All of us had had enough at that stage. I didn't want to go looking at his pet project.'

'What was that?' Sibanda asked.

'His warthog study,' she replied. 'We all wanted to go back to the lodge, particularly after seeing that poor warthog dying on the end of a wire – yuk – but Barney seemed to know where he was going and nothing was going to stop him. It was as if he knew all along that the body was in the valley.'

'Go on,' said Sibanda.

'You know what I think?' she said. 'I think that dead guy was a poacher, trying to find food for his family, and Barney shot him and left him for the vultures.'

She is a venomous little madam, thought Sibanda, but she had given him food for thought.

'Or stabbed him,' she said. 'That would be clever wouldn't it? And you will never find the wound because the vultures will have eaten it away.' With that she reached into a side pocket on her designer safari shorts and produced a knife. 'I found this on the side of the road as we were walking. It's pretty old and beaten up, but look here, there is a letter B scratched into the blade, B for Barney.' Ruby handed him the knife.

Sibanda reached into his pocket and took out a plastic Zip loc bag. 'Drop it in here, young lady, please,' he said. 'When you go to the station to make your statement, your fingerprints will be taken as well. In the meantime, one of my officers will take you back to the exact spot where you found the knife.'

Chapter 4

Sibanda headed to the lodge car park. He hadn't bargained on the Land Rover having to make a side trip, but the location of the knife was key evidence. Ruby had found the weapon north of the valley. Whoever dumped the body had taken off in a vehicle heading south.

The detective relaxed his fisted hands as he reached the car park. The Land Rover was running in a reasonable fashion. The exhaust pipe rattled metronomically and the exhaust gases seemed pale and healthy. His sergeant, however, was emitting loud snores to rival a bellowing buffalo. He lay fast asleep in the front seat, the full weight of his body wedged against the Land Rover door. A wide-open mouth exuded a hint of drool dribbling along the path of his right jowl. The top button of his uniform trousers had eased undone. His troublesome stomach had expanded into the extra space, enjoying a moment of unrestrained freedom. The sergeant's personal exhaust gases must have been active. The surrounding air reeked of sulphur.

Sibanda checked his initial instinct to open the door and let the sergeant fall out of the vehicle. He never accepted sloppy or undisciplined behaviour, but Ncube had been awake all night. A wave of unusual gratitude for his mechanical expertise stopped him. He tapped on the window instead.

'Sergeant Ncube,' he said loudly.

Ncube awoke with a start and attempted to stuff his extra adipose flesh behind the suffering waistband and wipe the spit from his face at the same time.

'Um, sorry,' he stuttered, 'I...'

Sibanda cut him off. 'Ncube, we've had a development. One of the witnesses, Ruby Bernstein, found a knife not far from the body. Can you take her back to the scene and identify the exact spot. Check for anything else of interest at the site. I will be waiting in the car park when you get back.' Sibanda turned his head to establish the absence of onlookers and said sotto voce, 'And don't switch off the engine.'

The detective walked back towards the lodge, hoping to catch the manager in his office. His old lecturer used to say environment told you more about a person than an hour's interrogation.

'Newly acquired wealth is a giveaway,' he would say. 'Obsessive cleanliness or complete disorder are excellent pointers. Check for any rearrangement of furniture or fresh paint, cleaned carpets. Watch how the suspect behaves. He should be at ease and at home. On the other hand, anyone overly relaxed and too friendly could be putting on an act.' The advice had served Sibanda well in several cases. He had a good eye for detail.

John Berger's office was a study in bland. He occupied it with authority and conviction. He rose from his padded swivel chair and showed the inspector to a sofa and coffee table and joined him.

'Nice working environment,' commented Sibanda.

'Yes, the whole lodge has been refurbished, my office included.'

'Don't you own the lodge, then?' asked Sibanda.

'No, I'm just the manager. The Barton family built Thunduluka years ago. You must remember Thandanyoni Barton, Inspector.'

'The name is familiar, but we've never met,' he said, 'remind me who his is.'

'He ran this lodge in the '80s. In fact, he found the site and built from scratch. Back then he established a bush camp, comfortable with lots of character, but the tourism industry moved on. Competition is fierce. Safari lodges have become less Hemingway and more Disneyland. Tourists seem more concerned with the location of the spa and swimming pool. Even the traditional hunter's pot has been replaced by fancy food arranged on an odd shaped plate. I miss the good old days. More than a few old safari hands, Thandanyoni included, must shudder at the changes. We are on the slippery slope to Follywood.'

Sibanda had been jolted by the name Barton. He wondered if *she* might be related to him. They hadn't talked family history. Families remained a taboo topic for them both. They came from Zimbabwe with enough baggage to fill a million conversations.

Uncomfortable silences or mindless chit-chat about the state of the English weather didn't feature. They spoke instead about home, politics, history, wildlife, their nostalgia for biltong, Mazoe Orange, Tanganda Tea, Hwange Park, the Matopos, Great Zimbabwe, Jade soap, Zambezi mud, the burnt-blue winter skies, the jacaranda-lined streets, the glorious summer rains and the infinite starry nights. And they laughed and occasionally mourned. Those memories were what sustained Sibanda when times got rough or the Land Rover curled up its toes.

'So, why did Thandanyoni leave the lodge?' Sibanda hoped to reel in information without revealing his own interest.

'You don't know the story then?' Berger asked. 'Before your time I suppose. In 1985 this area of the country was crawling with dissidents. Independence brought liberty to some, but others were being marginalised. Local dissidents targeted tourists from time to time, but the attacks were opportunistic and rare. Thandanyoni continued to operate this lodge despite the troubles. He was an old bush hand, vigilant and had a weapon. The game park is a huge tract of land. To reach this part on foot would mean traversing wildest Africa at night. Not a safe place for the faint-hearted.'

'But they came anyway?' Sibanda interrupted.

'Yes, they came armed to the teeth: AK 47s, grenades, Sam 7s and bandoliers bristling with ammo. One of them was hurt in a bad way. They must have been desperate. The staff from the camp tried to deal with them, feed them and patch up the wounded man without letting Barton know because the situation would become tense if he got involved. Remember both sides had weapons. Of course, they underestimated Thandanyoni.'

'In what way?' Sibanda asked.

'Well, as a supreme bushman, he didn't miss a trick, could track a beetle over a boulder. If something was amiss in the camp, his nose would twitch. He called one of the staff members to his tent. She spilled the beans.'

'And then?'

'He was as cunning as a troop of baboons, diplomatic and incredibly brave. He went unarmed to the kitchen tent. He spoke to the dissidents in their language. I'm sure they were shocked because not many white men can speak Ndebele so fluently, better than a tribesman. Look, I don't know all the details, but somehow he managed to persuade them not to kill the clients in camp or take them hostage, and then it all went wrong. A fire-fight broke out; most of the dissidents got away. Thandanyoni was wounded horrifically. The Police Internal Security Investigation Unit got involved – the dreaded PISI. All the camp staff were jailed for collaboration with *The Boys*. Thandanyoni ended up in intensive care. They still arrested him and kept him under surveillance.'

'How do you know all this?' asked Sibanda.

'One of the old cooks still works here. He passed the story on, although he doesn't like to talk much. Seems he wasn't much of a hero in the episode.'

'Where is Thandanyoni now?' Sibanda was keen to learn about this possible connection to his Impossible Dream.

'He gave up safaris. He is teaching at Kestrel Vale School. The lodge sat empty for a couple of years. The lease was given to the company who still run it today.'

Sibanda steered the conversation back to the present. 'Which area was your anti-poaching team deployed to last night?' he asked.

'On a patrol in the far north of the reserve around the Mabali Pan region,' Berger pointed to an area on a large framed map behind his desk. 'Hard, hot, dry country with thick bush. The reserve's black rhino population is concentrated up there, hammered by poachers. Our team spend most of their time in the area. We aren't covering the rest of the ground as thoroughly as we would like. Barney was on the tracks of a group of poachers when he came across the body.'

'Yes, I understand so,' said Sibanda. 'He seemed to indicate to the Bernstein family the team should have been checking the Ntundhla Pan area. Are they armed, by the way?'

'Shotguns only, for defence. We don't shoot poachers, Detective, much as we sometimes might like to. I do the anti-poaching team's roster. I decide where they are going to patrol, when, and for how long. Barney just assumed they might be at the pan.'

'Who else knows the roster and knew they wouldn't be in the area where we found the body?' Sibanda asked.

'Most of the staff. They talk among themselves. Members of the team chat about their deployment.'

Sibanda was frustrated by the lack of progress. He needed the exact cause of death.

'One last question, Mr Berger. Do you recognise this?' Sibanda pulled the plastic bag containing the knife from his pocket. Sibanda watched him carefully for signs of recognition, but his face remained expressionless.

'No, sorry, Detective, never seen it before. Nice piece of steel though, looks like an American make, a Buck knife perhaps, popular with the hunting fraternity. Built to last. Did you find this near the body? A murder weapon perhaps? I am beginning to assume this was not a death from natural causes.'

'No to both questions, Mr Berger. Just routine procedure until we can establish the identity of the victim and cause of death,' Sibanda terminated the interview and any further enquiry.

A loud trumpeting scream cut through the atmosphere as though a thousand throats were being cut. Both Sibanda and Berger recognised the distinctive shriek of elephant discontent.

'They must be at the waterhole.' Sibanda glanced briefly into the car park. Ncube hadn't returned yet. He could steal time to indulge his passion. 'Don't forget to send all the staff in for fingerprinting,' he addressed Berger and then he was through the doors and striding towards a lookout point.

Sibanda spent as much of his free time as possible at waterholes watching elephants. This one at Thunduluka was an unexpected bonus in his working day. His consuming elephant obsession went back to one childhood night. As a small boy he guarded the mealie fields, chased the monkeys and baboons raiding the unripe stalks and banged loudly on a large water-filled drum with a metal stake if elephants came. This chased the ghostly thieves and woke the village men to come and discharge an old WWI Martini-Henry in their general direction. The shot had no hope of ever reaching the elephant let alone penetrating the skin, but the noise and smoke scared the creatures away. Often Sibanda, the boy, would delay the warning signal to watch these graceful monoliths, allowing them a few mouthfuls before he hammered the drum and they plunged seamlessly into the island of stalks with barely a puff of pollen to mark their passing.

That night had been moon-filled, still as the stars, quiet as the heavy blanket of air that had cushioned him to sleep. He had woken convinced he had been shaken awake. The platform in the middle of the lands was his bed, a wooden island bathed in golden light as he dozed off. Now it was pitch-black. He rubbed his eyes, terrified they had failed him whilst he slept. When they adjusted to the gloom, an enormous bull elephant blocked the moonlight. Standing within touching distance of the platform, two matched creamy-white ivory tusks swept in a sensuous curve almost to the ground. Sibanda, so close, could make out the fine tracery of the growth pattern on the tusks and the hairline cracks that came with maturity. They had been mascaraed by countless hours digging for roots or rubbing along bark. The bulk of the elephant's large body blotted out his horizon.

Sibanda barely dared to breathe. When he did, his nostrils were filled with the smell of raw earth, trampled herbs and the pungent, musky scent of wild Africa. He could taste the fear in his mouth, a sharp, metallic tang. His body alert and trembling, inch by inch, he levered upright, never for a moment taking his eyes from the glorious beast that stood next to him.

In an act he came later to realise was supreme idiocy, he reached out and touched the dark, deeply creviced skin. He was as bewitched as the fairy tale Sleeping Beauty. She went to sleep for a hundred years. He finally woke up to the elemental splendour of his own land and the creatures that shared his planet.

He did not hit the drum that night, but watched spellbound as the elephant plucked a few choice mealies from the crop with a delicacy born of habitual theft, ate them and disappeared into the darkness as stealthily as he had arrived. Sibanda's neglect earned him a good beating for sleeping on the job. He nursed his bruises the next day. The punishment was well worth the breathtaking privilege.

Since then he had read everything about elephants that he could get his hands on. He spent countless hours watching their behaviour. He learned the largest elephant ever to exist was four metres high at the shoulder and ten metres from the tip of its trunk to the end of its tail. It weighed eleven tonnes. The young Sibanda was miffed it wasn't his elephant.

The detective turned to the small cow herd at the Thunduluka waterhole as they nervously drank and martialled the little ones. The adolescent males had been bellowing as they tussled with one another and jockeyed for best position, testing their mettle for the bigger battles in adulthood. The matriarch lifted her head, raising her trunk to sniff out danger signals. She stood motionless. The rest of the herd stilled at her soundless command, not a drop of water fell. Then, just as seamlessly, she resumed her siphoning. The herd dropped their trunks back into the pan, drinking like a band of drunken buddies, not caring if they slurped and burped. The lead cow had caught a faint whiff of him. She had dismissed the alert, habituated to human scent in this neighbourhood.

In a shop in England, where he browsed for a gift, a chattering collector of elephant ornaments insisted an animal with its trunk down brought bad luck. In reality it was the reverse. For the elephant, trunk down meant relaxation and unconcern, trunk up, a sign of stress, alarm and possible danger. This herd wouldn't hang around for long as cow herds took family protection seriously. The cover of thicker bush beckoned. A waterhole was a dangerous place for elephant children.

A couple of males, who eschewed all domestic concerns, cooled off in the shade of a clump of leadwood trees arranged like a natural sculpture garden to the left of the waterhole. The dove-grey tree trunks and branches twisted stylishly, topped with a flush of dainty lime green foliage as though manipulated by a Bonsai master. Thandanyoni certainly had an eye for beauty and landscape.

A young bull shuffled on his knees like one of Chaucer's pilgrims looking for an indulgence. His indulgence was salt. His left tusk mined a salt lick, as he hoovered up the precious grains with his trunk. Few people knew the role of elephants in manipulating landscape. They had dug for salt in this calcrete area for millennia. The holes they left eventually collected water and filled with dung. The elephants trampled, puddled and paddled, wallowed and rolled, deepening the salt basin, sealing the pan with both the fibrous cement mix and further windblown sediment added over time. 'Perfect synergy,' he mused.

Elephants were instinctive and successful miners, their dietary need for salt driving them to their labour. In East Africa they excavated huge caves in a mountain side in order to access salt. No Davy lamps for them.

They walked blindly into the deep, dark caverns. Using their tusks as picks, they chipped away at the salt rock and ground the mineral to powder in their mouths. Sibanda admired their Darwinian adaptation as much as their majesty.

A series of loud and irregular outbursts from the car park alerted Sibanda to the return of the Land Rover. No time for further rumination. 'Sorry guys,' he said aloud to the elephants, 'the Land Rover is nearing the end of its tether. I must go.'

Sibanda walked back past the row of enviable safari vehicles, admiring their khaki perfection and harmonious upholstery. His keen eye picked out a blemish, the tiniest of marks on the rear right-hand bumper, no more than the faintest nick, but it had trapped the colour of the offender in a minute smear of bright, metallic blue paint. Sibanda took note of the number plate and the shape of the dent with a quick sketch in his notebook. The Land Rover was already belching paroxysmic fumes and hiccoughing violently.

Sibanda jumped into the passenger seat – this was going to be a rough ride. He needed to concentrate, to pull some sort of scenario together before they got back to the station. 'So, Sergeant, did you find the location of the knife?'

'Yes, sir,' the sergeant replied, 'on the side of a path leading to Ntundhla Pan.'

'Anything else of interest around the area?'

'The path is well trodden by both animals and humans. The lodge staff use it daily fetching wood for cooking and camp fires. It's criss-crossed with tracks of every shape and size. Nothing that looked crisp though,' he added, glancing sideways for some sign of approval. At this point Sibanda began to stroke his chin and Ncube bit back further suggestions.

Sibanda had in fact retreated into his internal office searching for the 'Rubble' reference. It didn't take him long to find it. He had been in a small village not far from Nottingham. She was there investigating the history of a large, misplaced, Gothic minster that got stranded in its rural idyll when commerce and population grew faster in nearby Nottingham. They had agreed to meet for a weekend pub lunch.

It had been pouring with rain. A flurry burst in through the swing doors soaked to the bones of her desirable body. Droplets fell from her wild blonde hair. They splashed across pale, flawless skin and streamed down her cheeks like tears pleading to be kissed dry. She was laughing and brushing them aside with the back of her hand, totally unconscious of the devastating effect on all those who witnessed her drenched exuberance.

'Jabu,' she said, 'look at me, I'm soaked. What am I going to do?'

Look at me, he thought, as if he even had the strength to drag his eyes away from her.

In a flash, he had organised a towel from the manager and removed his own shirt from under his jacket. She disappeared into the Ladies, dried herself off and appeared a few minutes later in a halo of angel hair and his shirt. He almost lost his composure then, seeing her body touching the same fabric that a few moments earlier had been on his. He gave himself a phantom kick in the shins and began mentally reciting from the *Police Regulations Manual.* It sometimes worked.

He couldn't remember how the conversation had moved on to the boyfriend/girlfriend topic, but she volunteered quite ingenuously that she had a guy back in Zimbabwe nicknamed Rubble. They had been together since school. A knife twisted in his bowels. He was out of her league for a million reasons. He replied lamely that he was single and unattached. He hadn't met Khanyi then.

'Shit!' With some urgency, Sibanda sat bolt upright. Ncube slammed on the brakes which, thanks to new shoes, responded rather too enthusiastically. The engine stalled. Sibanda had forgotten to cancel his meeting with Khanyi's mother. They would all now be waiting in the village, clicking their tongues and enumerating his disrespect.

'Is everything alright?' asked Ncube.

'Yes,' he replied, without elaboration, not about to share his personal life with a member of staff. He took out his phone. The comforting bars had disappeared.

'Sir,' Ncube ventured, 'you are going to have to push to get us started again.'

'No,' replied Sibanda irritably, 'you are going to have to push. Get out.' He jumped across to the vacant driver's seat, engaged second gear, put his foot on the clutch and awaited motion.

It took several attempts and the assistance of Sibanda's right shoulder before they got up speed and the clutch plate could be released. The Land Rover jump-started like a spring hare with hiccoughs. The belated journey to Gubu continued.

'So, Sergeant, tell me what we have.' Sibanda began the review in the confines of the colourful cab.

'We have a body that may or may not have been murdered.'

'Definitely murdered, Ncube, and what have we got for a motive?'

'Possibly witchcraft,' he replied.

'Or, possibly not,' said Sibanda. 'This could be a body that has been doctored to make it look like witchcraft; a red herring,'

'A what, sir?' queried a perplexed Ncube.

'A red herring; it's a fish, Ncube, but don't worry, they are rare in the Zambezi. You won't need to design a lure to catch them. What clues do we have?'

'Not a lot really,' Ncube suggested. 'We don't have any identification yet. Very tricky. Maybe a missing persons report or the few scraps of fabric clinging to the body will help.'

'We have a splinter of blue paint on the body, possibly from the vehicle used to dump him,' Sibanda continued, 'what we don't have is time or place of death. Blue paint is on a Thunduluka vehicle. How did it get there? And then there's the Desert Duellers. Until we know the cause of death, the knife is a possible murder weapon.'

'Someone lost that knife, sir,' interrupted Ncube. 'The murderer would have thrown it deep into the bush if he wanted to get rid of it.'

'You are right, Ncube, so maybe not the murder weapon. Maybe Forensics will come up with a bullet, or powder residue, we'll test all the lodge weapons. We should have copies of the Thunduluka gun licences back at the station. That will tell us exactly how many they have and what calibre. Check on that.'

'Yes, sir,' he replied. 'And suspects?'

'It could be anyone at this stage. If it's a muthi murder, then it's been done for money. Berger and Barney Rubble don't seem strapped for cash, but who knows? The Bernsteins are obviously rolling in it. They are unlikely suspects. The lodge staff may be involved. Have you got the list? We need to check them against known criminals, if they have a record. Get on to it first thing.'

'Yes, sir, first thing,' said Ncube.

'And Ncube,' Sibanda hesitated as though making a decision, 'don't mention anything about the blue paint or the governor's vehicle. We will keep that under wraps. The whole of the region might be awash in blue vehicles for all we know.' Sibanda finished the conversation and turned the limping Land Rover into Gubu Police Station.

Sibanda dropped the Land Rover keys at the front desk. He went towards his office and the phone call he urgently needed to make. He was waylaid by Stalin Mfumu smirking with a pleasing day of bureaucracy behind him. Mfumu was as attracted to paperwork as a mosquito to blood. Sibanda liked that because the Chief Inspector stayed out of his hair. He spent his life pandering to head office's requirements for quadruplicate documentation, never set foot in either vehicle, never disturbed the creases in his uniform trousers, and relied on Sibanda and Ncube to do the leg work.

'What is the situation with the body near Thunduluka Lodge?' he asked Sibanda as they passed in the corridor.

'Most likely a murder,' said Sibanda, 'but nothing concrete to go on at the moment.'

'A messy business, wrap it up as soon as possible. I have left a docket on your desk,' added Mfumu, a little too casually. 'There's been a death out at a farm not far from Kestrel Vale School. A straightforward case, but you'd better go out tomorrow morning, first thing.' He strode off to his office.

'First thing,' Sibanda replied to the disappearing officer. Unexplained death was a workload. He was not going to make it to Khanyi's village. His marriage stocks were plummeting.

Chapter 5

Sunday-morning chapel was over and Simons (AKA Simple or Pie-man) and Wart had the whole day to explore the bush and leave behind the drudgery of school. With flawless planning they had avoided the possibility of being picked on by a sixth-former who needed his study cleaned with a toothbrush, his shoes polished to mirror perfection or, out of boredom, would find some mindless task to torment the juniors.

Last Sunday Wart and his friends had been entered into a 'rubber race'. They were lined up against other unfortunates and obliged to push an eraser along the tarmac with their noses. Betting flourished and laggards were beaten on their jutting backsides with thin, whip-like stalks of bamboo raided from the Rhodes House shrubbery. Wart managed third place thanks to the encouragement of two rather timely blows from Brunswick Major, a hero of the first-team front row. His biceps failed to fit into his school blazer and he was a legend when it came to the precision and vigour of his caning. He may have been a certified knuckle-dragger, but no one in the history of Kestrel Vale School, disparagingly known as Crow Valley by the inmates, would ever leave a deeper stripe than Brunswick.

The tail-end charlie of the race, Paul James, got the worst of it. In an attempt to avoid the bamboo cane, he chose to plough his face into the tarmac. By the end of the race his nose and chin were so skinned, bloodied and embedded with tar fragments he had to go to the San and then to hospital. School scuttlebutt varied during the week on the state of the wounds. They grew in severity as the rumours circulated.

What started as speculation of stitches ended in absolute, *God's honest truth*, confirmation of skin grafts; this from Stinky Stortford who had been in San at the same time with a severe case of ball rot. Most of the competitors had varying degrees of damage to their faces but no one commented on the proliferation of scabbed noses that week, least of all the teachers.

Wart and Simple decided they had to avoid further humiliation and set about thinking of a plan; on Monday, Simple came up with a beauty.

'Listen, Wart,' he said, 'follow me after chapel next Sunday. We'll go and speak to Spirit on some religious stuff. If we can keep him interested for half an hour or so then the heat will be off. The prefects will have chosen their victims by then. All we need to do is skirt the quad, take the long way round behind the rugby pitch and we'll be free for the afternoon.'

'Oh, bummer! Not *Spirit*,' said Wart. Spirit, alias The Reverend Jones, was Wart's nemesis. He took Bible studies. As an avowed atheist, Wart showed no interest in his subject and came bottom of his class. Wart teased Spirit mercilessly. Spirit's ears would make a doorpost seem audio-gifted. He relied on hearing aids that barely functioned. They whistled at inappropriate times. The batteries often died in the middle of his lesson. Spirit banged the contraptions in an attempt to revive them and left the boys unattended to find replacements. The class relished these unsupervised moments.

Of course, it didn't take the heathens in the class long to cotton on to a splendid diversionary tactic. Spirit would ask for a volunteer to read a Bible passage. One of the band of *God Sceptics* would oblige, reciting loudly in a piping treble. Slowly, the reader lowered and deepened his voice. In the end, he was mouthing the words in complete silence. Spirit never understood the hilarity that accompanied the removal and shaking of the hearing aids, but he somehow understood that Wart was the architect of the disruption.

'You need to believe it,' Simple continued, 'Spirit is our only hope of escape. Wart, you had better have a bloody brilliantly researched bit of the Bible to discuss with him.'

Wart spent more hours with his head in the Bible that week than in his favourite and much-read *Oxford Book of Science*. Nothing, however, grabbed his attention or his interest. The New Testament was far too tame to mount a half-hour diversionary skirmish. King Solomon and his tribe of foreign women gave some food for thought. Seven hundred royal wives and three hundred concubines would provide ample ammunition given Spirit's momentous sermons on chastity and the sanctity of marriage. Wart read on to find God was none too pleased either with Solomon and his gargantuan fornicating habits. Seems he agreed with Spirit.

On Friday, Wart got to *Proverbs*. His eyes were drawn to chapter X verse 30: *The righteous shall never be removed: but the wicked shall not inhabit the earth.* Eureka! The Old Testament, a book of complete spiritualistic tat, hadn't let him down. Here was meat for a good half-hour's discussion without too much effort. Wart could rabbit on about Hitler inhabiting the earth for far too long. He survived over forty assassination attempts while Burlington's sister, too young to be anything but righteous, died of meningitis at eight years old. Poor Spirit would be tied up in knots.

'Think about it,' he practised on Simple. 'Jesus, righteousness incarnate himself, got nailed, at a young age, to a bit of wood. Pontius, his executioner, went on to enjoy a long successful political career. My coup de grâce is Paul James and his mangled face. James is a Spirit groupie, a committed Christian and God-botherer, and yet he's the one in hospital. Half an hour will fly by.'

All went according to plan, unusual for anything Simple had a hand in. He didn't earn his nickname for nothing… After the service had ended and the prefects had ushered the rest of the school away to participate in their weekly amusement, Wart and Simple cornered Spirit in the vestry and engaged him in argument. To be fair, Spirit seemed content to listen to Wart's rant with little interruption. Wart had to dig deep and waffle to use up the time.

'Well, Molesworthy,' he said, 'you do have an interesting slant on the rewards of sin and the penalties of innocence. I hope this creed will take you far in life and give you all the joy and recompense your heart may desire.' Mrs Spirit came and claimed her husband. They walked away companionably, arm in arm, through the nave. Spirit paused before the chancellery door. He glanced over his shoulder with a look that spoke of immense sorrow and disappointment. It stopped Wart in his rush to escape. Then the hearing aids began to whistle. Their shrill siren keened around the stones and statues like a lost ghost. The spell was broken. Wart turned to run.

'Wart, hurry up, we'll get trapped if you don't move that sorry backside of yours.' Simple broke into Wart's thoughts. They made a dash for it, through the school gates, with the delicious prospect of a whole Sunday of freedom before them.

By the previous Tuesday they had already decided to cycle to Robert McClean's farm. Robert McClean was a legend in the district, a giant of a man with thick black hair and ice-blue eyes. He and his wife welcomed any boys who managed to score a gate pass. The boys treasured their visits to Zebra Hill Farm. They itched to ride the McClean's horses around the property looking for game. On a good day, they hunted birds with one of McClean's shotguns. If any of them managed to bag a couple of guinea fowl or francolin, they would be heroes to the hungry hordes in the dorm.

Wart and Simple hared along the bush trail, pedals pumping, bodies low over the handlebars to avoid the flying beetles and cicadas whose bony carapaces could inflict quite a sting at speed. They raced as though chased by the whole first-team pack. Complete safety lay with the farm gate at their backs.

A figure stepped out of the long grass onto the path in front of them. They thought it was a sixth-form ambush. They rammed on brakes and came to a dusty, stone-showering halt, their hearts thumping with the wildness of a tribal drum at an African wedding. It took some time for the taste of terror to leave Wart's mouth. Sole stood in their path. He was harmless, just an isibonda, a vagabond.

Sole was a well-known character in the district. Not quite right in the head, he wandered the bush from village to village in mud-coloured clothing glued to his body. He was covered from neck to ankle in filthy monkish garb. He had never changed his appearance in the longest living memory of Kestrel Vale School. The foetid miasma gave Stinky Stortford serious competition. Footwear baptised Sole. He wore boots with only uppers recognisable; the soles had long since disappeared. From time to time he changed the laces and re-threaded the eyelets with anything to hand, a scrap of string or torn fabric, even plaited tree bark. Those uppers became his pride and joy.

The juniors thought of Sole as their mascot. Here was someone in a far worse position than they were, a vacant mind who couldn't escape his fate. At least the boys could get a reprieve if they passed sufficient exams and progressed as planned through the school system. It seemed like an eternity to wait, but for Sole there was no end. Despite the bleak future ahead of him and his homeless, mindless wanderings, Sole was a happy, kindly soul. He grinned now, his wide, even smile shining like a bright half-moon through a dusty-grey night sky.

'I have eggs,' he greeted them.

'Jeez, Sole, you scared us to death,' spluttered Simple still gathering his breath.

'I have eggs, ngila amaqanda,' repeated Sole, taking great care to enunciate the skilful click on the 'q', a sound they were all practising as part of their Ndebele language class. Few of them would ever achieve the fluency. Wart and Simple leaned closer, still maintaining a sensitive nasal distance, to get a look at what Sole had on offer. In the bottom of an old jam tin lay three perfect specimens, a small, creamy-white egg, a beautiful greenish-blue and a large, red-speckled, beige one. Both boys wanted them all for their collection. With the posse closing in and no time to fight over the eggs, they decided to take one each. Wart chose the blue and Simple grabbed the speckled one. Hours of pleasure lay ahead identifying them.

'I don't have anything to trade,' Wart said. No one took advantage of Sole. They all gave him something for his eggs or guinea fowl chicks or the occasional night ape he caught. Sometimes the boys sacrificed precious tuck if the egg was rare, but payment could be as little as an empty jar or a pencil. Their Spartan lives produced little excess, but Sole took anything. Wilson Minor once traded a holed pair of underpants which Sole wore on his head for weeks.

'Me either,' said Simple, edgy, looking behind him now to check the prefects weren't catching up.

'Akula ndaba, no worries.' Sensing their urgency to get a move on, Sole shuffled into the long grass on a mission only he understood.

'We'll see you next week, Sole,' Wart shouted after him as he got back on his bike. He stood on the pedals to accelerate. Sole had melted away as he had arrived, like a wild creature of the bush.

The day at Zebra Hill Farm didn't disappoint. Mr McClean agreed to retell the story of the leopard he had killed on his veranda with only a knobkerrie to defend himself. 'With one good blow from this induku, lads, the leopard's skull was crushed. His eye popped out of the socket as easy as a ripe pea from a pod.' McClean placed a finger in his cheek to mimic the wet, sucking sound of the eye's expulsion – an effective exclamation mark to end his tale.

The boys loved the gory bits. They marvelled at the strength of the man. This is who they wanted to be when they left school: A man of the bush, a man of action, muscular and courageous like Mr McClean. They dawdled back to school, reliving the day and congratulating themselves on their clever ruse. They arrived just in time for roll-call. On the way, they looked out for Sole. They had some of Ma McClean's home-made biscuits in their tuck boxes. They planned to share them with Sole in payment for the eggs, but he rarely turned up in the same place twice.

Wart and Simple enjoyed the envy of their mates for several hours after their return. The rest of the dorm had been subjected to an endurance test that Sunday; forced to squat, thighs at right angles to a wall with their arms outstretched, a brick in each hand. The first to keel over was required to eat a tablespoon of vomit Brunswick Major had chucked up an hour earlier.

'Phew, I'm glad we avoided that one,' Wart said to no one in particular, 'who copped the vomit?' Various voices chipped in with the tale.

'Stinky, then he vomited it all back up again anyway.' Some laughter ensued.

'Then most of us retched and vomited in sympathy.' More laughter followed.

'It was a mess. The whole quad was awash with puke.' They were howling uncontrollably now.

'Even some of the sixth-form threw up!' This was the last straw. Wart battled to breathe through his hysteria. He noticed Paul James in the corner looking very glum with a bandaged nose. A large sticking plaster covered his chin.

'Hey James, how goes it?' Paul James had never had a nickname. They had tried various names. Nothing seemed appropriate. Religious and intellectual, he didn't fit in with the rest of the mediocrity in the dorm. 'How's the nose?' said Wart.

'Okay. They say I'll be scarred. I suppose the skin will heal eventually.'

'Why so miserable then?' Wart asked.

'Because, Wart, if I had been back in time, it would have been me grazing on vomit, not Stinky.' This was true. Paul James was the weakest specimen in the dorm. If Wart thought life was tough for him, it must be hell for James. In that moment, Wart hatched a plan which he shared later with Simple.

'Listen, Simple, we have to get away again next Sunday. We can't use Spirit a second time, too obvious, and I don't want to investigate the Good Book any further.' One week of trawling the sacred texts was more than enough for Wart.

'So what do you suggest? You know it's no use me trying to research anything. I can barely read, let alone make head or tale of the Bible.' A fact Wart didn't dispute. Simple was bottom of the D stream but his dad owned the largest car dealership in the country. Simple didn't need a brain, he was already made for life.

'Buffoon,' Wart said, naming the most demanding master in the school. 'Buff always reads one of the lessons in chapel. He will be there after the service. He's our delaying tactic.'

'I may be called Simple, but I'm not stupid! I am rubbish at maths. I got zero per cent in the half terms–'

'Yes,' Wart interrupted, 'I failed too, but James was top with ninety-eight per cent. Don't you see? James is bound to be able to come up with some interesting theorem or insoluble problem to tax old Buff. It'll keep us safe for half an hour. He can coach us to chip in from time to time with a sensible question. This way James does the swotting and we get a free Sunday.'

'Jeez Wart, I'm not sure about this,' said Simple. 'Buff is no pushover. He will smell a rat. We'll have to drag James along with us. He's as slow as a constipated sloth. We're going to get caught with him as baggage.'

'Trust me, Buff's ego will be flattered *any* boy in this school wants to talk to him, let alone discuss the finer points of geometry, trig or algebra or whatever James comes up with. Buff's the easy bit… James? Well, the poor guy deserves a break. Between us we can keep him moving.'

James's research into polyhedrons, which Wart thought was some kind of mythical, multi-headed, Greek, cave-dwelling monster, was a complete waste. On Tuesday, all gate passes were cancelled for the following Sunday. They found out why the next day. Whispers began [illegible] like soap through a duck.

[illegible] 'Shut up, Stinky, we don't know that,' said Wart, 'maybe he was just dazed, tried to defend himself.' Silence cloaked the room for a while after this. Wart and most of the others imagined the attack, the brutality, the blood, the splintered bones and the horror. It was the stuff of nightmares. The gory bits were made real. The question was asked that they had all had on their minds since first hearing the story. 'Why did McClean kill him? Surely he knew he was harmless, knew he

Sole jumped out of bed in alarm and, Wart suspected, confusion. His deluded mind would not have recognised the severity of his crime nor the imminent danger. Wart pictured the engaging smile he would have offered in his defence and the trust in those big eyes that saw the world as a child sees it. He wouldn't have understood why the knobkerrie rained

'Why did McClean kill him? Surely he knew he was harmless, knew he wasn't right in the head? I just don't understand.' Silence followed. They eventually slept, a cold, disturbed sleep.

Next morning, Wart's stomach churned. He felt constantly nauseous. He had never known confusion or anxiety like this before. Even standing outside the housemaster's study waiting for a beating would have been more comforting in its familiarity. Wart needed answers, they all did. The atmosphere in the school was sombre. The sixth-form had been juniors once too, recipients of Sole's generosity and mad gentleness. He had stood out in their brutal environment of beatings, cruelty, cold showers and sadism like the soft duvet he had died for. They mourned his passing.

During the whole of Buff's interminable maths class on the properties of something squared called a hypotenuse, Wart couldn't concentrate. the others imagined the attack, the brutality, the blood, the spl intered bones and the horror. It was the stuff of nightmares. The gor y bits were made real. The question was asked that they had all h ad on their minds since first hearing the story . 'Why did McClean kill him? Surely he knew he was harmless, knew he sprained his wrist.' Unspoken, both of them sensed he was going easy because of Sole. This abnormal consideration was unnerving. Wart would have preferred a good tongue-lashing.

They moved towards Spirit's class room and their weekly religious knowledge session. Usually, Wart would be planning a disruptive strategy. Today he wanted to listen to Spirit. Wart wasn't getting religion. He hoped Spirit would put everything into perspective, put up a defence for Robert McClean. Exonerate him. Explain how such an upright and solid man, their hero and role model, could murder a harmless simpleton.

'Open your Bibles at Matthew, chapter 5 verses 3 to 10,' said Spirit without preamble. Wart rifled through the wafer thin, rarely-thumbed pages looking for Matthew. James nudged him. He gave Wart a clue as to Matthew's position in the vast book. 'Read for us please Mr Molesworthy, if you will,' said Spirit.

Wart stood up. He began loudly and clearly: '*Blessed are the poor in spirit, for theirs is the kingdom of heaven. Blessed are the meek, for they shall possess the land. Blessed are they who mourn…'* He stumbled over the words. He could feel all the pent up emotions of the last few days bursting inside. His voice wavered pitifully on *for they shall be comforted.* Wart couldn't continue, his lip quivered. Any more of this and he would be blubbering. Spirit graciously took a moment to bang his hearing aids, although Wart suspected they were working perfectly. James rescued him and took over the reading. The class, already quiet, stilled further, wooden floorboards hushed their creaking expansion, ever-restless chairs settled. Flies, caught up against the windows, ceased their buzzing escape efforts. James recited what Wart later came to know as the Beatitudes in his strong but mellifluous voice. He ended with the powerful last verse: *Blessed are they that suffer persecution for justice, for theirs is the kingdom of heaven.*

'It was an angel moment,' said James later in the dorm as they all sat around discussing the class.

'What rubbish,' said Simple.

'Not rubbish,' said James, 'those really silent moments happen for a reason. You know we were all thinking about Sole. I think his spirit passed over us just for a minute.'

'Now you are speaking absolute horse manure, *Pastor James*,' Wart said, although something *had* happened in that classroom and it had changed him.

'Pastor James, ooh, Pastor James!' The chant went up around the dorm. That was how James finally earned his nickname and how they all came to laugh for the first time since the ghastly news had reached them. It was the start of the healing process.

Chapter 6

Jabulani Sibanda arrived in the office early the next morning, before the night shift had knocked off. He had to head off for Zebra Hill Farm and the suspicious death, but he needed time to investigate the sliver of blue paint, the only real clue along with the much-worn Buck knife. He weighed up Mfumu's probable wrath against the urgency of getting on the murderer's trail. He opted for the dressing down. On his way in to the station he had passed by Sergeant Ncube's house. It galled him, but he needed the bumbling sergeant's help and contacts on this one.

As he approached the township house, walled by a thick milk hedge, he heard a chatter of laughter and the early morning bustle of pots and babies. It reminded Sibanda of the cosy, communal squawking of a flock of red-billed wood-hoopoes whose raucous chirps had earned them the nickname of mahleka abafazi, the laughing women. Ncube seemed to have a whole nest of joyous fledglings and females to care for.

'Ncube, are you awake?' he called through the open door, aware no human being could sleep with the ear-piercing screams and laughing shrieks of the Ncube clan.

'Coming, sir,' said Ncube as he buttoned his trousers and tucked a much-washed vest into his waist band. He popped his head through the doorway apologetically indicating his shoeless, shirtless state, 'I am not due on duty for another hour.'

'I know, Ncube,' Sibanda replied irritably, 'but we need to get an early start. Today is going to be busy. Mfumu has lumbered us with another case. We can't afford to let the leads on the mutilated corpse slip.'

'You mean the paint, sir?'

'Yes, Ncube, the paint.'

'I feel unwell today,' said Ncube suddenly grasping the large expanse of flesh resting in a fat teardrop over the top of his trousers as though it could roll away and land with a splash at his feet. 'It's my stomach. It gives me a great deal of worry. Today it is paining horribly.' He added a groan of conviction and a grimace to match. The paint saga scared him.

'I don't care if you've a million maggots munching on your innards, Ncube, get dressed and get to the station now!' Sibanda's voice contained menace. Ncube scurried back into the house and began to search for his shoes and socks, which had recently doubled as cars and trucks for the male children of his brood.

The sergeant hopped along after the disappearing figure of his superior, pulling on shoes, buttoning his shirt and straightening his peaked cap. He muttered curses against the officer to whom he had been recently assigned. Why the continual rush? he asked himself. Does this man never relax? He should smell his own armpits, recognise his own faults. He has a temper like an old bull, his horns should be cut and a ring put through his nose. The diatribe of observations continued all the way down the dusty path to the station.

'Right, Ncube, contact your friends in the motor trade. Get them out of bed if necessary. Phone around everyone you know. See if they can come up with any information about blue 4x4s. Check out the local panel beaters. The vehicle concerned may have been involved in an altercation with one of the Thundulukas vehicles.'

'A what, sir? What has been altered?' queried a perplexed Ncube.

'The rear bumper of one of the lodge Land Cruisers has a smear of blue paint. Hit by the pick-up that moved the body.' Sibanda enunciated each word with sarcasm, 'The murderer will cover up any dent quickly.'

As Sibanda stalked off to his office to make phone calls of his own, Ncube, aware he had once again transgressed, began to dial his brother, the best place to start, although he would not take kindly to being woken up at this hour. Ncube sighed and punched in the rest of the number.

Sibanda looked at the phone in his office. He considered phoning Khanyi. Instead he dialled the vehicle registry. Every registration book noted a vehicle's make, model, year, colour, owner and address. A long shot, but they might be able to pull out all the blue 4x4s registered in the area. 'Blue' covered every colour from midnight to sky and a multitude of shades in between. The phone rang out several times before he smashed the receiver back on the cradle and cursed the unreliable time keeping of the civil service.

His office door swung open. A beaming Sergeant Ncube burst in.

'You look happy, Ncube,' commented the detective. 'Has your stomach ache improved?'

'No, sir… I mean, er… Yes, sir, my stomach has completely recovered, but there's some other good news.'

'Well, spill the beans, Sergeant.'

'Beans, sir? I don't eat beans, they cause me a great deal of discomfort. You know, they er… blow up my mathumbu. They make nasty, hyena breath explosions–'

'Okay, Ncube,' Sibanda interrupted before the description of intestinal gases became too graphic, 'just tell me the news.'

'Good news. My brother has a friend who works for Customs in the vehicle importation section. He phoned him on the off chance to discover if any blue pick-ups came through the border…'

'"Blue" is no good as a description, Ncube, there will be hundreds of them.'

'The blue paint we found on the body is the exact shade of the walls at Pumula Primary. My brother knew the shade immediately. His friend, Mathe, attended the same school.'

Sibanda merely raised his eyebrows.

'Anyway, sir,' continued Ncube, 'Mathe, the Customs officer, clearly remembers a batch of similar-coloured vehicles arriving five years ago, an unusual order. They had been specially spray-painted in Japan for a company that suddenly found it could no longer put a pot on the fire. They couldn't take delivery – Toyota Land Cruisers,' he added.

Sibanda smiled wryly at Ncube's colloquial take on bankruptcy. 'How many vehicles came in, Ncube?'

'Twenty-three.' Ncube handed Sibanda a piece of paper. 'I wrote down the name of the colour.'

'*Mediterranean Sapphire*,' Sibanda read out the laboriously copied words. 'Hmmm, seems our victim's final ride was on a jewelled sea.'

'Yes, sir,' said Ncube disguising any expression of confusion. The words *Mediterranean* and *Sapphire* were meaningless to him except he now understood one was a gem and one was a sea, and they were both blue. 'This is excellent news, don't you think, sir?'

'That we have to track down at least twenty or so vehicles?' Sibanda queried.

'That we don't have to worry the governor.'

'Ah, yes, I see,' said Sibanda, understanding Ncube's remarkable recovery. 'We may have to check him out at some stage. Let's keep the information to ourselves for now. In the meantime, get back on the phone to the panel beaters. They could give us a real lead.'

As Ncube left, Sibanda re-dialled the vehicle registry. Surely they had pitched up at the office by now. He glanced down at his watch. Chief Inspector Mfumu was due to arrive at the station shortly. He was a stickler for routine, immovable when it came to his orders. Flexibility was not a luxury he embraced. Sibanda would have to head off for the farm incident as soon as his superior arrived. He hit the keypad again, with some force, as if the extra energy could stir the receptionist at the other end. It worked. A laconic voice mumbled a morning welcome with practised disinterest.

'This is Gubu Police, Detective Inspector Sibanda speaking. Put me through to the officer in charge,' Sibanda barked. He was in no mood for niceties.

'Hold on,' came the short, charmless reply.

Several minutes passed with Sibanda seething and rubbing his chin restlessly. He almost banged the phone back down again. He had received a warning – any more broken phones and he would be charged with damage to police property.

An oily voice materialised, 'Progress Kanyombo speaking, how can I help, Detective Inspector?'

'I need a track on some *Mediterranean Sapphire* Toyota Land Cruisers. They entered the country between 2005 and 2007. It is not a standard colour. About two dozen of these vehicles were imported. I am particularly interested in any licensed in Matabeleland North. I want names and addresses. The information is confidential and sensitive.

'This will take some time, Detective,' drawled the voice irritated by the interruption to the morning office ritual of coffee and a newspaper.

'I don't have time, and you, Kanyombo, need to understand I know contacts in the tax department who will make your life a misery. If you don't sort this you might just get an unwanted visit.'

The phone fell silent for several seconds. Kanyombo wondered how this man knew he had an unlicensed tuck shop, run by his wife. It brought him in a very tidy undeclared income. 'How did you know?'

'Impukane ziyezwa, Kanyombo, flies have ears,' replied Sibanda. In reality, he did not have a clue about the man's financial dealings. He just took a punt knowing most civil servants had some business on the side to bolster their sub-economic wages.

'I promise, I will work on it myself, and come back to you later today,' said the shaken man.

Sibanda regretted his bullying tactics, but sometimes they were necessary. 'Thank you,' he conceded, 'I won't be in the office. Give your findings to Constable Zanele Khumalo and only to her.' This blue paint saga might well be dynamite, but it was their only solid clue.

Ncube returned to the office looking less pleased with himself, in fact he looked browbeaten. 'None of the registered panel beaters have anything to report,' he advised, 'and I think we should get going to Zebra Hill Farm khathesi, khathesi!'

Sibanda glanced up at this out-of-character insistence on immediacy. He registered the tension in his sergeant's shoulders. Only one of Chief Inspector Mfumu's frank, obedience lectures could have caused the sergeant's terseness. He saw no point in his adding to the man's misery. 'Right, Ncube,' he said with a large reassuring grin, 'then the claptrap Land Rover willing, let's be on our way.'

The Land Rover was surprisingly willing. They were out of the station yard before Mfumu could repeat his tirade to Sibanda.

'So, Ncube, no sign of a damaged blue Toyota?' Sibanda asked, as they drove along the road towards the farm.

'No, sir, but with so many back street panel beaters in the village, I will have to walk and check them out. They have no phones.'

'Good man, Ncube. I called the vehicle registry about the twenty-three *Mediterranean Sapphire* Toyotas.'

'Ha,' grunted Ncube, 'you are travelling only to get a dead donkey. You know there will be no result from that office. It's lighting a fire in the wind, a waste of time.'

'I have lit a fire alright, Ncube, right under the feet of the man in charge and I am hopefully not flogging a dead horse.' Sibanda laughed as he realised how often proverbs collided despite the cultural divide. 'Seems futility is the same in any language, Ncube,' he commented. 'Anyway our man promised–' Sibanda was interrupted by the radio crackling in the vehicle.

A faint female voice hissed, 'Gubu Base to Gubu Mobile, come in please.' It was Constable Zanele Khumalo, the female officer who handled the day-to-day paperwork back at the station. Sibanda relied on her discretion. She had never let him down yet.

'I hear you, Zee, but only just,' replied the detective.

'I am keeping my voice down, sir; too many ears about. You told me to be discrete.'

'Okay, what have you got for me?' Sibanda lowered his voice.

'Kanyombo of the vehicle registry has phoned. He said to tell you that of the twenty-three blue Toyotas in the country, five are registered in this region.'

'Do you have addresses, Zee?'

'One so far. He promised the rest later today. The name is Mr Ishmael Naidoo from the Naidoo Brothers Sawmill.'

The radio signal faltered and then died. Sibanda suspected that Constable Khumalo had cut him off from the prying ears of either Mfumu or his accomplice in idle bureaucracy and quires of paperwork, Assistant Detective Chanza.

'Naidoo Brothers,' he mused, 'isn't the turn off to that sawmill just down the road?' Ncube, still mulling over how his dead donkey became a dead horse, replied, 'I think so, sir, but the chief inspector will be as angry as iqaqa, a polecat, if we delay further. Perhaps we can investigate another day…' Ncube's voice trailed off. He recognised the beginnings of one of Sibanda's resolute moods from the set of his chin in profile. He chose not to press the matter further.

Sibanda remained silent and stony-faced as he turned the old Land Rover off the main road and onto a gravel track. A faded sign advertised the sawmill as being some five kilometres further on. They bumped over a corrugated, ungraded road, rattling the Land Rover viciously, exposing a multitude of loose-fitting parts and shock absorbers that absorbed nothing. Ncube sat listening to every squeak and rattle. He mentally noted the tightening up necessary after the trip. He strained to locate each new knock and jangle. He cursed the convoys of logging trucks that sped too fast along the road and created the wave-like surface in their wake.

Sibanda was oblivious to the orchestra of complaining metal filling the cab. He had eyes only for the magnificent teak forest they were travelling through. On either side of the gravel grew thick stands of the ancient hardwood. Rusty, velvet pods still clung to the branches. New leaf in seasonal shades was beginning to flush. Kalahari woodland at this time of the year was a riotous autumnal rainbow offering splashes from blood red to orange and from berry brown to ochre. Beneath the canopy grew tufts of showy golden yellow rhigozum. Sibanda breathed in the faint but tangible scent released by the flowers. He knew he was tense. He resented Mfumu's ability to bestow stress, to muddy his investigative waters with the sediment of pedantry. On this road with the mid-morning sun dappling the trees, and a soft breeze stirring the leaves, he felt his shoulders relax and his troublesome jaw ease, 'Do you know these trees, Ncube?'

'They are *Umkusu*,' replied an uninterested Ncube, far more concerned about the overworked bushes of the Land Rover's springs than the bushes that surrounded him.

'Yes, Zimbabwe teak. They produce a hard and beautiful, dark, reddish-brown wood. No wonder the Naidoo brothers located their sawmill here. When the London Corn Exchange was rebuilt in 1952, they needed a strong, durable wood to withstand the abrasive husks. They chose this tree. Parquet blocks from this forest now grace the floors of London. Quite a thought.' Sibanda glanced across at his sergeant for a comment, but he was in a world of his own, his ear cocked to the open window and a worried frown on his face.

Sibanda left him to his fears and drove on through the forest greeting each ancient bole, each fissured and cracked specimen, like an old friend. Slowly, almost imperceptibly at first, the forest began to thin. Sibanda detected signs of saw and blade. More and more stumps littered the ground with just the young, the soft and the commercially offensive left to shade the undergrowth and halt erosion.

Sibanda began to tense up again. He hated the destruction of native woodland. Some reports suggested Zimbabwe had lost over twenty per cent of its forests. It was in the top ten countries for deforestation. 'Another record we can do without,' seethed Sibanda aloud.

'Sorry, sir? I was not listening,' said Ncube, who had given up trying to register the dismemberment of the Land Rover.

'Well, it's about time you did,' snapped Sibanda irritably. 'What do we know of these Naidoo brothers?'

'The name has come across my desk,' said a hurt Ncube. How could he pay attention to the detective when the poor vehicle was suffering on this rough road?

'In relation to what?'

'Mohammed Naidoo is a suspected currency dealer. Rumour says the brothers use their logging trucks to smuggle goods through the border. Everyone in Gubu goes to them if they need a new phone or a radio.'

'And what about their logging business, Ncube? Licences all in order?'

'I can't say, sir. Forestry Commission handles that side of things.'

The conversation ended as they pulled into the sawmill. The Land Rover drove past a graveyard of rusted trucks, trucks up on makeshift logs, lopsided tractors, defunct engine blocks and a heap of broken saw blades, pipes and anonymous parts, the collateral damage of abandonment and the elements. The yard was a mess, an ugly fungal infection inflicted on a vulnerable environment.

Sibanda pulled over next to a blue Toyota in what passed for the yard's parking lot. He jumped out of the Land Rover and ran his eye over the obvious *Mediterranean Sapphire* paintwork. The vehicle was in a poor state with several dents and a rash of gravel chips on the bonnet and bumper. Rust had taken hold. Sibanda could see no fresh scrapes. 'What do you think, Ncube?' he asked.

'Hard to say, sir, without washing off all the dust. This vehicle is in a sad state. With heavy loads and many kilometres. It is wounded.'

Sibanda raised his brows, 'It is only a vehicle, Ncube, not an animal. It can't feel pain.' Ncube disagreed, but rather than argue with this complex man he just looked down and shuffled his feet. The saws which had been silent since their arrival started up again. The scream of the timber as it split into boards rent the air.

'Now, there's the sound of suffering, Ncube,' said Sibanda, 'a fifty-, maybe hundred-year-old tree being torn to shreds. Trees *do* have souls, Ncube,' he added, with a hint of irony.

‘If you say so, sir,’ said Ncube. The comment merely reinforced what he already suspected: the detective was as mad as a rabid goat.

They walked towards the intolerable noise and clouds of saw dust and chips. Not far away a welding machine hummed and flashed sparks into the air. Before they reached the epicentre of activity, a man approached.

‘What are you doing here? Get on your way,’ the man waved his arms indicating the exit. ‘This is private property.’ He was of Indian descent, short in stature, with a mop of thick black hair growing low on his forehead. His skin was pocked. His head popped up and down like an inquisitive tortoise investigating the outside of his shell.

‘We are from Gubu Police,’ said Sibanda. ‘We are here to investigate a murder.’

‘There's been no murder here. This is a sawmill. You've come to the wrong place.’

‘I am Detective Inspector Sibanda. This is Sergeant Ncube. We need to look around your yard – if it is your yard – and you are…?’ he asked.

‘Ishmael Naidoo. I own this business. You have no authority here. Do you have a warrant?’

‘Do we need one?’ asked Sibanda provocatively. ‘Do you have something to hide, Mr Naidoo?’

Ishmael Naidoo's head began to bob and weave. His already large eyes emerged from their lids like a frog's, exposing bloodshot whites, and irises so black it was hard to make out a pupil. ‘Do you need one?’ he repeated, his voice rising steeply. ‘You should know the law, Detective, of course you need one. Now, get off my property.’

During this conversation, Ncube had drifted towards the welding machine, and was currently chatting to the man behind the mask. Ishmael Naidoo swung around after his tirade. He became almost apoplectic, waving his arms in Ncube's direction, ‘And tell your sergeant to get out of here. This sawmill is busy. My men don't need distractions. It can be a dangerous place.’

There was a hint of a threat in these last words. ‘Mr Naidoo, I will ask a few questions. You need to think before you answer them, civilly, I can assure you,’ he said with unnatural calm. ‘This is well within my jurisdiction. Where were you the night before last?’

Ishmael Naidoo sensed danger. Something in his eyes, the way he stood and the way he spoke was unnerving. He was never on the back foot when it came to manipulating people, but this detective was different. Naidoo felt intimidated for the first time in many years. He wanted to launch into another bullying rant, but the detective's demeanour brought a bead of sweat to his narrow brow. 'With my brother, Mohammed,' he replied, almost meekly.

'Good – better,' said Sibanda. 'What time was that?'

'From about six, when I knocked off here, to about ten. We were discussing our business, and trying to find ways to improve turnover.'

'And after that?'

'I went home to my wife.'

'Can both these people vouch for your whereabouts?'

'Yes.'

'Mr Naidoo, does that Toyota belong to you?' asked Sibanda, indicating the blue Land Cruiser.

'It belongs to the business. I normally drive it.'

'And where was the vehicle the night before last?

'With me, I drove it from here to my brother's place, he runs our furniture store in Gubu, and then home.'

'Mr Naidoo, a man was murdered the night before last. We have reason to believe a blue Land Cruiser, similar to yours, was involved. Do not leave the district until our enquiries are over. Any cleaning of your vehicle, inside or out, will be deemed as an admission of guilt. Get in to Gubu Station sometime today to give fingerprints.' Ishmael Naidoo nodded his understanding. Sibanda turned and walked towards the Land Rover. He should spend more time interrogating this man, but the other incident had to be investigated before Mfumu started to bleat. He stopped to whistle Ncube to get a move on.

'He whistles you like a dog?' asked the welder.

'He doesn't shout,' replied Ncube. 'I am getting to know the shape of his call.' Ncube wasn't quite sure why he defended the detective and his ways, but he was not going to show disrespect in front of this workman. 'We, in the police, need these signs and signals for emergencies,' he improvised.

The welder shrugged his shoulders and then pulled his mask down and re-engaged the flame. Ncube hurried towards the Land Rover as quickly as his short legs and rotund body would allow in the thick grey

Kalahari sands that seemed to grab at his every step. He had one last glance at the blue Toyota before joining Sibanda in the police vehicle.

The Land Rover coughed into life on the third turn of the ignition and rattled through the heavily barbed and chained sawmill gate. Conversation was hard over the complaints of the Land Rover's inner workings. Sibanda spoke above the din. 'Could that have been the vehicle that transported our victim, dead or alive, Ncube?' he asked.

'It is the right colour. The tyres and tread are also correct, but worn. Difficult to be certain. The Toyota has been in several… altercations,' Ncube hesitated over this last word, and looked shyly towards Sibanda. He was quite pleased he had remembered it. Four English syllables were new territory for him.

'It has seen some life,' said Sibanda, unaware of his sergeant's linguistic bravery. 'Ishmael Naidoo is up to something, Ncube; I can just sense it. He was nervous about us being there. He's a natural-born thug and the vehicle fits the profile. Plus, he's engaged in cross-border trade. Check out those alibis as soon as we get back to Gubu.'

'I will, sir, although any wife would protect her husband. Her alibi might not be all that reliable.'

Sibanda glanced across at Ncube thoughtfully. With the household he was running, he had ample experience of spousal loyalty. Did his wives cover for him, he wondered. Aloud he asked, 'Ncube, did you pick anything up from the welder?'

'He claimed he was welding a fuel tank, but the cat was complaining loudly. His story doesn't ring true.'

'Why?'

'When you are welding a fuel tank, you need to take special care even if it is a diesel tank. The tank must be washed clean with lots of soapy water first. Gasses can build up. The tank will explode – a nasty business.'

A bit like your gut, Sibanda thought to himself. 'And the tank hadn't been washed? Maybe he was just careless.'

'Or lucky, like the steenbok that jumped out of the pot. No, he was too relaxed, not careful enough with his seams. That tank wasn't being welded to carry fuel or any liquid. My guess is it's a false tank used to smuggle goods across the border.'

'Body parts?' suggested Sibanda.

Ncube gulped. He attempted a silent belch. The resultant expulsion of air overcame even the clamouring of the vehicle. 'Sorry, sir, I cannot think on these things easily. I am sure that bits of body could be carried in such a tank. Concealed under the truck as a second fuel tank, never checked at Customs, it would be the perfect way to move a bag full of muthi.'

'Ishmael Naidoo and his brother are definite suspects,' said Sibanda. 'But we'll get nowhere until we find out the identity of our victim. Opportunity and motive are key. We need a link between the Naidoos, the victim and the market for body parts in South Africa.'

'You are right, sir, the man was frightened. He showed his fear in the neck like a frog. I could see his veins throbbing. He has something to hide.'

Silence entered the cab for a few moments as they both considered what they had turned up. Much to Ncube's relief the Land Rover reached the main road, still mostly in one piece, and continued its journey to Zebra Hill Farm.

Chapter 7

As Sibanda and his sergeant were investigating Naidoo Brothers Sawmill, so Isabelle McClean was dabbing concealer on her blackened eye. Four nights ago the argument had been terrible. He had punched her. Normally he used his open hand and slapped her on any exposed flesh. It smarted, but after a bit of ice and a night's sleep, the redness subsided. He always wanted sex on those nights, muttering words of passion which she barely registered. She went along with the motions and acted out satisfaction, but there was no pleasure, no tenderness, no shared giggles and teasing. She had, months ago, sealed herself in a protective shell. He couldn't hurt her any more emotionally. Brutality was his only weapon. Once he grunted his satisfaction, he would roll away and fall asleep. The alcohol that fuelled his rages also fuelled his bottomless, unrousable sleep, the only time she felt safe around him.

When the *punishments,* as he called them, first started, Isabelle had been confused and contrite. She owned up to sins she had never committed, to oversights that were his. She didn't understand her husband any more. He wasn't the lovely man she married, the doting father to their four-year-old twins, but a violent bully who picked on the fragile and heaped scorn, criticism and gutter language on her.

Her eye had turned purple. It showed, even under a thick application of make-up. She had told the first police to arrive that the tramp had done it. He had made her say that. Robert made her attempt some disguise before she went out and she had to get out. The twins clamoured for fresh air. She wanted to take her own stress out on them. She had never hit them, but of late her fingers sometimes itched. Violence was infectious, a need for the weak to assert themselves over the weaker. They all needed to get out of the house. 'Shake themselves off and give the birds a good feed,' she laughed, recognising the words of her mother. Maybe she would take the twins for a walk down by the river, have a little picnic with them. They loved to roll around on a blanket and to pick at food in the fresh air.

Friends phoned when they heard about the vagrant. They wanted to come over and help, console them, offer advice. She couldn't bear to retell the web of lies. She was useless at covering up. Someone would get to the truth.

Isabelle McClean required time alone to regain her composure. The image of the poor defenceless man beaten so savagely by her husband was her constant companion. His brain gaped through a large crater in his skull. His surprised eyes glazed over in death. A gentle mouth retained a startled 'o' shape like a choirboy about to launch into a soaring cathedral solo. The vision played over and over in her mind until she thought she would never sleep again.

She heard rather than saw the Land Rover drive up. Her heart sank. The engine's sound effects were startling. Robert, as a brilliant handyman, kept all the machinery going on what was left of the farm. He would never tolerate such a run-down vehicle.

Robert had always been given to outbursts of anger. She knew of his temper before she married him. It had not been a problem then. After a couple of hours all would be forgotten and forgiven. The twins had been conceived after one of his outbursts. They had laughed together at how fertile anger could be. Their calm attempts were barren.

The stress started when he received the farm eviction notice, a terrible body blow to this proud man. He never coped well from the first moment until the settlers began arriving to take over.

Robert was not a man to be defeated. He fought for what he considered to be his birthright. Great-great-grandfather McClean had been given this land by Lobengula, the Ndebele king, as reward for his services as a bodyguard. Robert McClean took his case to the courts. It had only incensed the authorities further. When all avenues were exhausted, and he had to accept defeat, his anger became violent and sustained. She hoped he would be polite to the visitors and not ridicule their transport. It must be the police. She was scared.

Robert McClean walked from his workshop, where he had been servicing his tractors and plough. It was time to till the fields and get the maize crop planted. He resented any delay in his well-planned schedule. The filthy, lice-ridden body had finally been taken away. He had told the police what happened. It was quite clear he was only defending his property. What more did they need to know? He wished he had laid off the booze last night. A clear head this morning would have helped. Looking at the vehicle, he relaxed a bit. He could easily outwit this pair of bumbling officers in their laughable Land Rover. If the stupid bitch he was married to stuck to the story all would be okay.

As they drove up, Sibanda knew a moment of envy. Zebra Hill farm was the sort of place he had dreamed of owning on those grey, grizzly days that punctuated life as a Nottingham cop. The city buildings crowded in on him. The endless stream of the downtrodden and their estate hoodlums plagued his life. He could have sketched this house from his dreams. It lay swathed in a sea of lawn, mature trees and flowering shrubs, with a view over the bush. A few artfully dishevelled granite boulders and blue hills peppered the near distance. How many times had he pictured himself on a shady veranda like this? His feet up on a nearby table, a shot of his favourite scotch, knocking ice cubes against crystal, Angel Hair sitting by his side, a herd of zebra grazing placidly, eyeing his lawn.

Sibanda didn't want to farm. He had watched his parents grub a hard living out of the earth. His father was a superb farmer, recognised by his peers as something of an agricultural genius. But even he couldn't control the weather, the price of fertiliser, the vagaries of schemes that didn't deliver on promises of tillage or seed. The endless toil and disappointment had killed him in the end. It left the family nearly destitute. All Sibanda wanted was a few untouched acres near the game park where he could build a home like this and surround himself with wilderness. Farming was the dominion of big companies and the ruination of small families. It sustained hope, but drained resources in an ever diminishing cycle of expectation and reward.

'Good morning, officers,' Robert McClean greeted them warmly with a wide smile. 'How can I help you today?'

'We have come about the incident yesterday morning,' said Ncube, his eyes swivelling as he tried to get a better look at the immaculate workshop. The sergeant's own workshop was a patch of shade under a teak tree in the station yard, a grubby tarpaulin as a floor, a battered tin trunk as a store room and a few old paint tins that housed an assortment of nuts and bolts.

'Good morning, Mr McClean, Detective Inspector Sibanda, CID Gubu Police. Do you think we could have a look at the room the vagrant broke in to?'

'Certainly Inspector, please come in,' said McClean. 'Just in time for a slice of my wife's Victoria sponge, fresh from the oven.'

'Sadly, we will have to forgo any refreshment at this stage,' said Sibanda, 'but thank you for the offer.' He sensed a wave of acute disappointment from the sergeant at his side. The waft of fresh baking was already in Ncube's nostrils. His saliva glands were imagining the first cream-soaked slice slithering easily across his tongue, calming the bile that came from all the talk about body parts.

'Could you lead the way?' asked Sibanda.

Robert McClean gestured to the kitchen door. The three of them entered through a screen door into a well-ordered kitchen exuding the delicious smell of fresh baking. McClean's wife was obviously accomplished.

'Good morning, Mrs McClean,' Sibanda said to a woman hovering near the kitchen range with two small tots clinging to her skirts. She nodded a shy, tentative greeting in his direction.

'This way, officers,' McClean said. He waved the policemen out of the kitchen and down the corridor to the bedroom. 'We have cleaned up a bit. The police who came out yesterday seemed very thorough. They didn't mention we would be having a second visit.'

The yellow police tape had been removed from the bedroom. The bed was stripped. The floor had been scrubbed. The parquet floors had been polished to an ice rink gloss. Sibanda had already noted the extreme orderliness of the workshop, house and garden. Someone was a perfectionist in the household. He admired it, but knew he couldn't survive in such a sanitised environment. With no signs of books or music, no children's toys carelessly strewn around the floor, no magazines on the tables, the house appeared soulless.

'Can you leave us for a couple of minutes while we take a look?'

'There's nothing to see,' offered McClean. 'We had to give the room a thorough clean-up. My wife and I could not stand the thought of all the filth and vermin that dirt bag had brought into the house. And the smell…' McClean wrinkled his nose in disgust. 'I didn't think we would ever get rid of it.'

'Well, it has gone now, Mr McClean; the room smells of fresh air and roses,' Sibanda smiled dismissively, willing the man to leave them to assess the scene of the incident undisturbed.

It worked. 'I'll be in the kitchen if you need me,' he said.

Sibanda began by closing his eyes and trying to imagine the drama that took place. Ncube stood by, fidgeting. The longer the silence lasted, the more agitated he became. The detective needed to open his eyes and look around, what was he up to? He seemed to be asleep on his feet. Ncube shuffled his own feet across the polished parquet. The rubber soles of his shoes producing teeth-setting squeals. It had little effect on the detective's meditation. The sergeant cleared his throat, hoping to startle Sibanda into action.

'Patience, Ncube,' was the response. Sibanda had taken in the dimensions of the room, the position of the bed and the wardrobe. He was trying to picture a number of scenarios including the one given to the police by the McCleans. He did not trust the local plods to do a thorough job. Not their fault; they hadn't been properly trained in gathering detail. He opened his eyes and began to look for clues that might have survived the detergent blitz.

'They seem to have done a thorough clean-up job,' he commented.

'They should not have removed the tape without permission,' said Ncube.

'I wonder if they were properly cautioned about not crossing it or removing it.' McClean seemed to indicate that nothing was said. 'Check on that when we get back, Sergeant.'

Ncube wrote a laborious reminder in his notebook. He began to examine the walls, windows and doors of the bedroom.

'What have you got, Ncube?' Sibanda asked after a few minutes, when he noticed the sergeant paying particular attention to an area of the wall at the back of the room.

'Not sure. It seems to be a stain of some kind.'

Sibanda moved to have a closer look. It could have been a splash of blood. It seemed quite a long way from the door where the body had been lying according to the police report. His knowledge of blood spattering, something of a science, was sketchy. Could it have flown that far?

Sibanda had familiarised himself with the McCleans' statements and the police docket before setting out from the station. Margaret, the domestic help, had come upon the victim asleep in the bed. She had screamed and run out of the room. Mrs McClean had been first to the scene. The victim had attacked her. She, in turn, had screamed. Mr McClean had come running. He hit the victim with his knobkerrie, killing him instantly. It must have been an unlucky blow, thought Sibanda, or else this man has more muscle than he knows.

'What do you think, Ncube? Justifiable?' he asked as he stood up and moved away from the wall.

'Very hard to tell, sir. I would have been afraid if I had found someone strange in my bed,' he replied.

'And it certainly wasn't Goldilocks, Sergeant,' said Sibanda. Ncube looked at him askance. The detective came up with odd comments from time to time.

'Sir, did you notice Mrs McClean?'

'Not really, Ncube, other than she seemed quite shy. Why?'

'Well, I thought she seemed… not so shy, but nervous and upset. The little ones seemed scared. A woman in her own kitchen is normally relaxed, happy and you know… enganakile, carefree. She did not even come over to greet us.' Sibanda thought for a moment. He trusted Ncube's judgement on women with a household full of wives and, if station rumour were to be believed, several girlfriends as well, all of whom adored him.

'Okay, let's see what we can unearth here,' said Sibanda. 'Interview the domestic, I'll chat with the McCleans.' Ncube set off in search of Margaret. Sibanda returned to the kitchen. Isabelle McClean was sitting next to her husband. Sibanda could see her full face. Someone had given her a serious beating.

'That's a nasty bruise, Mrs McClean.'

Isabelle self-consciously put her hand to her eye. 'It… it was very frightening,' she stumbled.

'I am sorry, Mrs McClean. Is it alright if I ask you a couple of questions?'

Isabelle looked at her husband. He nodded.

'You told the police the tramp hit you, is that correct?' asked Sibanda, now seated opposite the McCleans.

Isabelle looked away. She took a moment to answer. 'Yes, it was the intruder,' she said, turning towards her husband as if seeking approval for her words.

'He was like a wild animal and you were terrified, weren't you?' prompted McClean. 'That's when you screamed and I ran in.'

Sibanda was silent for a while. He had done a stint on domestic violence as a young officer and enough night shifts with Nottingham's Domestic Violence Unit to know, even on a white skin, that the ripening contusion on Mrs McClean's left eye was older than yesterday morning. He also noticed that Mr McClean was stirring his coffee with his left hand. His right hand was constantly shielded from view. 'I would appreciate it if you could allow Mrs McClean to answer for herself,' he addressed the farmer.

'My wife is very shy. She doesn't take to strangers; you are frightening her after all that's happened,' said McClean.

Isabelle was shaking. She was battling to hold on to her composure. Ncube was right, this woman was not comfortable. Sibanda was doing his best to make her feel at ease. There was more to her terror than a home invasion or irrational fear of the police. Her husband put his arm around her shoulders in comfort. Sibanda noted that he applied more pressure than a reassuring hug.

'Izzy has been very upset since the attack, Detective,' said McClean, standing now. 'I think she would be better off lying down in her room.' He gave his wife a tug on the arm, pulling her up from the sofa and herding her off toward the door.

'Thanks for your time, Mr and Mrs McClean,' said Sibanda as they walked away from him. Outside, his sergeant was waiting.

'You picked it up, Sergeant,' he said, as soon as they were out of earshot. 'There's something not quite right here. We are not getting the full story. Any luck with the domestic worker?'

'She is very tight-lipped, I think she is terrified. Her story is the same as the McCleans' in every detail. One thing, though, which might interest you. She is married to one of the cooks at Thunduluka Lodge. Come and look here.' The sergeant gestured to an old pick-up which was parked near the kitchen door. 'Look, there is that blue paint again.' He puffed his cheeks out a bit and swaggered importantly towards the vehicle. Could this be a vital clue? His pride was showing.

Sibanda took in the long, faint streak of metallic-blue located half way up the driver's side door. He squatted on his haunches to get a closer look. He ran his fingers along the scrape. He dropped his head in deliberation. 'Can these two crimes be linked?' Crime and coincidence were two Cs inextricably intertwined and never to be discounted, but this scenario stretched that concept to the limit. A murder in the game park with possible witchcraft implications and a random killing of a vagrant on a farm, linked by blue paint, a husband at one location and a wife at the other. It was tenuous at best, but needed to be investigated.

'Good work, Sergeant,' he tossed over his shoulder as he walked back to the house. In the kitchen, the boys were playing quietly and watchfully in a corner with Margaret. Robert McClean had returned to the sofa, his wife was absent.

'Sorry to bother you again, Mr McClean, just a couple more questions. Do you own the pick-up parked outside?' he asked.

'Yes, that's mine, but my wife uses it mostly.'

'When was the last time it was driven?' Sibanda asked.

'Last Friday. My wife went to town to do the shopping. I am pretty certain it hasn't been used since then. Izzy normally lets me know if she is going out,' McClean said.

I'm sure she does, thought Sibanda, you have the poor woman on a tight rein.

On a hunch, Sibanda produced the Buck knife from his pocket. B for Bob, he thought. It's a long shot but worth a try. 'Have you ever seen this, Mr McClean?' he asked, showing him the Buck knife found on the road. It had been dusted for prints and swabbed for DNA the previous evening. He allowed the farmer to hold it and examine it closely.

'No, sorry, Detective, it's not mine. It's been well used though and sharpened often, someone will be really missing this,' he said, running his finger along the blade. Sibanda had been glancing across at the children who were tussling over a toy car when he thought he caught a guilty glance from Margaret. It was fleeting and quickly disguised. Was it the knife that unnerved her, or her employer or the evidence she had given?

'Mr McClean, your pick-up has a streak of blue metallic paint along the near side door, did you know?' he asked.

McClean seemed genuinely puzzled. 'No, I'm very particular about my vehicles, I keep them in perfect order.'

'If your wife has any memory of a blue vehicle having parked near to her or having been involved in a collision, it may help us with enquiries into another case we are handling,' said Sibanda. 'One last question, Mr McClean. Do you have any weapons? Have they been discharged recently?'

'I do, Detective. They are well secured.' McClean led the inspector to his gun cabinet. 'Two shotguns and a .308. A couple of boys from Kestrel Vale came over last Sunday. They may have used some bird shot in one of the shotguns. They didn't bag anything. I haven't used them at all recently. I don't have enough land any more to hunt for the pot…' He left this last comment deliberately hanging.

Sibanda let it pass. Land redistribution was a hot potato. He was glad that he wasn't involved with the policing of it. He stepped outside and handed McClean his card.

'If you remember anything, get in touch.' He headed for the Land Rover and offered up his well-worn supplication for a clean get-away.

The Land Rover started up on the first key turn. Sibanda and Ncube were through the farm gate before they began to discuss their findings.

'The bruise on Isabelle McClean's face was not inflicted by the isibonda. I am certain of that,' said Sibanda. 'It's too ripe. There are already traces of yellow in the purple and black. That's at least a three-day-old injury. The husband is a nasty bully. He's too smug by half. What else do we have, Ncube?'

'Sir, the domestic, Margaret, is nervous. I am not sure she knows the whole truth, but she is sticking with the McCleans' story. I think her job depends on it. She has children and grandchildren to support. Her husband works at Thunduluka. She doesn't see him very often. I don't think there is any love lost there.'

'We know the victim reportedly fell near the door,' said Sibanda, 'because according to their story he was chasing Mrs McClean as she fled from the room. Despite their best efforts at cleaning up there was that possible speck of blood on the far wall.' He thought for a moment, rubbing his chin and taking several minutes before he spoke again.

'Ncube, here's what I believe happened. Margaret, going about her morning cleaning, disturbed the vagrant who leaped up from the bed. He retreated into the corner attempting to hide. Margaret naturally panicked and called McClean who charged in with his induku. He killed him in that back corner. Probably didn't even give him a chance to explain himself or surrender. They thought it best to move the body closer to the door to fit the story they had concocted.'

'That is terrible,' said the sergeant. 'Apparently the isibonda is well known in the district as a harmless half-wit. He has been wandering around these parts for some years. Never given any trouble. He wasn't going to hurt anyone. He was probably lost or confused.'

'Do we know his identity?' asked Sibanda.

'Not yet, sir. The station is on to it,' said Ncube.

Sibanda knew that proving a degree of manslaughter would be almost impossible unless either of the women came forward with the truth. The Zimbabwe Police looked leniently on the killing of interlopers inside a home, ruling it as justifiable. The country had inherited much of its legal and judicial system from the British. This was one area where they diverged like the Red Sea complete with Moses waving his staff.

'Look, sir, ihobo,' said Ncube suddenly.

Sibanda turned in time to see a long, black-tipped tail disappearing into the grass on the road verge. 'Also known as a slender mongoose.'

'Yes, and dangerous too. Mrs McClean must take care of her chickens with these things around.'

Sibanda laughed. He knew all about the myth of the slender mongoose and its reputed ability to trap chickens and suffocate them. His mother swore she had witnessed it. Even he had believed the superstition as a child. As he grew and began to take an interest in wildlife, he knew it was a physical impossibility for ihobo to catch chickens by the method attributed to them.

According to village legend, this creature lay in wait with its backside fanned open. Perhaps a gland under the tail disguised to look like a maize seed attracted the chicken initially, then *ihobo* would pounce on the chicken's head, trapping it in its anus. Once the witless bird had suffocated in the faecal passage, the mongoose dragged it away, still sucked into its sphincter, to devour it at leisure. That a creature barely bigger than a squirrel could do this challenged the laws of nature; that people actually believed this, challenged common sense. Sibanda had been unable to convince his own mother of the absurdity of the belief. He was not going to bother trying to convince his highly superstitious sergeant.

Berry Barton had been riddled with western superstitions. She tossed salt over her shoulder and avoided ladders. He teased her about this odd behaviour. She shrugged it off, laughing and claiming she had no idea why, or whether these actions staved off bad luck. She was not superstitious, she said, it was more of an insurance policy just in case. Her ancestors must have done it. It was now an inbuilt reaction, like jumping on a chair when a mouse ran past.

Sibanda had a flashback to a day when they had been walking together in Nottingham. An ambulance passed by, all lights flashing and the siren wailing. Berry had quickly grabbed her collar and held on to it tightly until the sound had disappeared down the road.

'Another bit of juju your long-lost ancestors have taught you, I suppose,' he had said. She laughed, knowing she had been caught out, and thumped him quite fiercely in the arm.

'Oh you,' she said. 'You are just too… too… rational. Let go a bit and give in to some of your inner demons. Believe in the impossible. Listen to your ancestors. They may not be a crazy as you think. Look,' she said, laughing and pointing to a wizened old man, carrying a walking stick and wearing a straw boater, 'isn't that a village goblin, a tokoloshe?' Before he could comment, she had sprinted off down the road, and leaped onto a number 98 bus heading for the university. She waved to him from the footplate. She blew him a kiss as the bus sped by. He caught it in his hand. He kept his fist clenched until he was obliged to haul himself onto a bus headed for the police station. The faint bruise on his arm sustained him through the next three weeks until they could catch up again.

The radio in the Land Rover crackled into life. Sibanda started guiltily. If he was thinking of anyone other than the two victims it should have been Khanyi, the girl he was shortly to marry.

'Gubu Base to Gubu Mobile, do you read? Over.'

'We have you fives, Gubu Base. Go ahead,' said the sergeant.

'Firstly,' said the gentle voice of Constable Zanele Khumalo, 'Forensics have come up with a cause of death for the Thunduluka victim. It seems he was suffocated. There was considerable alcohol in his bloodstream, possibly sleeping pills as well. They are awaiting secondary tests on that. Still no ID, I'm afraid, but he was between twenty-five and thrity-five years of age.'

'Time of death?' asked Sibanda.

'Between eleven and midnight is as near as they can get.'

'Did they come up with anything else?'

'No, but they are still working on it. We do have an ID on the vagrant though. His name is Mtabizi Mpofu from Munda village. We have sent someone from the station to advise the relatives.'

Oh God, thought Sibanda, Khanyi's village, Khanyi's name. Could this man be a cousin or a brother? He couldn't go barging in there now, claiming her hand. All the marriage arrangements would have to wait.

'Sir,' said Ncube, 'do you want to divert to Munda village?'

Sibanda thought for several moments. He should go to the village to be with Khanyi. She had never mentioned an isibonda in the family. He was fairly certain that if Mtabizi Mpofu was a relative then it must be a distant connection.

'No, Sergeant, I think we'll let the officers do their job, we can be better occupied elsewhere. We need to get back to the station to check Naidoo's alibi. With any luck by then Constable Khumalo will have more news on the other *Mediterranean Sapphire* Toyotas.

Chapter 8

She lay on her bed embracing the pain in her joints. She wanted to suffer. She wanted her crumbling bones to take away the ache in her heart. The throbbing agony would distract her from the anguish and sorrow which was ripping the soul from her very being. They had come yesterday to tell her he was dead, her blessed son, her child, her free spirit, Mtabizi, crushed by a blow to his skull. They said he had been attacking a white woman, had spent the night in their house, gone mad in the morning. She did not believe a word of it. This son of hers who cradled the nestlings when they fell from the nest, who was one with the birds and the wild animals, would never harm a living thing. He worshipped the world and all who stepped on its earth. His compassion was boundless.

She wished she had been able to keep him safe. She envied the grey penduline tit, a busy little bird that built a nest out of cottony plant down, the softest, fluffiest nest in the bird world, a complete ball of comfort. So soft and fragile a home that bits fell off as the nestlings stirred, or the wind blew too fiercely. The parents had to spend much of their time on building repairs. The nest was not only a downy cocoon, but a safe and secure haven. The adult birds could leave the nest often, in their search for patching materials. They had developed a secret zipper to enclose the vulnerable hatchlings in their velvet bubble. No marauder could discover the entrance. Mantini wished she had been able to find a hidden fastening and a velvet bubble to hide her children away.

Her son's behaviour puzzled her. If Mtabizi was wet and cold and needed a warm bed, why didn't he come home? He always returned to the village in winter on those frost-tipped, clear-starred nights, or in summer when the rains broke and slaked the earth. He slept in his own hut then. He had never sought shelter elsewhere other than under a friendly bush or in the leafy down of a tree's shade. What possessed him to break into a strange house, she could not know. Possession was the word she used. Her son must have been bewitched by some evil force. She suspected her sister, the one who always complained about him. She had no kindness in her heart. Selfishness was her master; meanness of spirit, her hymn. She was born cold. Not even the hottest fire made from the dense wood of the leadwood tree would drive the ice from her soul. She belonged in hell.

She had confronted her umthakathi of a sister, the witch. 'You chased my boy from the village, you who caused him to be murdered,' she had screamed at her.

'Be careful who you accuse, old woman,' her sister had said. 'I had nothing to do with his killing, I did not chase him. I did not like him, with his strange ways and rancid body, but I did not chase him. You should look closer to home.' She glanced at Kanku's hut.

It could not be Kanku. She refused to believe her beloved daughter had anything to do with this. Kanku, her unexpected gift who arrived long after she thought she could conceive, the miracle child who had sustained her through the difficult times when she could no longer work. Such a special baby born out of the ashes of blood, death and violence. A cuckoo child, her inkanku created from the sperm of a stranger as the Jacobin called overhead. It didn't matter if those memories surfaced. They could not be as hurtful as the keen edge of her grief. She let her mind wander again back to that fateful day *The Boys* arrived.

When she and Shadrek had run back to the kitchen area to warn the rest of the staff, they were too late. The staff were already sitting on the ground with their hands on their heads, *The Boys* standing over them with their AKs alert and pointing. The barrel of one rifle gesticulated to them to sit with the others. They complied silently, with economy of movement in case any excess effort might be deemed hostile. Mantini remembered her terror as clearly as if it was happening again, now in her hut. Time soothes the memory of birth pains, takes the edge off sorrow, but the remembrance of fear is eternally real. Her heart was pounding, skipping beats; breathing was difficult. Her throat started to constrict. Slowly she brought her emotions under control as she had that day.

'If one of you fucking bantwana besambane opens your mouth or moves, you are hyena bait. Now, you,' their leader said pointing to Moyo, one of the waiters, 'we need meat and drink; beers, quickly.' He kicked out at the young waiter, who leaped up and looked around helplessly.

'Sir,' he said, his voice wobbling with fear, 'the beers are locked behind the bar. The food for tonight will be issued in an hour or so. The only thing we have is tea and cake which we are going to serve the customers before they leave on their safaris.' The rifle butt smacked him hard across the face, a tooth flew. He began to bleed from his nose and mouth.

'Just do as I say,' the commander threatened. Moyo picked himself up and, holding his head, went to see what he could rustle up.

Mantini realised this group of dissidents was under pressure, being hunted themselves and probably high on marijuana. She had heard dissidents often smoked imbanje to bolster their courage. She had seen its effects before. Her brother grew a few plants in the bush behind his hut. He smoked it from time to time. She recognised the pin-prick irises of the stoned. They would be irrational and incapable of reasoning. She hoped they kept their heads and were able to placate these misguided warriors.

'Sir,' she said, 'I think I can help. That boy will find little. I have the confidence of the manager and access to his tent. I know where he keeps his keys. There is a first-aid box,' she added, nodding towards one of his companions slumped over on the ground with blood oozing from a wound in his side. During her small speech the commander had put the barrel of his rifle in her neck just beneath her chin. He pressed the cold steel firmly into her throat. She found it difficult to talk. She shook with fear, but she felt their lives depended on getting supplies. Someone had to volunteer.

Mantini recognised she had done the wrong thing by bringing attention to herself, but Moyo was young and new. Thandanyoni ran a carefully controlled camp. Bar stocks were locked away. He would come back empty-handed. The soldiers would be desperate.

The commander's eyes narrowed. He prodded the barrel of the AK even harder into her skin, using it to lever her upright. She had no choice but to stand. He led her away to one of the staff tents. Mantini knew what was coming next. These men had been chased and harried. The commander was like a hawk that had strayed into the territory of a family of fork-tailed drongos. The little birds were belligerent and aggressive defenders of their space. They flew high and dive-bombed the hawk's head and kept up the onslaught until the predatory bird retreated to a branch to gather his strength. She was that branch. She did not want to imagine who the drongos were, or what the commander had done to make them so angry.

'Take off your clothes, woman,' he ordered, 'and lie on the bed. Let's see if you talk so much now.' As she did so she felt as exposed and vulnerable as the featherless hornbill in her mud prison. She was not ashamed of her body. It bore the scars of four pregnancies and had fed four children. She might not be eighteen, with firm, proud breasts and rounded hips, but she had fought heroic battles to bring forth life. She wore her medals with pride. He wanted to humiliate her, to dominate. She allowed him to win those skirmishes. She was not frightened at the thought of being raped. She wanted to struggle, but she was terrified of the violence that might follow. She would be shot once he had finished the act. Her children would be orphaned and abandoned.

The commander did not remove his fatigues or his bandolier and grenades. He propped his AK against the foot of the bed and climbed on her. Since her husband had left for Johannesburg nearly three years before she had not allowed another man into her bed. Shadrek had made continuous advances, but he was already married. She was not prepared to betray another woman. When the soldier penetrated her, she bit back a gasp. Her body had changed in the last three years, it had dried and shrivelled. As the commander prodded and poked against her unwilling flesh, she felt unbidden tears and globules of sweat strain to escape as if fleeing her flesh like rats from a burning grain bin.

Mantini let her mind drift, hoping to hook a memory that would drag her from the present to a place of sanctuary. The rainbird called insistently in the acacia, but the reminiscence that came was of a red-billed oxpecker feeding on a donkey. The bird had gorged itself on the freshly blood-bloated ticks for which the donkey was surely grateful, cleaning out her ears and digging under her tail for the tenacious gore-siphoning parasites. Having discovered a harness sore, he began to probe the wound with his razor-sharp beak, digging deeper and deeper, tearing away needles of flesh until new blood ran down the donkey's flank. The old jenny shook her head and shivered her skin in an attempt to shake off the relentless probing. Each time the bird flew up a few inches and resettled, mining the growing wound like a scarlet seam of precious metal.

Eventually, she felt the relief of his sperm trickling down her leg, heard the commander's satisfied groans, and detected the soft retreat of the uncompromising beak. He collapsed on her, his head burrowing into her breasts. Not knowing why, but unable to resist, she took his head in her arms and cradled it like a baby. For a few seconds he relaxed, gave in to post-coital lassitude and the possibility of home and a family. She sensed it through his stinking camouflage, through the cords of his neck that slackened, through his hands that loosened their claw-like grip on her shoulders and through his hips glued heavily against hers.

The commander propped himself over her and looked into her eyes. He was young. A wave of pity for this umtwana driven to fight for a cause he was passionate about passed over her. He continued his soul-stealing stare as though she would be the last vessel to receive his seed. Then he blinked back to reality, rolled off her, picked up his rifle and pointed it at her head. She steeled herself against the bullet, squeezed her eyes shut, held her breath, mumbled a prayer. He did not pull the trigger. She would always wonder if her instinctive caress had saved her life.

He leant over her again, grabbed her roughly by the jaw and hissed, 'Get up, go and get the keys and don't tell anyone if you want to avoid a massacre.' She wiped herself as best she could on the sheet and got dressed. As she left the tent the eyes of the corralled staff were upon her. With a straight back and despite the burning pain between her legs, she walked normally towards Thandanyoni's tent.

She entered the tent as though this were a routine, bed-turn-down visit and went straight to the slender knee drawer of the desk where Thandanyoni always kept his keys. They were there. She exhaled the breath she had carried like a heavy pail of water all the way from the staff tent. As she went to pick them up she heard a noise behind her. It was Thandanyoni.

'I never took you for a thief, Mantini,' he said calmly.

'No, sir, I'm not,' she was shaking now. 'It's just I needed extra cleaning materials...' her voice petered out knowing she had made a vital mistake. The cleaning stuff had been issued that morning. She turned to look at him and shrugged her shoulders. 'I'm very sorry, sir.'

'Mantini, don't take me for a fool, I know something is going on here. The staff area is as quiet as the grave, which despite my best efforts, never normally happens. There should be a clattering and banging of cups. What happened to the afternoon tea service? They are here, aren't they?'

'Yes, they are here,' she replied with resignation, 'four of them.' Thandanyoni could pick up on the slightest sign, a hint of a wind change, a bend in the grass, a turned leaf; these were as loud as clamouring bells to this magayigusu, this man at one with the bush.

'What should I do? They have all the staff at gunpoint. They are demanding food and drink. One of them seems badly wounded.'

'Take the keys, Mantini, give them what they want. Give them a bottle of brandy each rather than beer, it will act faster and relax them. Take the first aid kit, help the wounded man. Tell no one that you have seen me. I will sort this out.'

Mantini made her way back to the kitchen. The staff were as she had left them. She handed the keys to Shadrek and told the commander he would be the best one to find supplies. As she passed the keys over she had only enough time to whisper, 'Brandy,' to the cook and hoped he understood. She averted her face from the commander's gaze, kept her eyes on the ground. To exchange looks with him might betray his rape of her or her betrayal of him.

'I have a first aid certificate,' she said. 'Do you want me to attend to your comrade?' In reality she knew the very basics. When the staff were sick she was the one they turned to. She doled out a few paracetamol tablets here and there, daubed the cuts and blisters, administered the occasional plaster, but that was her limit. Anything more serious went to the clinic in Gubu village.

'Yes, see if you can do something,' he said, as he frog-marched Shadrek towards the supply tent.

She knelt down beside the wounded dissident. He was pale and sweating. His temperature was soaring. He was barely conscious and only a child. Mantini propped him against her knee and urged him to swallow the Paracetamol. They would be of little use, but they might dull the pain and bring his temperature down. She lifted his shirt and examined the wound. This child would die. The wound was black and oozing, surrounded by a growing circle of hot, red, swollen skin. The rotting flesh stank. She took an antiseptic swab from the box and gently cleaned the wound. The boy groaned and began muttering that he could see elephants charging and they were all going to be killed. She tried to pacify him with the gentle words she had used on her own children when they were sick or could not sleep, but he was delirious and hallucinating. She covered the gaping hole with a wound dressing. This boy needed an operating theatre and a skilled surgeon to extract the bullet and cut away the festering flesh. She had done as much as she could.

The commander and Shadrek returned holding bottles of brandy and tins of ham, baked beans, peaches and bread. The commander had already downed nearly half a bottle of the spirit. He handed out the booty to his men. They began alternatively to drink and swill from the tins, tearing gobs of bread and dunking it in the juices. Mantini could see they were starving, had not eaten for days, too wary to light fires as they dodged their pursuers.

A noise broke the strained silence. Vehicles started up accompanied by the excited chatter of guests clambering aboard ready for their safari. Mantini realised Thandanyoni was clearing the camp of guests in case there was trouble. He would have covered for the lack of afternoon tea with some clever story. Once, the truck bringing in supplies had broken down and there were no eggs for breakfast. Thandanyoni explained it away by telling a wonderful tale of how a honey badger had broken into the kitchen, demolished the eggs and munched its way through the bacon. The clients were enchanted and delighted to make do with cereal, toast and marmalade. Better than a cooked breakfast, they had a story of African legend to tell at their smart dinner parties.

The commander raised his rifle. He became alert. There was a change in camp activity. He was watchful and nervous. He walked across to her where she was still kneeling next to the dying boy. He grabbed her by the neck, his rifle pointing at her stomach.

'Did you speak to anyone? Do they know we are here?' he spat at her. The rest of the dissidents stood up and cocked their weapons in alarm. Mantini spoke desperately through her constricted wind pipe. 'The afternoon game drive is departing,' she said, 'They always leave at this time. It's normal.' The commander relaxed his grip. She fell back next to the boy. Her legs were shaking. She trusted Thandanyoni, but even he could not rescue them from this.

As she lay there contemplating her death, she felt like the victim of a fiscal shrike. The shrike was the gangster of the avian world, a pugnacious, war-mongering bird, armed with an arsenal of lethal weapons – a powerful neck, a cruelly hooked beak and a hidden sharp tooth with which to dismember its prey. Sometimes it killed other birds, but more often it lived on grasshoppers and frogs. Even when sated it would continue to kill and maim, impaling its victims on long thorns or barbed wire, leaving them to die and rot and never returning to eat them. It was as if they were advertising their territory in some doomsday scenario, warning all those who ventured in of the consequences. These *Boys* were like that. They could slip away now, silently, leaving no trace, but Mantini knew they needed to mark their territory. She felt impaled.

Mantini continued to minister to the wounded boy, bathing his brow with cool water, exhorting him to drink, trying to keep him quiet and still his tortured mind. She had no idea how much time had passed but *The Boys* were visibly relaxed, slouching, their weapons at ease. The rest of the staff had lost the look of desperation. They were settling like condemned men into their captivity.

When she heard a cheery whistling coming down the path, the end was near. Thandanyoni was publicising his arrival.

'It's Thandanyoni,' she said, 'he's coming to check where we all are.' All but the wounded boy melted into the cover of the bush. She heard the click of their automatic rifles changing status. There would be trouble. She tried to look around her to see where her safety lay and, imperceptibly, she cowered down next to the fevered boy.

'Yeyi, madoda, kwenzakalani la? Why aren't you at work? Do you think this is a holiday?' Thandanyoni asked, in pure Ndebele.

'Hayi baba, kodwa sesilohlupho, there is a problem,' Shadrek replied for the seated group. 'We have ebesingazilindele, unexpected visitors.'

Thandanyoni nodded his understanding. The three soldiers reappeared, all three rifles trained on him.

'Angihlomanga, I come unarmed,' he said with his hands raised, 'I am alone. I mean you no harm. Your friend needs help,' he said pointing to the increasingly agitated boy on the ground.

'There is no help for him,' the commander replied.

'Ufunani? What do you want then?' asked Thandanyoni.

'Time,' replied the commander, 'and we will kill anyone who gets in our way. You will be first.'

'Commander, if you wanted to kill me you would have done so already,' said Thandanyoni. He pushed away the rifle barrel from in front of his face. 'I'm afraid you don't have much time either. I have just heard via our radio that National Parks have an armed patrol in the area. They usually call in for a beer or two. Take what you want from here and head south. The boundary is not far away. You will reach villages where you can hide.'

'Why are you helping us?' the commander asked.

'Akukho skhwehle esephandela esinye,' he replied.

The commander laughed at this and the tension eased. How could this white man know those deep sayings only the old people still used. No francolin forages for another, or he supposed the closest English proverb would be, God helps those who help themselves.

'How are you helping yourself, Thandanyoni?' he asked.

'I have no political axe to grind, Commander. And these people,' he said gesturing to the staff, 'are my responsibility. Plus, I have a camp full of American tourists. I don't want a gun battle here. I respect your right to dissent, but bloodshed is never the answer. Go talk around a table.'

The commander never got a chance to reply. The injured boy leapt up with the last of his strength and screamed. 'Machitigaza, Spill Blood,' he called out his leader's nom de guerre, 'basop, isilwane!' In his frenzied, delusional state he thought he could see lions attacking. He opened fire. Everyone scattered. Mantini turned to run as the hot casings, ejected from his magazine, hit her arms and legs. Moyo's head exploded like a ripe watermelon. Thandanyoni went down in a hail of fire before she gained enough momentum to get upright and flee. It seemed like an eternity, but was probably seconds. She felt as though she were wading through a mire of thick porridge, gripped and hindered by its sticky viscosity, so slow was her progress. She fell heavily, hitting a log as she went down, pushed from behind by Shadrek who used her back as a springboard to his own safety. She would be unable to move further, both her knees were badly twisted. As she awaited her inevitable fate, she looked back at the scene of isihogo, of hellfire, in time to see the commander put a bullet into the head of the delirious boy. The following silence was only interrupted by the groans of the injured. Mantini blacked out.

'Qoki, qoki, qoki'. There was someone rapping at her hut door. 'Gogo, Granny, wake up.' It was her niece who woke her from her sleeping torment to her waking nightmare. The realisation of where she was and what had happened hit her afresh.

'Ngena, my child, come in,' she said through renewed tears and heartache.

'Gogo, I have a message from Lindiwe,' she said indicating her cellphone. 'She is on her way back from Johannesburg for Mtabizi's funeral and will be here soon, Gogo. She will be here to keep vigil with the body.'

Lindiwe was her last daughter, born before her cuckoo child, Kanku. She had not seen or heard from her in a long time. It gave her a chink of joy in her heart. Her children might all be together soon even though two of them would be beneath the ground.

Chapter 9

When the ailing Land Rover pulled into Gubu Station late morning after visiting Zebra Hill Farm, Sibanda understood further forays would not be possible in the immediate future. The sawmill road had taken care of that. From under the bonnet, a steaming white cloud was hissing and spitting at him like a cornered caracal. Ncube leapt out of the vehicle, sucked his teeth, shook his head and looked accusingly at the detective.

'Sir, I think you may have travelled too fast; the radiator is boiling.'

'I can see that, Sergeant,' he replied tetchily, 'but it would help if the temperature gauge could indicate that before vaporisation set in. Right now the pointer is stuck in some perpetual marriage with the blue line. Perhaps you could make a special arrangement with it to reflect the temperature of the engine.'

The sergeant scratched his head. He tried to decipher the detective's speech, but failed. He had understood the sarcastic tone though. He wanted to snap back about the irresponsibility of someone having hammered the accelerator governor to pulp. An old lady such as this deserved respect and veneration, a gentle hand and a considerate foot. She needed to be coaxed and sweet-talked. Sibanda was always in too much of a hurry. The sergeant lamely commented that his brother in the CMED was expecting a similar model vehicle in shortly. He would be sending up a temperature gauge as soon as he could. It hardly mattered what he was saying anyway as the detective had turned his back and was storming into the station.

What he did not tell the inspector was that the unfortunate Land

Rover to be cannibalised came from the Hwange Town Police. It was booked into the CMED for its annual overhaul. The mechanic had been primed to exchange the working unit for the Land Rover's defunct gauge. The clandestine swop was going to cost Ncube a box of dried fish caught over two weekends and lovingly smoked by Nomatter, his second wife, who was gifted in the art.

Ncube focused his attention on a more worthy recipient of his consideration, the Land Rover. 'Now, Umchinawami, my baby,' he wheedled, 'what is the matter this time?'

Back in his office, Sibanda cooled off, gathered his thoughts, and went through the papers on his desk. There were several typed statements from the staff and guests at Thunduluka Lodge, and a comprehensive list of staff members. He checked through the list for the initial B. There were three possibilities: Bornwell Mpofu, Barbara Moyo and Peter Bhebhe. Shadrek Nkomo must be the husband of Margaret, the domestic at Zebra Hill Farm, who had mentioned her husband was a Nkomo.

Burrowing further into his pile, and discarding memos requiring him to submit reports, fill out forms, or pay attention to new procedures, Sibanda came across the fingerprint report on the Buck knife. Forensics had been able to lift one clear print and one partial print. Diagrams of both were included in the report. He dreamed then of the computer in Nottingham which, when fed fingerprints, would match them to a suspect in a matter of minutes. Gubu Police Station only had one computer; it was as ancient and cantankerous as the sometimes smoke-, sometimes steam-belching mechanical monster in the yard. It occurred to him that it really did depend on the Land Rover's mood as to which end it chose to expel its venomous vapours.

Police Constable Zanele Khumalo, who doubled as receptionist, family liaison officer, filing clerk and typist, was to the computer what Ncube was to the Land Rover. She had a brilliant eye for detail. She would be the one to sift through the fingerprints and laboriously make the visual comparisons to see if they could determine an owner. He should have a result in the foreseeable future if PC Khumalo wasn't tied up with Mfumu's obsessive paperwork.

At that moment, Constable Khumalo knocked and came into his office. She leaned back through the door jamb scanning the corridor left to right for unfriendly ears. Satisfied, she closed the door. 'I have the list of blue Toyotas and their registration and addresses,' she confided in a low voice. 'You are not going to like this, but one of them is registered to Micah Ngwenya, the governor.'

'I suspected as much,' said Sibanda, 'and Sergeant Ncube is already having nightmares about the future of his internal organs.'

'You don't think…' said Constable Khumalo, her eyes widening in alarm.

'It's a possibility that we have to face, Zee. That's why I need you to keep this to yourself for the time being. If Chief Inspector Mfumu gets wind of it he will whisk me off the case faster than a dragonfly off the water.'

'Here's the list of the others, sir.'

Sibanda took the paper and had a look. Ishmael Naidoo stood out as the prime suspect so far; Micah Ngwenya, Harry Burke, Brian Joseph and a vehicle belonging to Joel Dube, but which hadn't been registered for two years, were also on the paper. He noted the two Bs in the list. They might be worth checking out first.

'I know you are probably run off your feet, Zee, but please check out the fingerprints of anyone whose name starts with a B first. If we can nail down the ownership of that Buck knife, we are half way there. Oh, and Zee,' he called the constable back as she was about to leave his office, 'Ishmael Naidoo will be coming in sometime today to have his fingerprints taken. Check those as soon as you can. He's hiding something.'

'I'll do that, Detective, when I have a free moment. The chief inspector is on the rampage today. I'm holding all my papers with my teeth, you know, not a free hand to spare.'

Inspector Sibanda laughed at the image, picked up some of his own papers, and strode down the corridor to Mfumu's office ready to debrief the chief inspector as vaguely as he could. He had learnt fairly quickly the less the man knew the more successful the case would be. He knocked on the door and walked in.

'What do you have for me, Inspector?' Mfumu asked.

'Not a lot yet. Until we find the identity of the victim, it will be a battle to find the perpetrator. We have no idea of the victim's recent movements and associates.'

'Have you filled out all the necessary dockets?'

'The paperwork is nearly finished,' said Sibanda as he waved the totally unrelated papers in his hand across Mfumu's eye-line. 'This appears to be a muthi-related crime and I'm certain body parts were removed before the vultures got to work.'

Mfumu pursed his lips. 'We will have to keep this from the public for the time being, the publicity could be unpleasant.'

'We discovered a knife not far from the crime scene,' continued Sibanda, 'which may or may not have had a connection to the crime. The victim was probably murdered elsewhere and dumped in Thunduluka Vlei. There were vehicle tracks at the scene. From these we suspect it's a Toyota Land Cruiser.'

'There are many of those vehicles in this part of the world. What is the point of pursuing that? You'll be wasting your time and police resources,' stated Mfumu.

'Possibly,' conceded Sibanda, not yet prepared to disclose the distinctive colour, 'but it is worth keeping in mind. We also know the victim was suffocated, probably while drugged from a mixture of alcohol and sleeping pills. Forensics may be able to give us more details on the cause of death, but I'm not hopeful, given the state of the corpse.'

'You went to Zebra Hill Farm?'

'Yes, but the situation there is not completely clear either. The victim did break into the farmhouse, but there were some discrepancies.'

'What sort of discrepancies?' asked Mfumu with alarm. He thought this case was cut and dried. He wanted it cleared off his desk and in the filing cabinet as soon as possible.

'The intruder was a harmless vagrant, well known in the area, but I'm certain that Mrs McClean's injuries were not inflicted by the homeless man.'

'What makes you say that, I heard the isibonda hit her?'

'Unlikely,' replied Sibanda. 'The bruise on her eye was far too old and seasoned to have been inflicted by the tramp. It must have been done days before.'

Mfumu did not like the way this case was shaping up. It was becoming messy. Chanza, his nephew, had assured him it was an open-and-shut case needing little attention. He might have known that Sibanda would find reason to complicate matters. It was his speciality.

It would play havoc with his end-of-month statistics. This mess had to be cleaned up in a few days.

'I think you are muddling your facts here, Detective. I have seen the report. It was a simple break-in with violent intent. You will stick to that line of enquiry.'

Sibanda was not about to be dictated to when it came to a crime. He could barely conceal his anger. His jaw clenched, which to anyone who knew him at all would have signalled obstinacy. His voice took on a firm tone as he continued, 'In addition, the victim's body may have been moved. There is blood evidence on a far wall to suggest where the vagrant may have been cowering when he was hit. He was probably moved after death, dragged nearer the door to indicate he attacked Mrs McClean.'

'What are the witnesses saying?'

'The witnesses are sticking to their original statements. On their evidence it will be very hard to charge Robert McClean, even with manslaughter. It would probably never stick in court.'

Mfumu relaxed a little. This was more like it, he thought. Accidental death was a nice clean outcome.

'There's something else you need to know, Chief Inspector,' Sibanda had deliberately kept this bit of information until last. 'The victim from Zebra Hill is apparently related to my intended, Khanyi Mpofu. She lives in Munda village and so does Mtabizi Mpofu, the deceased.'

'Then you can have nothing more to do with that case,' Mfumu spluttered virtuously, 'you will be too emotionally overwrought and unable to think clearly. You will hand the dossier to Assistant Detective Chanza immediately.' Mfumu was delighted at this unexpected windfall. Perhaps this case could be wrapped up by month-end.

'Is that strictly necessary? I am perfectly capable of handling this case without becoming emotionally involved. I've never even met the vagrant, Mtabizi Mpofu.' Sibanda was furious. Sentiment never entered his work. He recognised another police regulation being brought into play. Mfumu could probably quote it to him chapter and verse. He needed little prompting to bring Prosper Chanza to the fore. He was the inspector's nephew, a dysfunctional nerd who hid behind owl glasses and embraced forms and filing with the enthusiasm of a dung beetle for a pile of wet elephant droppings. This was an office war he couldn't win. He wanted his powder dry for bigger battles to come. 'Perhaps you are right,' he conceded.

Mfumu looked up suspiciously at Sibanda's meek acceptance. He could smell a rat but as yet had no idea where the rotting rodent corpse lay. 'Any other leads on Vulture Man?' asked Mfumu warily, expecting the hidden rat carcass to show up on his desk at any minute.

Sibanda winced. He felt the name, however appropriate, was disrespectful. 'We have actually named him Mufi, the departed one.' He made the name up on the spot. The victim had some kind of identity now. 'We do have a couple of leads, nothing momentous. I am hoping to check one of them out this afternoon if that rust bucket outside will perform.' He deliberately didn't mention the possibility of a visit to the governor. It was too sensitive. Given Mfumu's reverence of high office and protocol, the visit might well be stalled or abandoned altogether. This revelation would be Sibanda's planned skirmish of the future.

'Keep me posted as soon as anything breaks. I'll have provincial HQ on my back. They will be nervous of another witchcraft orgy in the press,' said Mfumu. He picked up his ball-point pen and returned his meticulous attention to the form in front of him on his desk.

Sibanda strode out towards the Land Rover and Ncube. The sergeant had a cloth in his hand and was worshipfully wiping the Land Rover's windscreen where the angry water had condensed.

'All fixed, Ncube?' Sibanda asked hopefully.

'Yes, sir,' replied Ncube, in a tone that betrayed hostility. Sibanda sighed. He had absolutely no curiosity in knowing what was wrong with the steam-snorting dragon in the first place, but he recognised he would have to appear interested if he was to keep his genial sergeant on his side.

'Hop in,' he said, 'you can give me a run down on the repairs as we travel.' Sibanda drove gingerly out of the police yard. He would have to nurse the scabrous boneshaker all the way to the governor's house. It would add at least ten minutes to the journey. As he gently manipulated the pig-headed gear lever into third and even more tentatively into fourth, he remembered a movie he had watched as a kid in what passed for the local fleapit. It had been about a chauffeur driving a prickly, elderly lady around at a speed that would have given an arthritic chongololo a run for its money. The elderly lady was called

Miss Daisy. The perfect name for the bad-tempered hag he was driving. Ncube would be delighted that she was to be named after a flower. It would suit both of them.

'So Ncube,' he said with a wide grin on his face, 'tell me all about Miss Daisy.'

'Miss Daisy?' queried Ncube, 'Ngubani lo? I don't know anyone by that name.'

'It's the name of the Land Rover, Sergeant. I have decided to name her after a flower. You know the one. It is colourful, normally appears on bushes; pink, yellow and white ones to match the upholstery. It is hardy, lasts forever and doesn't need much water.' This last observation was pushing the analogy a bit. He had seen Ncube secrete a sghubu of water under his seat. Miss Daisy's water woes were obviously not over.

Ncube beamed, maybe the detective had a heart after all. Ncube began his story, highlighting his diagnostic genius. It began with a tightening of springs and bushes, and attention to the shock absorbers. Then came an examination of coolant system leaks that proceeded to the water pump, via the thermostat, timing belt, oil level and radiator hoses until it came to a grinding halt at the radiator cap. During the entire naming and checking of parts Sibanda felt he could get away with the occasional knowing nod of his head, interspersing a few double and triple nods, and a raised eyebrow. This allowed him to drift off and concentrate on what approach he was going to use with the governor. A lengthy silence prompted him to say something.

'So what exactly is the problem?'

'As I was saying, sir, I narrowed it down to the radiator cap. The gasket had blown, fallen to pieces, which meant the system was no longer under pressure, and not doing its job.'

'Excellent work, Ncube, the station would be stationary without you,' said Sibanda. He mentally approved of his own witticism even if the pun went sailing over his sergeant's head. 'How did you fix it?' he asked, without the least shred of interest in the answer.

'Rekin, sir,' he replied, 'we don't have a spare gasket at the station. My brother tells me it is unlikely he will ever locate a new one, so I cut one from rekin. It won't last very long. I have cut several more. They are under the seat ready to replace it when necessary.'

He should have known it; rekin was the glue of Africa. He sometimes felt the whole continent was held together by the stuff. Cut from old discarded inner tubes, it was used to replace gaskets and washers, was brilliant in binding any materials together, irreplaceable in hosepipe connections, puncture-repair kits, catapults, home-made sandals and myriad uses yet to be conceived. Africa, rural Africa at least, would disintegrate without it.

At the exact moment Sibanda, Ncube and Miss Daisy were pulling in to the governor's offices, Mfumu was receiving a phone call from Robert McClean at Zebra Hill Farm. The call intended for Detective Sibanda had been put through to the Chief Inspector.

'Good afternoon, Chief Inspector,' said Robert McClean, 'I'm actually glad I have you. Firstly, Detective Inspector Sibanda asked me to phone about the blue metallic paint scratch on my wife's vehicle. She has remembered that one of the two boys who visited from Kestrel Vale College last Sunday had a blue bike. She thinks it might be where the paint scrape came from. You know how careless boys are, Chief Inspector. They probably just parked the bikes up against her car. Detective Inspector Sibanda did mention the blue paint was quite important and might help with another case he was investigating which is why I am phoning back so quickly.'

McClean hesitated then before getting to the meat of the call. Mfumu was wily enough to know that the next few sentences would be the real reason McClean had picked up the phone. 'Secondly, Chief Inspector,' McClean continued, 'I wish to lodge a complaint against the detective. He reduced my wife to tears with his interrogation. She is a highly sensitive and nervous person. I'm afraid she was shocked by both the vagrant's attack on her and the detective's harassment. She has taken to her bed.'

'Would you like me to send our family liaison officer around, Mr McClean?' the chief inspector asked. 'She might be able to help your wife come to terms with her ordeal.'

'No thank you, Chief Inspector, she is currently too distressed to see anyone. I want her left alone to recover privately.'

'I understand, Mr McClean. Would you like to make a formal complaint against the officer concerned?' Mfumu asked.

'No, Chief Inspector, I have made my point and would like to leave it at that.'

Once he had put the phone down, Mfumu gave himself a few moments to digest the content of the conversation. Detective Inspector Sibanda could be infuriating, disorganised, indifferent to procedure, unimpressed by authority and given to volcanic outbursts, but he was not a bully. His interview technique up until now gave Mfumu no cause for concern. This phone call had been a chess move, an aggressive but strategic pre-emptive strike. Queen F1 to F5. Mfumu was familiar with this since he played regularly at the chess club in the village. He considered himself Gubu village champion, even though no such competition had been held and he could boast no laurels. McClean was on the attack for some reason. He wanted to stave off further investigation. Now why would he want to do that? Perhaps he had misjudged Sibanda. Perhaps there was something fishy about this case after all.

He let that thought mull for a moment before he moved on to the blue metallic paint reference. In his earlier meeting with Sibanda there had been no mention of any paint. If it was important in another investigation then it could only be the Thunduluka Valley murder of Mufi, the Vulture Man. Sibanda had no other current cases.

Why would Sibanda want to keep the blue metal paint detail from him? It only took a few seconds for that thought to reach its logical conclusion. Somehow the governor and his well-known vehicle were going to be involved. Sibanda was keeping that piece of information to himself. Mfumu would never sanction such an august figure being dragged into a squalid and squeamish murder case that involved vultures, body parts and witches. Most distressing was the thought this officer had lied to him.

Chief Inspector Stalin Mfumu began to fume. He did not often fume. He considered himself to be an even-tempered and balanced individual. At church on Sunday where he was a senior pastor at The Brethren of the Lord's Blood congregation, he preached the path of truth and honesty in all things. His sermon this very Sunday had been on just such qualities: *Put on the full armour of God so that you can take your stand against the Devil's scheme.* Ephesians, chapter 6 verse 11. He had exhorted his congregation with every fibre of his being to don the armour of the Lord: the helmet of righteousness, the breastplate of justice, the shield of honesty and the sword of truth to protect themselves against Satan, the *father of lies,* who would lead them astray on their path to salvation.

He had shaken the pulpit with his fervour and banged the lectern with his fist. He wanted to drive home the narrow path that must be followed on the rocky road to eternal life. He swept his congregation along with him. They had punctuated each of his metaphors with resounding 'Amens' and 'Yebo Lords'. It had been a particularly successful sermon, one that left the congregation inspired and uplifted. He had been exhausted, but enriched. Truth and honesty were the cornerstone of his life, the very reason he became a policeman. Lies and deceits were the devil's handiwork and now, to his shame, he had discovered that members of his own staff were keeping the truth from him. This was more than this measured man could contemplate.

Mfumu carefully rearranged the pencils on his desk, realigned his in-tray so that every paper was as one and readjusted his uniform to ensure a dignified and imposing persona. He was about to call Sibanda back into his office for a dressing down. The relationship between the CID, the Criminal Investigation Department and the police had always been fractious, but this was his station, he was the ranking officer. He should be kept clearly in the picture of all crime on his patch. Subterfuge was unacceptable.

'Constable Khumalo,' he shouted from his office. He heard the clatter of her shoes on the well-worn and patchy linoleum that led to his office. She opened the door, 'You called, sir?'

'Yes, get Detective Inspector Sibanda in my office, now!'

'I don't think I can do that, sir.'

'Why not?' he snapped.

'Because he has already left with Sergeant Ncube, sir.'

Chief Inspector Mfumu walked purposefully to the radio and called the Land Rover.

'Gubu Base to Gubu Mobile, come in please.' His request was met with silence. The detective and his sergeant were already in the governor's office. Miss Daisy sat alone, her radiator creaking and ticking as it cooled down from its blistering run on the drive to the provincial capital, Detaba.

The governor was not at all what Sibanda had expected. He had brushed shoulders with several prominent politicians due to his having won top honours at the police academy, and later being chosen for further study in the United Kingdom. Politicians all tended to look as though they had been standing in a fertile mealie patch; paunches, jowls and collar rolls illustrated their recent acquisition of plenty. Designer suits and ties advertised their status. Governor Ngwenya was cut from a different mould. Although middle-aged, he was still in fine shape, lean and muscular. He was a tall man, almost as tall as Sibanda. His suit was subdued, but urbane. It probably cost more than a detective's annual salary, but it was very discrete when it came to the origin of its designer. The detective was impressed with Micah Ngwenya despite his preconceived ideas.

Sibanda had left his sergeant outside the office chatting to the governor's secretary.

'Sir,' he said as they entered the office, 'my legs are wobbly like those of a newborn impala, my mouth is as dry as the Kalahari sands and my body is running like the Zambezi. I do not think it is wise for me to greet the governor like this.' Sibanda could see the pale grey uniform shirt turning to a deep charcoal as the sergeant's troublesome personal cooling system failed again.

'No, Sergeant, you are right. Talk to some of the governor's staff. Get some background information.' He was learning that Ncube could be relied upon to worm his way into the confidence of any woman. They often had the most revealing details to divulge.

Sibanda was ushered into the governor's office and offered a chair. He was grateful for a few moments to look around the office while the governor answered a phone call. It was tastefully decorated in neutral shades, but made absorbing by the art that graced almost every surface. It would take a lifetime to get bored with this room. Every view offered some delightful African antique piece or quirky artwork. It ranged from naive wire art to exquisite African carvings. Berry would have been enchanted. This man had a good eye. In addition, nearly every spare patch of wall was hung with pictures of trees, photographed in spectacular light or from an unusual angle. They were a collection of living sculptures. When the governor turned to face him, Sibanda felt warmth in his presence. There was something about his face both attractive and familiar. He reminded Sibanda of someone he knew, but he couldn't put his finger on it.

'Are you the photographer, sir?' he asked, after the niceties of introduction were over, pointing to the gallery on the walls.

'Yes, I am,' Ngwenya replied. 'Do you take photographs, Detective?'

'No, but I'd like to. I haven't any good equipment yet.' Sibanda thought about his dismal attempts to photograph wildlife with his phone camera. They couldn't begin to compete with these crisp, charismatic creations. 'Why trees?' he asked.

'Ah,' sighed the governor, 'I spent a lot of time in the bush at one time in my life. Trees were my companions; they hid me, sheltered me, kept me warm and fed me. At times I survived on Umkhemethswane, the monkey orange, Umtshwankela, the chocolate berry, something of a misnomer I can tell you, Imiswi, the waterberry and Umthunduluka, the sour plum, to mention a few I am grateful to. I find them exceedingly beautiful. You may have noticed I have instigated a vigorous tree-protection campaign in the province. I am proud of that.'

'I seem to recognise the leadwood,' said Sibanda pointing to a particularly arresting photograph.

'You might well,' said Ngwenya. 'That particular one grows very close to Thunduluka Lodge. It means a great deal to me – a long and complex story from our recent dark ages. I went back there when I had a good enough camera and photographed it several times in different lights and seasons. It's my favourite. A masterpiece don't you think?' Sibanda nodded in sincere agreement.

'Of course, the tree itself is amazing. Our ancestors used it instead of metal, before iron or steel came to the continent. The wood is the best firewood you will ever burn. The ash doubles as both limewash and toothpaste. I was obliged to use it myself for several weeks at one stage. The taste leaves a lot to be desired, but the result is just as effective as the stuff from a tube.'

This was nothing new to Sibanda, but he was impressed that the governor was so well versed in African dendrology.

'Now, how can I help you, Detective?' the governor asked.

Sibanda abandoned the line of questioning he had planned, which was to be a gentle and roundabout tactic, and plunged headlong to the heart of the matter. 'I am investigating a murder that took place, not far from that tree,' he said, pointing to the photograph of the stylish leadwood. 'We have reason to believe a metallic blue Toyota Land Cruiser may have been involved. There are several in the district, but yours is one of them.' Having dropped his bombshell, Sibanda sat back in the chair. He waited for the ensuing explosion.

'I rarely use that vehicle any more, Detective. I have two government-issue vehicles, a Mercedes and a Jeep Cherokee, plus a chauffeur. The blue Land Cruiser is normally based at my ranch, Hunter's Rest.' The reply was measured and without rancour. 'Who was the victim?'

Sibanda took a brief moment to digest the name Hunter's Rest, 'I'm afraid we don't have an identity yet, but the body was badly mutilated, probably for body parts and disfigured by vultures. It is a difficult case.' Sibanda paused a moment before continuing, 'I have to ask, Governor, where were you on Monday night and the early hours of Tuesday morning?'

'I was in Harare at a presidential reception for the visiting president of Togo. I flew back to Bulawayo on Sunday and was driven back here in my Mercedes on Sunday afternoon. My secretary can give you all the details.'

'Finally, sir, who has charge of your blue Toyota at Hunter's Rest? Who drives it normally?' Sibanda asked.

'My son, Bongani, Detective Inspector. He is my farm manager.'

'I will need to interview him.'

'Of course, although I happen to know that he was probably on a date. He is a young man and…' the governor looked knowingly at Sibanda. His voice trailed off. Sibanda got his gist.

'Thank you, Governor; I will visit your son.' Sibanda stood and made as if to leave.

'If you ever get that camera, come and see me. I will give you a few tips.' He smiled warmly. It wasn't a throw-away line. The governor was genuine.

On the gentle journey back to Gubu, Sibanda debriefed Ncube. The secretary had proved to be a mine of information on the governor and his family.

'It seems, sir,' confirmed Ncube, 'that the blue Toyota is now a farm vehicle driven by the son. This son is a bit ihlongandlebe, you know… wayward. He failed at university in America. He has come back home like a cringing jackal. The governor has him working hard on the farm. They don't get on too well. There have been several very public arguments in the office.'

'And what else did you find out about the governor?' Sibanda asked. 'He certainly doesn't appear to be the fearful politician that he is painted, more a reasonable family man and a conservationist. On the other hand, there was something about him that bothered me, Ncube. Perhaps he was a little too smooth and accommodating. There was definitely something… as much as anything, he reminded me of someone I know.'

'According to his secretary, he has a lion's reputation,' said Ncube. 'He was a very dangerous commander in the Civil War. Ruthless, they say. Killed first and asked questions later. He left a trail of terror and destruction in the area under his command. Went by some frightening war name, Machitigaza, Spill Blood, but his secretary seems to worship him. Normally, I would trust her judgement because women have a sixth sense when it comes to character. What I can't understand is the governor's fearsome reputation. How can there be two such different sides to this man?'

'Well, Ncube, women can often be seduced by money and power. The governor is a good-looking, wealthy man.'

The sergeant looked askance at the detective wondering what had happened in his life to make him so cynical.

Sibanda drove for some kilometres thinking hard about possible motive and opportunity. There was still a strong possibility that the blue Cruiser was a key clue. The ranch, Hunter's Rest, bothered him. The governor had been allocated the ranch. It must have been taken from Barnaby Jones's family. Barney was bitter, no doubt about that. Could Barnaby Jones have set up the governor or his son? He would have both the opportunity and the motive. He must keep that in mind.

The Land Rover pulled successfully into the Gubu Police Station yard.

'Two excursions in one day,' said the detective, 'something of a record, Sergeant, keep it up.' He headed for his office. At the reception desk, PC Khumalo gave him a conspiratorial look.

'Watch out,' she said, 'Cold War is on your case. He has been pacing up and down ever since a phone call from Zebra Hill Farm. He says I must let him know as soon as you are back.' Cold War was the nickname that everyone in the station gave to Chief Inspector Stalin Mfumu. It suited him. He certainly knew how to retreat behind an iron curtain when the mood took him. He often drew that curtain firmly between the police and CID. 'Oh and by the way,' she continued, 'no luck yet with the prints and the names beginning with B and no sign of Ishmael Naidoo.'

'Thanks, Zee. Stall Mfumu for a couple of minutes if you can,' he said, 'I need some breathing space.' He walked to his office. He needed to call Khanyi. Now there was a death in her village. He wanted to be with her to comfort her and assist the family. This was going to delay their wedding plans. His mother would be distressed. She couldn't understand why he wasn't settled already, why there were no grandchildren. He didn't really understand himself although he suspected that the illusive Berry was part of the delaying equation. Was he settling for second best? Yes, probably, but if Khanyi was second best, it was a very tight-run thing. She was stunning. He picked up the phone.

'Hi Khanyi, it's me, I'm just calling to check how you are. Sorry for not getting in touch sooner. The last few days have been chaotic. My case load is ridiculous. Please apologise that I wasn't able to get to the meeting with your mother.'

'Jabu, it's impossible to arrange anything with you. There will always be another case, another robbery or a car theft. Will I always be second best?' she moaned.

Sibanda recognised that her thoughts mirrored his from a few moments earlier. He felt enormous guilt. Changing the subject, he said, 'One of the cases I am involved with concerns someone from your village. He was a vagrant, an isibonda, Mtabizi Mpofu. Was he related?'

Khanyi was quiet on the other end of the phone. She said nothing. The silence became uncomfortable.

'Khanyi, are you still there?' he asked, sensing a problem.

Finally Khanyi spoke, 'Jabu, there is something I need to tell you. I am finding it very difficult,' she hesitated and took a deep breath as though diving into deep waters. 'Mtabizi was my brother. I didn't want to tell you before in case you were disgusted at his dirty habits. I was so ashamed of him.'

'Khanyi, I am so sorry,' he was speechless for a few moments. 'I really didn't know.' At that moment he realised he knew very little at all about Khanyi's brothers and sisters. She hardly mentioned them. 'I am a bit disappointed you didn't tell me about him,' he said, with some sadness. 'Do you think I would judge you and your family because you had a brother who is soft in the head?'

'I didn't know, Jabu, I was confused.'

Now it was Sibanda's turn to become silent and as the silence grew so the difficulty of re-establishing the conversation became more difficult.

Khanyi broke the silence. 'I misjudged you, Jabu. I am sorry.'

Sibanda, a little calmer now, but still saddened by her lack of trust, asked politely how they were all coping with the death.

'My mother is a mess, Jabu, she hasn't left her hut. We are all so worried. My sister, Lindiwe, is coming up from Joburg. She won't be any use. She's...' Khanyi hesitated for a moment. 'She's... difficult. She and my mother fight whenever she is here. There'll be more stress. We have arranged the funeral for Sunday. Please say you will be there.'

'Listen, Khanyi', he said, when he finally spoke, 'I haven't got time now, I am going to have to run. Mfumu in on the warpath and I'm his target. I will try and make the funeral. Don't worry. Love you.' He tacked the two words on the end, like an obligatory afterthought.

'Love you too,' she responded. He sensed a wall had gone up between them. Her reply was equally strained.

As Sibanda put the phone down, he heard footsteps in the corridor. It was PC Khumalo. 'Jabu, you had better get into Mfumu's office now. He's looking like a spitting cobra about to ambush.

'I am on my way,' he replied.

Chapter 10

In all, despite the horrible drama of Sole's death, it turned into a good week for Wart and his friends. Firstly, the jacaranda season was officially over. Probably only Scott House Old Boys would fully understand the joy this brings. To everyone else, jacarandas are a spectacular South American import covering the avenues and squares of the country with a carpet of lilac flowers to soothe cement monotony. To Scott House juniors they were perpetual blossom-shedding trash-dispensers. The juniors' duty was to keep the house quad and pathways scrupulously devoid of even one mauve petal. This meant a continuous day and night roster of brushing. As fast as they swept them up, so the blossoms rained down again, tenfold, like one of Spirit's biblical plagues. It was another of those pointless tasks designed by seniors to keep the boys' minds busy and their bodies tormented.

Yesterday, Ma Baker, the rotund, mousey English mistress, was teaching Wart's class about Greek myths. Wart felt the gods dreamed up some very creative tortures to inflict suffering on their own juniors. They were in consultation with Kestrel Vale sixth-form who could be equally inventive when the mood took them. She talked about some poor bloke named Sisyphus who was condemned to continually roll a huge rock up a hill only to have it roll down again just as he was about to get it to the top. When Wart suggested to Ma Baker that it bore a marked resemblance to the history of Scott House, the sweeping of jacaranda petals and suffering juniors, she ignored him. She moved on to another gruesome Greek torture concerning a man chained to a rock having his liver constantly pecked at. Wart had his hand up in a jiffy.

'Have you eaten in the school dining hall recently, miss?' he asked. The whole class collapsed, they certainly got it. Ma Baker glared speechlessly. He was saved from certain detention by the bell.

Secondly, Spirit and Wart had what Spirit called an 'adult' conversation, interrupted by the whistles and squeaks coming out of his ears. For once Wart found it irritating rather than funny. He resented the disturbance rather than welcomed it. It was not often that a master treated juniors as an equal. Wart was rather relishing the manly spotlight.

'The time has come, Molesworthy,' he said, 'to call a truce. I understand you are an atheist and while it is a sadness to me, I do accept it. Perhaps I am getting too old for this world and its modern scientific thinking. All the writings of Dawkins, Hawkins and Hitchings, whilst very clever and supremely well written, do not convince me that we would behave with thoughtfulness to one another without a moral code to refer to. Our simian past is far too close to dispense with the beast in us, as illustrated by recent events.'

'Yes, sir,' Wart nodded sagely, although he would need to refer to the walking dictionary that was Pastor James, now AKA Macca, to fully understand what he was on about. He had heard of Hawkins, but Dawkins and Hitchings sounded like interesting authors to explore. Wart made a mental note. Pastor James's nickname was still evolving. It changed to Pasta within a few hours and then just as swiftly became Macaroni, hence Macca. Some kids were already testing out Spaghetti. The permutations were endless.

'You must understand, Molesworthy, like it or not, much of western philosophy, philology, literature, law and morality are based on Judaeo-Christian belief. I don't know what you are planning as a career, but it will be touched in some way by this creed. After all, if you want to argue against Christianity then you need to understand it first. So the time has come, my boy, for you to knuckle down and take responsibility for your future. I don't expect you to believe in the Lord, but I do expect you to respect the code that has shaped our western civilisation. You have a good heart and you are a leader, Molesworthy. It's time to behave like one.'

Wart came out of Spirit's study on a bit of a high. He knew then he was going to go easy on him. He was beginning to like the old codger, besides which, Ma Baker was shaping up to be a much more rewarding target.

The next bit of good news came via Stinky. It seemed Wart had finally been granted hallowed membership of the Birding Club. Stinky had wormed his way in thanks to his elder brother, Stench, the club secretary, who had manipulated the waiting list for him. Wart had had to wait in the queue. The word was that Job Nkala from Rhodes House was emigrating mid-term to Australia with his parents and a space had become vacant.

Clubs were supposed to occupy the boys in the late afternoons, after sport practice. Most of them were mind-numbingly boring, but the Birding Club was first prize. It was run by Buff Barton who might turn decimals into dross and cause fraction-friction headaches, but when it came to birds, he was untouchable. He was a legend. Wart was over the moon.

When good news comes, it seems to arrive in a cluster, like a flock of violet-eared waxbills. When Peewee Marufu came haring into the dorm with the news that almost the entire sixth-form was going to be absent for the week, the Scott House second-year boys threw an impromptu celebration. All eleven of them leapt on their miserably narrow, sad and sorry excuses for beds and bounced, whooped and hollered until Brunswick Major came in with a cricket bat, lined them all up and gave each a belting cover drive for six. Wart was able to sit with some semblance of comfort after two days. Spaghetti walked around with a pillow for a week.

Brunswick's euphoria-dampening blows came at an opportune moment. Wart was just beginning to think that maybe some higher power was rewarding him and his mates for their grief and confusion, saying, 'Hey guys, you've done it tough this week, let me give you a break,' but Brunswick successfully killed off any fling Wart may have been having with the Lord.

'Wart, listen, it's me,' Simple woke him from compulsory afternoon bed rest with a loud, spitting whisper in his ear. Simple had just come from fagging for Dumisani Dube. Wart didn't normally spare a thought for Simple's welfare, but he had definitely copped the short straw when it came to fagging duties. Dube had just been voted the sixth-former most likely to graduate as a serial killer. He was, without a shadow of a doubt, the most evil, sadistic, warped-minded student ever to grace Kestrel Vale and, if legend was to be believed, the school had witnessed some manic psychotics in its day. Wart's religious non-beliefs were even further strengthened by the fact that Dube had been nominated for the Good Citizenship Award, quite a significant end-of-year accolade dished out at final assembly. 'No comment,' Wart had said to himself.

'Wart, wake up, you lazy dog,' Simple hissed again.

'I'm awake,' he said. 'What's the fuss and why all the secret whispering?'

'Because we can't afford to let what I have just learned become public knowledge too quickly. This is nuclear,' he huffed.

'Okay, keep your hair on, calm down and give me the info,' Wart said.

'Well, I was in Dube's study, polishing his shoes and washing his socks and jocks, when Ball Hair Williams burst in. He could hardly breathe with excitement.' Simple recounted the scene with as much drama as his whisper would allow.

'Dummy,' Ball Hair had said to Dube, 'get your nose out of those books and up to the window, quick. The new history teacher is walking past and she is a Babe.' Ball Hair then hauled Dube up to the window and squashed his nose against it, 'Get a squiz of that babelicious beauty,' he had said, 'and you are not going to believe it, but she is Buff Barton's daughter.'

'Did you get a look?' Wart asked.

'Are you mad?' Simple replied, 'Dube had already catapulted several golf balls at my head for making too much noise with the washing water, but Buff is showing her around. They should be strolling past Scott House any minute now.'

Simple and Wart, as casually as possible, made their way to the meagre window which was the sole light provider for the form-two dorm, and scanned the quad. They didn't have to wait long before the slightly lop-sided figure of Buff appeared, accompanied by what could only be described as a vision.

Instantly, Wart was in love. He looked at Simple, who had a dazed look on his face. His lower jaw hung open as though sucking in the big ones after a punishing cross-country run.

'Jeez, Wart, she's stunning. What a hot chick, smokinnnn',' said Simple, doing his signature Stanley Ipkiss impersonation, as soon as his brain reconnected to his mouth.

'That'll do, Pig, that'll *certainly* do,' Wart muttered under his breath, with his own movie reference from *Babe*. It never seemed more appropriate.

'Right, Simple,' Wart said, 'as soon as we can get out of here, we are registering for History Club.' Until now this club had been more or less memberless and shunned.

'Done,' said Simple.

'What do you mean?' Wart asked.

'I put our names down already on the way back from Dube's. We only just made the list. We were the last two names. Suddenly the whole school is history mad,' said Simple with a grin on his face that even a call-back from Dube wouldn't erase. Wart never understood why Simple was languishing at the bottom of the D stream because at times he was an absolute genius. Wart laughed. He hadn't been happier since he had landed in this godforsaken joint two years ago. He had read somewhere that happiness requires only three elements: one, something to do, and he didn't really get that because he and his mates were constantly occupied. More leisure time would have made them far happier. Two, something to look forward to. This was an easy answer. The holidays away from this hell-hole. And three, someone to love. Wart understood love was what had been missing in his life, the piece of the jigsaw puzzle that, once clicked into place, would make the picture complete.

Wart's bliss lasted a good hour. It translated into a rash of wickets at cricket practice. Simple must have been feeling the same because he was smashing the ball all over the ground. They were both benefitting from the extra spring in their step.

Wart saw the first-former approaching out of the corner of his eye as his developing doosra skittled Mozzie Sithole's wicket. He knew it was trouble. He had a nose for these things. The first-former was interrupting the uninterruptable net session. This was unprecedented.

Normally, when punishments are meted out there is a serious protocol to be followed. First call on beatings is the dorm prefect; should he feel the crime warrants it, he passes the offender on to the head of house, from there to the house master and only in very rare and extremely serious cases does anyone ever visit the consecrated ground of the headmaster's study.

Jake Joubert, the cricket coach, called Wart over, 'Molesworthy, you are wanted at the headmaster's study immediately.'

'What right now, sir?' he quivered.

'Yes, just as you are, Molesworthy.' Wart managed a quick glance of terror in Simple's direction. Simple returned the look and made a throat-slashing signal with the thumb of his batting glove. It didn't help. Wart vowed to get him for that.

As he walked up the path from the field to the daunting building that housed the administration section of Kestrel Vale, Wart ran every single possible misdemeanour through his mind. It couldn't be Spirit, they had a truce and he was a gentleman of principle. Could it be the zero per cent he got on Buff's last maths test? Unlikely, that had happened before and Buff delighted in administering the beating himself. Ma Baker and the pecked liver/dining hall reference? Surely not, wit is the last refuge of the oppressed schoolboy. They wouldn't take that from them, would they? Could someone have infiltrated Wart's imagination and pictured just what he planned to do with the gorgeous Miss Barton? No, not even the Crow Valley Mind Police had perfected that technique. Best not to mull over it, he thought, wait for the reality.

Was there enough time to nip back to the dorm to put on his specially designed underpants? They were padded with foam and had served him well in his punishment career so far. They didn't nullify the pain, but they took the worst of the sting out of a lethal bamboo cane. He had been thinking of patenting them and going into production with his sister. In the end, he just plodded on dolefully, inventing obsequious excuses for anything and everything imaginable.

'Come in, Ben,' said Dr Prendergast, 'and take a seat.' The use of his first name, the welcoming tone of his voice and the offer of a chair alarmed Wart. The situation must be graver than he thought.

'This is Detective Inspector Sibanda. He is here to ask a few questions.' Wart stood and, being hatless, tugged his forelock and shook the detective's hand in what he trusted was a faultless and grovelling greeting. He hoped to gain some reprieve in Headmaster Ghastly's eyes for his good manners. Why had the headmaster called in the CID?

The man seated to the left of Ghastly was tall and lean with the appearance of Zoom Mangwende, the speedy first-team wing. He looked as though he could sprint into action in a heartbeat. He had flawless deep-golden skin that radiated fitness and high, well-defined cheekbones that Wart's freckled, chubby, chipmunk chops envied.

'Ben, I believe you cycled to Zebra Hill Farm last Sunday,' said the detective.

'Yes, sir,' Wart replied nervously. He was not sure where all this was going but he had watched enough crime movies to know that brevity under interrogation is best.

'What colour is your bicycle?'

'Blue, sir.'

'Metallic blue?'

'Yes, sir.'

'And your friend Henry Simon's bike is red?'

'Yes, sir.'

'Okay, Ben, relax,' said the detective. He winked out of sight of Ghastly. 'You are not in trouble. I need information on your movements last Sunday.' Wart suspected then that the detective had been to a Zimbabwean boarding school. His backside had also experienced an evil assortment of punishing weapons. He knew the drill. He wouldn't drop Wart in it.

'I understand, sir,' Wart said, and he winked back conspiratorially. He had an ally.

'Ben, did you see the local vagrant last Sunday?' he asked.

'We met Sole on our way to the McCleans' farm. He had birds' eggs for us.'

'Sole?'

'Yes, that's the name we all know him by because of his worn-out shoes. We never found out his real name.'

'Did you notice anything different about him that day?' the detective asked.

'He seemed his usual cheery self. He smiles all the time, you know, he never grumbles despite his lot. Always has something to give us. He never begs from us, never asks for anything.' Wart spoke about him as if he were still alive because for him, he was. Sole would always wander the bush welcoming the spring winds and the summer rains. He embraced life with such grace that death could never claim him. Whenever a lilac-breasted roller perched on a low sapling, wind at his back, turquoise feathers ruffled, Sole would be there, bent over, tying his laces; whenever the Heuglin's robin sang its sunlit song to the morning dew, Sole would be humming in harmony, and whenever the peregrine falcon soared overhead on a warm afternoon thermal, lazily eyeing the earth below, Sole would be flying wingman. 'No, sir,' Wart said eventually, 'there was nothing different about him that day.'

'And the McCleans, Ben, how were they?' asked the detective.

'They seemed fine, welcoming as usual.

'Did you see Mrs McClean?' the detective asked.

Wart thought for a while, and then replied, 'Actually, no, come to think of it, we didn't see Mrs McClean, but she must have been in the kitchen baking because Mr McClean gave us some of her freshly baked biscuits to bring back to school. Mr McClean was on the veranda having a few beers and he told us some amazing stories about his hunting exploits. We went off to ride his horses around the farm.' Wart tried to remember as much as he could about the day.

'How many beers, Ben?' Sibanda asked.

Wart took a moment to answer. If he was going to be honest he would have to say he saw a large mountain of discarded cans at McClean's feet, but he knew he was going to lie, or at least be vague. 'I'm not sure, sir, we were only with Mr McClean for about thirty minutes before we went on our ride.' The detective looked a bit subdued, as though Wart had welshed on his side of their unspoken bargain. Wart compromised with, 'quite a few, I think.'

'Right, Ben, do you think I could have a look at your bicycle?' asked the detective. Wart glanced across at Ghastly who nodded his head, signalling approval. Once out of Ghastly's den a huge surge of relief swept over him. He began to chat easily to the detective. He had been right about his education. The detective had been to another famous torture establishment, Marula Tree School. Detective Sibanda told Wart tales of his school days as they walked to the bike shed. The stories further curled Wart's already bothersome hair. They continued to swop school horror stories until they reached the shed.

'That's it,' Wart said pointing out his trusty steed.

'And a fine specimen too,' said Detective Sibanda as he examined the bike.

'What has my bike got to do with Sole's death?' Wart asked.

'Nothing,' he replied, 'we are actually investigating another case where blue paint is significant. I want to eliminate the McClean's vehicle. Did you lean your bike against one of the vehicles at the farm?'

'Am I in trouble for damaging the McCleans' car?' Ben answered the question with a question of his own, another technique he had learned from his holiday diet of crime movies.

'No, far from it,' said Sibanda, 'you may actually help the McCleans by telling the truth.'

'Okay then, maybe. We were in such a hurry to escape Sunday persecution that when we reached the farm, we just threw our bike's down and ran into the farmhouse.'

And there it was: a tell-tale white smudge on Wart's back mudguard where it had slid down against the McCleans' pick-up. They walked back to the car park and Detective Sibanda's vehicle. Wart asked him what it meant to find that his bicycle had left blue paint on the McCleans' car.

'Well, it means that they are most likely not involved in a second case I am investigating,' said the detective, 'and that is enough information for now, Ben.'

'Just one more question, Detective Inspector.' As his teachers already knew, Wart was difficult to stop once he got rolling. 'Did Mr McClean murder Sole? Was he defending his family or was it some kind of accident?'

Sibanda looked down at Wart and took a moment to frame his reply, sensing it meant a great deal to this wise and inquisitive boy. 'It will be difficult ever to know the answer to that, Ben,' he said. 'I have my views, my conclusion, and I expect you have yours. Sometimes life is not as cut and dried as we would like it to be.'

That seemed to satisfy Wart and brought an end to his questions. Instead they chatted amiably about life in general. Wart was hugely impressed to discover that Sibanda was a bird-watching tragic like himself. They discussed a few of the local species. Wart realised he was in the presence of not only a master twitcher, but a tree genius as well.

They were so engrossed in conversation about the similarities and differences between the masked weaver and the spotted-back weaver, both of which had established nesting colonies in rival bamboo clumps, busily weaving their exquisitely complex houses, that they failed to notice the pair walking towards them. Detective Inspector Sibanda looked up and suddenly halted mid-sentence. He had been animated about the architectural differences of the nests, describing in particular detail the contrasting entrances built by the two closely related species. Wart looked up, puzzled by the break in commentary, and thought for a moment that the detective was going to turn away from the approaching couple and take another path, but then he stood his ground and spoke.

'Berry,' he stuttered, as he addressed the young lady accompanied by an older man, 'I didn't realise you were back.' Wart noticed the colour drain from Sibanda's face and wished his would behave similarly. His already high complexion blushed to a lucky bean red as he stood in the presence of his newly acquired passion.

In seconds, the detective had regained his cool composure, so later, when Wart was recounting the scene and the conversation to the dorm, he wasn't sure he had witnessed any change in the first place.

'Jabu, what are you doing here?' the new teacher said with obvious delight. 'You left the UK in such a hurry. I didn't know how to contact you. Dad,' she turned to Buff, 'this is Jabu Sibanda. We met in Nottingham where we spent time together reminiscing about Zimbabwe. This is my father, Buff Barton, he teaches maths here. I am joining the staff to teach history.'

The men exchanged handshakes. Sibanda, having returned seamlessly back to normal, said, 'I'm actually here to check up on this young man,' indicating Wart who was hanging back, at his side. Wart, never a fan of the boy wizard, wished at that moment that he could shrivel up and disappear in a mist of Hogwarts magic. He could feel himself wriggling under the spotlight of Miss Barton's pale-blue gaze, like a blindworm excavated unexpectedly from its burrow. He never realised that love could be so painful and discomforting.

'Ah,' said Buff Barton, 'I might have guessed it would be you in trouble, Molesworthy,' but there was no malice in the observation. If Wart had been more alert and less overcome he might even have picked up a gentle hint of humour.

'Yes, sir,' Wart said and, desperately trying to gain some credibility in the eyes of his new love, added cheekily, 'seems like I am the arch criminal you all make me out to be.'

Buff Barton laughed heartily and Wart, unaccustomed to anything other than Buff's maths persona, felt a sense of shock. Unexpectedly, he had seen through the hard façade of the teacher and was getting a tiny glimpse of what might be hidden on the other side.

'Jabu, you and my father have a lot in common,' said Berry, 'he is also a complete bird nut. His nickname for years has been Thandanyoni, Bird lover.'

'I have heard of you, of course, sir,' said Sibanda, 'you have a legendary reputation. Actually, I have just been at Thunduluka Lodge investigating a case. They still talk about you. They told me that you were badly wounded in an incident in the Civil War.'

'Detective, never call it a civil war. That has to be the ultimate oxymoron. Civil and war are two words that should never be spoken in the same breath. Yes, unfortunately, I was involved in a shoot-out. I took five bullets in my left leg at close quarters. Most of the bones were shattered. It was an accident really. The soldier who shot me was only a child; off his head with fever and gangrene.'

'That sounds like a really serious injury,' said Sibanda, desperately trying to keep the conversation moving.

'I was enormously lucky to keep my leg,' said Buff, 'although it is fairly useless to me now. I can no longer guide or do safaris. I spent a long time in intensive care and was very fortunate to come under the care of a brilliant orthopaedic surgeon. Everyone wanted to amputate the mangled thing, but he insisted he could save my leg and look,' he said, pointing, 'it's still here and it works well enough to get me around the school and chase reprobates like this one,' he ended, tousling Wart's hair.

'Afterwards, I believe you were jailed,' said Sibanda.

'Yes, that's true too,' said Buff, 'but it's not something I really want to talk about here,' he added, indicating Wart. Barton didn't wait for a comment, but turned to the school boy. 'Right, Molesworthy,' he continued, 'you and I have a date with a failed maths test I think. Shall we proceed?' And he ushered Wart away towards his study. Wart looked over his shoulder at the detective as if pleading for help.

'Mr Barton, do you think Ben could meet me in the car park in about ten minutes? I still have a few questions for him,' said Sibanda, honouring their unspoken pact.

'Of course, Detective, I'll make sure he's waiting for you.'

As they walked away, Sibanda heard Wart ask, 'Why can't I hear about your time in jail, sir? Was it awful? Were you tortured?'

Buff looked down at Wart in the way the old sometimes regard the young and their artless naiveté; their lack of ability to empathise with the pain and suffering that they had yet to encounter and said, 'Many years ago, a wise woman gave me a very valuable piece of advice, and I suggest that you, of all people, Molesworthy, should take heed of it.' Thandanyoni Barton had a wry smile on his face as he quoted Mantini's words, 'She said, *Numbers are for money, books are for stories and names are for living things*. This means, to you, young man, if you are interested in the material things in life, study your maths; if you want stories, go and read a book, don't pester me; and since you've joined Bird Club, learn the bird names. For now, go and wait in the car park for the detective. I will catch up with you later…'

Wart ran quickly to the school car park and stationed himself beside the odd-looking Land Rover parked on a slope that must belong to the detective. He was hopping from leg to leg with impatience. He could not wait to get back to the dorm with all the hot news. His status would be considerably elevated by the fact that he had been the first to meet the luscious Berry Barton and, puzzlingly, a completely new and quite jovial Buff Thandanyoni Barton. In the meantime, he would use these few minutes to plan a horrible revenge on Simple.

Sibanda and Berry began to talk easily to one another. It hadn't taken them long to fall back into their old banter. They caught up quickly on the details of their lives in their year out of contact. She had completed her history degree and teaching diploma, returned a few weeks ago and taken this job at Kestrel Vale.

'Didn't you ever think of staying over there, better pay and conditions and an easier lifestyle?' he asked.

'Never,' she laughed with surprise, 'I was always coming home, although some might think otherwise. This is my land, my country and my destiny. I need the warm grey Kalahari sands ingrained under my toenails, my ratty hair tangled by fierce September winds and my nose filled with the magic smell of fat, sizzling raindrops on a year's accumulation of dust. Where else in the world could I get that, Jabu? Drizzle, on acres of paving and a few windblown, soggy leaves is no substitute. I am an addict. Zimbabwe has always been my drug of choice. Wrong-coloured skin, that's my problem. Besides which,' she added, 'I knew you were here,' and she tipped her head back, laughing helplessly.

The detective smiled wryly, he knew it was a joke and it made her comment all the more painful for him.

'And you?' she asked. 'Surely you got offers over there.'

'No elephants,' he replied succinctly.

'Ah, yes, the love of your life,' she sighed and they walked companionably towards the car park and the waiting boy.

Chapter 11

'Three wives…' Sibanda contemplated the concept and shook his head trying to rid himself of the image. 'How on earth do you keep them all happy?'

'That's the real, real secret,' said Ncube with a growing smile. It displaced his chubby cheeks and caused them to expand beyond the jawline. It forced the extra bulk both down towards his collar where it corrugated evenly over the stiffened fabric and up towards his eyes. They were reduced to twinkling slits, leaving the impression of a face dominated by a mouth full of teeth. 'I don't keep them happy, they keep each other happy. We are a happy family,' and as he chortled away, his jelly belly wobbled and tapped against the steering wheel.

Sibanda, in the passenger seat, took a few moments, wondering if he could ever be married to Khanyi and Berry at the same time, imagining the sort of household that might ensue. Both were feisty, independent women, but he could only picture fireworks, besides which a plural marriage wasn't in his make-up. Still, it was a fascinating concept for any red-blooded male and he pursued his questioning, 'Why aren't they jealous? How come they are all content?'

'Well, you see, sir,' Ncube said, warming to his subject, 'the skill is in choosing the right wives. My first wife, Blessing, was arranged.' Sibanda smiled wryly at Ncube's choice of phrase, it made his wife sound like a bunch of flowers, placed just so in a vase, but he didn't interrupt and Ncube continued. 'Her parents consulted the local matchmaker and she suggested three men who might be suitable. I was the one she chose.'

'So you had no say in the matter?' Sibanda asked.

'Yes, of course I did, I could have discretely turned down the suggestion, but I was honoured to have been chosen. My parents encouraged me, I was at that age when…' he hesitated and glanced sideways at Sibanda. 'You know,' his voice became conspiratorial, 'when…, well, let's say… the imbuzi, the goats, were beginning to look like intombi enhle, like comely maidens.' Ncube laughed heartily at this admission. His gut threatened to seriously interfere with the steering and send Miss Daisy careering off into the bush, although there seemed little chance of that as the dirt road they were following was deeply rutted from a long association with donkey carts and Miss Daisy could have been on rails, so cushioned by walls of sand were her tyres.

Sibanda laughed too, a rare, shared laugh. It was an open, if unspoken, secret among young Ndebele boys that goats were good practise for the joys of the marriage bed to come. 'And was it love at first sight, Sergeant?'

'Ah, sir,' the sergeant sighed and clicked disapproval through the side of his mouth, 'love is not something for the eyes, it is a matter for the heart, nor is it to be rushed or quickly judged. Love is like a diesel engine, at first, shiny, new, a bit stiff, a little bit proud, but as it runs in and needs attention, the occasional oil change, a new filter, so it loosens up and begins to purr gently, to give reliability and greater efficiency, until eventually it is as smooth as the inner thigh of a king's virgin. And that is how it was between Blessing and me. By the time of our first child we were like two cylinders side by side in an engine, pumping away in total harmony.'

Sibanda coughed discretely at Ncube's inappropriate metaphor and wondered if he had any idea of the openly sexual picture he was painting. One look at the innocence on his face cleared him of smut. 'And all the lobolo, the bride price, Sergeant, how did you manage that three times on a policeman's salary?'

'Well now, that is the best part of the arranged marriage. The matchmaker not only takes family and interests into consideration, but the delicate matter of money as well. She knew what I could afford to pay. She knew what Blessing's parents expected, and so the deal was done. I bought mamazala a new dress and hat and my father-in-law a new jacket and shoes. A few extra blankets and some cooking pots and Blessing was mine.

'Wife number two?' prompted Sibanda, who envied Ncube's bargain basement lobolo. He knew that for Khanyi he was going to be paying over the odds. She was an educated prize and many head of cattle would have to change hands to cover the bride price.

'She is Blessing's cousin, Nomatter, an orphan. In fact it was Blessing's suggestion that we take her in to the family.'

'You mean that your first wife actually nominated your second wife?' said Sibanda, in some surprise.

'Yes, sir, by now we had two little ones and another due to join us soon. Blessing was very large by the time the third child was coming. Her legs and ankles were swollen like those of an elephant cow, her back ached and she was perhaps a little irritable'

A look of hurt flickered briefly across the sergeant's face, but disappeared just as quickly as he continued, 'I suggested help, she suggested Nomatter, who was all alone in the world with nobody to look after her. She was seventeen and homeless. No other relative could take her in. It was the perfect solution for her to come to us, and to look after the little children while Blessing concentrated on the baby. Nomatter was a gift to the little ones and to Blessing, and a joy to me. Blessing could see our growing closeness and she urged me to take her as my wife. There was no lobolo to be paid as she had no relative other than Blessing, and even the chief agreed it was… how do the mukiwas put it…? A win/win situation.'

Sibanda sat back against the striped canvas of Miss Daisy's passenger seat and ruminated on Ncube's good fortune. A free wife was a rarity even in these more enlightened times. He knew that in most populations it worked or had worked the other way around with a dowry provided by the bride's family being the norm. 'Just imagine that,' he said out aloud, 'getting paid to get married.'

'Sorry, sir?' queried Ncube.

'Nothing, Ncube, I was elsewhere for a moment. Tell me about number three.'

'Well, we were in the same situation again. Nomatter was pregnant with her second baby. The first one had been a difficult birth and we didn't know if the child would thrive; she was sickly and Nomatter was exhausted. The clinic sister said she should rest, put her feet up. Blessing was pregnant too with her fourth at the same time and couldn't help much. She said we should get someone in to help and asked Nomatter if there was anyone she would like to invite into our family. You see, she had chosen Nomatter and she felt it was Nomatter's turn to pick a companion.'

'A companion, a nursemaid, I can understand, Ncube, but another wife?'

'What is a man supposed to do?' asked Ncube resignedly. 'Sukoluhle is beautiful and irresistible. I couldn't help myself. Both my wives were pregnant and… you know, how shall I say it…? Not able to share my blankets.'

'What did your wives think? Weren't they angry?'

'No, not at all, they weren't the problem. In fact they had secretly planned it all. Nomatter told me later that she had chosen Suko as a gift to me because I had been so understanding and kind to her. The problem was Suko's parents. By the time they discovered the situation, she was also pregnant. There is no doubt I had been a little behind with my duties. Dereliction is the right word, is it not, sir? I hadn't been to visit her family, nor paid anything, not even respect to her parents. After Suko had little Samson, her father came and took them back to their village.'

'Ncube, how many children do you have?' asked Sibanda with some distaste in his voice. Overpopulation was one of his hobby horses. He had seen first hand the teeming streets and overcrowded tenement blocks of Nottingham, witnessed the crime bred in clogged estates, and mourned the disappearance of open space as it was swamped by a mire of bricks and cement in an attempt to house a rash of overbreeding. His country was much larger, but he feared for the free-roaming herds and the life-breathing forests if Ncube was anything to go by.

'Eight, sir,' replied Ncube proudly, puffing out his already inflated chest, 'and Suko is shortly expecting her third.'

Sibanda refrained from the belittlement and sarcasm that would normally have followed such a revelation; they were, after all, on their way to a funeral. Instead he asked, 'So you got her back, then?'

'Those were very hard times for us all. Blessing and Nomatter cried endlessly, the abantwana too. Her parents were demanding damages and lobolo and we couldn't find the money. Then I was posted here to Gubu that was far away from Suko's village. We were in torment. I tried to appeal the transfer, but you know the system, sir, the superintendent had a relative. He wanted him at his station so I had to move on. It all turned out for the best, though. In the end, Blessing began to sell roasted mealies to the buses on the Victoria Falls road and Nomatter stayed home and learned to smoke fish that I was catching in my off time. Gubu was happy to have a fish supply. Slowly, together we saved enough to buy ten goats and the phone Suko's parents were asking for, and she came home to us.'

'And now your family is complete, Sergeant?' Sibanda was curious to know if Ncube was going to continue to burden the planet with his offspring.

'Only God knows that, sir, and much as I admire Constable Khumalo – by the way,' he lowered his voice in awestruck aside, 'have you noticed the way her glorious cheeks fight with each other under that turquoise uniform skirt? Very off-putting during work hours – and I think she is attracted to me, I cannot afford another wife unless I am promoted.'

Sibanda could restrain himself no further and blurted, 'Well you won't be getting any recommendations for promotion from me, Sergeant, if by that I can save the world from any increase in the already overpopulated Ncube clan.' Under his breath he added, 'And rescue the talented Zanele from life in a harem.'

The sergeant looked wounded, his face unfurled and realigned itself so that his eyes were now visible and his jowls rested in a singular, impressive roll on his collar. The atmosphere was instantly less jovial and the conversation petered out. Sibanda took the lapse as a welcome moment to gather his thoughts. He had asked Ncube to drive the Land Rover because he felt it gave him more gravitas to appear at the funeral with a driver. This would be his first introduction to Khanyi's family. He could have come on his own, but he trusted neither the damned vehicle nor his own ability to keep it running.

Curiously, the Land Rover's multi-coloured cab was fast becoming his office and he found that the pastel stripes of ice cream tones and varying widths helped focus his thinking process. For the time being, he put aside his own complex issues; Ncube's far more convoluted arrangement put his personal life into perspective. It was time to review the last couple of days.

The interview with Mfumu had been stinging. He had defended his position. Things had been said on both sides that probably should have been best left unsaid and all over a tiny speck of *Mediterranean Sapphire* paint. He sensed Mfumu's relief when he finally advised him that the governor was very amenable and no longer had the vehicle anyway. He had deliberately kept that gem and the fact that there were multiple *Mediterranean Sapphire* Toyotas in the region until the very last, knowing much of Mfumu's tension was about how his interview with the governor went and whether he was implicated or not. He had kept him sweating. It was good to know that Cold War could be rattled, that behind that immaculately starched shirt beat the heart of a man with insecurities. Station politics were all about tactics and knowing which buttons to press and when to press them. Sibanda now held a valuable piece of the Mfumu puzzle. It might well be useful in future encounters. He never mentioned that the blue Toyota was now with the governor's son, that piece of dynamite would keep.

He had then had to spend half an hour with that weasel, Chanza. He passed on the information about the removal of the police cordon, the suspected blood splattering, Mrs McClean's bruising and the domestic's twitchiness, but he sensed, like his uncle, the assistant detective would be already at his desk filing a report and closing the case. It was frustrating; Sibanda would have liked to dig deeper.

The visit to Kestrel Vale School had also been unsettling in more ways than one. Ben Molesworthy, with his combination of adolescent angst and inquisitive schoolboy cheek, reminded him so much of himself at the same age. Ben's patently transparent crush on Berry Barton was a timely prompt to keep his own hopeless obsession well concealed. The visit did clear up the blue paint on the McCleans' car. McClean was not involved in Mufi's murder, but the man was nevertheless a murderer. Rage, bitterness and alcohol were a toxic mix. They had fuelled McClean's heavy-handed attack on the hapless Mtabizi. Proving intent rather than self-defence would be almost impossible, certainly with Chanza at the helm, but this was Khanyi's brother and although he couldn't actively participate in the case, he would be following it closely. There was something he had missed with that case and he hated leaving anything half finished. He would have to concentrate on the Mufi murder now.

Progress with Mufi's case was slow and losing momentum –

something would have to break soon. The knife was the key. If they could match the print, and perhaps link any DNA on it to the victim, that would at least be a start. Ishmael Naidoo's fingerprints were not a match, but that did not mean he wasn't involved. The prints could belong to an accomplice, one of his employees, perhaps. The vehicle, though, fitted the bill, and he would get Forensics to examine it with the attention of ants on a honeycomb once he had checked out all the blue vehicles on the list. After the funeral he was hoping to head off to Harry Burke's smallholding to eliminate the next possible Toyota. First, though, he really needed to ID the victim. They would get nowhere without some kind of a link.

'Ncube, have we turned up likely missing persons yet?' he asked, breaking the stony silence in the cab. Outside were ominous coughing and spluttering noises, but inside no words had passed between them for an uncomfortable length of time.

'Only a missing woman and her child from Hwange town,' he replied stiffly, still offended by the detective's comments regarding his family, 'and a couple of teenagers from Lupane. Maybe this man was also a vagrant, an unwanted person with no relatives?' he offered as a peace pipe. Ncube could never stay cross for long.

'Unlikely, what remained of his clothes were clean and fairly new. Besides which, the remains of his body indicated a healthy and well-fed adult. Hardly an isibonda. No, Ncube, someone, somewhere is missing this man and yet they haven't reported his disappearance. That's got to be our focus. Why hasn't Mufi been reported missing?'

'Perhaps they don't know that he is missing,' the sergeant suggested.

'You are getting close, Sergeant. I think this man's colleagues and family aren't aware yet that they have a problem. He could be a travelling person, a salesman or a businessman on a trip–'

'Or,' interrupted Ncube, 'a criminal, lying low and keeping away from his contacts.'

'Possibly,' said Sibanda, 'but my bet is on someone away from home. He has got to be reported missing shortly. How long has it been now since we discovered the body?'

'Not even a week, sir.'

'Mufi will have his real name in a couple of days,' Sibanda said with conviction.

'Sir, we are approaching Munda village,' said Ncube. 'That must be it there, on the left.'

Sibanda looked up and saw a kraal, a cluster of huts in the distance. Neighbours from surrounding kraals were converging on the small settlement, dressed in their best. The men who had them wore suits and ties. The women were in skirts and headscarves. Many mourners carried Bibles and prayer books in their hands. Many had bent backs. Bony knuckles clutched to the handle of a walking stick. They all walked with intent, mostly silent, bearing the brunt of the full sun with the odd, prized umbrella here and there used as a sunshade. Sibanda recognised these people. He did not know them, but he had seen them in and around every village in his region. They were hard-working northern, rural Matabele, their skins burned to the colour of ripe sorghum and shiny like the polished teak of an ancient elephant rubbing post. They were a spare people with not an ounce of extra flesh; every muscle and sinew defined by a lifetime of hard toil in the fields, by the disappointment of failed crops in drought and by the death of their cattle from disease. If their bodies reflected penury, then their faces radiated generations of determination and the ageless wisdoms of stoicism and good heart.

Ncube pulled up under the shade of a mopane tree and Miss Daisy hissed to her usual steam-spitting stop. Sibanda, for once, felt relaxed about the old crock and her embarrassing appearance and failure to start; there would be no judgement of her condition in these parts. Face value meant just that. Snide comments and backhanded sniggers were unknown in this culture.

He looked across at Ncube, who was adjusting his jacket and attempting to get it to meet across his considerable girth without success. His fingers moved on to his tie. The mangled knot was doing its best to keep the over-washed shirt collar in place. The collar had no hope of buttoning at the neck, it too was under serious strain. In a community where fat was marked as a sign of wealth, the villagers would be mightily impressed by Ncube's girth. They wouldn't notice the groaning seams of his suit, the missing buttons that had pinged into space years ago, and the trousers that barely reached his socks and clung a little too intimately to the parting in his buttocks. There would be no judgement. The sergeant would be made warmly welcome and accepted as if he were close family in the age-old Matabele tradition.

'Leave Miss Daisy,' he said, as Ncube walked towards the steaming bonnet. 'There are enough people around to give us a push start when we leave.' Ncube nodded his head in acknowledgement of all that meant.

As they walked across the still unploughed dusty field to the huts, the sound of singing greeted them. It was a hymn dominated by the high, reedy voices of the women and the rich contrapuntal bass of the men. One group was singing naturally in thirds, so that a lilting harmony softened the chant. The voices drifted out from the death hut where the mourners had been keeping watch over the body and singing an endless requiem of solemn songs throughout the night. Khanyi and her mother would be in that hut.

'Jabu, over here.' The detective turned and was surprised to see Khanyi walking towards him. She stood out like a sable amongst impala. She was tall and elegant, her head swept back from a graceful neck in youthful arrogance and her clothes were sophisticated and understated. They haven't come from the Gubu General Dealers, he thought. Old Mr Barghee only dealt in Java print, some shweshwe design cottons and brightly patterned polyester, that with very little movement could generate enough electricity to light up a whole village, but then Khanyi's stylishness was what attracted him to her in the first place.

'Jabu, I am so glad that you are here,' she said, 'this has been an awful time for me.'

'My poor darling, I'm sorry,' he said. 'This week has been manic at work. A crime spree in the district. I have been so busy chasing up leads, mostly out of phone range, but you've been in my mind every spare moment. How are you coping?'

'I'm not,' she replied. 'I find it so difficult to understand, I didn't really know Mtabizi. I am much younger than my brothers and sisters and Mtabizi started his wanderings before I had a memory. I wish this could all be over.'

'Why aren't you in the hut with your mother paying your respects, keeping watch?' Sibanda asked.

She exhaled a little moue of discontent through her perfectly formed lips. 'I couldn't stay in there any longer. It was so hot and stuffy with all those people crammed in. The endless singing and wailing nearly killed me. I was just so tired. I came and slept in my hut.' She repeated her pout as if asking for forgiveness, she knew he couldn't resist it, knew he wanted to suck and nibble on her lush, amethyst lips. She could see his eyes drawn to them. She flicked her tongue and the saliva she distributed as the tip slowly circled her mouth added gloss and volume to the already swollen edges. This was a calculating seduction. She was going to need his help and support.

The detective dragged his eyes away, aware she was trying to arouse him, but this was neither the time nor place. He was in Khanyi's village, with her people. It wouldn't do to show any outward sign of affection.

'You should have stayed. It is your duty as a daughter and sister,' he reproved.

'It's okay,' she said. 'My sister – you know, Lindiwe, the one I told you about – she arrived from Johannesburg in the middle of the night. She came straight to the hut to be with Mama, which meant I could sneak out.'

Sibanda turned away, disappointed at her disregard for tradition and loyalty. People were gathering in the narrow shade, leaning against the walls and talking quietly between themselves. To the left of the huts a fire had been built and two large pots were simmering on the smoky wood. A group of women were tending the fire and stirring the contents of the pots with a long wooden paddle. They were in the full sun and bent over the heat, their backs straining to smooth the stiff maize meal porridge that would feed the mourners when the ceremony was over. The sweat dripping from their cooked faces would add to the bitter tears that made up the funeral feast. Beer had been brewed and a beast slaughtered. It was important that Mtabizi had an offering for the spirit world so they would receive him joyously. The skin of the animal would accompany him to the grave and the meat would be eaten, unseasoned, by the mourners in deference to the spirits who didn't like salt. Eating and drinking were an integral part of the ritual. An African funeral may be a banquet for the broken hearted and a libation for the next world, but it was also a reaffirmation for the living. Ncube would be in his element.

'Come, Khanyi,' Sibanda said, 'we need to join the rest. I can see movement at the hut door. They are preparing to take your brother on his last journey.'

'We haven't had time to talk,' she replied with some desperation. 'I need to see you. I need to tell you my problems.'

'We will talk, Khanyi, but not now,' he said firmly. 'You must think of your brother. It is his time.'

'No,' she almost shouted. 'This is not fair, don't you understand, Jabu? That bitch, Lindiwe is back and she is going to cause trouble for me. I am going to have to leave here and I have nowhere to go. You must help me.'

Sibanda ushered her back towards her hut and privacy. 'Shhh,' he admonished. 'Calm down, Khanyi. Whatever is the matter? Surely this can be resolved later. This is no time for family squabbles.'

'I have to leave now, Jabu,' she said with panic in her voice. 'I am scared of Lindiwe, she is evil… not normal.'

'Look, Khanyi, there is nothing she can do here with so many people around. Let's go and join the mourners and then we can try and sort this out later. I can't stay too long anyway. I have to be somewhere else this afternoon, but I can come back and pick you up after that.'

'Later will probably be too late,' she said, resignedly, and realising there was no convincing this man of the urgency, she moved away towards the gathering crowd.

Sibanda followed her, disturbed by her outburst, but glad she was seeing some sense. He couldn't imagine what her problem was, but he would be keeping his eye on Lindiwe. If she made any sort of trouble for Khanyi he would intervene.

The mourners were gathered on either side of the hut door, men to the right and women to the left. They were still singing, and as one voice flagged and lost power, weakened by the choral marathon, so another would take over with a fresh hymn and a fresh lead.

A group of men had remained outside the death hut throughout the night, stoking the fire that the women now cooked over. In years past their role had been to keep intruders away, to chase the abathakathi, the witches, who wanted to steal the body for their evil ways, but only a few of the old men remained to witness those beliefs. For most, it was a time to discuss the future for the bereaved family, to talk politics, discuss the price of cattle and lament the state of the crops.

The women had spent their night in the death hut with the corpse and his possessions. They emerged slowly and blinked as they made their way into the bright sunshine, retying wraps and blankets around their waists, rubbing their faces and wiping away the night's tears. Last to emerge was Mantini, bent almost double, every step a pain-racked offering to the son she had borne. By her side, supporting her fragile body, was a younger woman. Sibanda assumed this was Lindiwe.

The waiting men entered the hut, and the detective knew they would be hoisting the coffin onto their shoulders for the walk to the graveyard. He glanced across the swept, compacted sand to an area beyond the huts. He could see a patch of disturbed ground. A mound of rich, red-ochred earth lay in a pile on the surface of windblown Kalahari sand, like a bloody gash on elephant hide. The grave had been dug. His ever inquisitive mind thought for a moment how interesting the geology was in this ancient aeolian sand-covered land, but his indulgence was only for a moment before he refocused on the solemnity of the occasion.

Ncube was standing next to him. 'My condolences, sir, for the very sad loss to your intended.'

'Thank you, Ncube, she is not taking it well.' He knew Ncube would have witnessed the animated conversation he had had a few minutes ago.

'She is only young, sir, and the young are far from death or so they think. She will settle. She will come to understand the rhythms and ceremonies that mark a life, the living of it and the dying end. She will embrace them as a mother takes a child to her breast. It may give discomfort sometimes as when the hard gums of misfortune clamp down on a soft nipple, and it may drain her very life's strength as when the child grows and sucks ferociously, but in the end she will gain comfort from the trial and the familiarity with the pain. That is how it is.'

Sibanda only had time to raise his eyebrows as the cortege began its slow procession to the grave.

Chapter 12

Mantini halted for a few moments as she followed the procession. Lindiwe stopped beside her.

'Are you alright, Mama, should I run and get a stool so you can rest?' her daughter asked.

'No, Lindiwe, I will be alright. Breath does not last as long these days. I will find more in a moment.' She needed to ease her back and get her balance. She felt like a francolin chick, newborn and unable to keep up with the volatile flock of siblings that mimicked their mother's every twist and turn. She was the laggard who was slow to follow the snaking, evasive path set by the hen. She would be the one plucked from the earth by a yellow-billed kite, shredded and eaten in those nimble talons, all that remained a gathering of discarded down feathers floating lazily back to earth, hanging on a breath of air, veering and shifting with each faint vagary of the breeze. The lightness of this thought penetrated her joints and gave air to her lungs. She felt an easing of the stiffness, enough to get her started again on the slight incline to the grave. She looked around for Kanku and then took Lindiwe's arm for support.

'Where is Khanyi?' she asked. 'I can't see her.' 'She is behind us, Mama, she has a red dress on, a dress to kill the sun, she is looking beautiful.' Lindiwe glanced down at her own appearance. She had a much-washed blanket wrapped around her waist and her shirt had little of the original colour or shape left in it. It had been mended under both armpits several times; cleanliness was its best attribute.

'She always looks beautiful,' said Mantini and Lindiwe felt a momentary stab of jealousy. She wanted to say mean things about her sister, and open her mother's eyes, but it had never worked before. Her mother was completely blind to Khanyi's faults. She could not see her for the selfish, manipulative person she had grown into. There was no point burdening her now with such information as she hobbled slowly to bury her son. She would not be believed anyway.

'I cannot understand why she left Mtabizi's side. It was her place to be in the death hut, and to be with him for his last night at home,' said Mantini as she leant heavily on Lindiwe's arm.

'Perhaps she was not well,' replied Lindiwe, unsure of why she was protecting her sister.

'Is she sick? I must go to her. Ubulawayini, what is the matter?' asked Mantini, looking around with panic in her voice.

'No, Mama, she is not sick, do not worry, she seems well now. In fact, she is talking to a young man.'

'It must be her intended, Jabulani Sibanda, a policeman of some sort. I have not met him yet. What is he like? Can you see him?'

'He is far away still, but he is very tall and light-skinned and he dresses well. I can tell that much. Mama, if he is a policeman perhaps we could ask him about Thulani.'

'What about Thulani?'

'Remember, Mama, I told you that he travelled back last week, before we knew about Mtabizi. He was coming to settle here in the village. He wanted to rebuild his old hut, settle down and start farming again. You know he was always so good in the fields and with the cattle. Being in Johannesburg, living in a shack with no sky to look at and neighbours less than a matchbox apart from him made him realise just how much he wanted to be back in the lands. He had saved a lot of money. He was going to buy a plough. He was coming home to plough, ready for the rains, Mama.'

'Ha, Thulani is like his father, he has probably drunk the plough and squandered the seed maize on women. He has never left Joburg,' Mantini replied.

'No, Mama, Thulani is not like that. He is a good man. Like me, he sent money and a letter home every month. It hurt him that you never replied. I was with him when he got on the bus. I saw him pay the fare. I am very worried.'

They had finally reached the burial mound. The service was about to begin. Lindiwe took her mother's blanket and placed it in the shade. She helped Mantini to a sitting position with her back against a tree and she stood beside her. Her uncle started to preach. Once again the men were on one side and the women on the other.

Mantini could not concentrate on the words of her brother or the other men who were now taking their turn to praise the Lord and the gifts he had given. They used sweet words to try to explain Mtabizi's life and the sudden mysterious rage he had vented before his death. She cared for none of this. She knew her boy incapable of hurting anyone. He was the gentlest of souls.

Mantini had not allowed them to wash Mtabizi's body, as was the tradition in the death hut. She wanted him buried as he lived, in the cloak of innocence that he loved so much, with God's grit beneath his nails and the smell of wild places bathing his body for eternity. They had argued with her, told her that Mtabizi needed to enter heaven in a pure state. She could hardly contain her anger and when her late father's youngest wife entered the hut with a bucket of water, she found the strength to pick it up and throw it over the fleeing woman. Only then did they stop trying to persuade her.

Those preaching were talking now about how Mtabizi was free at last, released from his earthly body and damaged mind; an equal, finally, in the eyes of those in heaven.

Fools, she thought, didn't they know that he had always been free, was superior to their chained minds and repetitive days? She hoped there were birds in heaven and not just those white, bloodless doves that appeared in the Bible. She prayed he could float in the lustrous iridescence of the plum-coloured starling, clothe himself in dazzling rainbow of the kingfisher and, wherever he was, listen to the rapture of the Mapostoli bird as the night drew in, asking the Good Lord for deliverance.

'Mama, it is time,' said Lindiwe. Slowly, she helped her mother to her feet and over to the graveside. The singers had begun to sing afresh and the coffin was being lowered into the grave. Mantini stooped stiffly and picked up a handful of earth. She spat on it, mixing her saliva with the red grains, ensuring Mtabizi a welcoming entry to the next world. 'Hamba khule uzikhonzele, go well and plead for us, my son,' she said, exhorting Mtabizi to ask for blessings for the living from the old ones who had gone before, 'and give my loving greetings to Skhathele,' and the tears came again as she remembered her eldest daughter, lost to her two years ago.

Each mourner in their turn threw a handful of soil on the coffin until the lid was spattered with a last, life-touched communication; a personal farewell to the departed that would stay close to him through eternity. Then the men took up the shovels stabbed into the displaced earth awaiting their moment. Rhythmically, to the renewed efforts of the gathered voices, they replaced the disturbed ground to its natural home. Every man waited his turn to blanket Mtabizi with his cover of perpetual peace; every man bent his back to the task.

'Look, Mama,' said Lindiwe, distracting Mantini from the fresh wave of grief that was threatening to overwhelm her. 'That must be Sibanda,' and she pointed to a man, stripped to the waist, plying the shovel with the ease of the young and fit. He stood a head taller than those around him and with each thrust of the shovel, rivulets of sweat dipped and splashed over his undulating muscles like grass stirred by a summer breeze. All who watched saw a grace and poetry in his labour and for a minute many forgot the occasion. They were transported from their sorrow and the gnawing thoughts of their own mortality to a place untouched by human transience, a place of eternal youth. The spell was broken as Sibanda gave up his shovel to the next in line and an imperceptible sigh floated up from the gathering.

Mantini looked from Sibanda across to Khanyi expecting her to be glowing in the reflected glory of this supreme specimen of Ndebele manhood, but she was unfocused, her eyes darting over her shoulder and down to the cellphone in her hand. She reminded Mantini of an ostrich pecking for seed and then raising and swivelling its long neck to look for danger. 'What is the matter with the child?' she asked Lindiwe. 'It is Mtabizi's funeral, has she no respect?' Lindiwe remained silent.

The grave was finally covered with branches and switches from nearby trees as a death seal, and the mourners took this as their cue to leave the graveside. 'Come, Mama, we must go and wash our hands with intelezi, the herbs will purify us before we return to the kraal and greet the mourners.'

At the graveside, Sibanda picked up his shirt and jacket and walked towards the bowl of water left for the men to cleanse themselves. Ncube walked alongside him. 'That was a good thing you did, sir. Khanyi will know that you sweated for her brother.'

'Thanks, Ncube,' he said, and then eyeing the cooking fire ahead of them felt compelled to add, 'Don't forget we can't stay long, we have to get to Harry Burke's smallholding and examine his Blue Toyota. Ncube, you had better go, the ingovu, the funeral meat, awaits.' Ncube needed no second prompting and hurried off toward the fire and the enticing smell of roasting meat. Sibanda walked toward the huts hoping to talk to Khanyi and to reassure her.

'Detective Sibanda,' a voice called. He turned to see Lindiwe approaching him. He took a moment to asses this 'evil' sister, watching her carefully. He prided himself on being a fair judge of character, and evil generally, he thought, didn't come in the sort of package that was walking towards him. Lindiwe was, to put it bluntly, short, stocky and lacking any sort of presence, let alone a malevolent one. Her hair was shorn unfashionably short; no dreadlocks or weaves softened her face, but despite this it was her most attractive feature. It was a horizon away from the symmetry of the golden ratio and yet the very lack of divine proportion gave it an arresting character. The nose was too long, the eyes too wide and the mouth too big, but for all its lack of regularity, it demanded a second glance and would always get one.

'Salibonani, greetings, Detective. Can I speak to you for a moment,' she asked as she reached his side.

'Yebo, yes, of course,' he replied civilly and smiled in spite of his initial hostility.

'I am Lindiwe, Khanyi's sister,' she said, introducing herself. 'I do not like to bother you, off duty, at a time like this, but my brother, Thulani, has gone missing. I am very worried. It is so unlike him not to be in contact for this long,' she said. Sibanda immediately felt a jolt in his stomach like the kick of a donkey rebelling finally against the whip, but he kept all indications of alarm from his face. It would be far too cruel a coincidence for this family to lose two sons so violently in one week. He could not contemplate it.

'How long has he been gone?' he asked, donning a mask of professionalism.

'He lives in Johannesburg, but was moving back home. I put him on the bus to Bulawayo early last Thursday morning,' she said.

'Perhaps he only got as far as Bulawayo and hasn't travelled up here yet. Maybe he is visiting friends,' Sibanda suggested.

'I don't think so, Detective,' she replied. 'He sent me a text to say he was on the final leg home.'

'When did you get the message?' he asked, glancing around in time to see Ncube weaving his way back to a chair with a plate of meat piled so high that it required the balancing skills of a Chinese circus act.

Lindiwe reached down the neck of her shirt and fished a phone from between her breasts. 'Saturday morning last week,' she said, examining the screen. 'He was on the bus heading home when he sent the message, but he never made it. Mama has not seen him.'

'And you have heard nothing since?' he asked.

Lindiwe shook her head. 'I have tried and tried to phone him, but either his phone is dead or he is out of range.'

'I will need details,' he said, with a growing sense of foreboding. 'Can you come to the police station tomorrow morning? We will go through the procedure to register a missing person.' The detective, despite the urgency to know if Mufi and Thulani were one and the same, felt this family needed time to come to terms with the loss of one son and brother before he even hinted that another might have met the same fate. One more anonymous night would not hurt Mufi.

'Thank you, Detective,' she said. 'Won't you come over and meet my mother? She would like to greet you. Khanyi is with her.' Sibanda looked over to the hut and saw the red fabric of Khanyi's dress splashed against the ochre walls like blood spilled on the baked earth and his sense of foreboding deepened. He and Lindiwe walked together towards the old lady seated on her wooden stool against the hut wall and Khanyi who was by her side.

'Mama,' said Khanyi, 'this is Jabulani Sibanda.'

'I am pleased to meet you, Sibanda,' said Mantini. 'I have heard much about you from my daughter. I am sorry we should meet today.'

Sibanda squatted on his haunches so that he could talk on a level with this old lady whose grief had carved rills of distress in her face and sluiced her eyes with the bitter waters of anguish. 'I too have heard much of you,' he replied. He took her knobbly old hands in his, 'And I too am sorry that a day such as today is our first time to meet. This is indeed a wretched moment for your family. I want to offer my deepest condolences.'

Mantini nodded her head in acceptance of his sympathy. 'You are a policeman, Sibanda, perhaps you can tell me why that white man has not been charged with the murder of my son.'

'Gogo, grandmother,' he said, giving her the name that her revered age and status demanded, 'my colleagues are still investigating, but it is a difficult case. Mtabizi broke into the farmhouse and the farmer, according to his story, was defending himself. Can you think of any reason why he might break into a house? Would it have been for food or perhaps shelter? It was raining hard that night.'

'He always came home when it rained,' Mantini said. 'He was nearly forty years old. He had been wandering since he was twelve and his habits never changed. He slept in the bush most nights. He didn't mind the cold in winter, but Mtabizi never failed to come home to his hut if the rain was fierce or there was a storm. He was terrified of thunder.'

'Something or someone must have got in the way of his homeward journey that night, but we will get to the bottom of it, I promise you, Gogo.' His eye, trained to interpret body language and discomfort, caught a flash of red in his peripheral vision. Khanyi was shifting her position against the wall. She knew more than she was saying. Sibanda stood up. 'I must take my leave of you. I am sorry that I cannot remain for the feast,' he said.

'No, you must eat something, Detective. You cannot leave our home without tasting our hospitality, Mama will be most upset,' said Lindiwe.

'Thank you,' he replied, 'I am honoured, but I suspect my sergeant has eaten enough for both of us. He will have done double justice to the ingovu. I need to be elsewhere, I am in the middle of investigating a…' Sibanda hesitated, he had nearly said *a murder*, but he knew that Lindiwe would latch on to that and worry, perhaps needlessly. 'A serious incident in the district,' he continued, avoiding Lindiwe's eyes, 'and I must take my leave. Khanyi,' he smiled at the beautiful girl before him, 'perhaps you could walk with me to the Land Rover.'

Out of earshot of the hut, and out of sight behind the Land Rover, Sibanda asked, 'What on earth was going on before the funeral, Khanyi? You were almost hysterical.'

'I told you, Jabu, it is Lindiwe, she is out to cause trouble for me,' she replied sulkily.

'She doesn't look like trouble to me,' he said. 'She seems quite normal and reasonable.'

'Normal,' Khanyi snapped, 'normal – she's far from normal, you don't know her, she's…' and then she fell silent as if choking on the words to follow.

'She's what, Khanyi? How can I help you if you can't tell me what's wrong?'

Khanyi turned away from him as though what she had to say could not be said to his face. 'She doesn't like men,' she hissed under her breath.

'Ah,' was all he replied. He understood her turmoil now. Homosexuality was completely taboo in Africa. It was seen as a sickness or, even worse, a lifestyle choice. Gays were reviled, hounded, labelled 'perverts' and even imprisoned for their love.

'Listen, Khanyi,' he said, 'it's not how you think it is. I know the prejudice of our people, but you should try to overcome it. It's backward.'

'How would you like it if you had an isiphukhuphukhu for a brother and a moffie for a sister?' she asked.

Sibanda winced. Khanyi's choice of epithets marked her as a bigot. It distressed him. 'Why are you so scared of Lindiwe. She can't hurt you.'

'She knows that I know,' she said.

'What do you know?' he asked.

'I caught them, her and that disgusting Angelina from the next kraal,' and she indicated a cluster of huts no more than two hundred metres away, 'at it, you know, kissing and stuff. They took off the next day and no one has seen or heard from them since, until now.'

'Come on, Khanyi, you are being unreasonable. Live and let live,' he said with growing frustration at her intolerance. He decided to change tack then. He would have years ahead of him to convince her of her narrow-mindedness. Maybe one day they could travel together. It would open her eyes, soften her hard-line stance. He held her chin so she couldn't avert her eyes and softly asked, 'What happened that night, Khanyi, the night that Mtabizi broke into Zebra Hill Farm? You saw him, didn't you?'

She hesitated for a moment and tried to look around to check for prying ears, but Sibanda held her face firmly. 'Yes,' she replied, unable to lie under his intense gaze. Tears welled up in her eyes. 'I did, but Jabu, you mustn't tell anyone.'

'What happened?' he asked gently.

'I saw him that night. It was raining heavily, lots of lightning and thunder. Everyone was inside their huts, the weather was so bad,' she said.

'Why didn't he go to his hut and take shelter there?' Sibanda asked.

'I put my head out of the doorway to check on the rain. I saw him or rather smelled him coming. He was already wet and those rags that he wore stank, somehow the dampness of him had made his stench more repulsive than usual. He smelt like a bag of rotting vegetables. I couldn't have him hanging around the kraal the next day because...' Khanyi covered her face and sobbed.

'Because what, Khanyi?' Sibanda persisted. He let go of her face now, sensing her distress was too great. He took her in his arms. She held him tightly and began to mumble into his shoulder.

'Because of you,' she said. 'You were coming around the next day and I couldn't bear the thought of you knowing that I had a mad tramp for a brother. I was ashamed.'

Sibanda could feel her wet tears on his collar and registered each sob as it trembled through her body. He did not want to press her further to relive the encounter that took place that night. What had she said to make him turn away from the comfort of his home to seek out shelter in that inhospitable farmhouse among strangers? She would have to come to terms with that herself. He continued to hold her until the tears subsided, all the while wondering why this girl, his fiancée, was so different. She seemed so fragile and defenceless, and yet she had judged her brother as shameful. He was beginning to find her puzzling, beginning to doubt his own judgement of her.

'Khanyi, when the time is right you are going to have to tell your mother,' he said. He held her at arm's length. 'She will understand.'

'No,' she protested, 'I can never do that, you don't understand.' She pulled away from his embrace. It had not been Sibanda she wanted to hide her disgusting brother from, but she could not tell him that. Let Sibanda believe it was his fault, then he might not think so badly of her. She remembered the night clearly. She knew she could never tell her mother or Jabu that she had shouted at Mtabizi to go away. When he stood motionless, surprised by her outburst, she had picked up some stray bricks and a large log still smouldering from the cooking fire. She hurled them at him until he darted away through the bush. The last she saw of him was courtesy of a jagged flash of lightning that flared through the night sky. It outlined his shape as he ran, wild dreadlocks flying and flinging off droplets of rain in his wake. She had not planned the outcome but she was not really sorry either, nor was most of the village, she was sure. They may have wailed at the funeral, like a bunch of hypocrites, but he was the drought on their landscape, the blight on their maize, the tick on their livestock. Her tears, like theirs, were those of the crocodile.

'That must be your choice, Khanyi. I won't tell anyone. It must come from you,' Sibanda said. 'Is there anything else you are not telling me?' he asked.

'What do you mean?' she asked.

'Well, I have just heard from Lindiwe that you have another brother, Thulani. Why have you never spoken of him? Is he gay or mad as well?' Sibanda was battling to keep the edge from his voice.

'Whatever she has been saying is all lies,' Khanyi was threatening to become hysterical again. 'Didn't I tell you that she was going to make trouble for me?'

'She didn't make trouble, Khanyi. Your name never came up. She simply mentioned she hadn't heard from Thulani for some days. He was on his way back home,' he said.

'Well, I have already told Lindiwe I haven't seen him,' she cut in hastily. 'Maybe he is still travelling. Those buses break down all the time. Anyway, I don't care.' She turned and flounced away back towards the huts, her red skirt swinging in time to the long woven braids which hung down her back. Sibanda watched her go, his mood darkening with the knowledge that he had not been able to reach out to her.

A discreet cough from a few metres away signalled the arrival of Sergeant Ncube. 'I thought perhaps you were waiting for me, sir,' he said.

'I was, Ncube,' Sibanda replied curtly. 'Now let's get this heap of scrapmetal on the road.'

The sergeant recognised that the detective was in a foul temper, doubtless put there by the beautiful, wilful ntombi that had just walked away seductively. Her firm hips, a little skinny perhaps for his taste but nonetheless enticing, had swayed tantalisingly beneath a red haze, suggesting further delights and secrets to discover. She was trouble, there was no doubt about that, but what fun the detective was going to have taming this wilful leopard.

He turned to the vehicle parked on the roadside and under his breath he whispered to the Land Rover, 'Please, Miss Daisy, just this once be a good girl and start first time.' But Miss Daisy had caught the atmosphere and was playing hard to get. Her starter motor stammered and spat. She issued no soothing words. Ncube turned the key and pumped the accelerator several times, all the while coaxing his love with murmurs of endearment until even he recognised that the battery was beginning to die. He looked across at the detective with shame on his face. 'She won't start, sir, we are going to need to get help to push-start her.'

Sibanda got out of the cab and slammed the odd-coloured door so hard that it rebounded loudly against the Land Rover body. Ncube scrambled out to check on the door's status. He had searched for hours in the CMED yard for that door and celebrated joyously when he discovered it. He had worked meticulously to get the mismatched hinges to conform and open smoothly. He had adjusted the catch so that it talked gently to its home on the chassis and barely complained when clicked into place. This rough treatment from Detective Sibanda was an outrage, no wonder his woman strode away as though stung by a scorpion. The man had no touch. The rest of the day was going to be a trial.

Chapter 13

Miss Daisy was bumping happily along the dusty road heading to the smallholding of Harry Burke. She had made her point, and in doing so had caused considerable delay. She had taxed eight strong men with a good half an hour's exertion as they pushed her backwards and forwards through the thick sandy furrows of the village road attempting to gain enough speed to satisfy the starting requirements of the temperamental madam. Eventually Ncube had lifted the bonnet and, while one of the volunteers held it aloft, he had tinkered, all the while whispering secret endearments to this unpredictable mistress. Finally, in a gesture of appeasement, he replaced the gasket in the radiator cap even though the old one was still maintaining the pressure. 'There,' he said, 'a nice fresh seal for you. Now, please, Miss Daisy, don't give us any more trouble. The man behind the wheel is very angry and we don't want to upset him further, look what he did to your door.' Ncube glanced up at Sibanda drumming his fingers against the steering wheel with a face as black as thunder in a midnight storm and he offered up a further entreaty before emerging into the sunshine.

Ncube gently closed the bonnet, nodded to the gang of willing shoulders toiling under the hot sun and urged them to get their backs into it one more time. 'Yebo, madoda, tshova, shove guys,' he exhorted, his own arms locked onto the passenger door-frame. 'Futi, futi, some more.' Slowly the ancient Land Rover moved forwards, creaking and groaning. The soft sand of the road made it almost impossible to achieve any great speed, but the pushers put in a supreme final effort and managed to reach a half jog. With the men at as full a stretch as was likely, given the circumstances, and their strength beginning to wilt, Ncube realised this was their last hope for some time and shouted to Sibanda, 'Now, sir, NOW.' With the gear engaged, Sibanda lifted his foot from the clutch. The Land Rover lurched, clunked, coughed and then spluttered into life. The sergeant ran alongside and managed to haul himself on board with more agility than a man of his girth deserved so that Miss Daisy did not have to stop for him.

'Are you in, Ncube?' Sibanda asked.

'Yes, sir,' he replied, gasping for air, and with his last ounce of effort pulled the door closed. He turned and, through the cloud of churned sand and dust, waved to the group of helpers who were grinning back at him with the pleasure of a successful result. Ncube reached under the passenger seat and hauled out the plastic bottle of water he normally kept to replenish Miss Daisy when she got overheated. He felt he could borrow a few mouthfuls without putting the journey further at risk. One handful he reserved for his face, to wash away the dusty porridge that his sweat and the grey Kalahari sand had plastered on his cheeks.

'I have my uniform in the back, sir,' he said. 'Perhaps we could pull over somewhere ahead and I could get changed, I cannot be on duty looking like this.'

Sibanda looked across at the dusty, crumpled, brown blob sitting next to him radiating a humid and slightly rancid smell that was doubtless permeating the deckchair canvas and nodded. 'But I won't be switching off,' he added.

'No indeed, sir, please don't do that. I could not push Miss Daisy in this sand on my own.'

'Sergeant, as soon as we have wrapped up this case you absolutely will have to get down to Bulawayo and sort out this… this… umdidi of a Land Rover.'

Ncube inwardly swallowed his displeasure at the use of such a foul term to deride this fine vehicle. The detective, he thought, might be a man among men, fearless in the bush and a policeman with extraordinary instincts, but he knew nothing about machinery, was scared of it and that was the plain honest truth. 'Yes, sir,' was all he replied.

Sibanda changed tack. 'I was talking to Khanyi's sister at the funeral. She was telling me about another of her brothers, Thulani. He is missing;

started out from Johannesburg last week and hasn't got home yet. Not answering his phone'

'You don't think it's…' Ncube trailed off.

'Unfortunately, yes. It's a fair possibility that Mufi is Thulani Mpofu. We have had no other significant missing person reports and he is unusually out of contact.'

Ncube simply clicked out of the side of his mouth. It was a sound that was used to variously indicate disappointment, frustration or annoyance, but in this instance it perfectly reflected the sergeant's disbelief and sorrow. 'Ayi, ayi, no, that can't be,' he said. 'That family has had enough bad luck. Did you notice the grave next to the recently departed?' he asked. 'That belongs to his late sister, Skhathele, and the uncle was telling me that his own son is seriously sick, he was in one of the huts, too ill to come out for the funeral. He will die any day now, ayi, ayi, ayi,' he repeated his disbelief and his voice trailed off as he shook his head.

'Let's not get ahead of ourselves, Ncube,' said Sibanda, attempting to calm his overwrought sergeant. 'Maybe we are barking up the wrong tree. What we need to do now is focus on finding the right blue Toyota.'

Trees again, thought Ncube, the man is obsessed with them. Aloud, he merely mouthed the standard reply he used when the detective spoke of misplaced oddities such as dogs and trees, 'Yes, sir.'

Sibanda pulled over under the shade of a wild wisteria growing on the side of the road. Its shade was sparse but what it lacked in umbrage it made up for in appearance. This indigenous looker was covered in a showy display of pale-mauve flowers that easily rivalled the jacaranda. Sergeant Ncube prised himself out of the still-running vehicle and went to the back of the Land Rover to change into uniform. He never even glanced at the glorious display just inches above his head, saw the beginnings of a lush lavender carpet beneath his feet, breathed in the sweet, peppery scent of the fallen blossoms or glanced at the matching lilac-breasted roller that perched on a nearby fence and added a flash of pale pink and turquoise to the violet-tinted landscape.

Sibanda observed this lack of interest. 'I suppose, for you, beauty is just a well-rounded buttock, Ncube,' he commented idly, as he waited in the shade. Ncube, with a freshly starched shirt crackling in his ear, never heard the detective. The effort of trying to keep his balance on one leg as he pulled on his trousers had deafened him to all but his own grunts.

Sibanda's phone rang in his pocket. He had installed the call of the fiery-necked nightjar as his ringtone. It suited who he was and where he worked and was not out of place in this opalescent shade. '*Good Lord deliver us, good Lord deliver us*,' it repeated softly but insistently until Sibanda flipped it open, saw it came from Gubu Police Station and put it to his ear, 'Zanele?' he asked.

'Is this a good time to talk?' she asked hesitantly. 'I have just had some news from Forensics and I thought it better not to use the radio, I wasn't sure if this was to be private like the paint.'

'To do with Mufi?' he asked eagerly.

'Yes,' she replied, 'they have found a remnant feather in his windpipe.'

'A vulture feather?' Sibanda asked.

'Seems not,' she replied. 'They actually can't identify the feather, is that important?'

'Could be,' he replied. 'Tell them to keep testing and, Zanele, ask them to send over some of the bits of clothing. We may have a lead on Mufi's identity. I don't suppose you've had any luck with the fingerprints?' he added.

'Not yet, sir, I've been busy typing reports and returns, but I'll get on to it shortly.'

'And keep pressing for the DNA result from the knife.' As he snapped the phone cover shut, he felt for the first time in days that the case was moving ahead. Hardly had he returned the phone to his pocket than he heard a text message arrive to the chattering ringtone of a flock of disturbed guinea fowl. It always made him smile. Ncube was now doing battle with his buttons and gamely urging them to remain in the hole they had been designed for. Sibanda could see that the skirmish was becoming a lengthy war and so he chose to read the message. It was from Berry. His heart skipped.

'Hi Leo, u avail Saturday pm 4 skool excrsn? Need hlp. 6th fm awy. Police presence essntl. Bg bnd of sptty adlscnts. Ugh! Izithelo.'

He immediately recognised her disenvowelled style. She had it down almost to perfection. It was spare and economical, lacking any fuss or fluff, just like her. He smiled as he interpreted the invitation. She had used their nicknames for each other. Occasionally she called him Leo. Her Ndebele was good enough to know that his surname, his totem, Sibanda, translated roughly to big cat. She had given him a Latin makeover. As soon as this familiarity slipped into their friendship, he began to call her Izithelo, the closest he could come to Berry in Ndebele. He would help her out, he knew that, even though it would bring another dose of that exquisite mix of pleasure, pain and guilt that he recognised as an addiction.

'Sir, I am ready,' Ncube interrupted his thoughts.

'Let's go, Ncube, time and tide wait for no man.'

Ncube noticed the new spring in the detective's step, a lightening of his mood, but failed to understand what the sea had to do with their current status in the middle of the bush, in the middle of the country, about as far away from a coastline as is physically possible. He rolled his eyes conspiratorially at Miss Daisy, but all he said was, 'Yes, sir.'

'Where is this small holding we are heading to, Ncube?'

'Once we hit the tar, it's about another ten kilometres. Constable Khumalo says that Harry Burke grows vegetables he delivers to Gubu once a week.'

'His blue Toyota is probably the delivery vehicle. Have you seen it around the village?'

'I would remember it, if I had.'

'Or perhaps you mistook it for the governor's vehicle, when it was actually the vegetable truck of Harry Burke or the furniture truck of Ishmael Naidoo or the vehicle of one of the others on the *Mediterranean Sapphire* list. No wonder you think the governor is everywhere, with eyes in the back of his head, and an evil bastard.'

'Perhaps, sir, but, whatever you think of him, he has a face and a red heart, he is known by the people to be unusually fortunate in getting rich and he can be as angry as a honey badger attacked by a snake.'

'I thought you were going to rely on his secretary's judgement of sainthood, Ncube.'

'I am confused, sir. I can't make up my mind. I'm like a kudu with two heads.'

'Reputations are often enhanced in the telling,' said Sibanda, 'like a viral Chinese whisper. Stories change, with each gossip adding their own colour to the tale in order to make it more meaty and scandalous. I found the governor to be charming and a committed conservationist on the surface at least. We know he's capable of killing, his war record tells us that, but is he capable of murder?'

Ncube thought for a moment and tried to understand what the Chinese had to do with the governor's reputation. He was probably doing some shifty deal with them, perhaps a mining concession. He must tell his wives when he got home; that would give them all something to think about. 'Sir, take the next turn-off.' They had nearly missed it with all this talk of mining deals.

They took off down another bumpy track. It was sand-cushioned and kinder on Miss Daisy's gubbins than the sawmill road. She did develop a rather alarming roll as the deep sandy ruts rocked her and her inmates from side to side. Sibanda had the stability of the steering wheel to keep himself upright but Ncube had to brace his arms against the dashboard. This gave rigidity to his bones, but allowed his cumbersome stomach rolls to wave from side to side, which he found to be very disturbing.

'It can't be far now,' said Sibanda, understanding the sergeant's discomfort. 'I can see rows of cabbages coming up in the distance.'

'I hope so, sir. I feel like a hippo caught in a pool of churning water.'

Sibanda laughed and realised he had forgiven Miss Daisy for her recalcitrance. The thought of spending time with Berry added to his good mood. 'I can see a farmhouse ahead, Ncube, and some plastic covered seed houses.'

On either side of the vehicle fields of cabbages and tomatoes ranged in disciplined rows like a red and green army facing one another. A central pivot was delivering arcs of water to the thirsty troops and Sibanda felt the temperature drop as he passed through the aisle of coolness. It was a welcome relief. The day had been typical of October, hot and long.

Sibanda searched for an incline or any slope that might help the headstrong Miss Daisy to start without the circus performance that had just occurred. The driveway that fronted the house seemed to tilt temptingly to the east and he parked a little past the house on what he thought looked to be the steepest part of the gentle slope. 'That will have to do, Ncube, you should be able to ease Miss Daisy into a gentle roll without too much effort, don't you think?'

Ncube eyed the slight gradient and knew it would take more effort than the detective imagined, but the beast hadn't yet fallen on its horns, it wasn't a completely hopeless situation. 'Yes, sir,' he replied acceptingly.

A man in work overalls, gumboots covered in mud and barely holding together and a large floppy hat walked up. 'Salibonani, madoda,' he greeted them. 'Sorry but we don't sell vegetables from here, we only wholesale them. Mr Burke doesn't like visitors just to arrive like locusts on a mealie field.'

'As you can see we are not locusts or any other biblical plague,' said Sibanda, his mood darkening. 'We are from Gubu Police, and would like to chat to Mr Burke. Is he here or is he beset by boils?'

The man in the gumboots looked across to Ncube for a clue, but the sergeant was just as confused and he shrugged a question mark with his shoulders.

Sibanda repeated the question with increasing annoyance, 'Where is Mr Burke?'

Mr Gumboot answered with more deference now he knew it was the police. 'He's probably round the back, checking on the seedlings, follow me.'

At that moment the radio in the Land Rover crackled, 'Gubu Base to Gubu Mobile, come in please.' It was Constable Khumalo.

'Get that will you, Ncube, I'll go and find Mr Burke,' and Sibanda strode off to the back of the house, to the seed houses he had spotted from the road. As he stepped inside the first plastic house he was aware of a change in climate. It was steamy and hot, but a constant, fine spray from overhead misters kept the temperature tolerable. At the end of the house Sibanda could see his quarry, a large man with his back to him, directing a legion of workers with trays of seedlings, this way and that. He walked towards him along the rows of trays, admiring the uniformity of the seedlings and their vigorous growth. With all the workers turned and focused on this interloper, Harry Burke twisted around to see what had grabbed the attention of his staff.

'Hello,' he said. 'Do you mind not coming in here? These seeds are delicate little fellows and don't take kindly to strangers shedding diseased spores and bringing in weeds.'

Sibanda felt immediately guilty, he should have recognised the clinical nature of the work and the need for hygiene. He had seen a tray of chemicals at the door for shoes and deliberately avoided it, sanitising his soles would have taken a few extra seconds that he didn't have to spare, but more than guilt, he felt shock at the sight of Harry Burke. He was an exact double of Barnaby Jones with perhaps a thirty-year age gap. The jackal-pelt hair was the same, but threaded with more silver and he had Barnaby Jones' same square jaw and piercing blue eyes that were looking at him. 'My apologies' Mr Burke, could we perhaps chat outside? I am Detective Inspector Sibanda from Gubu Police.'

Harry Burke led Sibanda to the back veranda of his house and offered him a chair. 'I thought I was done and dusted with police visits, Detective. Have you come to take the rest of my few remaining acres?' Harry Burke said this in a resigned way as if he had already accepted his fate.

'No, not at all, Mr Burke, I am here to check on a vehicle which I believe belongs to you,' said Sibanda, who could now understand why this horticultural empire had consumed even the normal back and front gardens of the modest farmhouse. 'I can see you are cramped for growing space as it is; how many acres did they leave you?'

'Thirty, around the house, but it will do, I get by, and with intensive farming techniques I can turn a profit. Believe it or not, the loss of my land has forced me to become more efficient and creative with my land use. I think I have done pretty well, don't you?'

Sibanda nodded his admiration for the achievement, but chose to stick to safer ground. 'Mr Burke, do you own a blue Toyota Land Cruiser?'

'Yes, I do.'

'And where is it right now? Could I take a look at it?'

'Sorry, Detective, I have loaned it to my nephew. He has had it for the last few days.'

'Where was it three nights ago?'

'My nephew has actually had it all week. He's a young lad, Detective, and his girlfriend is in the area so I think he needed a reasonable vehicle to drive her around.'

'That's very generous of you, Mr Burke. Do you normally lend out your vehicle?'

'I never married. My sister's children are the only ones I have to spoil. Barney's a good lad and we have a close relationship. I like to think of him as my son.'

'Is that Barnaby Jones from Thunduluka Lodge?'

'Yes,' said Harry Burke, with some surprise, 'do you know him?'

'I have met him recently,' said Sibanda, 'and let's be honest, Mr Burke, you do look like peas in a pod.' Harry Burke laughed with the pride of a father and tilted his head like a flycatcher glimpsing himself in a reflective window. 'My sister and I are twins and people do say that Barney and I look like father and son.'

'Does Barnaby keep the Toyota at Thunduluka Lodge? I was there a few days ago and I didn't see it.' Sibanda could feel a familiar tension as he pondered the 'girlfriend' reference and he felt a kick of familiar jealousy in the pit of his stomach, but for now he needed to put Berry to one side and to get on with the job at hand.

'No, I don't think so. He rents a cottage about ten kilometres down the road towards Gubu on the edge of the game reserve and he usually parks it there. To be honest, it is more his than mine nowadays. Why are you interested in it anyway?'

Sibanda felt that the truth might be counterproductive. Harry Burke was obviously close to Barney Jones and he might just tip him off before he and Ncube had a chance to get a look at the vehicle closely. Young Ruby Bernstein had sensed something not quite right about Barney's attitude and if Ncube was here he would have advised him to go with the girl's instinct. 'We have had a report of a stolen blue Toyota,' he lied, 'so we are just trying to eliminate all the legally owned ones in the district.'

'I have the licence and log book if you need to see them,' offered Harry Burke.

'No, that's fine, Mr Burke. I won't waste any more of your time,' Sibanda added rather abruptly as he rose from the veranda chair and made to leave, 'and thank you for your cooperation.'

Harry Burke watched Sibanda walk away, aware that something he had said had upset the detective. He had been polite, willing with his answers, and accommodating in all ways. He turned to walk back to his seed beds and shrugged his shoulders, realising that the older he got the less he understood the young and their moods.

With a little help from the gumboot-wearer and Ncube's left shoulder, Miss Daisy rolled down the gentle slope away from the farmhouse and coughed into life.

'We have a new suspect, Ncube,' said Sibanda, his foot heavy on the accelerator, pushing Miss Daisy to her limit on the sandy track.

Hanging on for all he was worth, Ncube managed to ask, 'This man Harry Burke?' He was finding it difficult to speak, as the breath was bounced from his body.

'No, his nephew, Barnaby Jones, the guide from Thunduluka Lodge. He had the blue Toyota in his possession on the night of the murder.' He added, 'Harry Burke is a double for Barnaby Jones, I knew they had to be related from the first time I set eyes on him.'

'But what could be the motive, sir? It is unusual for a white man to be involved in witchcraft; they don't understand the first thing about muthi and the power it can give a person.'

'No, Ncube, you are right and that's what makes it the perfect crime. Hunter's Rest used to belong to Barnaby Jones' family. It was taken by the governor in the land redistribution exercise. I noted Jones' hostility and bitterness when I first questioned him. He, like all of us, knows that the governor owns a distinctive blue Toyota and luckily for him his indulgent uncle Harry owns an identical model. This is what I think happened, Ncube: Barney borrows his uncle's car, picks up a hitchhiker, possibly Thulani Mpofu, recently returned from South Africa, takes him to Thunduluka, suffocates him, makes it look like a black magic murder, makes sure bits of blue paint are found on the body and one of the lodge vehicles and then leaves the rest to our imagination. Perfect retribution.'

'But, sir,' queried Ncube, somewhat astonished by the detective's enthusiasm for this scenario, 'surely this matter is still lying in the path and you cannot go chasing after two impalas at the same time. What about Ishmael Naidoo?'

'I'm convinced, Ncube, that Jones is our man.' The detective pressed even harder on the accelerator as he said the name, as if his foot was on the suspect's neck, 'and we need to get to his cottage as quickly as possible.'

'But, sir,' tried Ncube again, 'we may never get there driving like this, Miss Daisy will rattle to pieces like mealie stalks in a storm.'

Sibanda just glowered. 'Stop wittering about this vehicle, Ncube; it's just a heap of metal designed to get us from one place to the next, and we need to get to that cottage before Barnaby "cartoon character" Jones gets wind of what's going on.'

'The cow kicks out after being milked,' muttered Ncube under his breath, 'and you, Mr Clever Detective, will not find the milk at this cottage or get to drink any. You are counting unhatched chicks and leaping to conclusions.'

'What's that, Ncube?' Sibanda asked over the squeaks and rattles.

'Sir, I was talking about the radio message from Constable Khumalo.'

'What did she have to say?'

Ncube deliberately mumbled a few words as inaudibly as possible.

'What was that Ncube?'

'I think you will have to slow down, it is impossible to hear over this din.'

Sibanda eased off the pedal and at that moment Miss Daisy hit a high ridge across the road and went sailing, all four wheels off the ground, before landing with a winding thud. Ncube felt every bone of his spine compact and crunch. Sibanda wrestled with the wheel to keep the Land Rover on the track and after several impressive fishtail skids he managed to get the skittish rump of the vehicle back under control.

It took quite some seconds for Sibanda to address his sergeant, and then it came with no apology for the speeding or reckless driving. 'What was that again, Ncube? What did Constable Khumalo have to say?'

Ncube had to admire the man, he hardly missed a beat. He, on the other hand, was still trying to find out if he was in one piece. 'She says that Ishmael Naidoo and his brother have been arrested,' he croaked breathlessly, in between trying to swivel from side to side to realign his vertebrae.

'Arrested? When?'

'About an hour ago and they are both pouring beans out.' Once again Ncube inwardly congratulated himself on picking up an English idiom.

'What are you talking about, Ncube? What is he doing?' asked an impatient Sibanda.

'You know, sir,' said Ncube, hurriedly realising he may not have quite got it right this time, 'it is as if they have been kicked by a zebra and are squealing.'

'Oh, they are *spilling the beans*, Ncube,' translated Sibanda. 'What about the murder?'

'Not yet, sir. Yesterday at the station, I alerted the road block on the Bulawayo road to check the Naidoo brothers' trucks and to check for false tanks. It seems that the first truck they stopped was loaded with a tank full of new phones. Customs have confirmed that they are undeclared and have been smuggled through the border.'

'Good work, Sergeant,' said Sibanda in a rare show of praise.

'Thank you, sir. I think those brothers realise that they have swallowed the egg of an ostrich and it is more than they can eat. We will hear shortly about the murder. They are nervous and will tell everything. I think we should go back to the station so we can be there when they confess. It is late now to travel further. I am not sure about Miss Daisy's lights.'

'No, Ncube, I am not convinced. I want to get to Barnaby Jones and find out what his story is. He was in the right place with the right vehicle, he has a motive, his name begins with B and there is an unidentified feather, Ncube, found in the victim's throat. If I am right about it, and I have a theory, then it puts the murder firmly at Thunduluka Lodge.'

Sibanda's foot slammed down on the accelerator again and the old vehicle lurched forward like a buffalo bull on its last legs, heading for water. Ncube rested his bruised body against Miss Daisy's seat and tried to relax. The detective was not seeing the obvious, there was something steering him in the direction of this Jones person like a dog chasing a car and barking at the wind of its passing. There were more obvious suspects, including the untouchable governor, the very thought of whom sent shivers through Ncube's complaining spine, and the Naidoos. Normally, the detective was clear thinking and brilliant in his deductions. Something was leading him badly astray and Ncube felt that it did not bode well. The detective was travelling the wrong path, a path that might well be washed away by dangerous flood waters.

Suddenly, Sibanda slammed on the breaks and negotiated Miss Daisy in a difficult U-turn on the narrow track. 'You are right, Ncube,' he said as he struggled to direct the vehicle across the sand ridges of the steep sides of the road, wrenching the wheel with brute strength and no finesse. 'We should get back to the station and eliminate the Naidoo brothers first before we go chasing after Barnaby Jones.'

Chapter 14

Gubu Police Station was busy, even for a late afternoon. Police Constable Zanele Khumalo was at the counter, studiously filling out forms in triplicate. This was a slow process as she was meticulous in the extreme. Her beautiful, if laboriously formed, round hand, upon which she prided herself, took much time to progress along the dotted lines and across the myriad columns. It needed firm and persistent pressure to ensure that the third copy was as legible as the first. Each contact of pen on paper was considered and measured like a chameleon dipping and withdrawing his prehensile toe as he progressed along a branch.

From time to time Constable Khumalo placed the tip of the ball-point in her mouth as if her saliva might revive the expiring ink supply. This was, in fact, a practice she had acquired at school where her soft graphite pencil had needed constant moisture to produce the dark lines her teacher favoured. Now this unbreakable habit served to give her a moment to ponder the next word to be written and to admire the perfection of the words already consigned to the page.

A squash of humanity sat patiently on a bench along the wall to her right; each one awaiting a turn to register the crime against him or her. The complainants had a mixed bag of misdeeds to report. A gaunt old man with a mangy beard and deeply pockmarked cheeks was currently detailing the theft of one of his cows. Constable Khumalo was examining his identity card and, number by number, transferring each corresponding digit into the box allotted by Police Standard Crime Reporting Form 24e/417B, until all eleven lined up in perfection. This took her several minutes. The lost beast may well have been butchered by the time the docket was opened. It would have been roasted and eaten long in advance of the top copy making its way to an investigating constable and completely digested and floating in a septic tank before the first step of intent was taken. The bearded man knew this, but his fatalism had been nurtured by years of disappointment in authority. Protest was futile, haste was unknown. The gentle pace of life in Gubu village was well established, and Chief Inspector Stalin Mfumu's motto of Diligence Above All held official sway.

Detective Inspector Sibanda walked into the office and interrupted the bureaucratic theatre. The audience in the stalls turned their eyes on him. He was the new act on stage. Anything was better than the bland, pen-pushing pantomime they had been watching for the last couple of hours. 'Any news on the fingerprints, Constable?' he asked.

Zanele Khumalo lifted her eyes and indicated the heaving bench of people stacked in a stoic huddle along the wall. 'Maybe tomorrow,' she said, with apology defining her lively features.

'Do the best you can, Zee. Now, where are the Naidoo brothers?'

'They are in the interrogation room, sir. Assistant Detective Inspector Chanza is with them.'

'And Zee,' he added, 'tell Sergeant Ncube, when he can pull himself away from fiddling with that scrap pile outside, that he must be here by 5:30 tomorrow morning. We need a very early start.'

Sibanda walked down the dingy corridor lined with the grimy handprints of many previous users, still kicking himself for his obsession with Barnaby Jones. Was it a jealous impulse that had sent him haring off towards his cottage or did the odds stack perfectly against him? Sibanda was finding it difficult to separate his own emotions from probability. This sort of thing didn't happen to him. He was normally clear-headed and decisive. He had to get a grip on his feelings for Berry Barton before she ruined his career and turned him into the sort of muddle-headed, barely functioning plod he despised. He supposed the fact that he had come to his senses and had turned the vehicle round was a point in his favour. He would need to build on that, but had he made the right choice? Barnaby Jones was a prime suspect with probably more opportunity and intent than Ishmael Naidoo and his brother. He desperately needed confirmation of the victim's identity and his last movements.

As he turned the door handle on what passed for Gubu Station's interrogation room, he took a deep breath, knowing that he would have to prise Chanza away from the suspects before he ruined any chances they had of getting a conviction.

'Good evening, gentlemen,' he said as he entered the grubby, paint-chipped room. No one replied to his greeting. Chanza grunted recognition. The Naidoo brothers merely glared at him from their chairs across the desk, sitting smugly like a pair of crows perched on a telephone wire, waiting for the moment to pick and scrape at an unrecognisable fur-ball plastered on the road. Somehow, Chanza had ceded power; he was just another road kill to them.

'Inspector Chanza, a moment please,' said Sibanda and he ushered the diminutive detective out of the room. 'What progress have you made?' he asked.

'It is obvious to me that the Naidoo brothers are completely unaware that their vehicles had been pirated for smuggling. I am calling the driver in for interrogation tomorrow. It seems he is the guilty party.'

'Perhaps it might have been better to question the Naidoo brothers individually so they had no chance to collude over their stories,' said Sibanda, frustrated by the detective's ineptitude. He barely restrained his anger, he wanted to shout and to give Chanza the dressing down he deserved, but it wouldn't do to alert the Naidoo brothers in the nearby room to dissension in the ranks. His hot air would be wasted on this fool of a man. Chanza would never learn policing; he had no feel for it. Sibanda had given up on the task of encouraging him months ago. The pint-sized toady would study, pass his exams and, because of tribal connections, be promoted.

'They are innocent and any badgering of the witnesses would have been unnecessary and pointless,' said Chanza petulantly. 'I was about to release them before you came barging in.' He glanced down at his watch.

'Is it a coincidence that the interrogation is completed as your shift ends?'

'I have nothing more to say,' said Chanza, walking away down the dark corridor, trailing his hands irresistibly along the paintwork, adding another film to the greasy layer, 'you can finish off here if you feel so strongly about it.'

Sibanda took out his exasperation on his tie by loosening it brutally and ripping the top button off his shirt. 'You'll keep, you sorry excuse for a cockroach,' he muttered towards the disappearing figure. He stepped back into the interview room. He understood that tonight was going to be a very long night.

At 2:30 am Sibanda walked back into his office and realised going home would waste too much time. He had stayed overnight at the station before. This night would be no different. He kept a blanket and pillow in the locked cupboard in his office. Officers sometimes chose to sleep on the bunks in the cells at the back, but bed bugs were now the most numerous inhabitants of the lock-ups. The blankets had never made an acquaintance with soap or water and the bunks' paper thin mattresses managed to attract a healthy population of the blood-sucking mites despite their paucity of comfort. He scanned the cupboard for a clean shirt, something he occasionally remembered to tuck under the files and papers for just such an occasion, but there was nothing. He placed the blanket on the cement floor and with hardly a thought for the arrogant, tree murdering Ishmael and Mohammed Naidoo, and their eventual confession of smuggling, he lay down for a brief night's sleep. It bothered Sibanda that they continued to deny murder. He had questioned them hard and long through the night hoping to get them to crack, with no result, but as he drifted off into a deep sleep, he took comfort from the fact that the Naidoo brothers were now in the cells, sharing infested blankets and stiffening on rigid beds.

Sibanda woke the next morning to the first light fluttering raggedly through the curtains and several early singers twittering their joy at the arrival of the dawn. He took a few moments to distinguish each unique song and took pleasure in identifying them before he hoisted himself up on his elbows and realised where he was. He had managed nearly three hours' sleep. He had barely moved. He leaped to his feet, grabbed his tie, straightened his jeans and threw on his jacket. In the kitchen he splashed his face. The constable on night duty boiled the kettle for him and made him a cup of coffee. The burnt orange granules indicated that this brand had never seen a real coffee bean. It relied on chicory to give it the muddy, washed-out flavour that echoed dishwater. Still, it was hot.

'I am here, sir, and ready to go,' said a sleepy Ncube, still digging yesterday's Kalahari sand from the corner of his eyes.

'You look well taken care of, Ncube,' said Sibanda, noting the clean uniform and shiny Vaseline face of his sergeant.

'It's the little ones, sir, they do not sleep late in the morning so my wives are always up early. They sent this for you in case you didn't manage any breakfast,' Ncube handed Sibanda a well-washed tea towel containing two slices of buttered bread with a hard fried egg in between, slathered with tomato sauce. It was still warm.

'Thank you, Ncube,' said Sibanda. He was touched by his sergeant's wives' thoughtfulness. It was a long time since anyone had considered his wellbeing. 'Now, let's get going.'

As Sibanda wolfed down his unexpected breakfast, he realised that he hadn't eaten anything in nearly twenty-four hours. It certainly hit the spot. 'What do you know about the muthi market, Ncube?' he asked, in between mouthfuls.

'Well, sir, Blessing, my first wife, is very good with herbs, bark and roots. She has a cure for every ailment. It was passed down from her grandmother. She keeps us all healthy with infusions and pastes. The little ones are always clear of rashes and never seem to get colds or infections. When Nomatter's last baby, Theodora, was very sickly and the clinic seemed unable to make her better, Blessing took herself off to the bush for a few days and came home with a basketful of natural remedies. Just as we thought we were going to lose the little one, she began to strengthen and to suck properly. Within a week she was screaming with the power of a baby elephant and we knew she would survive.'

'Traditional healing, banned during colonial times as witchcraft, has been legal again since 2006, but I was thinking more about the market for body parts, Ncube.'

The sergeant gulped audibly. 'I don't know very much, sir, except that huge sums of money change hands.' Ncube swallowed hard, trying to keep his breakfast from resurrection.

'It's big business. They estimate that between three and five hundred people a year are murdered in ritual sacrifice to satisfy market demand in South Africa. That's over one victim a day.'

'That many?'

'That's just the tip of the iceberg. If you take Africa as a whole then the numbers are frightening: Nigeria, Liberia, Tanzania… it's all over the continent. In Tanzania the predilection is for albino flesh. One limb alone brings in thousands of dollars. Albinos rarely venture out.'

Ncube sank into Miss Daisy's ice cream upholstery, seeking comfort and protection. He didn't like the sound of the word 'predilection', it had an ugly ring. If he could have shut his ears to the information that was to follow in the next few minutes he would have been saved the embarrassment of dribbling vomit down Miss Daisy's door, but he wasn't to know that yet, nor to realise the horror of what he was about to hear. It would change his carefree attitude to his children and their freedom. It would make him an over-protective parent, grandparent and great-grandparent for the rest of his days.

'It's children they go for mostly, Ncube,' continued Sibanda, 'I suppose they are small and easily manageable. You see, the organs have to be harvested from the living for the muthi to be at its most potent. The louder the victim screams as their eyes, liver, breast or tongue is cut away, the more potent the medicine. The sexual organs are the most prized, particularly those of a fully grown, fertile man. The dying screams as his genitals are sliced off bestow mighty sexual prowess on the recipient of the muthi.'

'Do you think our victim was alive when... when,' Ncube couldn't continue.

'Probably, and even though he was drugged and drunk, he undoubtedly gave his captors the agonised noises they were hoping for. I expect they had to muffle them and in doing that, they suffocated him.'

Ncube could feel the bile rising and burning as it entered his throat, but still managed to splutter, 'Why are we investigating the Indian and white community, surely this is a black man's trade?'

'Mostly you are right, Ncube, but the Indian community is not averse to charms and fetishes. They have been known to pay for the hands of a wealthy business rival. Fairly recently I read a report of a white police officer stationed at a morgue who harvested human fat to sell on to nyangas who dabble in the black arts. I know it's a bit unusual. Dead bodies are not normally considered any good for muthi. It's the screams of the living, tortured children that add the magic to the flesh.'

'Surely this can be stopped,' said a highly distressed Ncube, 'surely these evil people can be easily identified and arrested. Who would even pay for such muthi?'

'You would be surprised to learn, Ncube, that even upright pillars of the community have been caught. A bishop and his wife had a child mutilated and killed just because a nyanga advised them that this would bring the congregation back to their church.'

Ncube was just beginning to gain control of his urge to vomit. He felt sure that he could subdue the warring demons in his stomach until the detective continued with stories of a barbecued head to ensure success and a plastic bag full of body parts being dragged through the streets by a dog. This coincided with Sibanda taking a bite of his sandwich and squeezing a few drops of tomato sauce out of the side. The sauce fell onto his hand and he licked his fingers. Ncube put his head out of the window and dispatched his own breakfast to the early morning mist.

Harry Burke's blue Toyota sat at the front of the old thatched cottage and the sun now well above the horizon was laying golden glints in shafts across the bonnet, picking out metallic specks so that the whole effect was of stars shining in an evening sky or jewels floating on a still ocean. Sibanda thought briefly how apt the name of the colour was. He jumped out of the Land Rover. Ncube somehow poured himself out. He was still a little grey and his stomach muscles were complaining about the recent ejection exercise, but on the whole he felt much better. He rinsed his mouth with a swig of water and followed the detective.

'Interesting, Ncube, take a look at this,' said Sibanda, running his hand over the right front mudguard. It was quite severely dented and the trim was missing.

Ncube squatted down on his haunches and took a close look at the damage. 'This is more than a gentle altercation, sir, it is a complete alteration,' and he chuckled, pleased with his first-ever wordplay. He had been thinking about the similarity of the words for some time, and finding the opportunity to use them was as good as catching a ten-pound bream on a two-pound line.

Sibanda looked closely at the sergeant and smiled wryly. 'You are right, Ncube, this much damage couldn't have been caused by the Thunduluka vehicle, although, can you see that little scrape there?' he said, indicating a graze low down on the front of the mud-guard, 'That is our match, I bet you.'

'The tyres are right, sir, Desert Duellers.'

They were both still examining the damage when Barnaby Jones walked out of the front door of the cottage, 'Hi guys, can I be of help? Is this about the stolen vehicle?' He had just woken up, his hair was tousled and his eyes were still bleary with sleep.

'Not exactly, Mr Jones, but could we have a chat?

'Sure, come inside.' Barney led them through the quaint thatched porch to the cool dark room that lay beyond. 'Take a chair, Detective, Sergeant. Can I get you something to drink?'

'A soda water for my sergeant and just a glass of water for me, please,' said Sibanda before Ncube had time to open his mouth.

'I see you were interested in the damage to the vehicle,' Barney called out from the kitchen as he poured the drinks.

'Yes, how did that happen?' asked Sibanda.

'I'll tell you if you promise not to tell my uncle.'

'Go ahead, you have my word,' said Sibanda to Barnaby Jones as he walked into the room with a tray of drinks.

'A close encounter with an elephant,' said Barney grinning sheepishly. 'I was with a friend in the park. We were in the middle of a herd I am familiar with. I had a few pods – you know how they love acacia pods – and threw them out of the window to get them in closer so that my friend could get good photos. The light was perfect, gentle, yellow and yet crisp. The elephants were behaving brilliantly. They were close to us, but completely unconcerned. The calves were in among the mothers' legs, playing, wiggling their trunks as though they were unsure of what to do with them, falling over and generally being quite amusing. I was so engrossed I failed to notice a young bull, feeling a bit left out. He obviously believed if he shook the vehicle he might dislodge more pods. He was gentle, only gave me a bit of a shove, but the damage, I'm afraid, is horrible. Uncle Harry might not understand...'

'So you were in the park with your girlfriend when this happened?' asked Sibanda stiffly. 'Can she give you an alibi?'

'Did I say my girlfriend?' asked Barney, a little confused. 'It was actually just a friend; a bloke, Chris O'Connor. I'm sure he will give you the same story.'

Sibanda felt it was time to bring the interrogation into focus. 'Mr Jones, we are actually here to investigate a murder. It is now known that the body you found in the valley had been drugged and suffocated. We have evidence to suggest that the blue vehicle outside was involved. Can you give me a thorough run down of your movements from late Sunday evening until you came across the body on Monday morning?'

'Whoa, Detective, that's impossible, I am the only one that has driven this vehicle in the last week.'

'Exactly, Mr Jones, which is why we need to know who you have been with, what you have been doing and who can vouch for this.'

Barnaby Jones sat down, running his fingers through the thick mane of silver-black hair that topped his handsome face; he looked worried and nervous. A tic developed above his left eyebrow, something Sibanda picked up on straight away.

'I stayed at the lodge on Sunday night,' he said, addressing Ncube, whose round face seemed more understanding than the tight-lipped detective's. 'I had an early morning game drive the next day with the Bernstein family.'

'Who knew you were at the lodge?'

Well, John, the manager, knew I was there. He had booked me for the early game drive. I am freelance, Detective. I only work at the lodge when asked to do so.'

'Did you use the blue vehicle?'

'No, one of the lodge vehicles came to get me. I don't always have the use of this vehicle. I have a very old and unreliable Land Rover I don't use if I don't have to. Routinely, they pick me up.'

'So, the blue Toyota was never at the lodge.'

'It has been there before, but not for some weeks.'

'Okay, Mr Jones, did anyone share your room at the lodge? Can they give you an alibi that you didn't leave that night, waylay the victim, murder him and use the blue Toyota to dump his body in the valley under the cover of darkness?'

'This is ridiculous,' he protested. 'I slept alone that night, but I can promise you I didn't murder anyone. The first time I saw the victim he was vulture bait.'

'But no one can guarantee that, can they Mr Jones? Are you aware that the governor has a vehicle identical to your uncle's?'

'I've seen a few around, the same colour,' Barney hedged.

'He took your parents' farm, didn't he?'

'Yes, but what has that got to do with it?'

'You are bitter about it, aren't you, Barney?'

Barney remained silent, but averted his gaze from the detective.

'Did you plan this murder to incriminate the governor, to get your revenge? Same car; ferocious and fearful reputation. It would have been easy,' Sibanda suggested. He stood up. The aggression in his voice rose until he was a decibel away from a full-throated shout.

Barney stood up, his own anger boiling, and took a step towards the detective. 'This is absolute rubbish and you know it,' he said to Sibanda. 'What is your agenda here? Pick on the white man, harass him until he leaves, until he's tired of struggling and just wants out? Well, you picked on the wrong man here, Detective.'

At that moment Ncube intervened. He could see fists curling and body attitudes hardening with neither man prepared to back down. 'Perhaps now would be a good time for you to tell us everything about that morning,' he said, calming the situation down with his gentle manner, 'and how you discovered the body. Please take a seat, Mr Jones. We are just trying to get to the bottom of this murder.'

Barney Jones returned to his chair and slowly regained his composure. Sibanda did the same and Barney began the story of his morning walk.

'I woke very early, probably a quarter to five. I was at the morning fire by five. The Bernsteins came shortly after. We had a safari breakfast of rusks and coffee. We started out just at daybreak. I picked up fresh leopard spoor quite quickly. I followed it along the road for a kilometre or so and then she turned into the bush. We got out of the vehicle to track her on foot. It was a good track, the light was perfect and the ground soft. We caught up with her just in time to see her charge into the small family of warthogs. It was over in a second, but it was an amazing sighting. The clients were very lucky, that sort of thing doesn't happen every day.'

'Did she make a kill?' asked Sibanda, caught up in the story despite himself and imagining himself there.

'No, and I was glad of that, although I felt a bit sorry for the leopard. It looked as though she had milk and probably a couple of cubs to feed. I think I mentioned my interest in warthogs to the clients and the research project we have on the go. I talked about poaching and the fact that warthogs are easy prey for dogs and snares. I know that Ruby Bernstein became agitated. She's a bit of a do-gooder, I suspect, without knowing anything about the dwindling warthog population and their vulnerability. She gave me a really hard time, said I was putting animals before people. She's a bit of a teenage vixen. Anyway, I gave them all a run down on the project and the warthogs we have been monitoring. I took them to check one of the burrows.'

'When did you spot the vultures?' Sibanda got to the point.

'Not until we actually reached the burrow. The vultures weren't thermalling, they were gorging themselves on the ground. I made the clients move very stealthily and slowly, hoping that we would see the warthog munching on the nearby grass. It was also going to give me the opportunity to check on one of our animals.'

'Not to check on the progress the vultures were making with the corpse?' Sibanda was needling now.

Barney hesitated for a moment and then took a drink from his glass; Sibanda noticed that his hand was shaking. 'It was a morning safari, Detective. I was trying to make it as interesting as possible.' He continued with his tale. 'I could smell the kill from fifty metres away, an acrid mixture of blood and the hot, musty scent of adrenalin. Bill Bernstein spotted the vultures. At first, I was convinced it was the warthog they were eating. I didn't check carefully enough. Pearl Bernstein was the one who saw the feet.'

'Is that when you radioed in?' asked Ncube.

'No, not then. Pearl Bernstein became hysterical. It was infectious. Ruby the daughter also cracked and Bill was shaky.'

'Why didn't you stay with the body and try and chase the vultures away? Because you wanted to cover up your handiwork?' Sibanda was honing in for his own kill.

'No, Detective, I did not harm anyone,' replied Barney emphatically. 'I had three panic-stricken clients to take care of. By this stage, Pearl was hyperventilating. I suggested I run back and get the vehicle. That led to more shrieking and frenzied crying. I had no option but to walk the group slowly to the vehicle. They were my clients and my first priority. There was nothing I could do for the dead man.'

'How did you know it was a man? No one has mentioned the gender of the victim.' asked Sibanda.

'I don't know if the body was a man or woman, Detective, I guess I just used *man* as a generic term.'

'Why are you shaking, Mr Jones, are you nervous about something?'

'I have nothing to be nervous about, Detective, but I did have a bit of a party last night, hung one on. My girlfriend was here and we…'

'Thank you, Mr Jones, we don't need any details about your private life,' interrupted Sibanda. He glanced at his watch. He knew Lindiwe Mpofu would be in the office this morning regarding the disappearance of her brother. He did not want to keep her waiting. The sooner they knew the identity of the victim, the sooner they could pin the murderer down.

'Do not leave the district, Mr Jones, and do not touch the vehicle outside.'

'I need to get it fixed before my uncle finds out that it is damaged.'

'Believe me, Mr Jones, you have more to fear than your uncle's displeasure.'

Chapter 15

'I'm going to take a short cut back to the station, Ncube,' said Sibanda. 'I don't want to miss Lindiwe Mpofu, in case Thulani, her brother, is our murder victim.'

Better a short cut than charging along like a mad zebra, thought Ncube, but all he said was, 'Good idea, sir.' Had he known what was in store he might well have changed his mind and sacrificed Miss Daisy's peace and quiet for his own.

Sibanda turned off the main road onto a dirt track that would lop fifteen minutes off the journey back to Gubu. It cut across the edge of the park. Strictly speaking it was an illegal entry point, only for park staff, but Sibanda knew it well and had used it before.

The morning light was dappled and without the strength yet to stab through the shade and curl the leafy canopy. A cool breeze was swirling in Miss Daisy's cab. Sibanda and Ncube were discussing the recent interview with Barnaby Jones. Sibanda was listening with half an ear to Ncube's thoughts about who was now top of the prime suspect list, but his main focus was on the track in front of him. His eyes had picked up lion spoor from last night. It looked like a good-sized pride. He felt a familiar excitement in the pit of his stomach.

'I still think the governor… Jones is probably… the Naidoo brothers seem shifty…we still have three vehicles to check…'

'Look, Ncube, ahead.'

'What, sir?'

'Lions,' whispered Sibanda, as he edged the vehicle towards the pride. Ahead of them, twenty lions of differing ages lay spread like a tawny tablecloth across the track. They had found the deep shade of an umtchibi tree and were dozing after the night's hunting. Sibanda drove the Land Rover as close as he could and switched off the engine.

'Sir,' hissed Ncube as quietly as his voice would allow, 'do you think this is wise? Do we have the time… we may not be able to…' but he realised he was wasting his breath, Sibanda was so engaged with the sight in front of him he wouldn't have heard a steam train bearing down on him.

Some of the cats lolled with all four legs splayed, some had their heads resting on the rump of a slouched sister. A mother was licking her blissful, purring cubs, their fat bellies witness to a recent feast. A large black-maned monarch was slumped next to the carcass of an eland bull. Various princely offspring hung back from further bingeing, chased by the black-mane's menacing snarl. This was now the king's table and his only. They would be welcome to the leftovers once he was sated. One of the young pretenders, bored with the wait, spotted the Land Rover and took a few paces towards it. His eyes, previously slit and dozing, now opened widely. Two of his brothers followed him. This newcomer had more potential than the long wait for a few sinews.

'Sir, start the engine, they are attacking,' hissed Ncube.

'Relax, Ncube, they are just curious.'

'Look, that one just flicked his tail, isn't that a signal to ambush us?'

'Don't panic, Ncube, they have just eaten, they can hardly move, look at their stomachs.'

'They are coming very close, sir, I don't like it.'

'They are youngsters, Ncube, and hardly a worry. We don't want to upset the male, though, by getting too close to his kill. Seems like it was a big eland. They will be here for some time.'

The young males sniffed the wheels of the Land Rover as they walked past. Ncube could keep still no longer. He attempted to hide under the seat. He only managed to get part of his body in the foot well. His head and shoulders remained at the level of Sibanda's knee. His eyes fixed themselves on Sibanda's face, checking for signs of alarm.

'Don't be ridiculous, Ncube, just stay calm and quiet. They won't bother us.' The young males had now settled behind the vehicle. There would be no escape in reverse.

Sibanda didn't want to disturb the contented family group. He planned to leave the road, to work his way through the bush and around the pride. But Miss Daisy had other ideas.

'Get back on the seat,' ordered Sibanda, 'you look like a squashed baboon quivering down there. We are going now.'

Ncube carefully and delicately unfurled himself. He stealthily levered his bulk back onto the seat inch by inch, never taking his eyes off the ginger haze that surrounded him. Sibanda started the Land Rover. It coughed unpromisingly. Again, it coughed, and with each wheeze the lions became more aware. Several previously uninterested heads turned in their direction.

'Sir,' wailed Ncube, as silently as possible, mouthing the words. His terror was absolute. 'Miss Daisy isn't going to start. We are stuck. We will have to wait until the lions have eaten their fill and just hope we aren't on the menu.'

'Be quiet, Ncube, we can't wait here all day. These lions aren't going anywhere in a hurry, let me think.' Sibanda was getting irritated, firstly with the hold up and secondly with the irrational fear of his sergeant.

'I'm sure it's an airlock, sir, there is nothing to be done.'

'How would you normally fix an airlock?'

'Under the bonnet. I would turn the bleed screw while you pumped the accelerator, but nothing would get me out of this cab with these man-eaters on the loose.'

Sibanda rubbed his chin and went silent. Then, 'Listen, Ncube, I would get out and do this if I could, but I have no idea where to find the bleed screw. You're going to have to have a go. I'll turn the Land Rover side on to the pride. That way you will have protection from the front. I'll open my door to protect your back. I'll have the wheel spanner here in case…' He didn't finish, he couldn't find the right words to disguise the worst-case scenario.

'How can you turn Miss Daisy if she won't start?'

'Watch and learn, Ncube,' he said cheerily. He cranked Miss Daisy in first gear with his foot on the clutch. Every time he took his foot off the clutch, Miss Daisy stalled and lurched forward. Sibanda repeated this manoeuvre several times until he had bunny-hopped the bulk of the vehicle away from the pride.

'Now, Ncube, tell me you have the right-sized screwdriver.'

'I have it here, sir, and a spanner, but I cannot get out of this vehicle. It is not my duty.'

Sibanda lost his temper. He knew Lindiwe would be waiting. They couldn't afford to lose any more time waiting here in this remote part of the forest. 'If you do not get out of this vehicle right now, Sergeant, then I will open your door and push you out in full view of the pride, do you hear me?' The menace was enough for Ncube to nod his head shakily.

'Right, you need to slide to my side and get out of this door,' Sibanda decided on second thoughts that this was anatomically impossible. The idea of Ncube's now shuddering vastness sliding across him was not a pretty thought. 'I'll climb into the back. You can climb out of the door, leaving it open. I'll get behind the wheel and keep an eye out from here. If there's a problem you'll have to dive into the back seat.'

Again, Ncube merely nodded. His mouth was too dry for words, and any that escaped might be disrespectful. Sibanda clambered nimbly into the back seat. Ncube slid with some difficulty across the gear lever and handbrake into the driver's seat. Warily, he placed his hand on the door handle and began to depress it as silently as possible. Any sound would bring the beasts from hell upon him.

'Hurry up, Ncube, you aren't diffusing a bomb, get on with it,' snapped the detective.

Once outside the vehicle, Ncube felt as naked as a baby. He edged to the side of the bonnet and reached his hand around to the catch. He daren't look at the lions at all. Moving in slow motion, he prised open the bonnet lid and wedged the spanner. This gave him just enough room to get his head inside with an edited, but scarily panoramic view of the restless lions. Working mostly by feel, he located the bleed screw easily. He knew intimately every nut and bolt, switch and screw in Miss Daisy's body. He loosened it carefully and then gave Sibanda the thumbs-up without removing his head. This was the sign for Sibanda to start the engine. There was little response. Ncube knew it could take several minutes for all the air to be expelled. He wasn't sure the detective understood that.

Back in the cab, Sibanda was beginning to feel some stress. The longer it took to get the vehicle started, the greater the degree of danger. The wheel spanner he was holding in his hand was more a prop than a weapon. He knew he had the horn which would temporarily halt a charge, but it was still a risk. 'What's happening, Ncube? Get a move on.'

'I think we are nearly there. Am I still safe?'

'Yes, as houses.'

'Keep turning her over, sir.'

It was some minutes before Miss Daisy spluttered into life. Sibanda was relieved. A couple of the big females were beginning to feel threatened by all the activity. Ncube was wrung out. His legs barely carried him the two paces back to the safety of the cab. He dragged himself back to his seat and collapsed in a motionless heap. No words passed between the two for the remainder of the journey back to Gubu.

'Sir, Lindiwe Mpofu is here to see you,' said Constable Khumalo ushering Khanyi's sister into the room. Sibanda rose from his chair and shook hands with Lindiwe. 'Welcome,' he said, 'please take a seat.'

'I am here at your request, Detective Sibanda. Have you any news of Thulani?'

'No, nothing yet, but I need more information so I can file a missing person's report.' Sibanda did not want to alarm Lindiwe unnecessarily. The fragments of clothing were in his desk. He hoped they wouldn't be needed. He began his questioning. 'How old is Thulani?' he asked.

'Thirty-three,' she replied, 'he is the closest in age to me.'

'Height? Weight? Distinguishing features?' he asked.

'All fairly average,' she replied, 'but he does have a scar on the right side of his top lip. He fell out of a tree when he was young.' She had the memory in her eyes as she spoke.

Sibanda smiled at Lindiwe to hide his concern. If her brother was Mufi, then the scar was gone, probably already across the border and concocted by some nyanga, some witchdoctor, into a potion allegedly able to give the purchaser better oratory or more seductive speech. 'What was your brother wearing when you last saw him?' he asked.

Lindiwe took a moment to reply. 'Jeans and some kind of a checked shirt, blue as well, I think. They were new. He wanted to look his best for Mama when he arrived. He wanted to show her how well he is doing.'

Sibanda's worst fears were being realised. The tattered, blood-stained clothes nestled in a plastic evidence bag in his drawer matched that description, but he continued to go through the motions of registering a missing person. 'Is there anyone back in Johannesburg that he could have been in contact with? A wife or partner?'

'No,' Lindiwe replied emphatically, 'Thulani's wife died two years ago, she had been sick for some time. He doesn't have anyone else. After she died, he moved in with me. I helped him care for his kids. I think that's why he made up his mind to move back to Munda. He wanted his little ones to grow up in the village. He wanted them to go to the local school and enjoy the freedom we had when we were little. Joburg is no place for children. It is a dark, grey city, murky, like the inside of a smoke-filled kitchen hut, but with little soul and no tolerance of strangers. No matter how long you live there, you are always a foreigner. You have heard of the waves of xenophobia, I am sure?' she asked.

'Yes,' he replied, remembering newspaper reports he had read of extreme violence against not only Zimbabweans, but every displaced African population that had washed up there.

'Well, after the first violence and burnings Thulani decided it was time to come home. He has been planning it ever since.'

Sibanda knew the moment had arrived that he could not put off further. 'Lindiwe,' he said, 'I am investigating a murder, and the victim so far has not been identified. I don't want to alarm you, but from your description and the timings, it could be Thulani.'

Lindiwe fell silent. Thankfully, there was no hysteria or wailing as might be expected, no rending of clothes or tearing of hair. The woman in front of him remained calm, her distress only displayed by tears welling. Then she asked, 'Do you have a body, Detective?'

'Yes, but it is…' he hesitated briefly, 'mutilated and unidentifiable. I do have some clothes from the victim. Perhaps you could take a look, in your own time, and tell me if you recognise them.' He pulled the bag from his drawer and passed it over to her. She barely took a glance at it before she broke down in tears, and lowered her head onto his desk in sobbing anguish. Sibanda moved around his desk and laid a hand on her heaving shoulders, knowing that little comfort could come of it. He left her briefly to call Constable Khumalo, dragging her away from the fingerprint search. The needs of this doubly bereaved girl were more important.

Constable Khumalo bustled around and swiftly produced a cup of well-sugared tea and a couple of loose biscuits.

Eventually, Lindiwe lifted her head. 'Those are Thulani's clothes. I would know them anywhere. How was he murdered?'

'We don't have all the details, but it seems he was drugged with a mixture of sleeping pills and alcohol, and then suffocated. He would have known very little about it,' said Sibanda kindly. The truth that Thulani was tortured to death would never reach the family from his lips.

'You said the body was mutilated?' The tea in front of her was going cold.

'Yes, but again, we have not had the final forensic report. We suspect that Thulani may have been murdered for body parts and then his body moved to the national park. Vultures and scavengers inflicted further damage,' he said.

Lindiwe began to sob again, absorbing the horror, but it was a calmer, more resigned grief. Sibanda felt confident enough to send Constable Khumalo back to her acquiescent plaintiffs.

'If Thulani was taken to the park after he was killed, where was he killed?' Lindiwe asked through her tears.

'We don't know that yet,' replied Sibanda, realising that he had very little of substance to offer. 'Do you have a recent photo of Thulani?'

'Yes, I do,' she replied, opening her bag and pulling a picture from within the cavernous depths.

Sibanda looked at the image in front of him, so like his sister's, and reflected on the shredded face that until now had haunted him. It was comforting to finally humanise the scavenged corpse, but strangely unsettling in that this was to have been his future brother-in-law.

'This is a start,' said Sibanda. 'We will begin by checking all the buses that come into Gubu from Bulawayo. There are only three or four and the drivers are regulars. Maybe one of them remembers him. Perhaps if he had his seed and plough money on him, he might have been followed from the bus station.' Sibanda rubbed his chin for a brief moment before continuing. 'Did Thulani have any enemies or recent fights? Did he owe money? Is there anyone you could think of who would want him dead?'

'He was a gentle man, Detective, he never quarrelled with anyone… except…' she hesitated.

'Except?' he prompted.

'No, it doesn't matter,' she said.

The detective looked directly into her wide eyes. 'It may be really important, no matter how trivial it seems to you.'

Lindiwe took several moments to reply, as if morally weighing up the information she was about to reveal. Her anguish was reflected in her hands that continually twisted the handkerchief she had been using earlier to mop up her tears. 'He and Khanyi didn't get on. I'm sorry.'

'Don't apologise,' he said. 'In what way? Did they argue a lot?'

'Well, Thulani was always phoning Khanyi. He wanted to speak to Mama, but she would never let him. She always said that Mama was sleeping or that she was in the fields, but you have met my mother and you can see how stiff and sore she is. She never leaves the village.'

'Perhaps she was sleeping,' he offered, 'or didn't want to speak to Thulani.'

Lindiwe brushed aside the possible explanation. 'Thulani had been sending money to Mama to help her condition. He wanted her to get treatment at the hospital. Every month-end on pay day he sent money. Now I find that she never got any of it.'

Sibanda instantly knew what Lindiwe was suggesting. Could Khanyi have been taking the money? Is that why she wouldn't let her mother talk to Thulani? He didn't want to believe it. He looked across his desk at Lindiwe. Was she as devious as Khanyi had suggested and was somehow trying to make trouble for her sister or was she telling the truth? 'Do you have any proof that the money was sent?' he asked. 'Any receipts?'

'No, Detective, I don't. You know how it is. No one uses the banks any more, and there is no telegraphic service in this part of the world. My brother used a "runner". I don't know who he was. A friend, I think.'

Sibanda recognised the practicality of what Lindiwe had said. One of the best ways to keep afloat these days was with a mini bus and trailer, plying backwards and forwards to South Africa as a runner. In these uncertain times, a continuous stream of the disaffected, the disenfranchised and the desperate paid for a taxi ride to the South African border and beyond in the hope of finding work. Once established, they sent groceries, clothing and money back to their families via the returning driver. The system worked well, although border-jumpers ran the terrible double risk of being eaten by crocodiles as they attempted to cross the flooded Limpopo or being fleeced by the more deadly human reptilians that waited in ambush for them on the other side. Sibanda sighed, this grey market would be difficult to penetrate. 'I expect there is little chance of us tracking down the runner,' he said, 'and less chance of him admitting to running foreign currency across the border.'

'I will try and remember something, but Thulani never discussed the details with me. He just told me that he had sent money.'

'Do you really think that Khanyi harmed her brother?'

Lindiwe sat in thoughtful silence and then she added, 'I don't know, probably not. I don't think she physically attacked him, Detective, but she may have stopped him from coming home to the village, to Mama.'

'What do you mean?' he asked. Sibanda had an edge to his voice now; he sensed another revelation was about to shatter his calm and the picture of the girl who was to be his wife.

'Mangwenya, our grandfather's last wife, told me that she saw Khanyi the night that Mtabizi was killed. He had come home to sleep in his hut because there was a fierce storm. She saw Khanyi throwing rocks at him and screaming at him to leave.'

'You think she also threw rocks at Thulani?' he asked, sarcasm creeping into his voice, fuelled by dread and disappointment.

Lindiwe got up and gathered her bag as if about to leave. 'Detective, I am sorry to have burdened you with this. You are her fiancé and this is difficult for you. I must go home now and break the terrible news to Mama. She cannot take much more and I fear for her health and sanity.'

Sibanda immediately regretted his cynicism. Sometimes he could bite off his tongue. It seemed to have its own acerbic life and had let him down more than once in the past with its wilful independence. 'Please sit, Lindiwe, I apologise. I am as concerned as anyone.'

Lindiwe remained standing. 'Detective, has it never occurred to you that Khanyi dresses extraordinarily well for a village girl whose family attempt to grub a living from a few acres of drought-prone sand?'

Now it was his turn to remain silent, all the while the focus of Lindiwe's defiance. He kept his inner turbulence from his face and in particular from his eyes. He had learned over time to control their naturally expressive disposition. He had developed an ability to both glaze and hood them simultaneously. So, while on the outside he appeared passive and in control, his insides felt like one of the churning whirlpools downstream of the Victoria Falls. When he eventually replied, having shrugged his lips, raised his eyebrows and shaken his head slightly, it was merely to reply, 'No.'

Sibanda felt he had not lied to Lindiwe, but he realised that he had been lying to himself. He had always known that Khanyi was a stylish girl. Even yesterday at the funeral when he went to her village for the first time, he had not connected the dots, had not recognised the poverty of the village, its shabby air of make do and mend, contrasting with Khanyi's continual stream of expensive elegance. Could she be a thief?

Lindiwe interrupted his thoughts. 'Khanyi may not have chased Thulani but she found some way to keep him from the village and from Mama. I am sure of that. I know it because…' she hesitated again, and again her moral scale teetered, '…that is what she did to me.' This statement seemed to lift a large load from the short woman's broad shoulders and she sat again, almost with relief, at having vocalised words fenced for years in the diamond mesh of her stoicism.

Sibanda was not sure he wanted to hear another story about Khanyi, but he sensed he was to hear it anyway. 'Tell me about it,' he encouraged with his tone, while his heart wanted to stop up the flow of hurtful words from the moving mouth in front of him.

'Firstly, Detective, you must know that I no longer care what anyone thinks of me, I am who I am, and I make no apologies. I am a lesbian.'

Sibanda realised the courage it must have taken to make this statement to an officer of the law in a country where homosexuality was still illegal, misunderstood and maligned. 'No apologies needed to me,' he reassured her, 'these are still morally medieval times in Africa, we have barely stopped shunning lepers.'

'I appreciate your understanding, Detective, but you know well that your attitude is not widely sown and if it became public knowledge…' she never finished the sentence.

'Go on,' he said.

'I knew from an early age that I couldn't bear the thought of a man dominating my life; the endless round of cooking and cleaning in the house, searching for firewood, carrying water, and the hard labour in the mealie fields which had been the lot of Mama and her Mama, my Gogo, before her. I could not accept the ways of my culture where a man can sit at home and drink calabashes of beer that I had toiled to brew, beat me at his whim, and then throw his drunken body on mine in order to spread his spawn and boast of his manhood. It was a disgusting thought.'

'Times are changing,' said Sibanda, feeling the need to defend his gender against the brutal accusation, although he recognised that there was some truth in Lindiwe's description. Briefly, he wondered what Ncube and his coterie of domestic bliss would make of Lindiwe's take on marriage.

'Yes, Detective, but not fast enough for people like me. I have a friend… a partner… a girl from the next village. I made the mistake of indiscretion. It was a wild unguarded moment and Khanyi saw us. She threatened to tell Mama, even go to the police unless I left the village for good.'

'She pressured you to leave?' Sibanda asked. 'Why?'

'She wanted Mama all to herself. She wanted to be an only child.' Lindiwe reflected for a moment and then asked, 'You know that she is only my half-sister?'

'Yes, I believe so.'

'I do not know who her father is. We never saw Mama with another man, other than my father. After he left her, she went to work in a safari lodge. There was a dissident attack and she was injured. Her knees were badly twisted. They trouble her painfully to this day. She came home to Munda immediately after being in hospital. Some months later Khanyi was born.'

'Did she work at Thunduluka with Thandanyoni Barton?' Sibanda asked on a whim.

'Yes, she spoke of him often. How do you know of him?'

'He works nearby at Kestrel Vale School. I met him recently.'

'Mama will be amazed. She thought he died in the attack. He was shot several times. She thought he hadn't survived.'

'He is alive, and if not quite kicking, then stumbling along quite happily.'

'That is at least some good news to take back to Munda with me,' said Lindiwe, her face clouding over with the re-intrusion of the bad news she had just received. She remained still and silent for a few moments in thought, then asked, 'Do you know that Mama calls Khanyi, Kanku?'

'IsiKanku, the cuckoo?' Sibanda asked.

'Yes, she always said that Khanyi was conceived to the call of the rainbird, the first cuckoo to announce the rain, and it is a bit… ironic…? Is that the word? Because, as Mama has told me, the cuckoo disposes of its stepbrothers and sisters so that it can have the complete attention of its parents. Cuckoo children don't like to share. Kanku is a good name for Khanyi.'

At that moment there was a hesitant knock on Sibanda's office door and the sagging, timorous jowls of Sergeant Ncube appeared in the doorway. Sibanda thought he had never been so grateful to see the comforting rotundity of his sergeant's face.

'I am sorry to interrupt, sir, but you asked me to remind you about your meeting.' At this point Ncube opened his eyes to the fullest extent his weighted lids would allow, and began dunking his head backwards and forwards like a hen pecking frantically at a disturbed ants' nest. Ncube's theatricality was his attempt to inject hidden meaning into the words he had spoken. Sibanda realised that he was incapable of discretion, but felt no irritation, only gratitude for his presence.

'Come in, Sergeant,' he said. 'This is Lindiwe Mpofu and she has recognised the deceased's clothes as belonging to her brother, Thulani. We now need to get a DNA sample to be completely sure of the identity of our victim. Could you attend to that, please?'

Ncube and Lindiwe left Sibanda's office with Ncube clucking over the bereaved woman. Sibanda knew she was in good hands, Ncube was a compassionate man.

Sibanda himself was awash with conflicting emotions. His fiancée had transformed in a few short minutes from the mother-to-be of his children and lifelong companion into a manipulative blackmailer, thief and prime murder suspect. He picked up his phone and dialled her number, a disembodied female voice replied, delivering its irritating message of failure, 'The number you have dialled is not available. Please try again later.' He threw his phone on the desk in disgust. He could murder that woman; he hoped she had the good sense to remain anonymous. He probably wasn't the only one of a million, misconnected callers who harboured such feelings. Better though to focus his dark deliberations on an intangible. His thoughts were milling around, swarming through his brain like bees robbed by a honey badger. They needed to settle and refocus, assess the situation. He sat and rubbed his chin.

Sergeant Ncube knocked again and waddled into the office. 'We have taken the swab, sir, and Lindiwe is with Constable Khumalo. This is a terrible situation, two brothers murdered within a few days of each other. How can this happen? '

'It can and it has, Ncube. Whatever you do, don't mention the connection to Cold War. He will have me off the case as fast as fleas off a dead dog. I want to see this one through to the end.'

'Is that wise, sir?' Ncube asked. 'You are very close to the family.'

Sibanda ignored the advice and snapped into action. 'This is Thulani's photo, get it copied and get all available men out there checking the buses to see who brought him up from Bulawayo. Maybe one of the drivers remembers something. Check all the Naidoo brothers' drivers, maybe he hitched a lift back with them.'

'Yes, sir'

'Thulani apparently used a runner to bring money up for his family,' he continued. 'You have connections in the village, Ncube. See if you can ferret out who he used. Pass word around that we aren't raiding illegal operators or targeting currency dealings.'

'Yes, sir. Anything else?' Ncube could see that his planned afternoon fishing excursion with Phiri was going to have to be put on hold. He didn't think he could make it anyway. Those lions had knocked the stuffing out of him.

Sibanda's hand moved to his chin, his finger and thumb caressed either side of the clean lines of his strong jaw line several times before he replied, 'Yes, Sergeant, ask Constable Khumalo to phone Forensics and get them to check if the feather they found in Thulani's windpipe was this,' and he scribbled a name on a piece of paper and handed it to Ncube.

'Somet… molli… what is this, sir?' Ncube scratched his head attempting to read the words.

'*Sometaria mollissima*, Sergeant. Just give Constable Khumalo the piece of paper,' he said, his customary frustration now back in full swing.

'Yes, sir,' said Ncube, recognising and embracing the return of the status quo, and he left the office to attend to his tasks.

Chapter 16

It had been a second early morning for Sibanda and Ncube. Now they knew the identity of their victim, they at last had something concrete to go on. Sibanda was becoming impatient. No one in the village had seen Thulani since his departure for South Africa. One man thought he might have been on a bus with him, but he was the village drunk and his testimony was unreliable. If Thulani had returned when Lindiwe suggested, then he hadn't contacted any old friends. None of the cross-border taxi drivers were admitting to having carried him.

Constable Khumalo had unearthed some good news though. The *Mediterranean Sapphire* Land Cruiser that hadn't been registered for two years was a total right off. It had been wrecked in a head-on collision with a road train heading from Zambia loaded with copper ingots. It hadn't stood a chance.

'Sir, another bit of good news, I think,' said Constable Khumalo, popping her head around his office door. 'Brian Joseph has been contacted regarding his Land Cruiser and he says that he has converted it to a safari vehicle and spray-painted it safari beige. He is bringing it to the station this afternoon.'

'I won't be here, Zee, but ask Ncube to give it a careful going over. It might still have been able to produce the shard of blue paint from beneath its camouflage. Are the Naidoo brothers still behind bars?' he added.

'For now, but I don't know how much longer we can hold them. We have charged them with smuggling, but they have brought in a lawyer who is insisting on bail,' she said.

'Stall him if you can, I still think they are up to their eyes in this murder, I just need to connect them to Thulani Mpofu.'

'I'll do what I can, sir,' she said, 'and by the way I am nearly through the fingerprint pile,' she added as she left the office.

Right, thought Sibanda, just one more vehicle to check. He left the office and found Ncube tinkering with the Land Rover.

'I have found the source of the air leak, sir, it was very small.'

'Have you fixed it? That was a close-run thing yesterday with the lions.'

'Yes, sir,'

'With rekin, Ncube?'

'Yes, sir, for now at least, but my brother…'

'No more stories of "illegal borrowing", Ncube,' Sibanda interrupted, 'I don't want to be party to your illicit dealings.'

Ncube remained silent. He didn't know what *party* the detective was talking about, but he would have liked a party. All he had experienced were nightmares concerning screaming children with missing parts and a lion walking around with their limbs in his mouth. He had not slept well. Blessing had eventually given him a herbal tea that relaxed him. He had finally drifted off in the early hours. The little ones woke him soon afterwards.

It didn't take them long to reach Hunter's Rest. Ncube had taken advantage of the good road and the current silence of Miss Daisy's springs to doze off for a while. Sibanda noticed the heavy-lidded eyes of his sergeant, and he allowed him to sleep. He needed some quiet moments to try and figure out his approach to the governor's son.

Once through the farm gates of Hunter's Rest, Sibanda and Ncube searched for a suitable incline on which to park the Land Rover. They didn't have to wait long. Some distance from the farmhouse was an earthen slope scooped from the land. It had been deliberately fashioned as a loading ramp for cattle or game. It had also served generations of truculent non-starting tractors. Sibanda reversed the Land Rover up the steep slope and pulled hard on the handbrake. 'Will it hold, Ncube?' he asked.

'It will, sir I personally removed the handbrake cable and ratchet locking mechanism from a Land Rover belonging to the Donnington police that was in for a service when I was rescuing Miss Daisy. They were both in excellent condition.'

'Enough information, Ncube, I don't want to know about your nefarious trade. Do what you have to do, but keep me out of the loop,' said Sibanda, holding up his hand as if to block out the information and wash his hands of involvement at the same time.

'It's alright, really, the sergeant's wife at Donnington has a cousin who is the assistant to the head of the CMED and occasionally warms his bed. They will have a completely new handbrake system installed by now.'

'If you say so, Ncube,' said Sibanda sharply as he strode quickly down the ramp and headed off in the direction of the farmhouse. The sergeant scrambled after him, his shorter legs pumping frantically as the incline of the slope propelled him forward at a faster speed than he could cope with. Ncube caught up with Sibanda at the farmhouse gate, still twenty metres or so from the house itself. The detective had a finger and thumb wrapped around his chin. Ncube held back at a discreet distance awaiting his summons. It came after barely a few moments. 'Ncube, I would like you to scout around the place, locate the Toyota and get a good look at it before anyone knows we are here and check it for damage. I'll interview Ngwenya.'

Once through the elaborate gates, which had previously signified colonial splendour but were now hanging sadly off their hinges, they parted – Ncube towards the outbuildings and Sibanda to the back of the house and the kitchen door. He chose the back entrance because he suspected he would find a domestic who could announce his presence. Ngwenya should be out in the lands; he could chat sociably to the staff and get a good picture of the man and his lifestyle. The kitchen door was wide open.

'Qoki, qoki, knock, knock,' he called out, but there was no answer. The house appeared deserted. He poked his head into the kitchen. To his left was the scullery where the constant drip of leaking plumbing had left a brown silt mark on the stainless steel sink. The offending tap had long ago lost its spigot and was held closed by a large brick wedged over the top. A ribbon of ubiquitous rekin was stretched tightly around the barrel of the tap. Regardless, droplets of water squeezed through the rubber bandage with no respect for its purpose, adding further layers to the rusty tarnish. Sibanda registered the neglect and moved further into the kitchen, all the while repeating the traditional arrival call, 'Qoki, qoki.'

The kitchen had been scrubbed, but no amount of cleanliness could hide the disrepair. The oven door was held in place by an ingeniously fashioned piece of wire which hooked the door handle to a nail hammered into the wall above the stove. The enamel cook top was gouged spotless by endless applications of steel wool, or more likely handfuls of abrasive grit. Several windows were broken, the linoleum had cracked and, in places, relinquished its hold on the floor altogether.

Sibanda ambled back outside wondering if Barney Rubble had spent his childhood racing in and out of this very door. Had he led his nanny a merry dance, beseeching her for titbits from the baking? Had he been spoiled with the limitless love of black arms soothing his grazes and scrapes? Had those hands brushed away his baby tears and taught him to be a boy and then a man?

Barney Jones had to be bitter. It cannot have been easy to give up a ranch such as this. He would have grown up in the knowledge that he would take over from his father when the time came. He would have run a prize herd of cattle, watched zebra and wildebeest as they stole choice grazing from his Charolaises or Brahmans, accepted that the pleasure they gave could never be equated to the financial loss they inflicted on his farming activities. It was no excuse for murder, nothing could defend what had happened to Thulani Mpofu, but Barney Jones certainly had a motive.

Sibanda sighed for the loss of a unique opportunity. The idea of redressing the balance of land ownership was just; the execution, a tangle of corruption and ineptitude. He had hoped that his father, the master farmer, might benefit. He chided himself for his naiveté. Bloated politicians, colonels and cronies got the land. Most of Matabeleland had been given to Shona moguls, so that even the tribe whose blood had watered these arid soils was excluded… except for Micah Ngwenya with a power base that cut through tribal ties.

Overhead a pair of grey louries eating the purple-pink blossoms of a large bauhinia tree gave warning with their parrot-like squawking, 'Go away, go away.' It was a loud, atonal cacophony that was the bane of any hunter who had ever hidden motionless for hours awaiting the arrival of his trophy only to have it scared away by this avian picket. Sibanda looked up warily, knowing someone would be approaching.

An old man was walking towards him from an outbuilding, across the courtyard. His hands and arms were wet and he was wringing them, shedding foam and droplets as he walked.

'Salibonani, greetings,' he called out.

'Sikona, singatcholina Mdala,' Sibanda replied, 'I'm fine and how are you, old man? I am here to talk to Ngwenya.' The man in front of Sibanda was dressed in a suit of ancient khaki drill that had seen better days. It was washed almost white and bore the scars of many repairs. The patched knees had given way yet again and, with it, the resilience of the wearer. There seemed no appetite for further resistance to the inevitability of decay.

The old domestic retainer lifted his lugubrious face to Sibanda's, and from impassive eyes whose lower lids drooped to show the blood-lined inners, he indicated that Ngwenya was in the house.

'I did call out, mdala, but no one replied,' said Sibanda.

'He will be in the front of the house watching television. He won't have heard you,' said the old man.

'Not out on the ranch yet then?' asked Sibanda, 'or back from the lands for his breakfast?' he added.

'Never out on the ranch,' came the doleful reply.

'What? Never? How does the place work, then? Who is in charge?' asked Sibanda.

'Look around you, does it look like a working ranch? The cattle have not been dipped for months, the fences are all down, the pumps are broken, the waterholes dry,' said the old man wearily.

Sibanda had noticed signs of dereliction, but he had not realised the full extent of the neglect. The old man shuffled toward the house. 'I will tell Ngwenya that you are here,' he said. 'Who should I say is visiting?'

'Detective Inspector Sibanda.' He thought he saw a quickening of the old man's gait.

Sibanda used the cook's absence to reconnoitre the courtyard and surrounding buildings. The small outhouse was a laundry and inside an old-fashioned trough was full of soaking clothes. A washing machine stood idly by, exposed, corroded innards signalling a fruitless attempt by someone to get it working. Next door a small wooden entrance led into a dark storeroom filled with piles of salted, drying game skins. Zebra, impala, eland, giraffe and wildebeest hides were stacked stiffly one on top of the other like salted cracker biscuits in a packet. Sibanda looked away in disgust. Someone had been slaughtering the life blood of this ranch with impunity. There was no thought for the natural balance, or minimum numbers needed to maintain and restore populations. He doubted that much wildlife remained on this land. What a hail of bullets hadn't accounted for, wire snares would have finished off. He stepped back into the courtyard disheartened.

The old man came back to lead him through the once-graceful old farmhouse to the sitting room where Ngwenya was lounging in front of the television. He didn't get up, and barely registered Sibanda's arrival. His eyes never left the screen and its gurgitation of gyrating, loosely clothed rappers who belted out their belly ache, paying inordinate attention to their genitalia.

'Can I have a word, Ngwenya?' he attempted over the bass-heavy crump that was bouncing off the elegant cornicing and sash windows.

'Go ahead, Detective,' he said, still not averting his attention from the rappers.

'I must insist that I have your full attention,' Sibanda said, with authority. Ngwenya waved the remote at the screen and the sound muted, but the colourful clowns of street cred continued to jig and mouth their brutality.

'Your father has indicated that you are now in possession of his blue Toyota Land Cruiser,' he said.

'Yeh,' he replied, 'so what?'

'Do you keep the keys to the vehicle in a safe place?' asked Sibanda.

Ngwenya turned out his pocket and showed the keys to Sibanda. 'They are always on me.'

'Does anyone else ever drive the vehicle?'

'A couple of the guys on the ranch have licences. They sometimes drive into town to get supplies. Look, what is this all about, Detective? I am a busy man. Haven't you got something better to do?'

Sibanda ignored the question. 'Where were you last Monday night?' he asked.

'Probably stuck here in this godforsaken dump,' he replied, returning his eyes to the finger-brandishing figure on the screen.

'And the blue Toyota was that here as well?'

'If I was here, it was here, Detective.'

'Can anyone corroborate that?' Sibanda asked 'Someone on your staff?'

'Yebo, all of them,' said Ngwenya confidently, nodding his head backwards and forwards to the imaginary beat of the silent music.

'Have you ever seen this man before?' asked Sibanda showing him the picture of Thulani Mpofu.

'No,' replied Ngwenya barely glancing at the photograph.

'Could you have a good look? We believe this man is the victim of a brutal murder.'

Ngwenya dragged his eyes from the screen reluctantly and flicked them over the face of Thulani Mpofu. 'I said, no, and no it is, never seen him before. Is that all?' Before Sibanda could reply, he was cut off by the violent sounds of a loud disagreement coming from the kitchen. He could hear his sergeant's voice protesting, 'I am here on police business, let go of me. You have no right to…' the voice went silent, replaced by a couple of heavy thuds, then groans and the sound of breaking dishes. Sibanda raced back to the kitchen in time to see Ncube slide to the ground, taking the contents of the draining board with him. He was holding his stomach and gasping for breath.

'What is going on here?' demanded the detective, addressing a pair of farm labourers who were standing over Ncube with clenched fists. Behind him, Ngwenya, who had followed, finally finding a reason to divorce from the television, said, 'Who is this man and what is he doing on my kitchen floor?'

'This man,' said Sibanda, 'is Sergeant Thadeus Ncube of the Gubu police. He has obviously been manhandled by your men.' He leant down and assisted Ncube to his feet. The sergeant was beginning to breathe normally, but was still unable to muster enough air to speak.

'Moyo, Masuku, what is the meaning of this?' Ngwenya barked.

'We found this man in the garage, sniffing around the vehicle. We thought he was stealing the car.'

'Couldn't you see he was in police uniform?' Sibanda interjected.

'It was dark in the garage,' said one of the thugs.

'Then how did you know anyone was there in the first place?' asked Sibanda.

'We saw him enter the garage,' replied the other half of the violent double act.

'If you saw him entering, then you saw his uniform,' said Sibanda. 'Now give me a good reason why I shouldn't charge you both with assaulting a police officer.'

Ngwenya jumped into the fray at that moment, 'Never forget who this farm belongs to, Detective. I don't think any good will come of laying charges.'

'Mana, mana, wait, one minute, if I may…' said the surfacing Ncube, beginning once again to imagine his head on a weighted line trawling the Indian Ocean for golden mermaids. 'I am sure we can sort this out. It was a misunderstanding, madoda, wasn't it? Akula indaba, no harm done.' He continued to attempt to straighten his uniform and to deal anew with the buttons that had welcomed the temporary reprieve from their restraints. A trickle of blood began to drip from Ncube's left nostril and as he dabbed it with his handkerchief, he imagined the solace and comfort that he would receive this evening from his domestic triumvirate. Sometimes it paid to suffer.

'Okay, that's good,' said the governor's son, 'all sorted.' Addressing his staff he said, 'The police here want to interview you to find out where I was last Monday night. I am sure you will remember I was here.' The smile that had begun to remind Sibanda of his father's charm transformed with barely the twitch of an eyelash into a threatening grimace. 'Detective, Sergeant, if you'll excuse me, I have paperwork to attend to,' and he left the kitchen to return to his American gangster friends.

Sibanda knew he had been outdone. Any staff statements backing Ngwenya's alibi would be more or less worthless. He would have to gather them all the same. It did not improve his disposition. 'Ncube, are you up to taking statements?' he asked. 'I am sure that…?' he looked towards the khaki clad domestic, prompting him to fill in his name.

'Chaliss, sir,' the lugubrious man proffered his very English name with very Ndebele pronunciation.

'…Charles will offer you something while you take down the details,' Sibanda finished.

'Thank you, sir,' replied Ncube. 'I am fine now, but a glass of something would be most welcome.'

Sibanda left Ncube sitting at the kitchen table with his favourite orange tipple, taking statements from those staff who worked in and around the house. He needed to clear his head and think how he was going to proceed. He walked out to the weed-choked garden at the side of the house. Like the rest of the property, it was unloved. A few shrivelled lemons clung to a sadly abandoned tree that had embraced a black sooty mould in exchange for water. Overhead, a lethally invasive Zimbabwe creeper was surfing the canopy, reaching its pretty pink bells and tendrils into the gutters. A grove of toxic lantana, incubating deadly berries for distribution to the lands and sensitive rumens by an army of fruit-eating birds, added menace to the neglected patch.

Sibanda realised his quiet corner was not peaceful in the least. The heavy beat of Ngwenya's musical preference continued to blow through a window let high into the wall behind him. He was about to walk away further into the garden when the music cut off abruptly and was replaced by the shrill ring of a telephone. The call was answered by Ngwenya. Sibanda focused on the one-sided conversation.

'Hi, babe,' he said, followed by a silence while his caller spoke, 'calm down, it's going to be fine… No, not right now, the police are here… whoa, cool it, babe, really, it's all under control… In the village, outside Barghees… Yeah, I promise… Yeah, he was fine… I can't come right now, but as soon as they leave I'll meet you in the usual place… Love you too.'

Sibanda walked silently back to the kitchen in the hope that his eavesdropping had not been noted. There seemed to be a general gathering of interested onlookers around the kitchen door. He managed to slip back inside with no fuss.

'How are things progressing, Sergeant?' he asked.

'Just about finished.' Ncube closed his notebook. 'I will type these up once I get back to the station.' He glugged down the last of his syrupy drink and together they walked back to the waiting vehicle.

'What did you get?' asked Sibanda once they were out of earshot.

'Nothing, sir, they all said exactly what Ngwenya had told them to say. They are as frightened as caged hens with a jackal prowling. Ngwenya has them completely tamed. I thought for a minute that Charles, the cook, might sing sweetly, but he seemed to take too much notice of those two bullies.'

'Right, Ncube, we need to get Miss Daisy running. We are going to hide in the bush on the side of the road somewhere between here and Gubu. I overheard a telephone conversation between Ngwenya Junior and his girlfriend. It appears he is heading off to meet her as soon as we leave. I want to get on his tail and see where he goes. She seemed very upset from what I could make out. Something has gone wrong in her life. Could be, she is involved.'

'Just as well we parked on a slope then,' offered Ncube.

Miss Daisy, perversely, started at the first turn of the key without the help of downward momentum. They had not travelled far and were still several hundred metres from the main road when a figure leapt out of the bush and flagged them down. It was Charles.

'Sorry, sorry, to delay your departure,' he said, 'but I needed to talk to you away from prying eyes. I did not tell the truth in the kitchen. I was scared.'

'And now?' asked Sibanda.

'They do not know I am here, they think I am in the laundry washing the boss's sheets. The bricks at the back can be removed, no one else knows about it. I have used it before to…' he halted, knowing that admitting to theft of the boss's socks and the occasional pair of underpants was not best done in front of the Law. 'Well, I have used it before to take my leave without anyone knowing.'

'Go on,' Sibanda encouraged.

'Ngwenya did go out last Monday night. He went to visit his girlfriend. He didn't get back to the farmhouse until the early hours of Tuesday morning. His headlights flashed through the windows of my khaya and woke me up. I checked my clock at the time.'

'Do you know the girlfriend's name?' asked Sibanda.

'No, she only came here once, briefly, but she is very beautiful. I would know her anywhere.'

'Do you have a phone?' asked Sibanda.

From his apron pocket, Charles fished out an ancient brick-sized cellphone that had started life in the early days of the technology. 'Yes,' he said and, seeing the surprised look on the face of the detective, added, 'and it works.'

'Right, Charles, here is my number,' he said, scribbling it on a piece of paper. 'Call me if she comes again, or if anything else unusual happens in and around Hunter's Rest. Will you be safe getting back?'

'Ha,' said Charles, momentarily changing the hang-dog expression on his face for one of pride, 'these abantwana are useless, they may be strong, but they see nothing, notice nothing. I can run rings around them.'

Sibanda drove off, through the farm gates and along the Gubu road. It had been cleared of most of its undergrowth, but after about a kilometre they found a dense thicket and pulled off behind it.

'I'll leave the engine running,' said Sibanda, 'and let's hope Ngwenya doesn't notice any exhaust fumes.'

'This is a good day for Miss Daisy, sir, see,' Ncube said, looking behind, 'just a faint wisp.'

'Tell me about the Toyota, Ncube, did you find anything? Desert Duellers?'

'Yes, sir, it had those tyres. The vehicle had been recently washed and cleaned both inside and out. I can tell that is not normal. It is probably rarely cleaned because they had not even bothered to wipe it down and the lime from the water has left milky drops all over the beautiful bodywork. That car is not properly cared for; it is a disgrace,' complained Ncube.

'Can you stick to the facts, Ncube, and dispense with the automotive sanctimony. Did you see any dents or scrapes?' asked Sibanda.

'No, but look at this,' he said, ignoring the insult. He pulled a piece of crumpled paper from his trouser pocket. This operation required considerable wriggling, effort and manoeuvring to achieve given the narrow cab and Ncube's width.

'What is it?' Sibanda scrutinised the paper.

'It is fine water paper, sir, ultra-fine 1500-grit or perhaps 2 000-grit.'

'And so?' Sibanda asked, getting irritated by the detail and at his sergeant's failure to come to the point.

'See the blue stain on the paper?' said Ncube, 'It has been used to gently remove any different-coloured paint from the car body, leaving some of the blue paint on the sandpaper. I also saw bottles of a polishing compound and a blue-coloured wax. They would have used those to restore the shine and colour to the bodywork. This has been done recently. The polishing cloths and sponges were still damp.'

'So any damage has been covered up already?'

'I would say so, sir. I also checked the tray of the cruiser and some of the paint was beginning to flake. I think that's where Thulani could have got his speck of blue from.'

'Excellent work, Ncube,' said Sibanda.

'I also managed to pocket this, sir, before the thugs got to me,' said Ncube, and after further rummaging and much bouncing of Miss Daisy's springs, he triumphantly pulled a sizeable sample of the Toyota's blue paint from his pocket and showed it to Sibanda, like a child displaying a treasure to his parent, 'from a stone-chip near the headlights,' he said. 'I slipped my nail under it and it just popped off.' He grinned. 'Sukoluhle's brother works at a paint manufacturers in Bulawayo and they have just imported a machine so the ladies can match an exact paint colour to their curtains. Perhaps he can tell us if the two specks are from the same paint.'

'A spectrophotometer?' asked Sibanda with growing enthusiasm.

Ncube looked blank. 'No, just a machine to match paint.'

Sibanda shook his head in exasperation, 'I'm not sure that will be much use, Ncube, we seem to have three blue vehicles in the running for this crime and all of them were painted the same colour. But I suppose there might be some variation so it could be worth a shot.'

Suddenly Sibanda, looking puzzled, cocked his head to one side. He had picked up a noise outside the cab through his open window. 'What's that noise, Ncube?' he asked. The sergeant listened for a few moments. He clambered out of the cab making sure he wasn't visible from the road.

'Ah, sir, that is the sound of Miss Daisy's front right tyre hissing like a spitting cobra. I'm afraid we have a puncture.'

Sibanda cursed using words that Ncube refused to hear. He took a good look at the thicket he had chosen to park behind. In his rush to conceal the Land Rover, Sibanda had not taken stock of the surrounds. As soon as he saw the fluffy, pink-and-yellow flowers he cursed again. He had parked Miss Daisy in a patch of Chinese lantern, Ugagu, whose long wicked thorns could pierce the thickest rubber, even sturdy boots, inflicting a severe wound. Miss Daisy was bleeding air alarmingly.

At that moment the blue Land Cruiser flew past in a blur of speed and roadworthiness.

'Isithutha, idiot,' was all Sibanda could splutter, indicting himself for breaking one of the prime rules of the bush as he watched the flash of blue disappear over the horizon.

The wheel-changing exercise was a mammoth task. It required nearby logs to get the wheel off the ground. Miss Daisy's jack was a failure. Sibanda and Ncube toiled for an hour before they made progress. At least the spare seemed to be functioning. It seemed Bulawayo Central had unwittingly provided the reliable tyre.

Sibanda looked at his watch. He would be late for Berry's History Club excursion if he didn't get a move on. Should he even go? The case was beginning to break, he could feel it. He should really be following up on Barney Jones and now Bongani Ngwenya looked like a suspect. He needed to talk to Khanyi to get her side of her involvement with both Mtabizi and Thulani first hand. No wonder she was so agitated at their last meeting. She must have known that she would be rumbled. He should cancel Berry's excursion, but he wouldn't. He felt that two hours or so wandering among the ancient ruins and carved stones of his ancestors with Berry would give him time to think and pull the strands of this murder together better than a head-on collision with Khanyi. He looked at his watch again. He was grateful that he had borrowed his brother's car for the trip. His battered psyche could not stand any more turmoil, and that included a probable skirmish with Miss Daisy.

Chapter 17

'Be careful, Molesworthy, I think I'm going to fall, hold on tighter,' gasped Pygmy Horton in strangled tones, achieved only from being hung upside down with all blood concentrated on already distorted eyeballs and engorged tonsils.

'Stop panicking and get a move on,' replied Wart, 'I've got a good grip. Stortford and Simons are well anchored. Can you see it yet?'

'I think so,' replied the diminutive form-one who, due to his meagre stature, had been press-ganged into the break-in. 'Is it green?'

'Is it green?' Wart relayed the question to Simple who had hold of his left ankle.

'Yes,' hissed Simple, his nerves stretched to breaking point, his eyes swivelling in every direction like a paranoid chameleon, 'and tell that bloody mini-moron to get a move on, I can't hold on much longer. I told you to take your socks off, my hands are slipping.'

'He's got it,' said Wart, with some relief in his voice, 'haul us back.'

Slowly the two ankle-men pulled Wart from his precarious position, lodged, upended, through the high, narrow bathroom window that served Dube's study, and he in his turn dragged the wretched form-one from headlong suspense over Dube's pee-filled lavatory, clutching the canister of priceless deodorant.

It had been a daring daylight raid that would never have been contemplated if the entire sixth-form were not absent, off on some camp to teach them exam techniques or, more likely, to weed out the psychotic serial killers among them before letting them loose on society.

The first explanation of the absence came from Ma Baker, the second from Stinky who felt he was much closer to the mark.

Wart took possession of the precious aerosol, clipped the tiny and terrified squab across the ears and threatened torture beyond imagining if the story surfaced. Pyg Horton scuttled away back to the safety of the first-form dorm, grateful for a mere boxed ear.

It was the history excursion to Khami that had set the burglary in motion. The fusty smell of ten partially washed bodies, combined with Stinky's continuous replenishment of rancid malodour to the communal stew, had prompted Wart to attend to his own dodgy hygiene. Somehow, miraculously, since the arrival of Miss Barton in the school, he had begun to understand the necessity, even the desirability, of the application of soap and water in copious amounts, something his mother and her continual badgering had failed to achieve. He was not alone. Last night, the night before the much-anticipated history outing, there had been a flurry of sock washing. This was a rare event, even in a school where socks went missing at an alarming rate and where shared and repetitive usage was customary. Overnight, a sad collection of misshapen, heel-holed grey and navy polyester leg coverings spent the night steaming an infusion of toe-jam with a hint of foot-rot into the lungs of the Scott House, form-two dorm inmates.

By the morning Wart had realised that soap alone was not enough. 'We need some smelly stuff,' he confided to Simple. 'Have you got anything?'

'You are joking,' replied Simple. 'I would never waste tuck money on anything you can't eat.'

'We are not going to stand out and be noticed if we pong like barely camouflaged septic tanks,' said Wart.

'Dube always smells like an Italian bordello,' offered Simple.

'What does he use?' asked Wart.

'Some spray mist, body whiffer, eau de chick magnet.'

'Sounds just the job,' said Wart enthusiastically. 'Can you snare some?'

'Unlikely. He doesn't trust me with his study key any more, not since his stash of chocolate-covered caramel balls went missing.' Simple raised his eyebrows and feigned a look of complete innocence.

Wart well remembered the taste of the treats. They had been gourmet fare during a particularly bleak period of sugar deprivation. 'Okay, but we have to get into Dube's study and find that spray. In short, make a plan, Simple,' which is how they came to raid Dube's bathroom, via the tiny roof-light, during morning break.

Wart now had hold of the can, it was nearly empty and would probably only service two armpits and one groin, the other six smelly pits involved in the crime would remain fragrance free, and in the case of Stinky, like a hyena's sinkhole.

The others must not discover the perilously low supply, so Wart kept the sweet-smelling cargo close as the boys raced back just in time to disperse to their various maths lessons. Since the arrival of Buff's daughter at Kestrel Vale, Wart had been putting a real effort into Buff-the-birdman's classes.

Wart's last maths assignment, delivered by Buff's limping frame, landed with a thud on his desk. 'Not bad, Molesworthy, we'll make a mathematician of you yet,' he said as he hobbled on to the next delivery. Wart got sixty-five per cent. Perhaps this studying stuff did have some rewards after all, he mused, and that thought, plus his newly acquired aerospace ambitions, kept him occupied until just before the departure of the excursion bus.

'Hurry up, Wart,' said Simple, 'pass the stuff over.'

'Hang on,' said Wart, as he liberally sprayed his underpants in situ. He deliberately passed the now nearly depleted spray can to Stinky, who used the last perfumed droplets to deodorise his left armpit. All that greeted his right underarm was the hissing of scented air. Stinky despondently passed the canister to Simple who shook it vigorously before lobbing it into the shrubbery in disgust, 'I'll get you, Wart, you festering, pustulous growth, you boil on a baboon's arse…' he shouted after the now-fleeing figure.

Wart halted long enough to begrudgingly admire Simple's creative curses and once again marvel at his D-stream status. He drew a cut-throat slash across his neck. 'Gotya back,' he crowed, as he leaped on the bus.

The journey took just under an hour, but the time passed quickly for the boys, who rarely ventured beyond the local confines unless chosen for a sport's team. Even Ravioli James, whose athletic inability confined him permanently to school, had abandoned sanctimony and was joining in with the general air of celebration. His eyes were glued to the passing scenery, greedily devouring each previously unseen feature as though it were a rare manuscript briefly on loan to a prestigious museum. Wart, on the other hand, had positioned himself directly behind Berry Barton and was examining every glorious hair on the back of her head. Perhaps she felt his intense scrutiny, or perhaps she smelled his clean and perfumed aura, because she turned suddenly and addressed him. 'Your friend will be coming to Khami with us,' she said.

'Who's that, miss?' he asked lamely, transfixed by her smoky-blue glaze.

'Detective Inspector Sibanda,' she said. 'I have asked him to come and keep an eye on you all, make sure you behave like gentlemen,' she smiled, and turned to face forwards.

This was not good news for Wart. He liked the detective, they could talk about birds, trees and the bush in general, but he and Miss Barton were old friends. They would monopolise one another's company to his exclusion. He needed a plan to keep them apart. He had researched Khami Ruins thoroughly, read everything he could find on the heap of rocks. He was determined to keep Miss Barton bombarded with questions that would make her notice him. After all, it had worked with Spirit. He could not see why Miss Barton would not fall for his ruse and be charmed by his knowledge.

As the bus pulled into the car park at Khami, so a low slung, red sports car pulled in beside them.

'Take a look at that hot number,' said Simple, the acknowledged expert in the automotive field. He addressed no one in particular and certainly not the unforgiven Wart. Twenty heads swivelled to take in the sight of Detective Sibanda alighting from the soft-topped Mercedes Benz.

'I bet he pulls with that,' noted Juju Dube, younger sibling of the hated Dube.

'Shut up,' hissed Wart to the assembled boys. 'Don't give him any cred by staring, his head will swell.' But Wart himself needed considerable willpower to pull his own gaze away from the man and machine, both sleek, streamlined and made for one another like a cheetah and its sinuous coat.

Berry Barton rescued the situation with a brusque call for the boys to proceed along the path towards the Hill Ruins and to wait at the top. She turned to Sibanda, who was draped against the door of the Merc, watching her martial and dispatch the boys, not a little aroused by her control and authority, a side of her he hadn't seen before.

'Glad you could make it,' she said, and in the same breath, 'nice wheels.'

'Not mine, I borrowed it from my brother, Xoli. It was a tight run thing,' he said. 'I may not be able to stay the course; I'm in the middle of a breaking murder case. I can probably only manage an hour.'

'That will be fine, I'm grateful that you could come at all.'

'You don't appear to need me anyway, those boys seem pretty tamed. I never took you for a martinet.' He raised his eyebrows and allowed his lips to smile knowingly. It was flirtatious and he knew it.

'Oh, you are such a tease, Jabu,' she said, ignoring his allusion. 'Come, we had better catch up with the mob.' She turned to walk up the path.

Sibanda kicked himself for resorting to familiarity; would he ever learn? He hurried to catch up with her along the path. They quickly fell into old ways and chatted easily as they walked.

'So, you have never been here before, Jabu?' she asked.

'No, unbelievably, I haven't. I know very little about the place.'

'We are headed up to the Hill Ruins right now,' she said. 'This whole area is completely terraced, in-filled with granite and soil, thousands of tonnes of it, all of which had to be lugged up from the valley in pots and baskets. It was a monumental feat.'

'My ancestors must have been made of tough stuff,' he jibbed.

'No, Jabu, you lot are late-comers, colonialists, like the whites. Mzilikazi and the Matabele arrived long after this was built. In fact, we aren't even sure if he knew of its existence. The history of Zimbabwe is the history of colonisation. The original inhabitants were the San people, then came various waves of invasion, from the Torwa, through Rozwi and Shona, then Angoni, all of them colonisers, so you and I are not the only ones who can barely call Zimbabwe home.' Sibanda pondered this for a while. History could be unpalatable stuff at times, he thought.

'Do you see those three platforms over there?' she asked, pointing to three large flattened areas one above the other. He nodded his head.

'Well,' Berry continued, 'those are the foundations for the high-status huts that were built here to house the mambo, the tribal prince, and his family.' She continued to point out various features including the decorative herringbone-, checkerboard- and chevron-patterned walls that were the hallmark of the ruins, until they reached the boys who were waiting at the top.

'Miss, Miss,' called out Wart, 'is this Crocodile Pool where all the virgins were sacrificed?' His wooing had begun.

Berry glanced over the steep gorge into the Khami River, dammed in the 1920s to supply water to the early settlements. 'We don't know that they were virgin sacrifices, or indeed sacrifices at all, but some anecdotal evidence exists to suggest that people were tossed to the crocodiles in the river during rainmaking ceremonies. However,' she raised her voice over a chorus of bloodthirsty sound effects, 'let's not get ahead of ourselves, gather round and let me set the picture for you.'

Sibanda watched from the rear of the group as Berry sat on a rock slightly above the boys, who found slabs of granite or convenient boulders to perch on as she began her tale. He listened intently, completely fascinated by the history of the ruins.

'While the rest of the world was still struggling out of the dark ages, Zimbabwe's golden age of architecture began,' she warmed to her subject. 'Elaborate and enigmatic stone cities flourished across the landscape, spawning tyrannical rulers and fabulously wealthy empires more flamboyant than their pale European counterparts. They basked briefly and gloriously in the African sun before fading without fanfare as all civilisations must. This is the story of one of them…' Sibanda and the boys remained in her spell as she talked of the Rozwi rebel leader, Chagamire, and his conquest of the region, of a dynasty of semi-divine, reclusive mambos with their twisting, secret passage ways and their life of imperial seclusion. She spoke of the wealth they created from trading with the Arabs and Portuguese who offered glass and jewellery, Ming porcelain, silver and firearms in exchange for priceless ivory, gold and slaves. By the time she came to the final days of Khami, when it was sacked and looted by ferocious Angoni invaders in the early nineteenth century, Sibanda was transfixed. The last of Khami's mambos, Prince Mandhlahla, who died valiantly defending his palace, haunted his dreams for some days.

'Any questions so far?' she asked.

Several hands shot up. Berry picked on Dube Junior, 'I thought slavery was a white man's trade, miss.'

'Not exactly, Dube,' she replied. 'Slavery had been around in Africa long before the white man got here. Europeans just took what was a small, but thriving, brutal inter-tribal custom and turned it into big business, you know, commercialised the whole thing and took it to the world stage. Evil under any guise,' she concluded.

Wart didn't wait to be picked, but blurted out his question. He was desperately keen to display his long hours of research. 'Miss,' asked Wart, 'is it true that once the mambo got too old to perform, he was ritually murdered by his most junior wife and then smoked and mummified?'

Sibanda did not get to hear the answer. He was interested in murder in any era, but at that moment his phone vibrated silently in his pocket. He walked a discreet distance from the story-telling before he answered.

'Sir, it is Constable Khumalo speaking. We have been trying to get in touch for some time. There are developments in the Thulani Mpofu case.'

'What have you got for me?' asked Sibanda.

'The phone call that the governor's son made…' Constable Khumalo hesitated.

'Who was it to?' he asked.

'Sir, it was to Khanyi Mpofu, and…' but she heard only silence on the other end of the phone. She waited a few moments before continuing tentatively, 'I have identified the fingerprint. It belongs to Shadrek Nkomo, the cook at Thunduluka Lodge.'

Sibanda took a few moments to bring his breathing under control before taking command. 'Any DNA results back on the knife yet?'

'No, sir, but Forensics have promised me something by this afternoon.'

'Good, now ask Sergeant Ncube to pick up Miss Mpofu and bring her in to the station. Keep it from Cold War for the time being. I will be back within the hour. Keep chasing the DNA results. If we can link Nkomo to Mpofu's DNA then we are starting to get somewhere.' He abruptly terminated the call.

Sibanda walked slowly back to the hilltop, using measured paces to regain his equilibrium. He walked along the once-covered passageway where, according to Berry, many had travelled before him only to disappear at the whim of a despotic leader – a climb to the guillotine, a slow march to the electric chair, a twisting walk to death by reptilian jaws… it was all the same really, each culture planned the pre-death journey with careful ritual and ceremony according to their ways, as if familiarity cleansed responsibility.

By the time Sibanda reached the summit, the ancient patterned stones and crumbling walls had worked their magic. He was calmer and completely focused. Berry sat ahead of him, alone, on a rocky outcrop named 'the mambo's seat'. 'Where did you get to?' she asked. 'Did I bore you witless?'

'On the contrary, it was riveting stuff' He looked around him at the now deserted area. 'Where have the boys disappeared to? Did you push them into Crocodile Pool?'

Berry laughed. He felt her infectious merriment wrap itself around his tensed shoulders, massaging the knots and gnarls that had begun to form and neutralising the bile of betrayal gathering in his throat. 'I have sent them off to the other nearby sites to explore and to perhaps sit quietly with their imaginations. They have all been brought up with a steady Harry Potter diet of witches and wizards, so they should be in their element imagining King Solomon's Mines, the Queen of Sheba or even the golden city of Ophir. Are you okay, Jabu?' she asked suddenly. 'You look a little pale.'

'I'm fine,' he replied smoothly, 'just not as fit as I used to be. The climb must have taken it out of me.' He realised that it was a lame excuse, but she seemed to buy it. 'Did I miss anything exciting?' he asked, changing the subject.

'Not much,' she said, 'just the bit where my Victorian predecessors got involved and destroyed this place, and other similar stone ruins. They were granted a mining licence to dig for gold in ancient monuments. They brutally ransacked buildings and destroyed loads of archaeological evidence. Vandalism for nothing, except here at Khami, in a cellar, where they discovered the mambo's treasure. They melted it into ingots to feed the rapacious maw of Industrialisation. Just think how eloquently all those gold ornaments, jewellery and artefacts could have spoken of this forgotten civilisation. If I could get my hands on them, I would kill them, they were just a bunch of barbarians.'

As he watched her anger grow, he thought of words she had just spoken, 'rapacious maw' and he sensed that he would like to get his own rapacious maw into the now seething Berry. He knew what rapacious meant but what on earth was a 'maw'?

'What's a maw?' he asked aloud.

'What?' Berry looked bemused.

'A maw, as in rapacious?' he asked.

'I'm not sure,' she replied, 'a claw? A paw? A jaw? Yes, that's it, a jaw or mouth, why do you ask?'

'An interest in words…' he suggested mischievously.

Berry began to smile again, this time with a hint of a blush, her anger forgotten. 'Oh, Jabu, you make me laugh; you are so good for me.'

'And you relax me, Berry,' he said. 'I would love to spend the day here with you, but I have to go back to the station right now. You seem to have the boys completely subjugated and under your spell. You don't really need me.'

'I know,' she said, looking at him intently and fixing him with eyes that matched the knowing grey granite of the hills. 'But I wanted you here.' The words fell between them, swallowed by the ancient walls and secret caves of the ruins, leaving a silence that brushed against the stones and hissed like the slithering whispers of the Mambo's courtiers in their ears. Sibanda stared back into Berry's eyes trying to read their message. He leant towards her and took her hand. The physical contact shook him unexpectedly. He tried to speak, but it was several moments before a rational thought reached his brain, 'Berry, I…' was as far as he got before a high pitched voice chirruped from behind him. It was Dube Junior. 'Excuse me, sir,' he said politely. 'I have seen a bird at the bottom of the hill. I don't recognise it. Can you help me?' In reality Dube Junior was not the least interested in birds, but he had been sent on a mission by Wart.

Juju Dube was the most compliant and amenable boy in the Scott House form-two dorm. Despite being well liked, he could never make up for the continual beatings and horrible tortures that his elder brother devised. Wart and his dorm mates were more like brothers to him than his own sibling. He would do anything for them. He had to try harder, though, to make up for his brother. They knew it, so he was the obvious choice for Wart's plan to disrupt the cosy tête-a-tête that was developing between the detective and Miss Barton.

'Do I have to, Wart? It'll be so embarrassing', he had said.

'Yes, Juju, do it for the honour of the dorm and the school,' said Wart. 'I'd do it myself but…' he broke off unable to think of a likely excuse.

Juju didn't understand the need to drag the detective away or what it had to do with the honour of the school, but his loyalty was unquestioning. 'Okay, I'll do it.'

As he walked down the hill in search of the bird, Sibanda turned and indicated to Berry that he would phone her. She nodded her head. The moment had gone and Sibanda was unsure of what, if anything, had passed between them.

'There it is, Detective,' Juju pointed out a handsome bird diligently weaving a circle of sticks and twigs onto a telephone wire. He watched it for a while and marvelled at the exquisite plumage of the crown, cheek and breast that bled from sunset red to sunset ochre – a gleaming jewel amid the desecrated ruin. Even this fellow's yellow highlights would disappear soon, swallowed by the full, flaming red of his breeding finery. Sibanda was reminded of what of Khami's heritage might have remained to fill out the story of the early inhabitants.

He sped away towards Gubu Station, having identified a red-headed weaver to his surprisingly uninterested audience.

The detective was met at the station counter by Constable Khumalo. 'Sir, Miss Mpofu is here, she is in the interview room. I haven't told Cold War anything.'

'Thanks, Zee, anything else?'

'Yes, the DNA on the knife is back and it is a match with Thulani's and the feather…'

'Has been identified as *Sometaria mollissima*, the common eider,' he interrupted.

'Yes, sir,' she replied with amazement.

'Thought so,' he said. 'Where's Ncube?'

'Right here, sir,' replied the rotund ball that emerged from beneath the counter with a sheaf of paper in one hand and a greasy rag in the other.

'Anything for me?'

'Well, we have questioned every bus and taxi driver in the village. It seems that Thulani Mpofu arrived at Gubu late on Monday afternoon, had a few drinks at the Blue Gnu beer garden before catching a taxi to his village around 7 pm. I have the statements from the two drivers plus some from fellow drinkers at the beer garden,' he waved the papers in his hand. 'And,' he added, 'Sukoluhle's brother says the blue paint samples are identical. He is sending me a print-out of the results.'

'Anything on the runner and the money?'

'No, sir, no one is admitting anything, certainly not any cross-border money deals.'

'Did you offer them a moratorium?'

The Sergeant looked puzzled, 'a mori… what… tori, sorry, sir?

Sibanda's impatience, fuelled by the stress of what awaited him in the interview room, finally boiled to the surface. 'Never mind, Ncube.' He waved him aside. 'For now, get that smelly, cantankerous old lady outside fuelled up, purring and waiting for me. It's going to be a long day.' Sibanda spat the words viciously as he strode off into the bowels of the station.

The sergeant stared after him, for once understanding the source of his outburst. 'Poor man,' he muttered, 'poor, poor man.'

Sibanda hesitated for a moment outside the interview room door. This was going to be the most difficult interrogation of his life. He would need to approach it with calm and control. He couldn't allow the jealousy and betrayal he felt to interfere with the need to find out what had gone on between Khanyi, Thulani and the governor's son. He took a deep breath and opened the door.

'Jabu, what am I doing here?' were the words that greeted him.

'You tell me,' he said, drawing up a chair opposite the already-seated Khanyi.

'I don't understand,' she said. 'Am I guilty of something?'

'Your brother Thulani was murdered and mutilated. Lindiwe has told you that, I am sure.'

'Yes, it is terrible; we are all shocked. Mama is refusing to leave her hut. We fear for her. You can't believe that I had anything to do with it. I never touched a hair on his head.' She began to whimper, staring down at the desk. 'You have to believe me, Jabu, the last time I saw him he was alive and well.' She was shaking now. 'I didn't murder him, I promise you, I am innocent.'

'Are you, Khanyi?' he asked. 'Do you have no blood on your hands?

If you want me to believe you then you must tell me the complete truth now. I will do everything I can to protect you.'

'What truth?' she asked, lifting her head so that the silent tears that had formed in her eyes began their inevitable descent over her lower lashes and onto her high cheekbones. At her chin, the drops hesitated as if loathe to leave such smooth and perfect skin behind, but the steady stream that followed those initial tears pushed relentlessly from behind, finally forcing the forerunners to leap off and splash onto the scarred and battered table that sat between her and her fiancé.

Sibanda watched the visible signs of distress on her face and softened his approach. 'I think you have seen Thulani recently,' he said. 'Take your time, but whatever you say, Khanyi, for your own sake, be honest.'

Khanyi's shoulders sagged with defeat. She looked at Sibanda, wiped the tears away with the back of her hand and began to speak. 'About a week ago, last Monday, in fact, he came to the village, just at last light. He had arrived at Gubu an hour or so earlier by bus and took a taxi the rest of the way to our village. He had been drinking and was staggering and almost incoherent. Mama was in her hut. It had been a bad day for her, her bones were playing up as usual, so she had gone to lie down. No one else was around. I saw him walking from the main track towards the kraal. I knew it was him instantly. You couldn't mistake his swaggering walk, even drunk. I suppose I panicked...' She fell silent then.

'Because you had stolen his money; the money he had sent to your mother so she could get help for her condition,' Sibanda filled in the blanks.

'She didn't need that money; she is just an old complaining woman...' Khanyi broke off and looked Sibanda in the eyes. She leant across the table and grasped his hands. 'I meant to pay it back, truly, I did, once we were married...' she left the fatal, damning words of future theft on the table. She unclasped Jabu's hands and clasped her own.

'What happened to Thulani? Why didn't he get to the village?' Sibanda asked her with more steel in his voice now. 'Did you chase him away like Mtabizi and Lindiwe?'

'No, what has Lindiwe been saying? I just told him that he couldn't stay that night. Mama wouldn't want him to stay in that state. I made him believe that she was angry with him for being away so long and would hate to see him drunk. I needed time to think, Jabu, to explain everything to Mama. I knew she would forgive me. Then Thulani could come home and it would all be okay.'

'So where did he go?' he asked.

'He was tired from the beer. He argued with me, said he couldn't walk back to Gubu. He was determined to talk to Mama. I told him it would be better if he came back in the morning and so…' she hesitated for a moment, nervous of the words to come before plunging on. 'I phoned a friend to pick him up.'

'A friend?' Sibanda asked. 'Do you have a name for the friend?'

'Jabu, I can't tell you who he is, but he wouldn't have hurt Thulani. He dropped him back in Gubu late that night.'

'Khanyi, you have to give me the name if you are to avoid charges as an accessory.'

'I can't, Jabu, you don't understand.'

'Does he drive a blue Toyota Land Cruiser?' Sibanda was pushing now to get at the facts.

Khanyi looked up sharply, 'How did you know…?' her shocked reaction gave away the truth.

'I know because I have a witness who can place you at Hunter's Rest, Bongani Ngwenya's farm. He owns a blue Toyota. You called him yesterday, didn't you? You were worried because you knew Thulani was missing and that Bongani was the last one to see him. He drove from Hunter's Rest to visit you yesterday afternoon. He is your *friend* isn't he?' Sibanda was putting two and two together. He hoped that the end sum of Charles' description of the beautiful girl, the hysterical phone call and the speeding blue Toyota added up to an accurate four. He paused for a moment to compose himself. 'You were having an affair with him, weren't you?'

'No, no, Jabu,' she protested, but her expressive eyes darted around the room with the fear of a trapped antelope searching for an escape.

'Don't lie to me, Khanyi,' he said. 'Forget where you are, in a police station, that doesn't matter right now; don't you think I deserve the truth?'

Khanyi looked at him. Her tears had dried and a look of resentment clouded her eyes as she sought to rationalise her behaviour. The same cloud drew in her features, distorting them. 'Alright,' she hissed through clenched teeth, 'I am seeing Bongani. He is very good to me; he brings me gifts. You never did that, Jabu, because you never really loved me. You love this job. You are married to a bunch of uniformed half-wits. You probably see more of that mafuta, that lump of lard, on the front desk than of me. You didn't even make it to meet my mother. Let's be honest, we were going nowhere. I thought marrying you would get me out of this hole, but that wasn't going to happen. Elephants mean more to you than I ever could.' She slumped back in the chair, exhausted from her outburst, defiant in her stance.

Sibanda chose not to reply. He scraped his chair out from the table, a noise that normally set his teeth on edge, but he never heard the irritating duet of wood on bare cement. He moved towards the door. 'You will need to make a written statement concerning your movements on Monday night last, and in relation to your brother, Thulani. I will send in Constable Khumalo to take it down. You will be required to remain in the area until our investigations are complete.' He made to leave the room, but turned to add, 'You are lucky. So far we have no proof of your theft, just Lindiwe's word. Whether you are charged or not depends on whether your family decides to press charges.' He closed the door firmly.

CHAPTER 18

Sibanda went back to his own office via the front counter, instructing Constable Khumalo to take Khanyi's statement and then to release her. He sat at his desk rubbing both hands either side of his face. There would be time to reflect on Khanyi's words later. Could he untangle her accusations against him, sort out the truth from the emotional blackmail? He needed to focus right now on his coming meeting with Chief Inspector Mfumu. It was unavoidable. It would be rough. Sibanda sighed at the inevitability and made his way to his superior's office, thinking on his feet as he went.

'Come in, Sibanda, I was just reading the latest instructions from Chief Superintendent July Chimombe. Have you taken a look at them?' Mfumu asked.

'Not yet, Inspector,' replied Sibanda. Given the yellowing pile of unread missives that lay mouldering in his in-tray, it would be unlikely that it would ever trouble his eyes. The wordy directives would remain obsolete, superseded by another memo, dumped into the bin and incinerated as a waste of precious trees and a toxicity of ink. Before Mfumu had the chance to disseminate the pearls of police wisdom sent from on high, Sibanda began to speak, 'We need to talk about the murder case–'

'Vulture Man?' Mfumu interrupted.

'Yes,' replied Sibanda with scarcely disguised irritation. 'The victim has been identified as Thulani Mpofu,' he continued smoothly, deliberately concealing the information that the victim also came from Munda village and was Mtabizi's brother. Chanza, *The Incompetent*, was not getting another of his cases. Mpofu was, after all, a very common surname in these parts.

'A local man?' asked Mfumu.

'Yes, just returned from a stint down south.'

'So he had some money on him, could that be the motive?' he asked.

'Possibly, although his ears, at least, were deliberately severed with a knife, probably for witchcraft purposes. It is reasonable to expect that the rest of his facial features and perhaps a few internal organs were harvested before he was left to rot as vulture fodder.'

Mfumu nodded, grimaced and moved quickly to erase the unpleasantness painted by the image. 'Any other evidence?'

'We have found Thulani's DNA on the blade of the Buck knife retrieved from near Thunduluka Lodge. The print of one of the cooks, Shadrek Nkomo, is a match for the one on the knife. We are off there now to bring him in for questioning. Forensics said the victim was drugged and suffocated. They have identified a feather in his throat as that of the eider duck.'

'Oh... um... excellent,' said Mfumu, but Sibanda could clearly see that his superior hadn't been able to make the evidential leap, so he spelled it out.

'The eider duck is a sea duck and, as far as I know, is only found in Europe, North America and, I think, eastern Siberia. It is unknown in Africa.'

'So how did it get in the victim's throat?' asked a puzzled Mfumu.

'The eider lines its nest with feathers from the female's breast. The feathers are apparently extremely soft. They are harvested, post-nesting, for stuffing pillows and quilts. Only for the wealthy though.' Sibanda thought unenthusiastically of the lumpy flock pillow that adorned his own bed. It had clumped and bunched. It numbed his ears and felt more like a sack of green apples than a resting place for his head. 'Nowadays feather pillows apparently come from domestic geese,' he continued, 'so eider pillows are rare, but then Thunduluka Lodge has been operating in the up-market arena for over 30 years. It may well have acquired some in its early days.'

'So, Vulture Man was suffocated with a pillow from the lodge, cut up and thrown out for scavengers?' Mfumu queried. 'Well, get on with it, go and arrest the cook, close the case and get on with the paperwork. It must be on my desk by tomorrow morning.'

As he was talking, Mfumu noticed a stray memo that had peeped a corner out of the meticulous stack in front of him. He tutted several times, picked up the pile and tapped it horizontally and vertically until the offending page retreated hastily back to harmonious rectitude. Mfumu looked up from his task, his face a portrait of satisfaction. He was surprised to find the tall detective still in front of him. 'Get on your way then,' he waved his hand in the direction of the door.

Sibanda took a deep breath. 'It is not quite that straightforward…'

Mfumu narrowed his eyes. So, he thought, at last, the rotten rat he had been smelling for some time was now on the table. Aloud, he continued, 'Don't tell me that this is another one of your messy cases, Detective.'

'Murder is only clean and uncomplicated in movies, Chief Inspector,' he said, paraphrasing an Alfred Hitchcock thought, and if anyone knew the ins and outs of murder, it was the unlikely, mild-mannered director. 'I don't think Shadrek Nkomo was working alone,' he added.

'Why not? He was on the spot, had the knife, used it to butcher the victim after suffocating him with an imported feather pillow. You said yourself that his fingerprint is on the knife. He probably needed the money. That was his motive. Have you looked into his finances?'

Sibanda ignored the question. Everyone needed the money. 'We have the problem of how Thulani got to Thunduluka Lodge. He was last seen at his village, dropped off by a taxi. I have a witness who can confirm that he was then driven away in the governor's blue Toyota Land Cruiser…'

'Not the governor,' Mfumu interrupted in disbelief, 'I won't have you bothering him again. You said the vehicle wasn't his any longer. How could you think he would be involved in murder? He is a man in highest office. He doesn't need a few dollars of seed money.' Mfumu had become agitated. His tension led him to his desk for signs of disorder. His fingers twitched with anxiety. They finally lighted on a collection of writing implements already martialled into immaculate size-order like a set of marimbas affixed each to the other in diminishing graduation. He had no alternative but to reverse their status, so that largest to smallest became smallest to largest.

Sibanda watched the troubled man fiddling in his restlessness for several moments before exonerating the governor, 'Not Micah Ngwenya, Inspector…'

Mfumu interrupted again, 'I thought as much,' he raised his previously fidgety hand, palm open, fingers stilled, signalling his relief. It was short lived.

'…his son.'

Mfumu spluttered, 'What do you mean?'

'The same witness can testify that Bongani Ngwenya, the governor's son, was driving the blue Toyota that night. He picked up Thulani Mpofu. The paint found on the victim's body is a match to the paint in the blue Toyota and, furthermore, the paint in the back tray of the Land Cruiser was flaking. Thulani was transported dead or alive in that vehicle. Given that the paint shard was discovered on his shoulder, there is every likelihood that he was lying down in the back of the pick-up,' Sibanda paused for a while to let the facts penetrate.

'That doesn't mean the governor's vehicle went anywhere near Thunduluka Lodge where you say the murder took place,' Mfumu protested.

'This morning, I visited the governor's ranch, Hunter's Rest. There was evidence that the Toyota had recently been damaged. Someone had worked very carefully with water paper, polish and paint to disguise the scrape. One of the game drive vehicles at the lodge had come into contact with a blue vehicle. It all adds up.'

'You went to the governor's ranch without telling me…?' Mfumu was strangely still, a more ominous sign, Sibanda thought, than his compulsive squirming, but he plunged on. 'I have interviewed the son. Despite witnesses to the contrary, Bongani Ngwenya insists that he never left his ranch, Hunter's Rest, last Monday night. He is lying and covering up, there has to be a reason for that.'

Sibanda was right, an unnaturally calm Cold War was a harbinger of nuclear activity. His tirade, when it came, began as a facial tsunami with wave after wave of spittle and snot shooting from every relevant feature. The volume of the ear-bashing rose and clamoured until it consumed the paper hills, threatened the alignment of carefully labelled files and caused the ranged pens to quiver and rebel against their classification. Sibanda had long ago found it useful to perfect the art of selective hearing. When the question came, he was not altogether sure that he was still on the same page as the inspector, having missed every word of the rant.

'How are you going to sort this out?' Mfumu spat.

'I am going, now, to arrest Shadrek Nkomo. I expect you will send someone to pick up the governor's son for questioning.' With a move that he considered to be a brilliant outflanking manoeuvre, he added ingenuously, 'might I suggest Assistant Detective Chanza…' He can take any political flack. Checkmate, Inspector Boris Spasky, he revelled inwardly.

The second tsunami was more vicious than the first. Great waves of bile and fury carried the discarded words of rage and hurled them in a deadly jumble of antagonism and wrath around the ordered office until it was submerged in verbal chaos.

Sibanda chose that moment to exit the office and head for higher ground. He had worked with Mfumu long enough to know that despite any political fallout, the inspector would do his duty. Sibanda suspected his superior officer had only read two books in his life – the Bible and the Police Regulation Manual. He was pretty certain that when push came to a hearty Miss Daisy tshova, Mfumu would take his lead from the latter.

Miss Daisy herself was, for once, not under any threat from Sibanda's pedal-flattening foot as he and Sergeant Ncube drove through the park toward Thunduluka Lodge. It was early evening. The fading African day was casting its enchanted light on the trees and grasses. It dusted the first yellows of sunset across the ancient landscape. Sibanda was convinced the rains could not be far away. They had only tantalised so far with local outbursts. He sniffed the air through the open Land Rover window and the faintest hint of Berry's '*fat, sizzling raindrops on a year's accumulation of dust*' reached him on a wisp of a breeze.

'The rains can't be far off, Ncube,' he said.

'No, sir, they are coming and this year, surely, they will be bountiful.'

Both men sat and contemplated the joy of drought-breaking rains while Miss Daisy trundled along the dirt road that skirted Thunduluka valley. Ncube saw his wives in the lands with their hoes, furrowing and weeding as the young, green mealie stalks forced their way through to the light, tossing aside stones and barely crumbled earth in their eagerness to embrace life. Blessing and Suko would have their newborns strapped firmly to their backs. Each time they bobbed up and down with the motion of the hoe, the lulling the little ones received would penetrate their bones, forever tying them to the land and the rains and the harvest of Africa, like an opium poppy trapping the unwary.

Sibanda remembered a particular season when the rains came late. He had been a boy of nine or ten, old enough to understand the tension in his parents, but still young enough to anticipate the adventure brought by heavy storms and unbridled water cascading over rocks, filling rivers, scouring mud pools and reinvigorating the land. There would be great scarab beetles to harness like oxen, a span of them pulling matchboxes full of pebbles, each one named like the great trek oxen – *Nkulumane, Busumani, Chalibeki* – and then raced against other boys' teams. There would be dams to swim in and rock slides greased with the soapy resin from beneath the bark of the *isiskhukhukhu* bush to slip down. He loved the mud, the tactile pleasure of sculpting animals and baking them in the hot midday sun. Sibanda specialised in elephants. That year he made a whole herd that lasted well into the dry winter months before they lost ears and legs and trunks and eventually crumbled to dust. When the rain came at last, Sibanda saw years drop from his father's shoulders, witnessed the lines in his face soften, saw his eyes come alive. He vowed never to forget the smell of water on hot earth and the sound of the soft hissing of rain as it greeted the grass and leaves, slaked their thirst and washed away their weariness. He finally understood the universal euphoria of an African summer.

Miss Daisy and her thoughtful passengers meandered on past herds of impala, barely disturbing their grazing. A group of zebra trotted only a short flight-distance away, followed by a snorting, high-stepping male keeping a round, beady, white-flecked eye on his harem. A bat-eared fox scurried across the track ahead of them, waiting in the long elephant stalks until they had passed, its ridiculously pointed ears and wide eyes peering through the clump with the loveable appeal of a stuffed toy. In the distance Sibanda spotted a herd of elephant lumbering towards a well-earned drink. They held their trunks down, heads nodding to the rhythm of their gait. Large dragging feet disturbed dust that drifted across the dying sun. It refracted colours of orange and fiery-pink, in contrast to the dull grey of their hide and the khaki of the bush. After a long and bitter day, Sibanda was about to greet old friends. The tension in his jawline and neck melted with the soft, late-afternoon light. A rare smile crept onto his lips.

As Sibanda's strain melted, so Ncube's apprehension grew. He had also spotted the grey monsters in the distance. He felt the first prickling of sweat under his collar because he knew what would happen next. The detective would drive right into the herd, nudging Miss Daisy closer and closer to the waterhole. The Land Rover would take her place at the pan like one of the shadowy drinkers, closed in on either side by a great heaving wall of wrinkled flesh – a mechanical member of the herd. Sweat began trickling down his back. His armpits were awash. Miss Daisy was no protection against tonnes of surging, milling, unpredictable wild creatures whose massive, curved, white teeth could pierce an aluminium body with the ease of an *umkhonto* spearing the soft belly of an ageing enemy. There was no certainty that the elderly Land Rover could speed them from danger should one of the seemingly placid beasts turn vengeful. His own gut rumbled in terror. 'Sir?' his voice questioned tremulously, 'can we spare the time to spend looking at elephants? Remember the lions…'

'No, you are right, Ncube,' Sibanda said reluctantly, 'we should press on. Get Nkomo's version of events.' He drove, grudgingly, past the drinking giants and turned in to the lodge gates.

Sibanda wasted no time in getting to John Berger's office. He found him behind his desk staring at a computer screen, 'Ah, Detective, back again,' said the manager, looking up over a pair of glasses jammed crookedly, at an angle of rare usage, on the end of his nose, 'I hope your week has been more productive than mine. I have been stuck here juggling figures to placate the directors.'

'Interesting, to say the least,' answered Sibanda for whom the previous few days had seemed like a lifetime: Two murders, a funeral, meeting up with Berry again, quizzing the governor, and all the drama with Khanyi added up to a decade of experience. 'You don't seem too busy,' he continued, glancing towards the lodge and the empty chairs and sunbeds.

'No, thank goodness. We are a bit short-staffed. Barney, our senior guide… you remember him, he was the one who first spotted the body… well, he resigned and left a couple of days ago.'

'Any reason for his sudden departure?' Sibanda asked. The case wasn't wrapped up by any means. Could Barney Jones be involved somehow?

'He is going back into farming. Seems the politician who jambanjaed his ranch, Hunter's Rest, has invited him and his dad back to farm again, in a sort of shared arrangement.'

Sibanda digested the Shona neologism that represented the land grab. He was heartened that sense was prevailing. It was a tragedy to exclude such hard-won farming experience and if Bongani Ngwenya's efforts were anything to go by, it was none too soon. Partnership could be the way forward.

'Still, it seems a hasty departure, he was here a few days ago,' he said with his wary detective's hat on.

'Rubble had some leave owing to him so he took it and left early. I think he plans to take his girlfriend away to the Victoria Falls for a few days before getting started on reviving the ranch and the house. It's in a bad state, I gather.'

'I was there recently, it could do with a makeover,' said Sibanda curtly. His mind was already focusing on Barney's planned break with his *girlfriend*. He was gripped with a chest-tightening jealousy. He stood motionless like a leopard. Every muscle and sinew was locked in stealth, primed to pounce. His eyes narrowed, claws unsheathed, skin tight – a killing statue. He heard John Berger ask him something. It took a second asking to break his concentration. 'Sorry,' he said, 'I was elsewhere. It has been an interesting week, as I said earlier,'

'Is there anything I can do for you, Detective?' the manager repeated his question.

'I would like to interview one of your staff members, Shadrek Nkomo,' he replied.

'What's the old man been up to now?' Berger asked, as if Nkomo was a perpetual source of minor irritation.

'That's what I'm here to find out,' said Sibanda. His tone indicated an end to the pleasantries. 'Just a couple of queries, Mr Berger. Do you have feather pillows at the lodge?'

'Yes, we do. It's pretty standard to have one feather, one foam, on each bed. We replaced most of the pillows when the lodge was refurbished a couple of years ago,' he replied.

'Any eider pillows?' the detective asked.

'Unlikely,' replied Berger. 'Nowadays it's all goose down, although the old feather pillows from Thandanyoni's day have probably made their way to the staff quarters. They may have been eider.'

'One last question,' said Sibanda. 'Do you have sleeping pills on the premises?'

'I'm fairly certain that we don't,' said Berger, 'but I will ask my wife. She handles all the health issues and the medicine cabinet.'

'Please check with her and let me know,' said Sibanda.

Berger stood up to leave in search of his wife. When he got to the door, he hesitated and stood for a moment in thought. 'You know, now I come to think of it,' he said, turning to address the detective, 'sometime last month a client complained her sleeping pills had been stolen. I didn't give it too much credence. She was a bit of a ditherer, you know, the nervy sort who thought there were elephants under her bed and lions between the sheets.' He looked puzzled. 'Why would anyone steal pills? A camera, iPod, phone maybe, something small that can be converted to cash. I never heard of pills going before.'

'That's what I hope to discover,' said Sibanda. 'Can I use your office to interview Nkomo?'

'Be my guest, Detective.'

Sibanda was currently sitting in the office's deluxe, padded swivel chair, a far cry from the wooden back-mangler that graced his Gubu Station desk. He had established Shadrek Nkomo's identity and written some meaningless notes on a pad in front of him. Keeping a suspect waiting always heightened the tension, made them restless, nervous and slightly off balance. A sullen but visibly distracted Shadrek Nkomo sat on the opposite side of the desk feigning calm. Sibanda had seen it before, an expression of unconcern plastered across the face of guilt. In many cases, the mortared coating barely disguised the cracks of culpability. Only the top dogs of crime could act out innocence with aplomb. Nkomo was a rural cook. Guile was not in his recipe book.

Sibanda had sent Ncube to search Nkomo's room. It would be riddled with clues. This man was not the head of a witchcraft smuggling syndicate. He wasn't the brains behind the scheme. He was probably seduced by a gambling habit, reduced by alcohol and racy women, or just exhausted by the drudgery of trying to make ends meet in a country whose ends had been pushed so far apart that it felt as if no one, not even Ncube's genius tailor, Phiri, could quilt them together again.

Sibanda stood and walked towards the window. He could hear the Jacobin cuckoo, the rainbird, calling with a tuneless, grouchy, atonal rattle that put a lilting song in the heart of many who were already looking skyward. He thought, as he stared, of Khanyi, her mother's rainbird, her inkanku. He understood why she had done what she had done. She too was not a career criminal, just a desperate girl who had traded her morality and family for a ticket out of rural African purgatory. She was more of a victim of time and place than the manipulative thief she would be judged as.

Sibanda continued to gaze to the horizon, darkened now with battered blue rain clouds, bruising the multi-coloured prism, bleeding into the haze like black tears washing the face of the sun. He dragged his eyes from the unfolding drama on the skyline and turned to address the hapless cook clutching the seat of his chair with the grip of a drowning man and his straw. 'The rains are here,' he said, 'it will be a good season.'

The old man nodded, acknowledging with a slump of his shoulders that he had seen his last rains as a free man. He continued to grasp at his strand of floating grass. 'Why am I here? What have I done?'

Sibanda threw the Buck knife onto the desk, it skipped like a stone before resting inches from Nkomo's face. 'Have you seen this before?' he asked.

'No, I do not know that thing.'

'Your wife recognised it, Nkomo.'

'My wife?'

'Yes. Margaret. She works for the McCleans, doesn't she?'

'My wife?' he repeated, as if he didn't realise he had one. He looked genuinely confused.

'It has your fingerprint on it, Nkomo. How do you account for that?'

Nkomo remained silent for a minute and then changed tack. He picked up the knife with surprise. 'Oh,' he said, 'I didn't recognise it at first, it looks different, but I see now that it is a knife from the kitchen. I wondered where it had gone. I have been missing it.'

Sibanda skipped the obvious fact that it was a hunting knife, not a kitchen utensil. He asked something that had puzzled him since

Shadrek Nkomo's fingerprint had claimed the weapon. 'Why does it have B scratched on the blade?'

The old man smiled. This was an easy question and his answer was ready, 'It belonged to Thandanyoni Barton. He gave it to me when he ran this lodge kudala.' Nkomo extended the penultimate syllable of the word, and raised his tone to emphasise just how long ago that was.

The knife had probably been lent for some task, never to be returned to its rightful owner. Conversion by stealth was not deemed as theft in Africa's lexicon. The detective reached into his pocket. He pulled out the picture that Lindiwe had given him. 'Have you seen this man before?' he asked.

Nkomo barely looked at the photograph before replying, 'No.'

'Look again, Nkomo. Look carefully this time. This is a picture of Thulani Mpofu, the man who was discovered in the valley last week, mfucuza by vultures. Are you sure you have never set eyes on him before?'

'Awami angizake ngiwabeke kuye,' he protested, continuing to deny all knowledge of the man.

Sibanda began to prowl around the office. Nkomo had to rotate his head to keep his eyes on him. Standing gave him dominion over the seated man. Movement gave him the power to unsettle. The cook was not going to cave in easily. He was no hero. Berger had told him he had behaved like a coward in the dissident incident in the '80s. Someone had a hold over Nkomo that was more terrifying than the threat of a mere detective and a murder charge. He pressed on. 'Do you know what DNA is, Nkomo?' he asked. The old cook shook his head. 'Well, I'll tell you.'

Sibanda thought for a moment, trying to find a simple way to describe to this simple man the amazing technology that had revolutionised crime scenes around the world.

'Our body is made up of cells, Nkomo,' he began, 'each one tinier tenfold than the egg of the intwala, the nit, that currently inhabits that greying hair of yours. Like the egg of the inkukhu that you fry every day for your customers' breakfasts, your cells have a yolk. In that yolk lies your DNA. It is unique to you.'

Sibanda paused for effect. He let the words penetrate. 'Do you know, Nkomo,' he continued, beginning to enjoy the challenge of the description, 'every single one of your cells holds the same recipe. The cells in your eyes or your lungs or your toenails have exactly the same ingredients. They have just been mixed differently. Imphuphu, mealie meal, can be cooked many ways, isitshwala, amaqebelegwana, ilambazi, sadza, dumplings, porridge, depending on the amount of water and salt that you add. Your DNA is the same. It can make up different types of cells to act as ears or a heart. Wherever you find DNA in your body it will always be identified as belonging to you.'

Sibanda turned to face the suspect. He looked him directly in the eye, their noses almost touching, 'Clever people have discovered a way to take a tiny bit of your body – a hair, a drop of blood or saliva or a bit of skin. They put it in a mixer, add a few drops of this and that. Under a microscope they can work out your very own, personal recipe. After blending into a soup, DNA looks like nothing more than a spiral ladder like the pod of the umlaladwayi, the acacia tree that is the roost of the secretary bird. It is a more accurate identification than a fingerprint.' Sibanda drew away from the trembling Nkomo, and with a touch of menace added, 'Thulani Mpofu's DNA, his personal life recipe, was discovered, along with your fingerprint on that knife. Now, what have you got to say?'

The suspect sat facing forward, obdurate, lips sealed. A haunted look displaced the coating of innocence on the weather-worn face, dissolved by a fine film of sweat that had broken out of every pore. Sibanda allowed the silence to grow and swell until it swamped the office and echoed against the walls like a submerging hippo sliding soundlessly into the depths. It threatened to drown the guilty man in its wake. He had lost his straw; he had nothing left to cling to.

At the very moment the silence became lethal and Sibanda felt sure his culprit would talk, the office door was head-butted open. A large, bustling Sergeant Ncube stumbled in bearing several plastic bags in either hand. 'Sorry to interrupt, sir, but I think you should see these things,' he said, indicating the bags he had dumped unceremoniously on the desk.

Sibanda glowered, his face crumpled with irritation at the lost opportunity. He snapped in exasperation, 'Sergeant, your timing is worse than Miss Daisy's. This had better be good, really good, believe me.' He allowed the barely veiled threat to settle on the desk next to the sergeant's booty.

Chapter 19

The change of expression on Sergeant Ncube's face reminded Sibanda of a whipped puppy. He immediately felt guilty until Ncube indicated, with unusual animation, that Miss Daisy's timing was actually immaculate. He had adjusted it himself with the very hands that now waved expressively in front of him.

'Sergeant,' Sibanda said, with a hint of familiar sarcasm, 'I don't think we need to share the flawed character of a clapped-out Land Rover with Nkomo here. Perhaps we could leave the mechanical niceties until later. What have you got in those bags?'

Ncube, once again, missed some of the meaning, but he understood the purpose. He let his arms drop to his sides. 'I haven't touched these things with my hands, sir,' he said sheepishly, embarrassed by his outburst. He would not hear any criticism of the Land Rover and would defend her at all costs. 'They are items I found in Nkomo's room. They may be important to this case. There is a feather pillow, a pair of new trainers, some bedding with rusty marks on it and quite a lot of money from beneath the mattress; more than a cook earns, anyway,' he added.

'Right, Nkomo, you know what DNA is now, so if any of these items has been near the victim then his personal mark will be on it. The scientists will find it.' Sibanda picked up the bag containing the shoes and examined it, mentally measuring up the size against Nkomo's foot. 'Are you Cinderella or the Ugly Sister? What do you think, Sergeant Ncube?'

The sergeant was once again flummoxed by what the detective was asking him. The man seemed to speak in strange tongues at times. He had learned silence was the best option in response to these questions that twisted and writhed like a severed mamba head. The detective was already in one of his moods. Ncube did not want to incur his wrath or the sharp edge of his irony more than necessary, so he took the middle road, 'I am not sure, sir.'

'Take off your shoes, Nkomo,' Sibanda demanded. He took the sole of one of the trainers, still in the plastic bag, and laid it against the bottom of the cook's foot. He registered the paper-thin socks and the sour aroma drifting upwards from the horny toes before pronouncing, 'I thought so, the Ugly Sister.'

'Are you saying these are not Nkomo's shoes, sir?' asked Ncube, confused by the gender the detective had assigned to the cook.

'They don't fit him, Ncube. They are too small.'

'You couldn't resist it, could you, Nkomo? After you murdered Thulani Mpofu and disposed of his body for the vultures to clean up, you stole his shoes. They were missing from the crime scene.

He threw the bag to Ncube, who added, 'These look like very expensive shoes, sir, not the sort stocked at Barghees in the village.'

'No, Ncube, you are right. These shoes came from Johannesburg on the feet of Thulani Mpofu.' Sibanda closed in on Nkomo. 'We will find Mpofu's DNA on these shoes, and since the victim was suffocated with a feather pillow, I suspect we will find his DNA there too; his last breath, maybe some saliva, it will be all it takes.'

Nkomo began to sweat profusely. He was shivering in the chair. His head had sunk into his hands. Several suffering groans escaped his tightly clasped fingers.

Sergeant Ncube made a move towards the anguished man. He was a gentle soul at heart, sometimes at odds with the ruthlessness required of a police officer in the Zimbabwe Republic Police. Nkomo, despite the callous murder, was a human being in distress. It behoved this portly peacemaker to comfort him no matter how heinous the crime. 'Come now, umdala, old man,' he soothed, 'tell us the truth of what happened.'

'Ayi, ayi, ayi, I can't,' the wailing continued.

'Umgane wami, my friend,' counselled Ncube, 'this pain and terror cannot leave your body until the words of truth leave your lips.'

This seemed to dampen the old cook's distress. Slowly he sat upright and composed himself before blurting, 'I murdered that man. I put the pillow over his face and then carried his body to the valley.'

Sibanda looked at Ncube and nodded his thanks. The nod also indicated that he would take over now. 'Thulani was discovered to have sleeping pills in his blood. Did you give him those?' asked the detective.

'Yes, yes,' he said in defeat, 'I put them in his drink; it made it easier to mbokotha him with the pillow.'

'Where did you get the pills?'

'I took them from an old salukazi who stayed at the lodge.'

'About a month ago?' queried Sibanda. The old man nodded his head.

'So you have been planning this murder for over a month, before Mpofu even decided to get on the bus from Johannesburg?' Sibanda suggested. 'Premeditated?'

'No, it wasn't like that,' stammered the cook. He put his head back in his hands and began his moaning again.

Sibanda let the inconsistency of the sleeping pills drift. He changed the questioning. 'The victim's body was discovered at least three kilometres from the lodge. Are you telling me that you carried him, all on your own, to the spot where we found him? You are not in your prime any more, Nkomo, this must have been very difficult, almost impossible I would say.'

Nkomo never lifted his head. The moaning continued in soft undulations like the distant call of a lioness to her cubs.

Sibanda intoned with a prosecutor's flair, 'Ngikubeka kuwe ukuba, I put it to you, Nkomo, that you had help, that, in fact, you were just the accomplice, the umncedisi.'

Nkomo came to life at this suggestion. 'No, it was only me, I did this thing on my own,' he said, thumping his chest to indicate his solo guilt.

Sergeant Ncube, who had remained watchful during the questioning, intervened. 'Nkomo, you have the build of a grass stalk, your back is bent and your haunches are withered. Your arms are those of the spider. You could never carry a body all that way. Tell us who set this all up, umdala, tell us who stole that poor man's insides and his manhood and where they went. It will go easier for you if you tell us everything.'

Nkomo slumped in his chair as if his body had been squeezed by a giant python and then discarded, winded and broken. All the fight had been crushed from him. He began his story in the monotone of inevitability. 'He said I would be cut up for muthi if I told anyone what had happened. I would be fed to the crocodiles; the witches who rode hyenas would come for me. He knew nyangas who had magic strong enough to send a plague of chameleons to walk all over me, clinging with their evil toes, unfurling their long sticky tongues and wrapping them around my naked body.' Sergeant Ncube shuddered involuntarily. His sleep would be troubled by such images for a long time to come; he could think of nothing worse.

Sibanda simply asked, 'Who threatened you like this?'

'It is a long story, Detective,' the old cook replied.

'We have time, Nkomo,' said Sibanda, looking out through the window at the gathering gloom and threatening clouds.

'It began many years ago, kudala, before you were born,' he began. 'I was ijaha, a young man then. I was already working at this lodge. Those were uncertain times for our country, like now, I suppose, except that back then everyone had weapons. They showed their discontent in violence. A group of dissident soldiers came to the lodge, running from the government troops and ready for trouble. We gave them food and beer, but it was not enough to stop the bullets. One of them was wounded and badly delirious. He began shooting without any reason. He killed my friend, Moyo, and wounded others. I was lucky, thanks to the intervention of their commander who put a bullet in the head of the fevered, young boy before he could kill more of us. They all left then and headed for the villages on the park boundary. Before they left, the commander told me to tell the government soldiers who would follow up that they had headed back into the park, back to the wilderness. That is what I did. They were never captured. Reconciliation and the Unity Agreement followed soon after. Everyone was friends again.'

'Micah Ngwenya?' Sibanda injected the name. He instinctively understood the link.

Nkomo showed no surprise, he realised that this man somehow knew everything. 'Yes, our governor now, was the commander that saved my life, then. Some years later, when he was climbing the political ladder, he came back to the lodge with his young son to show him the area he had patrolled as a rebel, during the Troubles. We recognised one another and he thanked me for my loyalty.'

'What happened next?'

'After that, he came back more and more. As the boy grew, he spent time with me. He hated the bush and was not interested in the trees and birds. He was a disappointment to his father. I had an old television in my room. He would bring taped cartoons. We would watch them together while his father wandered around with his camera and binoculars.'

'You are talking about Bongani Ngwenya, I assume,' interjected the detective.

'Yes, but then I lost contact with him for a long time. He went to boarding school and to university in America. He returned a few months ago. He came to visit me. He had grown into a very restless young man, angry and irritable like the small badger that lives on honey and attacks even the old dagga boys, the solitary buffalo bulls. Last month he told me he was tired of staying on his father's ranch. I knew staying in the bush would be like a life sentence for him…' The old man stumbled on these words, realising that this would be his own fate.

'Go on, umdala,' urged Sergeant Ncube.

Nkomo continued, 'He asked me to find some sleeping pills for him, said he was having difficulty sleeping since his return. So I took them from an old woman client. I could not understand his need. Why would anyone want a pill to make them sleep after a hard day's work? I would need one to keep me awake.'

'Did Bongani Ngwenya bring the victim to the lodge?' Sibanda wanted to focus Nkomo's story and to get to the heart of the crime.

'Yes, last Monday night he arrived quite late with a man I had never seen before. The man, Mpofu, was returning from Johannesburg where he had been working. I knew straight away that he had been drinking. Ngwenya told me that his friend needed somewhere to stay for the night, and to sober up before he went home. We are not allowed to have guests in our rooms. I protested that I could lose my job, but Ngwenya said he would make it worth my while. I went to the kitchen to do my evening shift. When I got back they had both been drinking heavily. Ngwenya had brought a case of beers with him. Mpofu was sleeping like a dead man.'

'But he was still alive when you got back from the kitchen?' Sibanda asked.

'Yes, but he might as well have been dead. The drink had made him senseless. It was then Ngwenya asked me if I had the sleeping pills. I took them from my drawer and gave them to him.' Nkomo's voice wavered to a halt. He seemed unable to continue, unable to recount the horror to follow, to contemplate the horror that would surely be inflicted on his personage once the confession was in the open. 'I can't go on,' he stuttered painfully. 'Ayi, ayi, ayi, I cannot do this.' His head fell back to the comfort of his worn hands and his groaning resumed.

'It is no use, sir,' said Ncube. 'This man is terrified. I myself would remain silent with such a curse hanging over me.'

Sibanda realised the dread of the night and the terrifying familiars of the spirits were a far more powerful threat than anything the human mind could conjure up in the way of persuasion. Pain and torture were impotent against the more powerful force of the imagined dark arts. Sibanda had never resorted to violence during an interrogation, although he knew of others, Chanza, in particular, who used it on a regular basis. It was distasteful. He was not about to start now on this pathetic old man. He walked over to his sergeant and, in a whisper so quiet that the sergeant had to strain to hear, said, 'Follow my lead on this one, Ncube.' The sergeant imperceptibly dipped his head.

'Nkomo,' he said, addressing the cook in a confident voice, 'you will have noticed I have powers. I can see things that others can't. I can smell things when there is no scent on the wind, and I can hear the bats when they talk to one another with their stories of heavily laden fruit trees and bountiful insects.' He looked across at Ncube and indicated he should confirm these skills.

Ncube had no trouble with this task. He had suspected all of this for a long time anyway. 'Nkomo,' he said, 'this is all true, I have seen it with my own eyes. This man has an unnatural cleverness given to him by his ancestors. He has powers that you can only imagine.'

Sibanda glanced across at Ncube with a look that said, 'Enough, don't get carried away.' From his pocket he produced a key ring, a lion's claw, edged with silver. Berry had given it to him for his birthday that year in England. She said her father had shot the lioness himself, an old and toothless animal, a danger to human life. The silver, Berry said, had come from a nugget discovered by her father during his early prospecting days. It was a precious possession. She wanted him to have it. He had carried it with him ever since. Sibanda covertly unhooked his house keys from the ring, and placed the claw in the palm of the superstitious old man.

Nkomo looked up. 'What is this?' he asked.

'This is the claw of isilwane, the king of the beasts, the most feared animal on earth. No ordinary lion, Nkomo, this was from the lion, Aslan.' Sibanda internally muttered his apologies to CS Lewis, but he hadn't time to create a legend of his own. Aslan pretty much filled the bill. 'He ruled vast kingdoms over the seas, and had powers beyond all knowing. When I have this with me, I am invincible, like the great Zulu king, Shaka. I need fear nothing. It is rimmed by the silver wrought from the bowl of Umlimo, the rain god from the granite caves of the Matobo Hills. The bowl that collected the first drops of water given to Mother Earth. This thing is a sacred talisman that gives me powerful protection. Take it, Nkomo,' and he wrapped the old cook's hand around the key ring, 'it will give you a safeguard against the abathakathi and their hyenas, and the chameleons.'

Even Ncube was not prepared to comment on the tale the detective had told. It could well be true, he thought, but to Nkomo all he said was, 'Now you are safe.' He said it with such genuine conviction that the old man began to spill out the details of the murder as though a long unused tap had suddenly been turned on, releasing a reservoir of pressure. The waterfall of words shocked even Sibanda as he listened to how the young Ngwenya had crushed the sleeping pills, mixed them with beer and poured them down the semi-comatose man's throat. He waited for them to take effect. Sergeant Ncube remained until now spellbound by the story, but remembering the knife, the fingerprint and the DNA awoke to ask, 'Was it you who removed the victim's body parts?'

The old man gripped the key ring with fierce intensity, pressing the claw deep into the flesh of his palm. 'Yes,' he said, 'Ngwenya told me to fetch a knife, said that as a cook I should know about butchering. He reminded me what would happen if I didn't help the spirit mediums. They would remember, he said, and haunt me forever. I sliced off his nose and ears with Thandanyoni's old knife, but I failed to take out his eyes and tongue. There was too much blood and the man was screaming despite the drugs. I think I must have passed out. I came to with Ngwenya slapping me and shouting that I must stay awake or the tokoloshes, the goblins, would get me.'

Nkomo went on to describe how, with a pillow, Ngwenya had smothered the lifeless drunk until he became a lifeless corpse. Nkomo claimed that he had tried to stop the suffocation, but that he was powerless against the youthful strength of the governor's son, and scared beyond reason at the threat of the witches and their requirement for muthi. It was a potent mix of political privilege and supernatural force that a weak man like Nkomo was unable to resist.

'When I woke up again he had already wrapped Mpofu in my sheet. I could see blood oozing from where his stomach should be and… lower down.' Ncube shuddered and wished he hadn't asked the question.

'What happened next, old man?' asked Sibanda.

'Ngwenya gave me an ice cream container covered in blood and told me to clean it up and to hide it at the back of the freezer. I never looked inside, but I think it contained the body parts of that poor man.' Sibanda remembered the iced water he had drunk the morning when he had first arrived at Thunduluka Lodge. The ice cubes that he had so readily appreciated had probably solidified inches from the congealed and slowly freezing facial features of Thulani Mpofu. 'There is always a worm in the apple of paradise,' he said, more to himself than to his distracted audience. 'Did you move the body, Nkomo?'

'I helped Ngwenya drag it to the door and then carry it to his vehicle. We removed the sheet first–'

'The blue Toyota?' Sibanda interrupted.

'Yes, and then Ngwenya drove it to the valley. We left the body there.'

'Did he hit one of the lodge vehicles?'

'He just touched one of them. I was terrified that someone would have heard the collision, but it was late by then and no one else was awake. I was grateful that it was only a small scrape. I thought no one would notice.'

A flash of lightning lit up the darkened office, followed by a deafening clap of thunder that startled all three men, so focused had they been on the telling of and the listening to the murderous tale. Sergeant Ncube jumped as if stung by a scorpion. One of his cousins had been struck by lightning and effectively fried. He had seen the body. He had never recovered. Sergeant Ncube knew well that statistics indicated Zimbabwe was high up on the table of lightning deaths. It had gone head to head every year with drownings for top of the fatality league until HIV/AIDS came and blew them both away like insignificant fluff.

'Is this the sheet?' Sergeant Ncube asked, indicating one of the bags he had brought from the cook's room, hoping to cover his disquiet with a question. He opened it up and displayed the stained bedcover to the cook. Sibanda thought how much it resembled the Shroud of Turin, bearing a faint rusty imprint where the organs had been incised. Their removal had stained the sheet with oozing bodily fluids. He knew exactly what had been robbed from the corpse.

Nkomo confirmed with a bowed head. 'Yes, I tried to bleach it, but I couldn't get rid of the stains. Ngwenya told me to burn it, but how was I to afford a new one?'

'Is the ice cream container still in the freezer?' Sibanda asked.

'No, Ngwenya collected it last night.'

'Did he say anything to you? Indicate what he was up to?' Sibanda asked.

'He was very excited, and just said that the plastic container was his ticket back to America. I was glad to be rid of it.'

'You went to check on vulture activity early the next morning, didn't you?' accused the detective.

'Ngwenya told me that the vultures would cover up for us. They would eat away all the evidence. The police would think it was just a stupid, drunk man who had wandered into the valley and been eaten by lions,' said Nkomo. 'I needed to check.'

Ncube shuffled uncomfortably at the scenario he had concluded. He kept his red face averted from the detective's eye line. 'You were unlucky, Nkomo,' he said. 'If Detective Inspector Sibanda hadn't been assigned to this case you could well have got away with it. This detective can see through walls.'

'Maybe if I hadn't dropped the knife…' the cook's voice trailed off. He realised his thought was futile. It was over. There was nothing more to say.

Sibanda glanced down at the old man's hand still tightly closed over Berry's key ring as if his life depended on it. It would be unkindness now to retrieve it. Perhaps it was time to let go of trinkets and memories that could never bring happiness, just an unrelenting desire for the unattainable. He was like a solitary African hunting dog hoping to pull down a buffalo. The prey was out of his league.

Another flash of lightning illuminated the faces of the three men. Sibanda's creased brow and tense jaw line indicated deep and troubled thought. Sergeant Ncube was trembling slightly, counting seconds under his breath and tensing for the inevitable bellow of thunder. Nkomo had turned a ghastly grey as he ruminated on his hopeless fate. The noise which suddenly broke the silence was not the rumbling of a boulder racing across the heavens, but the sweet, moonlit singing of the fiery-necked nightjar. Sergeant Ncube was the first to react. 'Your phone, sir,' he said.

Sibanda looked down at the number; he didn't recognise it. He left the office to take the call in private. 'Take over, Sergeant,' he said as he stepped into the promising night.

'Yimi, it is me, sir, Chaliss,' said the voice from the mobile phone.

Chapter 20

It took a few moments for Sibanda to remember Charles was the lugubrious cook from Hunter's Rest. 'Yes, Charles,' he replied, 'is this important? I am in the middle of something.'

'I think so, Detective, Bongani Ngwenya has left the ranch.'

'What do you mean, *left the ranch*? Gone for a drive? Gone into town?

'Gone for good.'

'Have the police been there yet?' Sibanda asked.

'The police?' Now it was Charles' turn to sound confused. 'No, we have seen no police since your visit.'

'Charles, it is important that you tell me everything you can remember about Ngwenya's departure. For instance, did he take his passport?'

'I think so,' said the wily old man. 'He emptied the wall safe of everything. He packed all his clothes. He even took some food from the deep freeze, said it was to sustain him on his journey. It was odd, really…'

'Why odd?' asked the detective.

'Well, he smiled at me as he said it, and he has never smiled at me before.'

'Was the food in an old ice cream container?'

'How did you know that?' Charles asked.

'Never mind.' The detective sidestepped the question and asked his own, 'How long ago did he leave?'

'Five or ten minutes ago.'

'Charles, stay where you are and phone me if anything else unusual happens. You have done a good job, siyabonga.'

Sibanda felt the first raindrop on his shoulder as he turned to go back inside the office. It hit hard with the thud of a leaden drop. It was followed rapidly by its twin, which laid claim to Sibanda's right cheek. He barely registered the moisture as it progressed down his face. 'Sergeant,' he instructed, as he thrust the door open, 'get this man cuffed. Read him his rights. You will need to phone the station. See if they can rustle up some transport to fetch you, or better still, see if John Berger can organise a ride in. I am taking the Land Rover. Bongani Ngwenya is making a run for it. If I'm quick, I can cut him off before he gets too far south.'

Sergeant Ncube barely had time to mutter, 'But, sir,' before Sibanda had disappeared into the night and an increasingly angry storm. What he had wanted to say was, 'But, sir, Miss Daisy may not like the rain, she has never been in such a storm since she came from the wrecker's yard. I am not sure if she is watertight. You may need me to keep her going,' but the detective was already behind the wheel, perched on the pastel pink driver's seat before Ncube's thoughts had time to form themselves into words.

Miss Daisy shot out of the lodge gates and onto the gravel track that led deep into the wilderness. Sibanda felt that he could get ahead of Ngwenya by taking a short cut through the remote area of the park, and then turning left along a rarely used dirt track that would intersect with Ngwenya's route to the border. The track he planned to take was little more than an elephant path connecting a couple of waterholes. It would be a risk, but there was no alternative. Gubu Station had no vehicle that could reliably chase a Toyota Land Cruiser. It was an open secret that the border was a smuggler's delight. Ngwenya would not be caught at Passport Control. Immigration would never even see his passport. The border was porous, at best a succession of illegal river crossings that obviated the necessity for official papers.

Sibanda quickly discovered to his irritation that the Land Rover's headlights were feeble. They would be of little use in the moon-smothering storm he was heading into. With each bump and dip of the ungraded gravel they flickered ominously. He hoped they would hold out. Travelling at this speed in game country was folly at the best of times. Without lights it would be lethal.

He was grateful in some ways his sergeant wasn't with him. His foot was flat to the boards and the speeding vehicle was producing rattles and squeaks of an increasingly intrusive nature, so Ncube would have been having a fit of the sulks by now and giving him the silent treatment. On the other hand, the sergeant's vast bulk at his side was reassuring. Two pairs of eyes peeled and trained keenly each on his own side, warning against a dazzled and confused kudu choosing that moment to leap across the track, would have been comforting.

More lightning flashed ahead, illuminating the road for some metres and allowing Sibanda a few moments' respite from his intense concentration. He briefly caught sight of a small herd of giraffe flared by the phosphorescence. They turned, disturbed by Miss Daisy's clattering progress, and swayed a few metres further away from the road, never taking their haughty noses off his progress. They served to remind Sibanda of the dangerous game of Russian roulette he was playing.

The detective cursed himself for having assumed that Assistant Detective Inspector Chanza would head out for Hunter's Rest immediately. The man had cultivated the art of the dilatory to perfection. He was known to dawdle and lag, shuffling papers and walking aimlessly around the office, issuing spurious instructions, until his shift was up.

Sibanda had known that Bongani Ngwenya was in this up to his armpits. He needed the security of Nkomo's confession to be sure. Had his obsession with Berry and his problems with Khanyi clouded his judgement? Why had he got so carried away by the thought of Barney Jones as the culprit? He had not been thinking incisively of late. The edges of his life were becoming blurred. He should have gone out to Hunter's Rest himself, immediately. Ncube could have cracked Nkomo on his own.

Large raindrops were beginning to bounce off Miss Daisy. The wind was bending the trees, waving branches like giant, green tentacles grasping at the night sky in a desperate lunge for the sweepings of the now rapidly falling water. He turned on the wipers and held his breath. The metal arms swung uselessly backwards and forwards in a repetitive arc, their rubber long perished to granules. The fast and torrentially arriving drops remained unmoved until they slid down the windscreen, confusing Sibanda's already obscured vision. He had no option but to slow down and as he did so, he let loose a string of curses that would have shocked even the hardened patrons of the Blue Gnu.

The windscreen was beginning to fug, adding another layer of difficulty to his progress. The vintage of the vehicle predated the luxury of a blast of cold air to clear the mist. It would have to be supplied by natural means. Sibanda rolled down the window hoping to equalise the temperature inside the old crock. It worked after a fashion. It cleared some of the accumulated condensation, but not enough. He needed a cloth of some kind to cut through the haze. All he found was a greasy old rag that Ncube kept for Miss Daisy's various ailments. It could only add oil to the cloudy mix, so he discarded it. In desperation, he ripped off his shirt and began to steadily wipe away the murkiness as he drove, one hand on the wheel and one on the windscreen. Rain poured in through the open window, breathtaking and needle-like. It ran over Sibanda's bare torso, stinging at first contact and then, seduced by perfection, changing moods and leisurely caressing his muscled frame.

He was travelling so slowly now that he caught a rare sight of an isambane, an antbear, zigzagging along on the verge. That he should almost be out-run by this trundling mongrel of a creature with its donkey's ears, hump back, pig's snout and kangaroo tail made him realise the futility of his chase, and yet he could not give up. Thulani Mpofu, his almost-brother-in-law, deserved his best efforts.

Think, you idiot, he said to himself, there has to be a way to clear water from glass.

He stopped the vehicle and hopped out into the storm. He bothered little about his already sodden state. He barely brushed away the ferocious drops that attacked his eyes and ears and sucked the breath from his lungs.

'At least the wipers work,' he thought, 'so I just need to replace the blades somehow.'

He began to rip his shirt into strips, and delicately bound them around the wiper arms. It would be a temporary measure; the fabric wouldn't last long, but it might do the trick for a while.

With her vision partially restored, Miss Daisy ploughed gamely on, racing through large puddles accumulating, particularly on the calcrete areas, where mini waterholes were forming. Sibanda noted that she aquaplaned quite stylishly for an old duck. It was down to her rain-soaked British ancestry. He replaced the strips once more. Despite the rain, friction was destroying them rapidly. He may not have enough material left to make the distance.

A massive lightning strike cracked open the sky in an ostentatious display of jagged brilliance, followed barely a second later by an ear-splitting peel of thunder. Sibanda was at the very heart of the fury, the epicentre of nature's anger. In that flash, he saw possible salvation with a glimpse of a granite outcrop not far ahead. It was a bizarre geological anomaly in the middle of the Kalahari sand veldt. Sibanda had no idea how it had got there or what forces had protected it from the millennia of abrasive sandblasting and blanketing, but he knew it might offer a solution.

Pouzolzia hypoleuca, it could work, he thought, let's hope some stray isiskhukhukhu, seed, has travelled and found a home here, as he remembered his childhood fun.

He pulled the Land Rover off the road and towards the rocky protrusion. His eyes lit on a small cluster of like-minded shrubs – the soap bush – obviously a dwindling and displaced population in this land of ancient sand, clinging, like all refugees, to its ghetto environment. He was glad it had survived. The green leaves displayed a silvery, white-velvet underside. As he began to strip the bark, so the resin he had used as a child to repel the water from his boyhood rock slides oozed promisingly.

It worked after a fashion, coating the glass in a sticky residue that both discouraged the rain and aided the bandaged wipers to perform. The view through the windscreen was distorted, giving a warped vision of the landscape and the occasional animal that ventured into sight – zebra with misaligned stripes, sable with contorted horns – but it enabled Sibanda to keep up his speed. The turn off was not far away; his back would be to the rain. Progress through the thick sand of the elephant path would be slower, but it was not far to the border road at this point.

The rain began to ease as the turn off came into view. It was barely more than a slight clearing on the side of the track that might have been overlooked by anyone other than the detective. He knew this area well from solitary camping trips stolen in his occasional spare time. He had found the track the previous year. He had marked it by a small grove of Kalahari apple leaf. The delicate sprays of lilac pea-shaped buds against the synchronised flowering of the deep yellow blossoms of a nearby camel thorn acacia had caught his eye. It was what had led him to the path in the first place.

As he turned off into the thickening Kalahari woodland, Sibanda felt more relaxed. He had dodged a collision with a buffalo, eland or other vehicle-wrecking animal. This was a positive. With time running short he needed to remain optimistic. He had seen the results of animal versus vehicles. It wasn't pretty for either party. An impala through the windscreen was capable of decapitation. A reedbuck could deliver a rapier thrust to the heart. It was best not to dwell on the outcome of an elephant pile-up.

Miss Daisy began a steady, if somewhat rolling, gait along the ancient elephant trail, ploughing over saplings and small bushes that impeded her travel. Twice Sibanda had to leave the vehicle with his axe to chop away at larger trees and logs that had fallen or been pushed across the path. Sibanda had factored this sluggish leg of the trip into his calculations. Time would be tight, but still tantalisingly worth the effort. He was punishing the Land Rover, hitting gullies hard, bridging trees a little too large and solid to be tackled, but he had to reach the road before Ngwenya.

Bongani Ngwenya, on the other hand, was speeding southwards on a good tar road with little traffic to speak of. The night was so filthy that most sensible people had stayed home. When he received the phone call from Khanyi, he knew the game was hotting up. It was time to move.

'Take me with you,' she had pleaded.

'Pack your things,' he had said, 'I will be with you within the hour.'

'I love you, Bongani.'

'Me too,' he had said, but he had no intention of picking her up. How could she think that he, the governor's son, could love a rural girl? There were chicks aplenty back in the USA, rich ones, ones that knew their way around the clubs and bars, sophisticated mamas with sass and style. Poor Khanyi, she was just a loser.

The storm was letting up a little the further south he travelled. Despite the fear of the dogs at his back, he eased up on his speed.

He hated men like Detective Inspector Sibanda, who had come to the ranch to interrogate him. He was just a police pig, satisfied to wallow in the Gubu sty, content to earn peanuts, eat swill and drive a battered skoroskoro that was an embarrassment. He had seen it parked on the cattle ramp, and recognised it as a heap of unreliable junk. Once back in the States he would own a very smooth ride, pimped to perfection. He knew where the money was – drugs.

When he first returned home, he had brought some cocaine with him stashed around his waist. Customs in Bulawayo was a joke, no sniffer dogs, no drug swabs, only an interest in electrical items and food. He was, after all, the governor's son. Who was going to dare to search him? His plan had been to make a pile of cash, be out of this hellhole in a few weeks and back on the fat drugs gravy train that ran through every US town and city.

How could he have miscalculated so badly? His father had told him lies, said the country was back on its feet, said that US dollars were the accepted currency and that money was flowing freely. What rubbish. It was the same old story, a few gogos with a grubby dollar, albeit now green in colour, wrapped tightly in their fists, doling it out for a loaf of bread as if the starchy staple was a precious gold ring studded with diamonds. There had been no economic miracle and certainly no money for luxuries such as cocaine. In the end, he had more or less given his stash away for pocket money.

This latest plan was far more lucrative. The true African drug of choice. Ground up human body parts. Powder, destined to transform the lives of all who believed in traditional healers and their muthi. He personally preferred the transformation of a quick snort of white powder up the nose. It was much less distasteful and far more effective. What a phoxo, a joke. He laughed to himself at the simplicity of the parallel. The frozen contents of the cooler box on the passenger seat would net him several thousand dollars, enough for a ticket back to the USA and seed money for his yet-to-be-born drug empire.

Ngwenya was so taken with his own ramblings he failed to notice a donkey straying onto the road. It was as black as the wild night that concealed it, with only its paler cross of suffering to distinguish it from the greasy, blackened road.

As Ngwenya slammed on his brakes and took evasive action, so Sibanda was doing battle on his narrow dirt path with an extremely angry elephant. The detective had known he was in trouble from the first minute he set eyes on the animal. A brief flash from the dying storm had alerted him to its proximity and its distinctive posture of turmoil. As the moon peeped coyly from behind a shrinking cloud, he saw the elephant's temporal glands. They were streaming on either side of his head, a sure sign of distress. This elephant was in musth, a Hindu word denoting the altered state that descended on sexually active male elephants occasionally. When it happened, they became solitary, irritable, highly testosterone charged and leaked urine constantly. Sure enough, the next excursion of the moon outlined the elephants dribbling, algae-coated penis.

'Yebo, Ndlovu,' he addressed the elephant. 'Ungathathazeli, keep calm,' Sibanda urged, while scanning his immediate environs for an exit strategy. He was hemmed in by thick bush. The only possibility was backwards, and that was no possibility at all. Miss Daisy could never outrun a charging elephant in reverse, even on a good road, let alone the narrow, twisting, rutted, log-strewn path he was now on.

'Okay, Miss Daisy,' he said, 'I hope you are up for this, hang on to your exhaust pipe, salukazi, old lady, this could be a rough ride.'

As the elephant dropped its massive head and raced down the path towards them, Sibanda revved the diesel engine to screaming pitch. He balanced the accelerator and clutch so that the vehicle stayed in one place, causing suffocating, black exhaust gases to cloud the Land Rover with the smell of partially burned diesel and exhaust fumes. All the while, Sibanda banged frantically on the driver's door with his flat palm, making as much noise as he could. Together, he and Miss Daisy looked like an emanation from hell. Undeterred, the elephant continued its angry run.

'You asked for it, Ndlovu,' was all he had time to say before he let out the clutch and charged the elephant head on. Had the elephant hit the ancient Land Rover, he could easily have pushed it backwards and flipped it on its side, but the effect of forward impetus and a screaming Miss Daisy, veered the beast away at the last minute and into the thick bush.

'Go and find yourself a big tree to take your anger out on, my friend,' said Sibanda as the elephant slipped past him and off to find another target for his hormonal petulance. Gingerly, Sibanda tested the clutch, he had done it no favours, but it seemed to have held up. There was still a chance.

Ngwenya had less luck with the donkey. Despite standing on his brakes and wrenching the steering wheel hard to the right, he clipped the poor beast of burden with his left front mudguard, dispatching it to a painless, well-earned rest. He pulled over shakily. That had been a very close run thing. His nerves were shattered. When he gathered enough composure to lift his head, he could see the donkey was dead, but he had also registered the ominous grating of metal on rubber. The blue Toyota could not travel further in this state. The mudguard was jammed hard against the tyre.

The governor's son assessed the damage and realised he was stuck. He couldn't pull out the indentation no matter how hard he tried. He spent a good fifteen minutes wrestling with the mangled metal. He was beginning to think about disposing of his carefully acquired assets in a nearby warthog burrow when he heard a repetitive squeak. It had the interval of an un-oiled bicycle wheel. He peered down the road into the gloom and saw a matching pedal-flash. It confirmed his hopes. A cyclist was approaching. He could help to fix the problem.

Sibanda shot out onto the tar road like a champagne cork. He had not realised he was so close to a lack of resistance. The bush and sand melted away like a homeless wisp of cloud on a winter's day. Suddenly, he was out in the open and on hard ground. He quickly surveyed the road. He had no way of knowing if Ngwenya had passed this point or not, but he needed to find an ambush spot. He had to still believe.

He chose to head north. The road was deserted. The rain had reduced to a whisper. The warm tar was steaming as it persuaded the recently formed puddles to return home to the air. Miss Daisy splashed along, coughing and spluttering with the early onset of a temperature, heralding who knows what disease, but in no hurry now. Either the blue Toyota was ahead of her or not. Sibanda scanned the verges with a barrier in mind. It wasn't long before he came to a bend that would give him an advantage. He pulled over and took out his axe and a couple of yellow, luminous, traffic control vests that had been carelessly abandoned from a previous duty. The air was cool from the storm. Sibanda enjoyed the physical exertion of hacking at branches and dragging fallen logs. It brought warmth back to his wet and wind-chilled body.

Ngwenya was once again behind the wheel of the blue Toyota. Together he and the cyclist, a young man returning to his village, had managed, with the aid of the wheel brace, to wrench the mud guard away from the tyre. Ngwenya had offered the young man a ride. He was now perched with his bicycle in the back of the pick-up, congratulating himself on his good luck. Ngwenya was more careful with his speed. He was concentrating on the road. The donkey had given him a real scare just as he thought he was on the home run straight to freedom and riches. The clouds had cleared and the moon was reflecting light off the rain-washed tar. He could feel himself relaxing. Once again he began to imagine his life as a drug lord, surrounded by the sorts of scantily clad, tit-wiggling, hip-stabbing dancers that he watched on his music videos. There was a bend ahead. He shook his head to rid himself of the arousing images. He must focus again.

Sibanda was sweating from the exertion of his efforts. The Land Rover was side-on in the middle of the road. On either side of it he had stacked bushes and branches to seal off the remaining tar and accessible areas of the verge. In front and behind the barrier, he had built a tripod with the yellow vests, striped with reflective tape, to alert motorists to the road block. It was the best he could do.

'Gubu Base, Gubu Base, do you read?' he asked.

Immediately the radio crackled into life with a response. 'I am here, sir'. It was Sergeant Ncube manning the base.

'Ncube, I have set up a road block on the border road about fifty kilometres south of you. I may need back up. Stay on the radio until I contact you.'

'Yes, sir, and just to let you know, Shadrek Nkomo is in the lock-up.'

'Good, is Chief Inspector Mfumu there?'

'No, sir, he went home early.'

'Well, Ncube, I don't think we need to draw the Iron Curtain and disturb a sleeping Cold War, do you?'

There was a hesitation on the other end of the radio. A dubious 'No, sir,' crackled over the airwaves.

'Okay, Sergeant. I can hear a vehicle approaching, over and out for now.'

Sibanda jumped out of the Land Rover. He took up a position behind a large teak tree whose girth had decided him on the position of the road block. As the oncoming vehicle rounded the bend, Sibanda knew immediately that it was the blue Toyota. The strengthening moon floodlit the metallic tint and cast a blue corona on the wet, mirrored road.

The Land Cruiser began to slow. Sibanda emerged from his cover and flagged the vehicle, indicating it should stop. For a moment he thought it was going to comply. Without warning it veered off left into the bush, trying to find a way around the roadblock. Sibanda hared after it on foot. The bush was thick and the Land Cruiser was battling to penetrate the snarl of large trees and lesser vegetation that had created a tight-knit community over the years. Every inch of viable ground was covered with shrubs and thorn bushes, trees and saplings. In between lay a mat of discarded branches and the rotting bodies of former stalwarts.

Sibanda hardly noticed the slap of branches and the rip of thorns on his naked torso as he sprinted in the vehicle's bouncing wake. He did notice the wide eyes of a man on the back of the vehicle clinging on for all he was worth. He barely dodged a flying bicycle as it cartwheeled out of the Land Cruiser and over his head, landing wheels-up in the fork of a tree, wriggling wildly like a cut snake.

The Land Cruiser only managed a few more metres before it came to a shuddering halt against the bole of a beautifully flowering gardenia that shook its white, deliciously scented petals over the blue Toyota, like confetti on a doomed marriage. Ngwenya was out of the vehicle with the ease of a plug from a ripened boil. He took off into the darkness, tripping over the tangled undergrowth and punching aside bushes. Sibanda was after him, hurdling fallen branches and ploughing headlong through the dense vegetation, oblivious to the grated effect on his body.

The governor's son was no match for the farmer's boy. Ngwenya rarely exercised except to posture in front of the mirror and match the finger contortions of his rap idols. Sibanda punished his body every day with strenuous exercise. He leapt on the fleeing figure from behind and brought him to ground. 'It's over, Ngwenya,' he said. The body beneath him twisted and thrashed, landing a punch on Sibanda's jaw.

'It will never be over, Ungxoza,' Ngwenya replied.

'I'll show you how useless, unreliable and dried up I am,' said Sibanda, losing his long-suffering cool at being referred to in such terms. He thumped Ngwenya soundly and repeatedly, landing blows to all parts of his body. When he got up from his knees, he landed a couple of well-aimed kicks to the stomach of the cowed murderer, one for Khanyi, and one for good measure. His anger abated, and energy spent, he took a few moments to draw breath. He noticed the wide-eyed spectator standing a few paces away. 'Buya Lapa, come here, jaha elihle,' he said. 'This is a police matter. I need you to watch this man. If he moves, hit him with this log.' He passed a handy truncheon to the bewildered cyclist.

Having checked that Ngwenya was in no fit state to run off, Sibanda made his way back to the Toyota. It was pretty mangled. He doubted it could move under its own steam. Someone would have to tow it away. It was an ignominious end for a good vehicle. He looked in through the window and could see a cooler box on the floor of the passenger side. By bracing a foot against the car body, he managed to wrench the door open and retrieve it.

Sibanda walked a few metres with the box, carrying it as though it contained an unexploded bomb. He set it down very cautiously and lifted the insulated top. Inside, in a nest of melting ice cubes, lay the innocuous ice cream container, its lid advertising a creamy chocolate chip delight within. Sibanda did not enjoy the irony. He placed his thumb on the protruding plastic lip designed to ease off the cover, and gently pushed upwards, just enough to expose a small corner of the contents. He quickly slammed it back down again. A large, bloody nostril had stared up at him, its partner squashed against the white plastic wall. It was all that was left of Thulani Mpofu's nose. Sibanda carefully replaced the container in the cooler box and carried it over to the Land Rover.

'Sergeant Ncube, are you there?' he asked on the radio.

'Yes, sir, are you alright? I have been worried that you have not come back to me.'

'We may need a doctor,' he said wearily.

'Why, sir, are you hurt?' said the sergeant with deep concern in his voice. Sibanda looked down at his upper body and arms which had been shredded by thorns and lashed by whip-like branches. They were streaming with blood. He had dozens of small cuts and abrasions, but it was nothing that a bit of antiseptic and a few plasters couldn't take care of.

'No, Sergeant, I am fine, don't worry about me,' he replied. 'But get a cell ready for Ngwenya.'

'You have got him then, sir? Is it he who is injured?'

'He crashed his car into a tree, so he has a few cuts and bruises, but nothing life threatening.'

'So who is sick?' asked the puzzled sergeant.

'It's Miss Daisy, Ncube. She has had a devil of a journey, speeding through water, over trees and nearly under an elephant. She's a game old bird, but she will be limping back to the station.'

The radio remained silent. All Sibanda heard was a sigh of pride and satisfaction.

'And, Ncube,' he continued, 'contact the Blue Gnu and ask them to deliver as much ice as they can spare.'

'Why, sir?'

'I am bringing Thulani Mpofu home.'

Epilogue

Detective Inspector Jabulani Sibanda pulled on the steering wheel again and attempted to get the Gubu Station Santana to stay on the road, something it seemed loathe to do. It was intent on dragging him into the oncoming traffic like a headstrong horse champing at the bit. He would tame this wilful beast yet. As he swerved left to right, he had time to reflect on the past few weeks.

The contents of the cooler box had been identified as belonging to Thulani Mpofu. They had been released with the body, just last week, for burial. Bongani Ngwenya and Shadrek Nkomo were behind bars awaiting trial. Publicity surrounding the case had been muted. So far the governor's name had remained untainted. The young Ngwenya had given up the identities of those evil, warped healers preying on the insecurities of the ignorant. The South African police had made several arrests and more were pending.

The governor may have remained untouched, but not so Sibanda. The reverberations of the case had been felt as far away as July Chimombe and the Minister for Police. Sibanda had been issued with a severe reprimand for breaching protocol regarding the governor. There had been the predictable memos about 'talent wasted', a 'disappointment for such an investment' and similar mouthings. He believed from friendly inside sources that the governor himself had intervened and saved him from a possible transfer, demotion, or worse – a desk job.

Mfumu's wrath had been predictably volcanic. It had taken two weeks for the eruption to cool. During that time everyone had kept their heads down. They had scurried around the office cleaning, polishing, filing, whitewashing rocks and generally rendering Gubu Station as close to perfection as the dilapidated building could achieve. The staff had even clubbed together to buy a new flag since the old one resembled tattered cobwebs. They had scraped and painted the peeling flagpole for its inaugural raising.

The Naidoo brothers had been released after three very uncomfortable nights in the cells. They received a massive fine for smuggling. The truck caught *in flagrante* had been confiscated. He felt, with a little pressure and given their criminal conviction, they might lose their logging licence. He knew it was like King Canute and the waves, but perhaps his efforts could slow deforestation and save at least one tree.

Miss Daisy was wrecked. Sergeant Ncube had been surprisingly understanding, if a little distant. Mfumu gave him a further raging ultimatum regarding the vehicular status of the station. He had quickly arranged with one of his wives' uncles, a senior railway employee, to load Miss Daisy on a train heading for Bulawayo where he and she were currently sharing CMED lodgings and scavenging once again for parts. Ncube was due back in a few days with or without his mistress. Sibanda had rather missed his sergeant.

Sibanda hadn't attended Thulani's funeral. He felt it best to leave the family in peace to grieve, and to come to terms with Khanyi's role in the deaths of her brothers. He had phoned Lindiwe to pass on his condolences. They had chatted amicably. He wasn't surprised to learn that the family had closed ranks and had chosen not to press any theft charges against Khanyi. She hadn't been totally forgiven, though. Lindiwe had arranged for her to travel to Johannesburg after the trial, to take up Lindiwe's old job as a domestic servant. That way she would pay back everything she had stolen and learn a little humility.

'She is already quieter and less sure of herself. I know she regrets what she has done,' Lindiwe said. 'Mama says she will never forgive her, but she will. I can see the way she looks at her when she thinks no one else can see. She is still her Kanku.'

'How is your mother?' Sibanda asked.

'She is very well, thank you. In fact, I haven't seen her so well in a long time. She has been to Bulawayo. We found an excellent doctor who specialises in bone diseases. With a course of injections and pills to drink, she is walking well. You should see her playing with Thulani's children, fussing around them, showing them all about the birds she loves. It is a joy to watch. She is smiling again and talking about the future.'

'And you, Lindiwe?' he asked. He had felt an affinity for this woman with difficult choices to make.

'I am fine, Detective. My friend… has moved back to her village. We see each other often. We are even talking about children of our own.' Sibanda didn't comment. There would be no need for IVF or sperm donors for this couple. They would easily find an unwitting, uncomplicated donor. Lindiwe would be fine and he wished her and her brood well.

He was about to hang up when Lindiwe said, 'The governor came to visit us, Detective.'

'I hope he didn't put you under any pressure,' said Sibanda, a little alarmed at this turn of events.

'No, he was very pleasant. He spent a long time with my mother, chatting about old times, I think. He came to see if he could help our family, if we needed anything, and to pay some compensation. It was, after all, his son who murdered Thulani. It was all a bit strange really,' she said.

'Why?' he asked.

'Well, it was as if they were old friends who had met up after many years. As he was leaving, my mother called after him, "Machitigaza". He stopped in his tracks, came back and spoke to her again, more urgently and secretly somehow. When he finally left it was as if a huge weight had gone from Mama's shoulders. Very odd. I didn't even know that she knew him.'

Sibanda had thought a great deal since about this conversation and it bothered him. His detective's instincts were telling him that there was a connection somewhere, some missing thread in all this that he had overlooked, some stored snippet at the back of his brain that refused to reveal itself. It worried him for quite a while, but then he let it lie. It would come to him sooner or later.

He sensed this morning there had been something of a détente in Cold War's demeanour. Firstly he had greeted him cordially and then he had summoned him into his office.

'Detective Inspector Sibanda,' he had said, while dislodging a minute speck of cotton from his uniform shirt, 'a couple of nights ago, Robert McClean, the farmer from Zebra Hill passed away. It seems he died in his sleep, inhaled his own vomit. Very tragic. We need a report, so could you go along and fill out the paperwork?'

The truth of the matter was, as he knew, Mfumu could not send Chanza out on the job. He had somehow failed to effectively clean up the Mtabizi case. No charges had been laid. That hadn't gone down at all well with head office. The murders of the Mpofu brothers had each in their own way caused Gubu Station to lose status in the hierarchy of rural police stations. It would be a very long time before they warranted such items as a desperately needed new computer, a lick of paint or a new Land Rover.

'I'll take the Santana,' was all he said, with what he considered was the stoicism of a martyr. It was enough to start the relationship repair job.

Sibanda pulled into Zebra Hill Farm and reminded himself how much he coveted the farm and its perfect setting. He found Isabelle McClean in the kitchen, her children playing about her feet. He wondered where Margaret was. He remembered her husband, Shadrek, was in jail. He really could have done with his sergeant here. He would be able to deal with all the complex female emotions that were surely reverberating around this house.

With the condolences over, and the social niceties that attend any death completed, Mrs McClean recounted the story of how her husband had drunk heavily the night before he died. She explained that he had become stressed of late and how his alcohol use was becoming a problem. She had been sleeping with the children for some days, because she could no longer tolerate his drunken snoring. Robert hated to be disturbed in the mornings after one of his binges.

'When and how did you discover the body, Mrs McClean?' he asked.

She took out a handkerchief and blew her nose, 'It was quite late yesterday morning, Detective. I realised that Robert hadn't stirred. He had never slept in so late before. I went to look for him and found him…' She put the handkerchief over her face, but no sobs came, just a dry moaning sound. Eventually she looked up and asked, 'Would you like to see the room? I haven't changed anything.' She looked him in the eye when she said this, acknowledging what he already knew about the scene of Mtabizi's killing. As they walked down the corridor to the bedroom, a faint waft of embrocation reached him. It intensified as he got closer to the room.

'Did your husband have any aches and pains before he died, any pulled muscles?' he asked.

'No, Robert was as strong as an ox and very fit. He never had a day's illness. I thought he would live forever,' she said. Sibanda walked into the room. Isabelle stayed in the corridor. It was much like any bedroom except the bed remained unmade. It was covered with dried vomit. The smell was sour, but still with that shadowy underlying odour of wintergreen. He checked the bedside tables for a tube of muscle rub, but there was nothing.

'Thank you, Mrs McClean,' he said. 'I have seen enough.' He walked back towards the kitchen to the sound of giggling, happy children. It was in sharp contrast to his last visit. 'Your domestic, Margaret, is not here I see,' he commented.

'No, she left this morning for Tsholotsho, her rural home. She has two grown up sons who are going to come and help us run the farm. Margaret has been very supportive during these last few difficult weeks. I don't know how I would have managed without her.'

'How has she taken her husband's arrest?' he asked.

'Shadrek was no husband to Margaret, not for some years anyway. She is feeling no pain.'

And neither are you, thought the detective, and it came to him then that Mrs McClean was truly enganakile, carefree. Ncube would certainly have picked up on that. As he walked through the kitchen, redolent of recent baking, he offered further condolences to Mrs McClean and the assistance of the Gubu Police should the need arise. He took his leave.

'Revenge is sweet and not fattening,' he said to himself with the tempting kitchen smells still in his nostrils. Alfred Hitchcock's genius seemed to have just the right thought for every crime scene. This was certainly the scene of a crime. He had no doubt that Isabelle McClean had murdered her husband, probably with Margaret's help. He knew exactly how they had done it. The clever thing was it could never be proved. He was not about to pour out Ncube's beans on the perfect punishment for a brutal, wife-beating, child-threatening murderer.

Mtabizi had been avenged. Justice had been served, on a cold plate perhaps and in a private dining room, but no less satisfying.

'Robert McClean was poisoned with Securidaca longepedunculata, the violet tree, umfufu,' he shared his conclusions aloud with the Santana, as it crabbed its way along the farm track, steering magnetically towards any suitable large tree trunk as if drawn by a death wish. He realised alarmingly that he genuinely missed the reassuring stripes and the noisy rattles of Miss Daisy in whom he would have preferred to confide. Was he becoming soft in the head like Ncube?

Sibanda reeled off mentally what he knew about this frequently used medicinal tree: the leaves, pounded with water and salt, are a very effective gargle; the bark can be used as a soap substitute; the roots for mouthwash and toothache, so, not poisonous at all. But the roots, pounded and taken intra-vaginally or anally, made it deadly and, before the arrival of western medication, it had been used for years as the favourite suicide method of despairing women.

McClean had been given this lethal enema, probably while in a drunken stupor. He had suffocated, in his weakened, febrile state, on the ensuing vomit. They would have found a piece of suitable tubing in McClean's well-equipped workshop. It would have taken the two of them, Isabelle and Margaret, one to hold the tubing in place and one to pour the concoction in from above. The odour of the old-fashioned muscle relaxant had been the giveaway. The roots of *Securidaca longepedunculata*, the poison tree, had a distinctive aroma of wintergreen.

Sibanda reached the main road and for a moment almost turned towards Kestrel Vale School. The urge to catch up with Berry was as strong as ever. He would have liked to talk to Thandanyoni, to give him the news of his old Buck knife and his unfortunate cook. He could perhaps even have chatted to the impudent Ben Molesworthy, but the pain would be intolerable. He hadn't phoned her as promised. She would have already been on her Vic Falls trip with Barney Jones. He was glad that Barney hadn't turned out to be the murderer. Berry deserved her happiness.

Overhead a pair of rainbirds were chirping triumphantly. They had fulfilled their destiny, installed their offspring in a nearby nest and summoned the rain. Jabulani Sibanda dragged the heavy steering wheel reluctantly to the left and headed back to Gubu Station.

Acknowledgements

My thanks go to Maureen Van der Horn, who encouraged me from the very beginning; to early readers, Rhett Butler, Jane McDuff and John Eppel, whose seal of approval gave me great comfort.

The blind faith, enthusiasm and unwavering support of Peter and Jan Arscott, Caerine Butler and Lulu Androuliakos was simply extraordinary.

I am grateful to Scribblers writing group, Mandurah, the kick start I needed, to the Odyssey writing circle who keep me on my creative toes, and to the Lembu girls, Tracy and Skha, who told me tales and gave me words. I should point out that any errors zoological, botanical, ornithological or linguistic are mine alone.

Lastly, my best thanks to Alan and Josh Elliott, the inspiration behind every word.